Praise for the Pyke series

'A story of high intrigue and low politics, brutal murder and cunning conspiracies ... tangy and rambunctious stuff!'

Observer

'The novel drips with all the atmospheric details of a pre-Victorian murder mystery – "pea-soupers", dingy lanterns and laudanum' *The Times*

'Pyke is violent, vengeful and conflicted in the best tradition of detectives. His story takes in grisly murder and torture, and uses 1800s London in the same way that hard-boiled fiction uses Los Angeles as a mirror of corrupt society' *Time Out*

'Gripping and atmospheric' *Daily Express*

'Well researched and enjoyably disturbing, *The Last Days of Newgate* is one of the few novels in the new wave of historical fiction likely to leave the reader clamouring for more'

Times Literary Supplement

'Novel of the Week: a riproaring addition to the bestselling Pyke series' Press Association

'He creates a vision of London ... so atmospheric that it is almost possible to feel the fog enveloping your face, to smell the stench from the gutters and to feel the danger in the rookeries' *Material Witness*

'Pyke is an intriguingly unfathomable character, and this is an excellent continuation of his dark journey' *Financial Times*

D0169537

Andrew Pepper lives in Belfast where he is a lecturer in English at Queen's University. His first novel, *The Last Days of Newgate*, was shortlisted for the CWA New Blood Dagger.

By Andrew Pepper

The Last Days of Newgate
The Revenge of Captain Paine
Kill-Devil and Water
The Detective Branch
Bloody Winter

BLOODY WINTER

ANDREW PEPPER

ANDREW PEPPER

FRANKLIN COUNTY LIBRARY
906 NORTH MAIN STREET
LOUISBURG, NC 27549
BRANCHES IN BUNN.
FRANKLINTON, & YOUNGSVILLE

PHOENIX

A PHOENIX PAPERBACK

First published in Great Britain in 2011
by Weidenfeld & Nicolson
This paperback edition published in 2012
by Phoenix,
an imprint of Orion Books Ltd,
Orion House, 5 Upper St Martin's Lane,
London WC2H 9EA

An Hachette UK company

1 3 5 7 9 10 8 6 4 2

Copyright © Andrew Pepper 2011

The right of Andrew Pepper to be identified as the author of
this work has been asserted by him in accordance with the
Copyright, Designs and Patents Act 1988.

All rights reserved. No part of this publication may be
reproduced, stored in a retrieval system, or transmitted, in
any form or by any means, electronic, mechanical,
photocopying, recording or otherwise, without the prior
permission of the copyright owner.

All the characters in this book are fictitious,
and any resemblance to actual persons, living
or dead, is purely coincidental.

A CIP catalogue record for this book
is available from the British Library.

ISBN 978-1-7802-2011-6

Typeset by Input Data Services Ltd, Bridgwater, Somerset

Printed and bound in Great Britain by
Clays Ltd, St Ives plc

The Orion Publishing Group's policy is to use papers that
are natural, renewable and recyclable products and
made from wood grown in sustainable forests. The logging
and manufacturing processes are expected to conform to
the environmental regulations of the country of origin.

www.orionbooks.co.uk

For Sadie and Marcus

Since then the smelters whose brick stacks stuck up tall against a gloomy mountain to the south had yellow-smoked everything into uniform dinginess. The result was an ugly city of forty thousand people, set in an ugly notch between two ugly mountains that had been all dirtied up by mining.

DASHIELL HAMMETT, *Red Harvest*

PART I

*

Dirty Town –

ONE

Snowflakes the size of half-shilling coins fell from inky skies, a few inches settling on frozen ground, the dirt and mud hidden beneath a dazzling layer of white. It made the town seem almost pleasant, lending it a magical quality it most definitely didn't deserve. The snow, which would be gone by the morning, a lie upon a lie. Welcome to Merthyr. Welcome *back* to Merthyr. Welcome to the dirtiest town in the kingdom.

Pyke passed through the army checkpoint without arousing the suspicion of the bored soldiers, two rosy-cheeked men who made Pyke think of his son Felix. Pushing this thought to the back of his mind, he kept his eyes focused on the snow. If the men had been instructed to look for him, he decided, they seemed to have forgotten. Their rifles were slung lazily over their shoulders and they were more interested in a young woman on the other side of the street.

He had just crossed Jackson's Bridge over the River Taff and continued now along Jackson Street towards the centre of the town. The icy weather had driven people indoors, leaving the streets nearly deserted. Perhaps, Pyke mused, the troops had also played their part. As he walked, he ruminated on the irony of it all. This was a situation he had conspired to bring about and yet, now it had come to pass, he did not welcome it with any enthusiasm.

With the snow and the eerie quiet, it felt like the end of the world; or perhaps just the end of *his* world. The shops in the town centre were still boarded up and the old courthouse was guarded by two soldiers. They stood on the steps, stamping their feet and blowing into their hands. Pyke checked the windows for any sign of light but he saw nothing. As he stood there, he tried to take in the full horror of what had happened inside. The building seemed deserted, a fact confirmed by one of the soldiers when Pyke asked to see Sir Clancy Smyth.

Did either of them know where the magistrate was?

The soldiers looked at each other and shrugged.

Mostly to get out of the cold, Pyke headed for the nearest pub, the Falcon on High Street. At the counter in the taproom, he pointed at a cask of ale rather than opening his mouth to order – doing so would draw attention to his Englishness. But no one paid him any attention, and inevitably what little conversation there was turned to recent events. The two men nearest to him were speaking in English. Pyke heard everything he needed to know within a few minutes.

Benjamin Griffiths was dead.

John Wylde had been arrested for his murder and was languishing in the station-house.

The two ironmasters were trying in vain to shore up their operations. Josiah Webb's Morlais works had temporarily been closed down and most of his family had departed for London. Jonah and Zephaniah Hancock, owners of the Caedraw ironworks, had retreated to their family pile in Hampshire.

The part of town known as China was under curfew and martial law, as were parts of Dowlais and Pennydarren and the areas bordering Caedraw's ironworks. Scores of Irishmen, some Welshmen and a handful of policemen and soldiers had been injured or killed in the disturbances. Yynsgall chapel in Dowlais and a Welsh Wesleyan chapel on High Street had been burned to the ground, while much of Quarry Row lay in ruins.

None of this was unexpected.

Pyke had travelled for a day without stopping and he felt exhausted – tired down to his very bones. After one mug of ale he felt light-headed; he decided not to have another, even though the fire spitting in the grate had been the first welcome sight of the day. Lacing up his boots, Pyke stood up and pulled his greatcoat around his aching body. The wound where he'd been shot hurt each time he moved too quickly.

Ignoring the bruises on his feet and the icy wind, Pyke retraced his steps as far as Jackson's Bridge. He passed through the same checkpoint and scrambled down the bank of the river to the path that ran along the edge of the canal. Snow was falling but it had eased enough for him to see the glow of the nearest cinder tip. Everything was quiet except for the clanking of chains at Caedraw. *Short of a strike, nothing, not a snowstorm nor a drought, would bring the works to a standstill.* Jonah Hancock's words.

Pyke walked in a southerly direction for the best part of an hour. He knew what was keeping him going but it remained something he wouldn't – *couldn't* – think about. Instead he focused on the next step and the one after that, his breath condensing on his woollen muffler then freezing. Eventually he came upon the house. Its name – Blenheim – a testament to the bloated ambition of its owner. It was just as he remembered it: not stately but smaller and more run down than it initially appeared. Approaching the house from the line of trees to the north, Pyke took care not to draw attention to himself, the snow muffling his footsteps as he made his way along the gravel path. Candlelight burned in what Pyke recalled was the window of the study. It told him that Smyth was at home.

At the front door, he paused for a few moments, readying himself, the tension in his stomach helping to restore the circulation to his feet. Then without warning, he lifted up his right boot and kicked the door open, the wooden frame splintering under the impact. Pyke crossed the threshold, the pistol already in his hand.

Alerted by the noise, the occupant of the study shuffled out to confront him, but it was the butler rather than the magistrate himself, a frail old man with arms like twigs. He saw Pyke's expression and the gleaming metal in his hand and froze.

Even though the first words that tumbled from his pale lips were 'He's not here', Pyke couldn't, wouldn't, allow himself to believe it. He had come too far and been subjected to too much.

Raising the pistol, Pyke pressed the end of the barrel against the man's terrified face and, just for a second, the rush of anger within him was so intense, so unexpected, that he almost squeezed the trigger. Instead, he asked where Smyth was, and when the butler didn't answer immediately, Pyke prised apart the man's gums and pushed the barrel so deep into his mouth that the servant began to retch.

Disgusted, Pyke withdrew the pistol. Whatever had billowed up inside him suddenly ebbed away like the parting of the tide.

'Where is he?'

The butler gave him a glassy stare. 'Ireland.'

Pyke nodded. Smyth had once talked about his ancestral home there. 'Tipperary?'

The old man's stare drifted over Pyke's shoulder. 'That would be my guess.'

'When did he leave?'

'Been gone two or three weeks now.'

'And did he say when he'd be back?'

'He didn't even tell me he was going.' The butler shrugged. 'If I had to guess, I wouldn't say any time soon.'

Later, as he watched the house from the same line of trees he'd hidden in earlier, Pyke thought about how he'd humiliated a defenceless old man who'd done nothing more than obey his master's wishes. He watched for an hour to make sure that Smyth wasn't there, but no one apart from the butler appeared in any of the windows. Eventually the old man closed the curtains and there was nothing left for Pyke to do. It would take him another hour to walk back to Merthyr and as Pyke set off, the wind howling shrilly in his ears, he kept coming back to the same thought.

Nothing at all good had come of his time in Merthyr. And nothing good was likely to come of it, either.

TWO

Michael Knox trudged across the spongy ground a few paces behind the agent. It was the first time he had met the new man and his immediate impressions weren't at all good. Knox had expected arrogance, of course, but given that the man's predecessor had been shot and killed, he had expected the agent to betray at least some doubt and perhaps even a little humility. Yet Jonathan Maxwell treated Knox like one of his labourers, barking orders and expecting them to be followed. He had even berated Knox for his time-keeping.

'Down here,' Maxwell grunted. He turned off the flint track and clambered down the bank towards the murky water of the stream. Dead leaves crunched underfoot and a solitary blackbird called from the branch of a tree. 'Nothing's been touched,' he added.

Knox had seen plenty of corpses, more in the last few weeks than he could count, but he had never led a murder inquiry. Already he felt the weight of responsibility. They walked around the body a few times, staring down at the stab wound in the middle of the dead man's stomach. Reading Knox's mind, Maxwell said, 'We looked for the knife but couldn't find it.'

'*His Lordship has specifically requested that you look into this matter.*'

Sub-inspector Hastings had gone to Knox's cottage to deliver the order in person. No other explanation had been forthcoming.

'*This is not a good thing,*' his wife, Martha, had said, as soon as the sub-inspector left. Knox was inclined to agree.

The corpse seemed untouched. It was a small miracle that a fox or rats hadn't feasted on the dead flesh. From the tree, the blackbird watched them in silence. Knox took a closer look at the body, watching his breath condense in the cold air. 'Do you know who he is?' he asked eventually.

Maxwell shook his head. 'A couple of the boys said he wasn't from around here.' He sniffed and wiped his nose on his sleeve. 'I'd say he was a vagrant, a poacher looking to steal from his Lordship's table.'

Just before Christmas, an unknown assassin had followed Maxwell's predecessor home and shot him in the face. During the spring and summer, acting on behalf of Lord Cornwallis, the man had overseen the eviction of more than a hundred families from their land.

Knox crouched down next to the dead man, trying not to get his knees wet. The deceased's lips were blue and swollen and his eyes were glassy. Knox put the man's age at forty or thereabouts. He had thick, dark hair and Knox guessed he had been quite handsome. The man was fully clothed, apart from his frock-coat, which lay tangled in the bushes near by. Knox riffled through the pockets. The fancy label inside the frock-coat indicated it had been made by a tailor in London.

'Who found him?'

Already bored, Maxwell was inspecting his pocket watch. 'One of the labourers.'

'I'll need to speak to him.' Knox hadn't found any money or possessions in the dead man's pockets – perhaps someone had stolen them.

Maxwell grimaced. Clearly he didn't like taking orders from a man of Knox's rank. 'Lord Cornwallis wants a word first.'

'With me dressed like this?' Knox gestured at his dirty coat and muddy boots.

'His Lordship was insistent.'

Knox cast his eyes down towards the body. 'I'll need someone to help me. I left my cart at the lodge.'

'You go and see his Lordship, I'll make sure someone brings the cart and body over to the house.'

'Tell his Lordship I'll be with him shortly.' Knox rubbed his sore eyes and tried to compose his thoughts. 'I should have a look around, see if anything has been left behind.'

Maxwell glanced at the darkening sky. 'Don't be too long. His

Lordship doesn't like to be kept waiting. He wants you to go straight to the drawing room.'

Knox found nothing of interest on or near the corpse. It stood to reason that the man had been murdered there, by the stream, but the blood had long since drained into the earth. The body hadn't started to rot but then it had been cold, especially at night and Knox didn't think the corpse had been there for more than a day. Once he had clambered up the bank, Knox lingered for a moment, watching the slow-moving water and wondering whether he had missed something important. Then he turned and started the short walk back to the main house.

Dundrum House was a four-floor Palladian mansion built from locally quarried stone, seven bay windows long. Knox found the place more intimidating than beautiful, its scale too grand for its surroundings, too removed from the world of the nearby village, as though to underline that its owner belonged to a higher class of men and could do as he liked.

Knox had visited his mother many times using the 'poor door' but he had never used the front entrance. His mother had worked in the kitchens for as long as he could remember and he knew the labyrinthine passages of the cellar far better than he knew the main house. He ascended the steps one by one and paused in the entrance hall. On the walls, Cornwallis's ancestors seemed to glower at him. The Moores had forcibly acquired the estate in the aftermath of Cromwell's rampage across Ireland two hundred years earlier. Since then the family had earned a reputation for muscular Protestantism and the current inheritor of the family title, Asenath Moore, the third Viscount Cornwallis, was cut from the same cloth.

When he entered the drawing room, Knox found Cornwallis warming himself by the open fire. A small, wizened man with a bald head shaped like an acorn, Cornwallis wore tan knee-breeches and a black cutaway coat. Greeting Knox with a curt nod, he sat down in an armchair next to the fire and regarded Knox without speaking, as if inspecting a museum exhibit in a vaguely dissatisfied manner.

'Your mother has kept me informed of your progress. It has been,

I'm told, quite satisfactory.' He removed his handkerchief and wiped particles of food from the corners of his mouth.

Knox bowed his head. 'Thank you, your Lordship.'

This show of deference seemed to please the older man. 'Maxwell tells me he's shown you the body down by Woodcock Grove.'

Knox knew better than to talk when a question hadn't been asked.

'I have no idea who this man was or what business he had on my estate. I think we can safely assume him to be a poacher and a vagrant.'

A vagrant, Knox thought, whose clothes had been made by a Savile Row tailor.

'I don't want word of this unfortunate occurrence spreading around the estate. For this reason, I took the decision *not* to solicit the assistance of the two sub-constables here in Dundrum. They're good men, both of them, but they're liable to blab.'

'I understand, your Lordship, but there will have to be an inquest . . .'

'That has been taken care of,' the old man said.

'Very good, your Lordship.' Knox tried to swallow. Unlike his own calloused hands, Cornwallis's were as smooth as marble. 'But it can sometimes be hard to keep such matters from the local people. The man who found the body, for example, will want to brag about it . . .'

'He'll be warned, you can be assured of that,' Cornwallis said, interrupting. 'No, sir, if word of this abhorrence reaches the ears of the village it won't have come from anyone on this estate.'

Knox took a short while to assimilate the threat. He was starting to see why Cornwallis had asked for him. 'You want the matter handled quietly.'

The old man's face brightened. '*Quietly*. That's exactly it. I couldn't have put it better myself.'

Cornwallis most definitely hadn't been quiet about the murder of his former agent. He had travelled to Clonmel to harangue the county inspector in person and had warned that troop reinforcements would have to be forthcoming.

Cornwallis stood up and wandered across to the window. 'I want you to take the body away. I don't want to see or hear of it again.'

It was said as though the matter was a trifling one. Knox could have pointed out that such an order was tantamount to interfering in a police investigation but it would have been futile to do so. Cornwallis's influence was such that there was no gap between his ambition and official policy.

'You will have heard some things – some unfair things – said about me in Cashel, I expect. That I am a monster; that I do not care about the well-being of the local people.' He paused and shook his head. 'Nothing could be farther from the truth. I'm here, am I not, even though my sons have chosen to spend the winter in London. I'm simply trying to attend to the matters of my estate as best I can.' Cornwallis tapped the heels of his boots against the floor.

An awkward silence ensued. Knox wondered why the old man had felt the need to justify himself.

'Will that be all, your Lordship?'

'Asenath. Call me Asenath.' He wandered across to where Knox was standing. 'You're a good boy.' Stretching out his hand, he tapped Knox gently on the cheek.

Knox shifted his weight from foot to foot and waited to be dismissed.

'Your mother has been a good and faithful servant to this family.' Cornwallis waved his hand, as though flicking away a fly. 'She's asked to see you. You'll find her in the kitchens.'

His mother took him in her arms, even though her hands were covered in stuffing. Knox was known by most of the women who worked there and they shouted their greetings. Pulling back from her hug, Knox surveyed his mother with affection. She was tall and elegant. Her thin, straw-coloured hair was tied up under a lace bonnet and her skin was blotchy from the heat of the kitchen. He still thought her a fine-looking woman, for her age, but each time he saw her, he worried that she seemed older. This time she also seemed thinner, but he reassured himself with the thought that there wasn't likely to be a shortage of food in Cornwallis's kitchen.

'How are you, son?' She wiped her hands on her apron and touched him on the cheek. 'And James?'

James was his son, her grandson. He noticed she hadn't asked after his wife. 'They're fine. Martha's fine, too.'

'It's the wee'un I worry about.'

Knox looked at the goose lying in front of her and the vegetables waiting to be cut. 'It's sometimes hard to believe people are dying of starvation.'

'Quiet, boy. You don't want his Lordship to hear you talkin' like that, do you?'

'You think what he's done, what he's doing, is right? Turning families out of their homes?'

His mother looked at him, half-amused. This was familiar ground and usually they chose to respect each other's different opinions of the aristocrat. 'Is it his fault the crops failed again this year?'

This time, Knox felt, there was a prickliness to her tone and he wondered whether he should speak his mind or not.

His mother sighed. 'I've served him for almost forty years and I swear, he's not a bad man. And he's been good to us, all of us, your brothers, your father, you too.'

Knox felt a pang of guilt. He hadn't seen his youngest brother, Peter, for a number of months and it struck him that with the spread of disease brought on by the famine he was more at risk than most. Peter had always been a sickly child but a bout of the pox when he was eight had nearly finished him off. Six or seven years on, his speech and mental faculties were still those of a young boy. As a result Peter had never been able to work and the family did what they could to protect him from the hardships of the world. Even their father did his bit, but it was Knox's mother who bore the brunt of the care.

'How is Peter?'

'You'd know if you ever paid us a visit.'

Knox didn't answer. He wondered whether his mother knew the real reason he kept away from the family cabin and why he hadn't made more of an effort to get to know his two much younger brothers.

As if reading his mind, his mother said, 'Your father's back has been playing up.'

Knox shuffled from foot to foot and looked around the kitchen. He didn't want to talk about his father. 'I should get going. I have to ride back to Cashel and it'll be dark in a couple of hours.'

His mother smiled and nodded. 'You take good care of yourself, son. These are terrible times.' Her smile evaporated, lines deepening on her forehead.

Knox wondered whether she knew that a man had been killed only a few hundred yards from where they were standing. 'Can I ask you a question before I go?'

Sarah Knox tucked in a loose strand of hair that had escaped from her bonnet. 'Of course.'

'It's about my position . . .'

As a rule, policemen weren't meant to take up positions in their native counties or the counties they were attached to by marriage. But eight years earlier, there had been a shortfall in numbers and a notice had been placed in the local newspaper. Knox had applied and had been accepted. He'd always thought that he had been accepted for the position on his own merit.

'When I first applied, did his Lordship put in a good word for me with Hastings?'

His mother retreated to the wooden table where the goose was waiting. 'I honestly don't know, son. I might've mentioned that I didn't want you to leave home. What mother wouldn't do that?'

Knox went over to her and gently touched her face. 'I'm not angry with you. But a few moments ago, you said we all owed his Lordship something and I just wanted to know what you meant.'

His mother sighed. 'I was referring to the wages he pays me, that's all.' Having made sure no one was looking, she picked up a thick cut of cured meat and stuffed it into his pocket. 'Don't say a word,' she whispered. 'Just take it, for you, Martha and the infant.'

Knox wanted to give it back but one of the other kitchen-servants had just come into the room. If someone saw what his mother had done and reported her, she could lose her job.

He went to kiss her on the cheek and, as he did so, she grabbed his wrist. 'You're a good boy, Michael,' she whispered, 'always was, and I love you very much, but this time you need to think about the whole family.'

The first potato crop had failed the previous autumn. On that occasion, the local authorities – in consort with the government in London – had made relief provisions and only a few people had perished. But when the crop had failed a second time one year later, the new Whig administration decided to leave the relief efforts to the traders, supposing they would import the necessary food. When the scale of the crisis became apparent, the traders tried to purchase additional maize and corn from Europe and the United States but prices had soared throughout the autumn and the first part of the winter. Now most ordinary people couldn't afford to eat and there was little that impecunious local boards could do.

Earlier in the year, Knox and other policemen had helped to protect convoys of wheat departing for Waterford and eventually England, where the grain would earn the greatest price. As far as he knew, the grain had reached its final destination, but in light of the current shortages, the decision to export so much food seemed immoral if not downright wicked.

He thought about the food he'd just seen in Cornwallis's kitchen and trembled at the injustice. Knox liked to think of himself as honest and plain speaking, but given the opportunity to confront the aristocrat, he had said and done nothing. He tried not think about how this reflected on his character.

The sky in the west was flushed with pale streaks of light and the air felt cool and damp on his skin. Knox kept up a gentle pace, keen not to drive the horse too hard, since Maxwell wouldn't have thought to feed or water it. Just before departing, he had talked to the labourer who'd first discovered the body. The man had told him nothing new and had strenuously denied taking anything from the dead man's pockets. With nothing but the wind for company, Knox's thoughts turned to the cured meat. He hadn't eaten in twelve hours and his stomach was swollen with hunger. Taking it from his pocket, he brought it up to his nose and sniffed. Knox hadn't seen, let alone eaten, meat for six months, and the urge to gnaw at it was almost too much to bear. Just one mouthful, he told himself. But if he ate a mouthful, he would end up gobbling the whole thing, and then how could he face his wife? Instead he returned the meat to his pocket, tried to distract himself by thinking about the body behind him.

About halfway along the old road a pauper scampered out in front of him, waving his arms. Knox thought it was some kind of ruse and that the man was part of a gang of robbers. He tugged the reins and went to retrieve his pistol. Quickly, though, he could see that the man was in distress; he was talking rapidly in broken Irish. Knox told him to slow down and explain what had happened. The man yanked Knox's arm and led him through a gate to his cabin, where a lantern was hanging on a hook by the door. In halted speech he said that he'd left for a week in order to find road-building work in Thurles. Pushing open the door, Knox could smell the rotting corpses. There were three of them, limbs tangled up in the middle of the room, their carcasses gnawed almost clean by rats. Knox stared at them, not knowing what to say. Next to him, the husband slumped to his knees and started weeping. Knox sniffed the air and looked for a shovel. If the women and two children had died from a fever it was important to bury them as quickly as possible, to halt the spread of disease.

He told the man that the cemeteries were full and the undertakers were turning people away. The man looked at him, hollow-eyed. Knox doubted whether he'd be able to pay what they were demanding.

Without thinking, he thrust the cured meat into the man's outstretched hand. Trade it for a coffin, he said, or just eat it.

The man looked down at the meat but said nothing.

Knox deposited the vagrant's body in the cellar at the barracks and walked the mile and a half back to his cottage on the outskirts of town. Martha was waiting up for him; she had been waiting for hours. His first thought was for the infant, James, but she reassured him that everything was fine.

'I thought something terrible had happened to you,' she said, embracing him.

At twenty-three, Martha was five years younger than Knox and much better looking. She had thick, black straight hair, pale, freckled skin and delicate cheekbones. He had met her at a town fair three summers ago and they had married the following spring. Their marriage had been condemned by both families but it had been harder for Martha, especially as the ceremony had taken place in an Anglican church. Until the birth of their son, Martha had worked in the Union workhouse. In recent months, however, with the assistance of a Quaker family from Cork, she had given up this position to help run a soup kitchen which fed those who had been turned away from the workhouse.

20227175

'Do you know how much the Cornwallis estate has contributed to the poor relief fund?' she'd asked him the previous evening. 'A hundred pounds. That's all. Over the whole of last year.'

When he hadn't responded, she'd added, 'It hasn't stopped him claiming for five and a half thousand against the public works scheme. And why? So he can pay his own tenants out of the general rate to square his fields and drain his land. Land, I don't need to tell you, which was taken from those who needed it most.'

Later, he told Martha what he'd seen that day and what had happened to him in Dundrum. Afterwards they lay in silence, listening to the tree branches tapping against the windowpane.

'People are dying and there's no corn in the depot, not here, not in Clonmel and not even, I've heard, in Cork.'

Knox thought about the provisions the constabulary gave its men but decided not to say anything. Martha, he suspected, didn't want or expect him to comment.

'On the way to the house this morning,' he said eventually, 'I passed the time imagining what I'd say to Moore, how I would stand up to him and make him see the error of his ways.' In private, this was what they both called Cornwallis, an obvious marker of disrepect. 'But when I had the chance, I did nothing.'

Turning around, Martha kissed him gently on the cheek. 'You have your mother and your family to think about.'

Knox listened to the sound of the infant sleeping. This was what his mother had meant. The family's well-being depended on Moore's patronage and the aristocrat had wanted to remind him of this. 'Moore ordered me to bury the whole matter. I said I would.'

Martha waited a moment before saying, 'And will you?'

'What choice do I have?'

Martha ran her fingers through his still-damp hair. He could see one side of her face illuminated by moonlight shining in through the half-open curtains. 'You're a good man, Michael Knox. When the time comes, I know you'll do what is right. That's why I married you. Well, it's one of the reasons at least.' She tapped him playfully on the arm.

Knox let out a sigh. It was true. He did always try to do what was right, but this time he didn't share his wife's optimism.

THREE

Pyke had begun to feel his age.

It was the little things, he noticed. Such as the pain when he emptied his bladder in the mornings and the fact that when he first staggered out of his bed, his joints were so stiff he couldn't walk without a limp. This morning he felt fuzzy-headed and disoriented. He had taken to drinking wine on his own, to ward off the loneliness, now that Felix, his only son, had left home. Dry-mouthed, he rubbed the crust from his eyes and yawned. He had opened a second bottle, he remembered, as he listened to the empty house creaking in the autumn wind. He would get up in another five minutes.

It had been harder to get going, Pyke had found, since Felix's departure in the summer. Perhaps it was simply that he no longer had an example to set. But Pyke hadn't been sleeping well for other reasons. A month earlier one of his sergeants, Frederick Shaw, had been killed during a botched raid on a warehouse, but not by of the one of the robbers they'd been hoping to apprehend. It was Pyke who had shot him by mistake. He had given his men orders not to enter the warehouse while he reconnoitred it but shots had been fired and chaos had broken out. Later, having listened to the evidence, the jury at the inquiry had declared the death to be an accident, but Pyke hadn't been able to absolve himself of blame. He had been distracted; his head had been thick from the previous night's wine; someone ahead of him had moved and he had ordered them to stop. He'd reacted too quickly or not quickly enough and now a man, one of his very *best* men, was dead.

The funeral had been terrible. Pyke had decided to attend it, at the bidding of the other detectives, but he hadn't known what to say

FRANKLIN COUNTY LIBRARY
906 NORTH MAIN STREET
LOUISBURG, NC 27549
BRANCHES IN BUNN.

to Shaw's wife and his young son. Throughout the service, he had listened to their sobs. Later he had visited the widow at home and had spent an hour with her, offering his sympathies and telling her what a fine man her husband had been. She had greeted him politely and seemingly bore him no ill will, but once or twice the mask had slipped and he'd seen what she really thought about him, the fear and revulsion. The boy had bawled throughout his visit. He would now grow up without a father and Pyke knew from his own experience the disadvantages this would bring. Pyke had assured Shaw's widow that she would receive a generous pension but he knew this wouldn't be enough to bring up the child. He'd left her an envelope with a hundred pounds stuffed into it. Blood money, he'd thought as he said goodbye.

'I called out to him. I identified myself,' Pyke said after the funeral to Jack Whicher, one of his detectives. 'Why didn't he react? Why didn't he let me know who he was?'

Whicher hadn't been able to give him an answer.

'I'm not sure I can do this any more.'

'*This?*' Whicher had put his hands up to his eyes to shield them from the dull glare of the winter sun.

'If I hadn't been there, in that warehouse, Shaw might well be alive now.'

Whicher shook his head. 'It was Shaw's mistake, not yours. If he hadn't gone into the warehouse, none of this would have happened.'

That conversation had taken place a month earlier, but if anything Pyke's disquiet had intensified. He hadn't been able to put Shaw's little boy out of his head, trying to imagine what kind of man he would grow up to be. It wasn't guilt he felt – he'd done a lot worse in his life – it was just how quick and needless it had all been. Yet the repercussions would last a lifetime: Shaw's boy would find this out for himself. It was at times like these that Pyke missed his uncle: Godfrey would have known what to say, how to put things into perspective.

Pyke got up and emptied his bladder into the commode. Downstairs, he lit the fire that his housekeeper, Mrs Booth, had prepared and waited for the kettle to boil on the range. As he broke three eggs into a jug and whisked the white and yolk together he wondered – not for the first time – whether he'd meant what he'd said to Jack Whicher.

Did he really want to resign his position? Could he afford to?

As an inspector he enjoyed a modest salary, most of which he spent on the running of the household. He owned the house in Islington and had inherited a small sum from his uncle Godfrey, the best part of which he was using to pay for Felix's education. From time to time, he took the opportunity to augment his income by keeping back some of the items recovered from robberies or by pocketing jewels or other valuables that no one came forward to claim. He was comfortable rather than well off, but didn't know whether he'd be able to support himself without his detective's salary.

Once he'd poured the boiling water into the teapot, he collected the newspaper and the post from the doormat and began to sift through it, looking for anything interesting. There was a letter postmarked Merthyr Tydfil. He read the name on the reverse and it took him a moment to place it.

Pyke hadn't thought about Jonah Hancock for five years. His wife, Cathy, had been the daughter of one of Godfrey's friends.

Tearing the envelope, Pyke couldn't think how the man knew his home address, until he recalled he'd written to Cathy to tell her about arrangements for Godfrey's funeral. She hadn't attended but had sent him a letter of condolence. Pyke tried to remember her as she'd been five years earlier, the last time he'd seen her: barely eighteen years old and pretty, her fine blonde hair arranged into ringlets. Pyke had seen for himself that she didn't love or even much care for the man she was about to marry, yet he'd said nothing. Perhaps it hadn't been any of his business. Still, if he was honest, he had known – he had always known – that she admired him and would have listened to him. At the time, he hadn't wanted to court intimacy with her; she was too young for any good to come of it.

Cathy had been attractive and flirtatious but he wouldn't have described her as sweet. She had always been too worldly, even as an eighteen-year-old. Instinctively she was aware of the effect she had on men, and Pyke couldn't pretend that he had been immune to her charms. At times, when she'd held his hand and laughed, he had felt a powerful tug in his stomach and she had seemed to realise this. Cathy was wasted on her husband. Jonah Hancock was dull and boorish at his best but he was also fabulously wealthy and had been looking for a young wife. Cathy, who'd been devoted to her father and was easily impressed, had consented to the arrangement. Pyke hadn't been invited to the wedding but he had met Cathy and Jonah Hancock a few weeks before it in London. The occasion had been pleasant at first but Hancock had drunk too much wine and, after lunch, Pyke recalled seeing them in the back of a phaeton, Hancock's arm around her, pulling her closer, Cathy struggling to free herself from his grip.

A year later, Pyke heard from Godfrey that Cathy had borne Hancock a son. Now, it seemed, from the content of the letter, that the young boy had been snatched by kidnappers.

It was odd, Pyke mused as he reread the letter, that Jonah Hancock and not Cathy had written to him. Perhaps Cathy had badgered her husband to write to him. Perhaps she had told him that Pyke was head of the Detective Branch. Or perhaps the man was just desperate. Pyke had gone through something similar with Felix, when he was about the same age as the Hancock boy, and he could recall how helpless he had felt. Now Jonah Hancock was offering him a thousand pounds if he would oversee the safe return of his son.

At first Pyke didn't seriously think about accepting the offer, despite the enormous sum of money being promised, but then he remembered that Bristol was on the way to Wales and he could stop there and see Felix, who had gone to study in Keynsham under a vicar they'd known in London.

Patting Copper, his three-legged mastiff, on the head, Pyke poured a cup of tea and sat down at the table. Perhaps it would do him good to get out of London for a while. He took a sip of tea and thought about the difference a thousand pounds would make to his bank balance.

Pyke knocked on the door of the Commissioner's private chambers and waited for Sir Richard Mayne to answer.

Mayne was sitting behind his polished, well-ordered desk. He looked relaxed and was talking to Benedict Pierce, the Assistant Commissioner. They stopped speaking as soon as Pyke stepped into the room, their eyes following him as he crossed the floor. Without saying a word, Pyke took out the letter he'd received from Jonah Hancock and placed it on the desk in front of Mayne. Now he was glad that Cathy hadn't written it: the ironmaster's sanction gave the mission additional legitimacy.

The Commissioner had silver hair, a firm mouth and quick, intelligent eyes. He had been supportive of Pyke mostly because he'd argued for the establishment of the Detective Branch and couldn't afford for it to fail. Still, their respective vision of the work detectives should perform was fundamentally at odds: Pyke had always argued that good detective work was founded upon the gathering of information from the criminal classes while Mayne worried that these encounters would inevitably corrupt the detectives under Pyke's command. Mayne could be taciturn but he was fair. Pierce, on the other hand, was a punctilious man who had climbed the greasy pole through a combination of flattery and viciousness. Pyke had hoped that his appointment as Assistant Commissioner – the youngest man to have held this post – might have mellowed Pierce, but the evidence pointed to the contrary. It was no secret that Pyke and Pierce despised one another and Pyke didn't doubt that if the man came upon something he could use against him, he would do so without a second thought.

Mayne passed the letter to Pierce and waited for him to read it. 'I've met Hancock's father, Zephaniah,' he said, when Pierce had finished. 'The ironworks they own is one of the largest in the country.'

Pyke just nodded. Mayne understood, without having to be told, that the kidnapping had wider political ramifications.

'So you think it's important that you attend to this business personally?' Mayne said, cautiously.

'Of course he does,' Pierce exclaimed. 'This man is offering to pay him a thousand pounds.'

Ignoring this outburst, Mayne stroked his chin, trying to assess the situation. 'Why did he write in person to you, Detective-inspector?'

Pyke explained that he'd known Hancock's wife and that he'd met Hancock himself just prior to the wedding five years earlier.

'You must have made an impression on him.' Mayne waited and added, 'Or her.'

That drew a slight smirk from Pierce. Pyke decided that the remark didn't warrant a response.

'Still, I'm inclined to approve the request – on the grounds that it's in the national interest.' Mayne turned to Pierce. 'Benedict?'

Pyke could see this had put Pierce in a difficult position. If he argued against it, he would be going against Mayne's wishes.

'I agree.' Pierce looked up at Pyke and smiled. 'I'm sure the Detective Branch can cope in the detective-inspector's absence.'

This was something Pyke hadn't considered – that Pierce might use his absence as an opportunity to interfere.

'Jack Whicher is more than capable of overseeing things until I return.' Pyke knew that Whicher – the ablest of his detective-sergeants – wouldn't give Pierce the time of day.

'I don't doubt that he is,' Pierce said, swatting a fly with his hand. 'But we don't need to rush into a decision right away, do we?'

'If I have your approval,' Pyke said, addressing Mayne, 'I intend to leave at once on the afternoon train to Bristol.' He'd already looked into the journey: he would stop and see Felix in Keynsham, then from Bristol he would catch a boat to Cardiff and take a train from there to Merthyr.

'Detective-sergeant Whicher has always struck me as a very capable detective.' Mayne drummed his fingers on the surface of his desk. 'How long do you imagine you'll be away?'

'It depends what I find when I get there.' Pyke paused. 'A month maybe.'

'That long?' Mayne regarded him sceptically.

Pyke reached out, took the letter and put it into the pocket of the frock-coat he'd just purchased from his tailor.

'If you're successful,' Pierce said, 'you'll be expected to register your reward with the Returns Office.'

'If I'm successful, a young boy's life will have been saved.'

Pierce's face reddened but he said nothing.

'I know one of the magistrates in Merthyr,' Mayne interrupted. 'A fellow called Sir Clancy Smyth – a good sort, from an old Anglo-Irish family.' He stood up, walked around his desk and accompanied Pyke to the door. 'Pass on my best wishes and tell him you have my fullest support.' He offered Pyke his hand and Pyke shook it.

Later, Pyke came upon Benedict Pierce waiting for him in the corridor.

'I just came to wish you happy travels.'

Pyke came to a halt a yard from where Pierce was standing and studied his face for a moment. 'If you'll excuse me, I have matters to attend to.'

Pierce didn't move. He folded his arms, the smile curdling at the corners of his mouth.

'Is there something else you want to say?' Pyke was a head taller than Pierce and stepped forward into the space between them.

'We both know why you're so keen to take this assignment. Don't think Sir Richard is blind to your motives, either.'

Pyke was about to say something but thought better of it. He went to open the door to his office.

'Pyke?'

Pyke tried to keep his irritation in check. 'Are you still here?'

But Pierce had moved off in the direction of the stairs.

Pyke caught the two thirty from Paddington and broke his journey in Bath, where he took the slower train to Keynsham. He arrived there after dark and made his way to the church, St John's, in the middle of the town. In the vestry, he found Martin Jakes attending to one of his parishioners. The elderly curate was dressed in a black cassock and when he spotted Pyke he extricated himself from the conversation and bustled over to greet him, smiling and shaking his head. 'You should have told us you were coming. Have you been to the vicarage yet?'

When Pyke said he had not, Jakes informed him that they would go at once, adding that Felix was proving to be a most able student.

Pyke nodded but secretly he'd been hoping that Felix's enthusiasm for a life in the Church might have waned in the months since he'd been there. This was not a reflection of the affection Pyke felt for Jakes – who he'd met a few years earlier and who, uniquely in his opinion, combined religious belief with a real concern for the poor. It was just that he hadn't envisaged Felix might actually want to become a vicar, and this brought into sharper focus his own lack of faith: not simply agnosticism, which he presumed described the perspective of most people, but a scepticism that bordered on total hostility. He'd always viewed the established Church as a bloated organisation intent only on maintaining its own privileged position in the world.

It was a five-minute walk from the church to the vicarage. There, he found Felix where Jakes had said he would be: sitting at a davenport in a sparsely furnished upstairs room, a copy of the Bible set before him. Felix greeted Pyke with a hug and berated him for not warning them of his visit. Now sixteen, Felix was nearly as tall as Pyke and he'd filled out considerably. With curly chestnut-brown hair, a clean-shaven face, soft skin, blue eyes and dimpled cheeks, Felix had turned into a good-looking young man. He listened carefully as Pyke explained why he was there, and then peppered Pyke with questions about their home in Islington, Copper, Mrs Booth, their housekeeper, and Pyke's life since they'd said goodbye on the station platform at Paddington station six months earlier.

Pyke hadn't written to Felix nearly as often as the lad had written to him and he'd been unduly nervous about this reunion. Part of him had been hoping that, having spent six months under Jakes's tutelage, Felix might have become disillusioned by the prospect of a life in the Church and would consider coming back to London – to take up an apprenticeship in, say, business or politics. Looking at Felix, Pyke knew immediately that this wasn't the case and it heartened and depressed him in equal measure. He didn't want his son to be unhappy but he knew that the more seriously Felix took his apprenticeship, the less likely he was to return home. Rather than admitting that he had missed Felix, Pyke told him that Copper had pined for weeks, which was true, and that the house was not the same without him, which was also true.

Felix studied him for a moment. 'You look exhausted. Are you quite sure everything is all right?'

'I'm fine, really. Just a little tired. I've probably been working too hard.'

'You always work too hard.'

'I've been promised some leave. I was hoping you wouldn't mind if I stopped here for a few days on my way back from Wales.'

'You know you're welcome to stay for as long as you like. We won't even try to make a Christian of you.' Felix laughed uneasily.

Pyke rubbed his temples. He'd experienced some pain during the journey from London but now it had developed into a full-blown headache. Trying to ignore it, he gestured at the Bible on the davenport. 'How are your studies progressing?'

'Good. And the Detective Branch?'

'Good too.' They stared at one another, unsure what to say next.

Pyke sat down on Felix's bed and looked around the room. He hadn't intended to say anything about Shaw but suddenly he felt compelled to mention what had happened. 'About a month ago . . . I killed a man, shot him in the back. Turns out, he was one of my men. Detective-sergeant Shaw. I'm sure you met him once. A good man and a good detective.'

Felix sat down on the bed next to him. 'So what happened?' he asked finally.

'We were raiding a warehouse in the East End. I thought he was one of the gang we were there to arrest.'

'It was an accident, then.'

'I shouted at him to stop but obviously he didn't hear me.'

Felix handed Pyke a handkerchief and Pyke took it and wiped the sweat from his forehead.

'Was there any inquiry?' he asked gently.

'The death was ruled an accident.'

'That's something, isn't it?'

'Shaw left behind a wife and a young boy.'

Pyke let his stare drift towards the window, the unfamiliar darkness. He imagined Felix lying there at night. Did the lad ever think of home? 'Do you think this will be your life, then?' He tried to keep the disapproval from his voice.

Felix regarded him with caution. 'I like what I'm doing, I suppose. I like the discipline; knuckling down to something I think is worthwhile. It isn't easy or comforting, though: giving yourself up to something, someone, you can't even see. It's the hardest thing I've ever had to do.'

As Pyke listened, he thought about how much the lad had grown up. 'You seem to be happy.'

'It hadn't really crossed my mind, whether I'm happy or not. But now you mention it, I suppose I am.' Felix looked at him and smiled. 'You never told me why you're going to Wales.'

'A child has been kidnapped.'

'A child?' Felix's expression changed. 'How old?'

'Four or thereabouts.' Pyke paused. 'I used to know the mother and father.'

'It must be a terrible time for them.'

'It made me think of what happened to you and your mother, all those years ago.'

Felix's face softened and suddenly the years fell away. 'I still think about her, you know. Sometimes I can hear her voice, the way she laughed, and but I can't picture what she looked like.'

'You were five years old at the time.'

'I know. But still, she was my mother.'

This was the longest conversation they'd had about Emily in years. 'You look a lot like her, you know. Your eyes and your nose, especially.'

Felix stood up, agitated, and then sat down. 'I wish we had a painting of her.'

'I tried to persuade her to sit for one but she told me she was too busy.' Pyke laughed.

Then Felix grabbed hold of Pyke's wrist and squeezed. 'Find this boy and return him to his parents.'

'That's exactly what I intend to do.' Pyke tried to show his gratitude at this unexpected show of support as Felix had never expressed much interest in his work.

'I know you will.'

Pyke thought about mentioning the thousand-pound reward but stopped himself at the last moment.

Later, on the platform, while they waited for the arrival of the Bristol-bound service, they were joined by Jakes, who assured Pyke he was welcome to stay for as long as he liked on his return from Wales. Taking Felix to one side, Pyke put his hand on the lad's shoulder and said he hoped – one day – to attend his ordination ceremony. It was the first time he'd given encouragement to Felix's decision. Felix just smiled. The train pulled into the station and blanketed the platform with steam. Kissing Felix on the forehead, Pyke whispered that he loved him and then took his suitcase and boarded the train. As it lurched forward, Pyke opened the window and waved at Felix and Jakes. It felt as if he were leaving a part of his life on the platform. *You have to let them go*, Godfrey had warned him shortly before his death. Now Pyke knew what he had meant.

FOUR

THURSDAY, 7 JANUARY 1847

Cashel, Co. Tipperary

Knox woke suddenly, startled by a noise beneath the window. He lay there, listening to his wife sleeping and to the sound of raindrops pattering against the windowpanes. He waited for the dog to bark but nothing happened so he climbed out of bed, taking care not to wake Martha, put on his robe, and looked at their child, who was fast asleep. Downstairs, Knox unlocked the door and peered out into the yard. The dog looked up at him from the shelter they had built and began to wag its tail. Knox stepped outside and patted the brown mutt on the head. It was barely light and the clouds overheard were ominous. At least it wasn't as cold as the previous two days, he thought, as he lit a fire in the back room. The dog joined him, even though it wasn't meant to come inside. Knox patted it on the head again and wondered how long they could keep the animal. It was useful to have a guard dog, Knox supposed, but they could barely take care of themselves, and another mouth to feed was a luxury. He had heard stories of stray dogs being killed for their meat, but as he patted the midriff of the animal at his feet, it struck him that Tom – that was what they'd decided to call him, after Thomas Davis – wouldn't make much of a meal.

Getting dressed, Knox turned his thoughts to the dead body he'd brought back from Cornwallis's estate. The day before, he had petitioned in vain for the sub-inspector to pay for an undertaker to embalm the body, at least to preserve it until someone had identified the dead man. But he had been told in no uncertain terms to get rid of it, something he'd promised to do as soon as he got to the barracks. If no one identified the man, Knox knew that the inquiry was as good as dead.

Upstairs he heard James cry, and almost immediately, his wife's footsteps crossing the bedroom to comfort him. Knox boiled a kettle of water, poured it into their mugs, along with some crushed nettles from the yard, and placed a saucepan of water on the range. Then he took the nettles out of the mugs, discarded them and measured half a cup of Indian corn before tossing the grains into the saucepan. His thoughts turned to the cured meat which he had given away to the man who'd lost his family. He'd done so because he'd felt sorry for him, and because it had seemed like the right thing to do, but now he regretted it. He had his own family to think about.

He took a mug of nettle tea to his wife, who was breastfeeding James.

'It's the coroner's inquest today.' Knox looked at her and James and waited for her to answer.

'And then?' she asked, finally.

Knox nodded. She was quite right. The verdict wasn't in doubt: murder by a person or persons unknown. How could it be declared otherwise? The real question was whether Hastings would want the matter investigated further.

James gurgled a little and continued to suckle on her breast.

'I don't know. It's not my decision.'

'Then why are you so worried about it?' Martha tried, not entirely successfully, to keep the judgement from her tone.

The previous day Knox had trudged around the inns and guest houses of Cashel, asking if anyone had taken in a man – very possibly an Englishman – whose description matched that of the corpse. No one admitted to having done so.

He stood there, staring out of the window that overlooked the yard. 'I can't explain it, Martha. I just feel like I owe it to him.'

Knox could tell that his wife didn't like his answer.

'I understand, Michael.' Her expression softened. 'Remember, we've been married nearly five years now.'

'But?'

'Moore gave you orders to drop the matter. What do you think he'll do if he finds out you're still digging around?'

Knox saw her discomfort. It was true that Martha was just as vociferous in her criticism of Moore as he was, at least in private, but now there was something else in her eyes. Could it be fear?

'If I say and do nothing, that man will have died alone and unmourned. Is that what you would want?'

'No, of course not.' She sighed and turned her attention back to the child. 'But I don't see how this one man is any different from the countless other men, women and children who are starving to death even as we're talking.'

Knox stared down at his muddy boots and listened to the rain outside.

'What you're doing, what you're proposing to do, is right. I'm not denying that. It's just we have other things, other people, to think about.'

After breakfast, Knox walked the mile and a half into town. It took him along a narrow track flanked by hedges as tall as he was, past the ruins of Hore Abbey on one side and the Rock of Cashel on the other. He entered the town and turned on to Main Street near the fountain. The barracks was a squat two-storey building that sat at a ninety-degree angle to the courthouse. He was instructed to report *immediately* to the sub-inspector.

'Constable Knox,' Hastings said, after he'd presented himself at the sub-inspector's door.

'Sir.'

Hastings was a dour Protestant, forty-one years old, married with three children, and as fair-minded as it was possible to be in the post he occupied. His moustache was trimmed and flecked with grey, and he made a point of donning the same uniform as the rest of them: a blue swallow-tailed coat and a pair of matching woollen trousers. His one remarkable feature was a glass eye: he had lost the real one in a brawl some time before Knox had joined the constabulary.

'Constable Knox, I wanted to ask about your plans for the disposal of the corpse lying in the cellar.'

'I intend to take it to the cemetery this morning.'

Hastings gave him a perfunctory nod. 'I'm afraid it won't be possible to bury the body there. They've dug a pit at the back of the workhouse. You're to take it there.'

Knox knew better than to question the man. 'Of course. Will that be all, sir?'

Hastings looked up from a document he'd been browsing. 'I believe the inquest is due to take place today.' Not waiting for an answer, he said, 'A verdict of murder will be returned. Since Lord Cornwallis asked you to attend to this matter, I see no reason to make alternative arrangements. It's Thursday today. You can have until Monday.'

Knox moistened his parched lips. 'You *do* know I've never conducted a murder inquiry before.'

Hastings had picked up a quill but he put it down on his desk and then sighed. 'Just do what you think is best, Constable.'

Knox nodded. The implication was clear: he was not expected to find out who'd killed the man or even who the victim was. He had been given the case because it was deemed not to be important.

'Good. That will be all.' Hastings turned his attention to the piece of paper in front of him but Knox didn't move. 'Is there something else, Constable?'

'There was one thing, actually, sir. There's a man in town called James Sullivan, owns a draper's shop. In his spare time, he has developed an interest in daguerreotyping. I thought I might ask him to capture an image of the dead man in case we need someone to identify him at some future point.' Knox waited. 'I imagine we would have to pay the man a small fee . . .'

Hastings sat back in his chair and folded his arms. 'Have you been listening to me at all, Constable?'

'Sir?' Knox felt a trickle of sweat snake its way down the side of his body.

'I want you to take that corpse to the pit at the back of the workhouse and dispose of it forthwith. Is there any part of that statement you still don't understand?'

Knox stiffened his back. 'No, sir. I'll attend to it right away.'

'See that you do it,' Hastings said, dismissing him with a wave of the hand.

The horse and cart were unavailable so he had to make do with a borrowed hand-barrow. The dead body had started to smell so Knox had to cover his mouth with a clean handkerchief before dragging it up the stairs to the rear of the barracks.

The route to the workhouse didn't take him past Sullivan's shop so he had to make a slight diversion. Knox passed a hatter, a brogue-maker, a stone-cutter and a tailor before he stopped outside the draper's window. There he covered the barrow with an old piece of cloth and entered the shop.

Inside, out of the cold wind, he told Sullivan – whom he knew quite well – what he had in mind and asked whether he would be interested in helping.

'Well, that's a mighty unusual request, sir, but I fancy I see your point.' The draper hesitated. 'We'd have to close the shop for a while. That would incur some cost. Then there's the matter of the copperplates, the iodine, the mercury.'

Knox tried to swallow. 'How much would two good plates cost?'

'Two?' Sullivan wiped his hands on his apron and did a quick calculation in his head. 'Shall we say a guinea, since it's coming out of the public purse?'

Knox had already decided to foot the bill himself but this was more than he had been expecting. He had saved three pounds, which was buried in the yard at home, but in light of the current difficulties, the idea of frittering away a third of this sum on two daguerreotypes seemed reckless to the point of stupidity.

'I was told not to go above twenty shillings.'

Sullivan eyed him suspiciously. Perhaps he thought that Knox had been given a budget and was trying to barter him down in order to keep some of the money for himself. 'I'll do it for twenty-three, not a shilling less.'

'You're not to mention this business to another soul. I mean it, James. Not even to your wife.' Knox folded his arms. He could feel his heart thumping against his chest.

'I can hold my tongue,' Sullivan said. 'Twenty-three shillings?' He spat on his hand and offered it to Knox.

'Agreed.'

After laying down the corpse in the back of the shop, Knox waited outside as Sullivan set to work.

The workhouse gates were locked but after he'd rattled them, Bill McDonagh appeared from around the side of the building, sleeves rolled up to his elbows. 'No more room,' he said, before he'd realised who it was and why Knox was there.

Knox looked up at the workhouse, which had been raised five years earlier on ground a few hundred yards south of the town. It was a building intended to deter rather than welcome: its austerity a reminder of the strict regime that awaited the men and women who had nowhere else to go. It had been full for a number of weeks but in defiance of the commissioners' strict instruction to cease all outdoor relief, hundreds of non-inmates were still being fed there.

'Yellow Bill' McDonagh was a gravedigger hired by the Board of Guardians to collect and bury stray bodies. Knox didn't know where the name 'Yellow Bill' had come from but it was how everyone in the town referred to him.

'That for me?' Bill asked, gesturing at the hand-barrow Knox had set down next to the gate. He spoke in Irish, even though Knox knew that he understood English quite well.

'I was told there was a pit here,' Knox said, making a point of answering in English.

Bill glanced down at the body covered by the piece of cloth. 'I've just come from it.' This time he had spoken in English.

'This one needs to go in the ground as a matter of urgency.'

Bill sniffed the air. 'Been a while, has it?'

Knox shrugged. 'I'll push the barrow, you lead the way.'

Bill wiped his nose on his sleeve. Like most Catholics, he distrusted the army more than he did the police, and seemed happy to take men like Knox at their word. 'I should warn you, Constable. It isn't pleasant in there.'

'I'm sure I've seen as bad.'

Knox let Bill walk ahead of him along a mud path that skirted the left side of the workhouse. It terminated at the edge of a giant pit which had been dug into the ground. On Bill's advice, Knox had already tied a handkerchief around his nose. Despite this, the stench of putrefying flesh was appalling. He stared into the pit and felt his legs buckle. There were, quite literally, dozens of bodies, limbs tangled together, flesh covered by quicklime. Rats crawled among the corpses. Nauseous, Knox had to look away. He took a couple of breaths and watched as Bill pulled back the cloth covering the body in the barrow.

'If it's all the same to you,' Bill said, 'I'll strip off his clothes before I toss him in the pit.'

Knox shook his head. 'No, he goes in as he is. Clothes and all.' He didn't want the gravedigger to see the stab wound in the dead man's stomach.

Bill looked up at him, squinting, and then shrugged. 'Suit yourself.' He went over to the barrow, scooped up the body and carried it to the edge of the pit. With a grunt, he pushed the body forward. Knox watched it fall. Bill went to collect some quicklime and sprinkled it over the clothed body. Now Knox understood why Bill had wanted to undress it.

Reading his mind, the gravedigger said, 'I wouldn't worry. A few more bodies, and they'll close up this pit and dig another one.'

Knox just nodded.

'Who was he, anyhow?'

'A vagrant.'

The older man's eyes narrowed. 'Aren't they all?'

The previous afternoon, Knox had taken the *Tipperary Free Press* to his nearly blind neighbour, Jeremy Brittas. Knox rented his smallholding from the Brittas family and twice a week read for the grandfather, who lived alone in the Mount Judkin house's lodge. Despite the old man's curmudgeonly manner, Knox relished these moments, as it was a chance to engage with a world beyond his front door.

Brittas liked him to read everything, even the notices for cold creams, macassar oil and pills to treat gonorrhoea. The previous day, the paper had reported more deaths in Skibbereen. On the same page, a notice for the new edition of the *Economist* magazine lauded the role that free trade had played in bringing about the moral and intellectual advancement of society. To Knox, it seemed like a bad joke.

'Has free trade put bread on anyone's table?' he had asked Jeremy Brittas. 'Well, has it?'

The old man hadn't an answer.

Knox had read some more of the newspaper. 'Why don't they report the deaths we're suffering here?' He had looked up almost accusingly at his neighbour.

Brittas had taken his stick and banged it into the floor. 'Read on, man. Read on.'

Knox had got to the end of the report about US President Polk's promise to increase his country's famine relief. He'd found himself nodding in agreement. '*Does America live under laws made by herself? She does. Does Ireland live under laws made by herself? She does not! Ireland pines, and starves and dies beneath the Upas tree of British Legislation.*' At that point Brittas coughed and Knox had looked up.

'Free trade might've made a rum job of feeding people but do you really think democracy would've improved the situation?'

'I'd prefer to die poor but with my head held high than poor and enslaved,' Knox replied.

'And if food was just handed out to folk, who would ever bother to work for a living?'

'But there is no work. That's the problem. No work and no food, at least at prices that poor folk can afford.'

Knox was still thinking about this exchange when Duffy, a constable from Roscommon, shouted from the door. 'Finally found you. They want us at the workhouse straight away. There's a mob gathered outside.'

Six policemen assembled in front of the barracks. All except for Knox were Catholics from hard-working families; they had come from all over Ireland and lived together in the barracks. It made him an anomaly, and while nothing was ever said aloud, Knox knew that none of them really trusted him, believing that he'd been appointed as an informer to the Protestant commanders. Nothing could have been farther from the truth. In fact, Hastings and the other head-constables had always regarded Knox with suspicion, wondering why he had been willing to work for the same pay and conditions as the Catholic constables.

Hastings appeared from the station and told the men to go to the workhouse at once and disperse the mob. He did not say how they were meant to do this or what would happen if the mob refused to go quietly. He didn't mention the word 'force' but it was implicit in everything he said. Why else had he instructed them to take their carbines?

A couple of days earlier, Knox had read about food riots in Clonmel. Now, it seemed, the same thing was about to take place in Cashel.

They trudged in silence along Boherclough Street past the Old

Court building on their left, and then the Fever Hospital. Knox couldn't speak for the others but he had already made a promise to himself that he wouldn't open fire on his own countrymen.

A mob of about fifty or sixty had gathered outside the gates of the workhouse and Knox and the constables had to push their way through, using the butts of their carbines to get to the gates. There, they found Michael Doheny, chairman of the Board of Guardians, trying to plead with the men. Some were brandishing pickaxes, others brickbats. Earlier that afternoon, it transpired, the workhouse had stopped issuing any outdoor relief. Doheny was promising to see whether any food could be found for them. He was a hero to these men. A few years earlier he had stood up to one of the largest landowning families and forced them to make good the rate they owed the town. He'd used the money to fund relief projects in Cashel which, in turn, had kept many men and women from starvation. Now, this source of income had dried up and the mood was desperate. Hands aloft, Doheny was pleading with the men to go home to their families.

'Home?' one of them yelled. 'We don't have a home. Not since we were turned off our land.'

'The workhouse can't take any more.' This time it was James Heany, vice-chairman of the Union, who'd spoken.

'We just want to eat.'

'My wife and baby haven't fed in a week,' another man shouted. 'If I don't get food, they'll die.' Further pleas were drowned out by the shouting.

Knox and the other constables fanned out in front of the gates. They were holding their carbines but hadn't yet turned them against the crowd. Knox tried not to think about what might happen if one or two of the mob tried to storm the gates. Were they desperate or hungry enough to do such a thing? He stared at the crowd, saw his own terror mirrored in their faces.

'I will personally make sure that supplies of corn are made available tomorrow for you to buy,' Doheny yelled through cupped hands, trying to magnify his voice.

'We can't *afford* the prices the traders are charging,' someone shouted back. There were murmurs of agreement.

Doheny held up his hands and waited for complete silence. 'I will personally make sure you'll be charged no more than two pennies for a pound.'

The market rate was now almost five pence for a pound of corn. Knox wondered how Doheny would make good on his promise but it seemed to do the job. Slowly the mob began to disperse, and the relief among the constables was palpable. Knox went over to congratulate Doheny. Grim-faced, the chair of the Board thanked him but said he still had to secure an agreement from the traders to sell the corn – if they had any left – at the low price.

A meeting to discuss the relief effort was due to start in the town hall on Main Street at eight, he added. It promised to be another stormy affair, as Lord Cornwallis and a representative of another large landowning family were due to attend. They would be asked to explain their unwillingness to pay for further supplies of corn, and Doheny wondered whether Knox and the other men would mind attending, in their capacity as defenders of the peace.

'They'll heckle Lord Cornwallis to start with, but mark my words, when he finishes, he'll have the whole room eating out of his hand.' Doheny – a man who had once organised a giant meeting in Cashel to agitate for the repeal of the Union and who fervently believed that Ireland should fight for independence – seemed more sad than angry at this prospect.

Knox hadn't eaten anything since breakfast but said he would be there. Doheny patted him on the back. 'It's hard, isn't it, when the side you're on is not the side you want to be on.'

Knox wondered whether Doheny knew that he, too, was in favour of Irish independence and had even named his dog after a man who had done as much as anyone to further this particular cause.

The town hall was full to capacity by the time Knox had pushed his way to the front of the room; a heaving mass of pale flesh and damp kerseymere exuding the smell of stale sweat and tobacco. On the stage with Doheny and the Board of Guardians were representatives of the Pennefather family and Lord Cornwallis, who'd travelled from Dundrum to address the meeting. The Pennefathers and the Moores were the largest ratepayers in the county and therefore enjoyed a de facto right to sit on the Board.

As far as Knox could tell, an argument had broken out about who would subsidise the corn that Doheny had promised the protesters earlier.

William Carew, a trader, was complaining that if they sold his corn at the low price, he would make a loss and would have to be compensated using some fund made available by the Board. Doheny told him there was no money left. Carew repeated that he couldn't afford to let the corn go at a loss. This led to further discussion about the ethics of the situation. Some accused Carew and his like of 'naked profiteering'. This drew hot denials from the traders and the shopkeepers. Others blamed the Relief Commission in Dublin, and no one had a good word to say about the new Whig government in London, especially when it came to Sir Charles Trevelyan, head of the Treasury, who had publicly stated that it was up to the local boards and landlords, not the government, to provide poor relief. But the debate was predictable, and after fifteen minutes of wrangling nothing had been agreed.

'*Dammit,*' Doheny shouted, eventually slamming his fist down on the table. 'While we're sitting here talking, men, women and children are dying every single day for the simple reason they can't afford to eat.'

He was staring directly at Lord Cornwallis and for the first time all eyes turned towards the gnarled aristocrat.

Cornwallis cleared his throat and rose to his feet, turning away from the rest of the Board to address the crowded room. His bald head shone under the glare of the gaslight.

'I come with a gift and a warning. The gift first: an additional one hundred pounds to the relief effort. This should, temporarily at least, defray the cost of the subsidy unwisely promised to the mob earlier today. But before I issue my warning, I feel compelled to clear up a few *misunderstandings* regarding the management of my estate. It is true I've been compelled to evict some unfortunate families from my land but only because the rent has fallen to such a low figure that the prospects for the estate have become imperilled. Reform is what's called for; diversification. The old system is dead. No longer can we rely on that lazy root, the potato, to provide for all of our needs. Surely the last year is proof enough of that? Now, on my estate, there is land given over to pasture and grain. But I hear other whispers, too, efforts to impugn my family's name. To some, I'm to be tarred with the same brush as other absent landlords. Apparently I care nothing for the plight of my tenants and sub-tenants. *An absent landlord?* Am I not here, addressing you? I am doing my bit, of course, as I should, but is it my responsibility alone to ensure that mouths in the county are fed? Look to the government. And before you think about pointing the finger in my direction, take notice of the money I have spent improving my estate, money which has filtered down to every single one of you.'

Cornwallis put his hands on his hips and stared out across the silent hall. He started to smile. 'Now to my warning. Should the Board attempt to raise an additional levy against my estate, I shall have little choice but to redesignate my land as belonging to the neighbouring parish, which will mean, of course, that I'll pay my rate there.'

As he sat down, the full implications of what he'd said started to ripple around the room. If Cornwallis withdrew his rate the work-house could not be sustained and would have to close, forcing all five hundred men, women and children on to the streets. The result would be calamitous.

Afterwards, Knox was so deep in thought he didn't notice Cornwallis approaching him until it was too late. The man's face was glistening with perspiration and Knox could smell the wine on his breath.

'I understand that your investigation is proceeding as per our discussion.' He reached out and patted Knox on the face. 'You're a good boy, Michael. Loyal as they come. I mentioned this to your mother earlier today. She is very proud of you.'

Knox looked at the older man's self-satisfied expression and had to rein in the urge to say what he really thought of him.

'I shouldn't wonder if it will be Head-constable Knox before very long. Who knows? Perhaps even sub-inspector one of these days.'

Knox stared down at his boots and again said nothing.

FIVE

TUESDAY, 17 NOVEMBER 1846
Merthyr Tydfil, South Wales

Pyke's first impressions of the town were not very promising and a brief walk around it didn't alter this perception. Merthyr was a squalid town trapped in a valley between three dirty mountains. If he'd arrived at night, someone said, the sight of jets of fire spurting up from the giant blast furnaces at the two great ironworks would have been impressive, but in daylight the place simply looked depressing, a grotesque man-made sore on an already bleak landscape.

In fact, to call the row upon monotonous row of squat back-to-back houses a town seemed to be a misnomer. Aside from a multitude of poorly constructed chapels, there were no public buildings or amenities of any note: no town hall, no fever hospital, no workhouse, no pavements, no gaslights, nothing to indicate that the civic spirit ran to anything more than letting the two ironworks do exactly as they wished. The High Street was pleasant enough, Pyke supposed, in a rather drab way, but he could see immediately that there were parts of the town where the squalor and degradation were as bad, if not worse, than anything he'd encountered in London.

On the train up from Cardiff, Pyke had sat next to a Chartist called Bill Flint. The radical had told Pyke that the town was booming on the back of a seemingly unquenchable thirst for iron, but that all the wealth was going straight into the pockets of the families that owned the largest ironworks: the Webbs of Morlais and the Hancocks of Caedraw. Merthyr, Flint had explained, was the biggest iron-producing town in the world. Wages were high, he acknowledged, compared with other parts of the country, but so were costs; private landlords were making a killing on rents and the truck system meant that workers had to spend their earnings buying overpriced goods at the company shop. What little remained went into the pockets of the publicans and brothel-keepers. At the last count, Flint said, there were five hundred beer shops and at least fifty brothels, the latter crammed into an area known as China. In turn, this had attracted swell mobs, pickpockets, thieves and gamblers from as far afield as Bristol and Liverpool.

Along the way, the police had lost control of parts of the town. But the ironmasters – to whom the police answered – didn't seem to be particularly concerned about gambling and prostitution and cared only about excessive drinking after payday when the workers didn't turn up for their shifts. It was the threat of industrial unrest that really frightened them, and there had been plenty of skirmishes over the years. The Merthyr Rising and the insurrection at Newport had been the most serious instances, and on each occasion soldiers had been called in to quell the unrest, with innocent men being shot and killed. On those occasions, Flint explained, the area had been suffering some of its leanest years and the men had been afraid for their jobs. Now, it was boom time and since there were more jobs than people to fill them, some of the radicals wanted to argue for higher wages. The town was awash with unsavoury types but the worst criminals of all were the ironmasters, Flint concluded. Perhaps not Sir Josiah Webb, who was well intentioned, but Zephaniah and Jonah Hancock were nothing short of pirates.

Pyke hadn't mentioned the kidnapping and Flint hadn't asked about it, or about Pyke's reason for visiting the town.

Before presenting himself at the Hancocks' home, he decided to call in to the station-house, a two-storey building on Graham Street. There, he found Superintendent Henry Jones, a well-spoken, energetic man in his twenties. Clearly Jones knew about the kidnapping but he hadn't been forewarned of Pyke's visit. He greeted Pyke and lamented the shortcomings of the force he oversaw in Merthyr, perhaps worried how the operation might look to a detective-inspector from London. When Pyke explained that he wanted to speak to Sir Clancy Smyth, the young superintendent suggested they wander over to the old courthouse.

'So what are your first impressions of our fair town?' Jones asked, as they crossed the street outside the station-house.

Pyke couldn't tell whether he was being ironic. 'Do you want an honest answer?'

Jones laughed nervously. 'It has its moments, you know. The Taff Valley is really rather beautiful.'

They walked for a while in silence. The streets in the town centre were quiet, with just a few drays and carts making deliveries.

'How many days has it been since the Hancock child was seized?'

'Five or six, I think.' Jones kept on walking. 'I think a ransom note was delivered to the castle the day before yesterday.'

When Pyke had first seen the Hancocks' address, he'd wondered whether the first line – Caedraw Castle – was an exaggeration. Since arriving in Merthyr, he had actually seen it from a distance, a grotesque mock-medieval pile perched on one of the hills overlooking the town.

'You don't seem sure.'

'As you'll doubtless find out, the Hancocks have their own way of conducting their affairs. For whatever reason, our expertise, such as it is, has not been required.'

'You don't know who sent the note, then?'

'I'm afraid I don't know what was demanded but I'm told the ransom note was penned by Scottish Cattle.'

'Scottish Cattle?'

'Most folk just call 'em the Bull.' Jones turned to face him. 'To some, they're defenders of workers' rights. To us, they're terrorists, plain and simple. These days, you're more likely to find folk from the Bull in mining villages farther up the valley. They killed a man once, back in the thirties, but I haven't heard much about them in recent years. Far as I know, they've never gone so far as to kidnap a master's child before.'

'You have your doubts about their involvement?'

'I don't know. Like I said, I haven't seen the ransom letter; I don't know what's being demanded.'

Ignoring the chill wind blowing off the mountain, Pyke looked up and down the street. Built from flint and stone, with two gable-ends and a porch covered in ivy, the courthouse was one of the oldest buildings in the town. Jones explained that it had once also been the family residence but some time after his wife died, Smyth had moved to an estate – Blenheim – about two miles farther down the valley.

Sir Clancy Smyth had a round, lively face and a brisk, no-nonsense demeanour. His friendliness seemed genuine enough, especially after Pyke mentioned that Sir Richard Mayne had passed on his best wishes, but there was something about his performance that wasn't quite convincing, a deadness in his eyes that seemed to contradict the curdling smile on his lips. He stood by the fireplace but kept shuffling from one foot to the other, as though being still was somehow beyond him.

'Look, Detective-inspector,' Smyth said, when the conversation turned to the matter of the kidnapping, 'whether I care for the family or not, it's true that the Caedraw ironworks is one of the largest of its kind. It employs three thousand men, women and children and the welfare of the whole town depends on its success.'

Pyke could tell at once that Smyth did *not* care for the family, and the fact that he didn't mind sharing this fact with a complete stranger suggested that the magistrate and the Hancocks were in open dispute.

As if to explain this, Smyth added, 'Zephaniah Hancock is, wholly without justification, contemptuous of our constabulary.' He glanced across at Jones. 'He might be more impressed by a detective-inspector from Scotland Yard. You could be our eyes and ears in the Castle. Of course, we want the same thing they want, the boy returned to his family. Everything else is unimportant.'

Pyke's thoughts turned to Cathy, as they had done on numerous occasions during the journey. Would she be happy to see him? Turning his attention back to the magistrate, Pyke considered what he'd been told. He wasn't convinced by Smyth's assurances but appreciated the man's candour.

'So what can you tell me about Hancock's wife?'

'She's much younger much than he is and a very beautiful creature. I wouldn't say it's an especially happy marriage but then again, I'm not sure I'm the best person to comment on such matters.'

Pyke looked around the room and wondered whether, as a widower, the man had any children. Would this be him in a few years' time? Pyke's thoughts returned – briefly – to Felix waving at him from the station platform.

42

'If you have no objections,' Smyth said, looking at Jones, 'I should like to be alone with the detective-inspector.'

Jones knew his place and nodded before departing, saying he would wait for Pyke in the entrance hall.

'Jones is a nice chap, honest and hard working, but I'm afraid he's quite ineffectual. The whole force is. As much as it pains me to say it, Zephaniah Hancock is right.' Smyth wandered over to the window and peered through the glass before turning around.

'In my experience,' Pyke said, 'policemen are only as effective or ineffective as they're allowed to be by their superiors.'

Smyth took the admonishment well. 'Of course, you're quite right, sir. Our mandate here has never been a strong one.'

'If you'll permit me to say it, Sir Clancy, you don't seem to care for the Hancock family very much.'

The magistrate turned around again and looked out at the street. 'That's a difficult statement for me to comment on, sir. Perhaps all I can say is that their general contribution to the civilisaton of this town has been less than I would like it to have been.' He paused. 'Did you know that Thomas Carlyle called Merthyr the most squalid place on earth? He was especially worried by the absence of a middling class of men, the kind who could bring some respectability to the town.'

'The Hancocks would doubtless claim they have provided work for the masses.'

'Indeed, and this is no small achievement. But if we can't take pride in our town, how can we expect others to do so? You've probably heard people talk about China. That's what they call Pontystorehouse or the Cellars. It's a squalid little area and at present we've all but ceded it to the gangs.'

Pyke recalled what Bill Flint had told him during their train journey from Cardiff.

'The rot starts in China,' Smyth continued. 'If we cut it out at the root, the town'll be able to breathe a little easier.' The magistrate realised what he'd said and tried to smile. 'I'm sorry. You didn't come all this way to hear me rant about our local difficulties.'

'Perhaps there's some link between the kidnapping and the trouble in China?'

Smyth smoothed back his silver hair with the palm of his hand.

'Perhaps — but then again I don't imagine any of the gangs would dare to launch such an open challenge to one of the ironmasters.'

Pyke watched a cart rattle past the window.

'Actually, Sir Clancy, I was hoping you could recommend someone I could use as a translator; preferably a man who isn't going to be intimidated by venturing into the more unsavoury parts of town.'

'Like China?'

Pyke shrugged but said nothing.

'There is someone actually. A good fellow called John Johns. He's a former soldier but don't hold that against him.' Smyth relaxed into his shabby armchair. 'To be honest, he's rather a queer chap, likes to keep himself to himself, but I'm told he's good with his fists and I know for a fact that he speaks Welsh like a native.'

'Where can I find him?'

'He rents a shack about a quarter of a mile out of town, on the road to Vaynor.'

As Pyke turned to rejoin Jones in the hallway, Smyth stood up and followed him to the door. Putting his hand on Pyke's shoulder he said, 'I don't mean to alarm you, Detective-inspector, but a friendly word of advice. Please watch yourself in your dealings with the Hancock family.'

Pyke was about to ask what he meant when Jones appeared and without another word Smyth turned and closed the door to his office behind him.

Caedraw Castle was a hideous construction with faux-crenellated walls and numerous turrets of different shapes and heights. Pyke didn't know which was worse: the ugliness of the building or the vanity it spoke of. Its proximity to the ironworks, meanwhile, was a stark reminder to those who toiled there of their lowly place in the world, for it meant that the Hancocks could keep an eye on their fiefdom from their drawing-room window, like a jealous master unwilling to let his mistress out of his sight.

It was dark by the time Pyke approached the Castle from the road and a damp fog was rolling in off the mountains. At the top of the hill he turned to face the works. It *was* an impressive sight, he supposed: jets of fire streaking up into the darkness from the top of the blast furnaces and the eerie glow of the tips that sprawled down the balding mountain on the far side of the valley. Even from this vantage point, the noise was prodigious too: the clanking of iron chains, the bashing of hammers, the grinding of water wheels. Turning back to the Castle, Pyke took a deep breath and tried to work out what was causing the butterflies in his stomach.

When the butler opened the door hatch and peered out, he told Pyke that the family was not receiving any visitors. Pyke introduced himself and told the man he'd come at the family's request from London to investigate the kidnapping. Eventually the door swung open and he was ushered into the gloomy entrance hall.

Jonah Hancock's girth had spread since Pyke had last seen him but otherwise the man was just as he remembered: a tall, commanding figure with sandy-coloured hair, and a strong lantern jaw. But it was his air of superiority that Pyke remembered most, as though everyone he talked to was a lesser species. He pumped Pyke's hand and then strode into the adjoining room, expecting Pyke to follow. A log fire was roaring in the grate and slumped in an armchair next to it was an old man. Jonah introduced Pyke to Zephaniah Hancock.

As he answered Jonah's predictable questions about his journey from London, Pyke's stare kept returning to the old man. He'd heard stories about Zephaniah Hancock's viciousness and opportunism and it was difficult to reconcile these with the emaciated figure hunched before him, a thick blanket over his legs. Wrinkled skin sagged from his face and gathered in leathery folds around his neck, and the few strands of ash-white hair that remained on his liver-spotted head were as fine as spun cotton. But the moment Pyke looked into his tiny, red-rimmed eyes, he saw that the old man's mind was undiminished.

Significantly it was Zephaniah who spoke first about the case. 'We haven't made the mistake of relying on the good men of the Glamorgan constabulary but, on the recommendation of Jonah's wife, we chose instead to solicit the assistance of Detective-inspector Pyke of Scotland Yard.' While the old man caught his breath, Pyke tried to work out whether there was a note of mockery in his voice. 'I hope you won't disappoint us. You don't need me to tell you what's at stake for this family.'

'I can't make any promises but I'll do everything in my power to make sure your grandson is returned to you safe and well.' He glanced over at the door. 'Perhaps you could start by telling me what happened . . .'

It was Jonah who spoke. 'Every week, always on a Monday, my wife Catherine takes the boy to place fresh flowers on our other child's grave.' He must have seen Pyke's expression because he added, 'We had a lovely little girl, Mary. I'm sorry to say she died two summers ago from consumption.'

'I'm sorry. I didn't know.'

Jonah nodded blankly. 'One of the drivers took them. It's a fifteen-minute ride to the cemetery at Vaynor. On the way back, just past the ruined castle, four bandits appeared out of nowhere, brandishing pistols, their faces masked by handkerchiefs. One of them seized my son, William. They dragged him into the bushes and warned my wife and driver not to follow. This took place a week ago yesterday.'

Pyke made a mental note of the reference to the cemetery at Vaynor. Wasn't that where Smyth had said John Johns, the prospective translator, lived? 'I'll need to talk to the driver, tonight, if possible. Your wife, too.'

Jonah exchanged a look with his father. 'I'll have someone summon the driver.'

'And have you received a ransom demand?'

'Aye.' Jonah rummaged in his trouser pocket. 'I'm assuming you haven't heard of an organisation called Scottish Cattle.'

Pyke shook his head. At this point, he didn't want them to know he'd already talked to Jones and Smyth. 'No. Who are they?'

Jonah found the envelope he'd been looking for but didn't hand it straight over to Pyke.

'Terrorists,' croaked the old man. 'They claim to be the voice of the working man but they're nothing but terrorists.'

'A few years ago,' Jonah said, 'there was a strike at the works. It was particularly nasty and coincided with a deep depression. Orders for our iron were non-existent and we had no choice but to cut wages and lay off workers. This was about a year after the General Strike, so tensions were still running high. You couldn't move in the town without running into Chartists from England spoiling for a fight. To cut a long story short, we shipped over from Ireland all the workers we could lay our hands on and rolled up our sleeves for a fight. The strike lasted three weeks. The strikers tried to blockade the works but our lads stood up for themselves and the furnaces remained lit. People on both sides got hurt but the strikers, egged on by the likes of Scottish Cattle, came off worse. Finally the strike collapsed and they came back to us, begging for their old jobs. Scottish Cattle were extremely bitter and accused us, unfairly, of all kinds of devious practices. The rancour remains to this day.'

'And you think this is why they kidnapped your son?'

'Actually, Detective-inspector, we aren't convinced that the Bull have our boy, in spite of the first ransom letter we received a few days ago.' Zephaniah kicked the blanket off his legs. 'Show it to him, boy.'

Jonah bristled at the old man's reference to him as a 'boy' but said nothing. Instead he handed the letter to Pyke. Briefly Pyke surveyed its contents.

Notice. Remember that the Bool is on rode every night, he will catch you at last. We hereby tell you we have your son. Be on the look out, pig. Raid your coffers of twenty thousand. Do as the Bool says or your son shall be kilt. You will believe it. O madmen, how long will ye continue in your madness.

Pyke handed the letter back to Jonah but kept his thoughts to himself. Even to a family like the Hancocks, twenty thousand was a sizeable amount of money. 'You said this was the first letter?'

'It turned up last Thursday morning. William was kidnapped on the Monday.' Jonah removed another envelope from his pocket and gave it to Pyke. 'This one came yesterday.'

Pyke inspected the envelope – Jonah Hancock's name was scribbled in black ink. The first thing he noticed was that the handwriting was different. 'So who delivered the letters?'

'Someone shoved the first one under the door in the middle of the night. One of the servants found it in the morning.'

'And this one?' Pyke held up the second envelope.

'After the first letter, we had men patrolling the grounds morning, noon and night,' Zephaniah said. 'A furnace-man was approached in a tavern in the town and offered a shilling to deliver a letter to the Castle. One of our agents questioned him thoroughly. We don't believe he was involved.'

Pyke slid the second letter from its envelope. He realised straight away that it wasn't simply the penmanship that was different.

Notice. The Bull is riding every night and he will catch up with you if you do not pay. Take one hundred in coin to the old Quarry near Anderson's farm. Leave it in the stone cottage on the Anderson's farm road. Do it on Thursday at ten in the morning. Just one man. Do not have the cottage watched. This is to make sure you know how to follow orders. The Bull wants twenty thousand in due course. Do as we say and await our instructions or the boy dies.

'It's not written by the same person.' Pyke handed the letter back to Jonah Hancock.

'I can see that.'

'I mean, it's not even written by the same class of man. The grammar is different for a start. This one was penned by an educated man trying to pass himself off as uneducated. Look at the differences. "The Bool is on rode" and "the Bull is riding". It's obvious.' As Pyke spoke, he could feel Zephaniah's eyes on him.

'What are you suggesting, sir?' the older man croaked.

'Who else knows that your grandson has been kidnapped?'

'We've tried to keep the news of what's happened to our immediate circle but inevitably people gossip. The servants are loyal and have been sworn to secrecy, but Catherine went and informed the constabulary so now every damned bobby in the town knows about it.'

Again Pyke wondered about the veiled animosity between the Hancock family and the chief magistrate.

Jonah was pacing around the floor. 'If this second letter was written by a different hand – perhaps even someone not connected with the kidnapping – why demand a paltry sum like a hundred pounds? Especially when the ransom has been set at twenty thousand?'

'I don't know. If the letters are from different people in the same gang, perhaps this is some kind of dress rehearsal, to see if you can be trusted.'

'And if they're from different gangs?'

'Then perhaps someone else has heard about the kidnapping and is attempting to turn this information to their advantage.'

Zephaniah eyed Pyke carefully from the armchair. 'So what do you recommend we do, Detective-inspector?'

'That depends on whether you've decided to pay the ransom or not.'

'Of course we've decided to pay,' Jonah said impatiently.

Zephaniah's tone was more conciliatory. 'The important thing is to get the boy back here where he belongs. Maybe, sir, you could be persuaded to take the hundred pounds out to the old quarry?'

Momentarily distracted by the sound of footsteps in the room directly above them, Pyke nodded without realising what he had agreed to.

'I'm still going to need to talk to your driver . . . and your wife.'

'I'll have someone fetch the driver. You might also want to find and question the boy's former nursemaid. Maggie Atkins. She left this household under a cloud.'

'What kind of a cloud?'

'We caught her stealing. In the end, we chose not to involve the police; we didn't want to make a scene. She always denied it, and was bitter about her dismissal.'

'Bitter enough to take matters into her own hands?'

'I just thought I'd mention it, Detective-inspector. I'll have one of the servants look out her address.'

Pyke glanced at Zephaniah and then let his gaze return to Jonah Hancock. 'It would be more helpful if you could summon your wife.'

Their eyes locked. Jonah licked his lips. 'I'm surprised she hasn't come down from her room to greet you.'

'Perhaps you would be so kind as to bring her down?'

The younger Hancock pondered this request then left the room. Pyke and Zephaniah Hancock stared uneasily at one another.

'Tell me, sir,' the older man said. 'Did you come up here directly from the railway station or did you perhaps call in on the station-house on your way?'

'The latter. I had a very brief chat with Superintendent Jones and Sir Clancy Smyth.'

The old man assimilated this news without reacting. 'In which case, I don't imagine you've formed a favourable impression of my family.' When Pyke didn't respond immediately, he smiled. 'Be that as it may, Jonah loves his son and there is nothing he – nothing *we* – won't do to ensure his safe return.'

None of the stories Pyke had heard about Zephaniah had portrayed him as a devoted family man. 'Do you have any other children or grandchildren?'

'I do have another son, but alas I see him very infrequently. He takes care of my family's ancestral home in Hampshire.'

'And is William your only grandchild?'

Zephaniah gave him a puzzled stare. 'My other son, Richard, has two children.' Then he seemed to relax and added, 'Look, I won't pretend I'm sentimentally attached to William, or children in general, but it doesn't mean I'm not concerned for his well-being. And William is the firstborn of the firstborn. Is it so wrong to want to see one's family name survive long after one's death?'

Before Pyke could answer, there were footsteps in the hallway. Jonah entered the room, closely followed by Cathy.

Seeing her for the first time in five years was both exciting and a disappointment. It was undoubtedly true that she had blossomed into a beautiful woman; her slender figure, pronounced cheekbones, ash-blonde hair and slim, pretty face were all reminders of the adolescent Pyke had once known. Nonetheless he saw straight away that the naivety and innocence he'd once associated with her had been replaced by an unfamiliar reserve. Before him was a woman whose expression was like the hard surface of a mirror: she smiled politely and held out her hand for him to shake. Drawn into her ambit, he smelled the sourness of claret on her breath as he tried in vain to find even the smallest flicker of warmth in her eyes. As he took her outstretched hand, she swayed towards him, whispering, 'You shouldn't have come.'

While Pyke tried to work out what she had meant, Cathy went over to join her husband. She was wearing a carefully brocaded white lace dress with puffed sleeves and a crinoline skirt. He noticed that Zephaniah had been watching their encounter.

'My wife will answer any questions you have tomorrow, Detective-inspector.' Jonah reached out and gently squeezed her hand. 'She is feeling a little tired, so if you'll excuse me, I'm going to escort her up to her bed.'

They didn't want, and didn't wait for, Pyke's sanction. He expected Cathy to look up at him on her way out but she swept by without acknowledgement.

'Don't take it personally, Detective-inspector,' Zephaniah said, grinning, after they had left the room. 'I do hope you'll stay here with us, sir,' he added, full of bonhomie. 'I'm afraid the accommodation in town is universally dreadful. It would be nice to have a man's company for a change.'

Pyke didn't miss this barbed reference to Jonah Hancock but decided to let it pass.

'It might surprise you to know that Catherine has always talked about you in very admiring terms.'

'I can't think why,' Pyke said. 'I hardly knew her when she was living in London. She was just the daughter of a friend of my uncle.'

'Indeed, sir. But who knows what passes for thought inside a woman's head. Perhaps she saw you as her knight in shining armour.'

The old man smiled. Pyke took the opportunity to change the subject. 'I believe a sum of a thousand pounds was mentioned if I ensure your grandson's safe return?'

'We men are always far happier to discuss money than women, aren't we?' Zephaniah tried to sit up straighter. 'Still, it wouldn't come as a surprise to you, I suspect, if I were to proffer the opinion that my daughter-in-law has always carried a torch for you, sir.' He held up his hand to stop Pyke from interrupting. 'Be that as it may, when your name was mentioned in the context of our difficulties, I took the liberty of asking about you. I found out that you've received two prison sentences, one for the non-payment of debts and one for murder.'

'I received a full pardon for the latter.'

'You miss my meaning, sir. I am always impressed when a man has risen above adversity. The fact that you are an inspector at Scotland Yard's Detective Branch suggests an impressive guile and determination, a survivor's instinct. I hope you won't think me excessively melodramatic if I were to suggest that the future of the house of Hancock lies in your capable hands.'

Pyke was tired from the journey but he knew he couldn't let down his guard. Zephaniah had gone out of his way to seem welcoming but Sir Clancy Smyth's warning was still ringing in his ears. Eventually he managed a thin smile. 'We'll get your grandson back, don't worry.'

'I don't doubt it, Detective-inspector,' Zephaniah said. 'I have every faith in your abilities.'

SIX

Knox had set off for Tipperary Town at first light, forgoing his breakfast because he hadn't wanted to wake the baby. He had walked the first couple of miles but just before the town of Golden, a dray had pulled over and the driver had offered him a place next to him. A mile or so beyond Golden they had passed a dead body lying at the side of the track. They hadn't stopped. The driver, a shoemaker from Cashel, had looked at Knox but neither of them had spoken. What was there to say? Eventually the body would be claimed by nature or the authorities. Knox had known it was wrong to leave the body lying there but it was someone else's responsibility. The driver had dropped him in the centre of the town and Knox had spent the next hour or two trudging around the various lodging houses, hoping that someone might recognise the man in his copperplate. He had described the man as an outsider, possibly from England, but by lunchtime, when he had had no success and was famished, he wondered whether his initial assumption – that the dead man had been a well-to-do traveller – was correct. No one in Cashel had remembered him and there was just one place left in Dundrum to check. After that, he would have to extend his search farther afield. Clonmel, perhaps even Thurles.

The wind was blowing from the north, and in spite of his greatcoat, Knox could feel the chill in his bones. The ground was frozen and the cold air stung his cheeks. Dispirited and exhausted, and with no food in his stomach, Knox thought about the inn in Dundrum and decided to call in on his family, perhaps even scrounge a little food from his mother. He set off at a brisk pace, enlivened by the prospect of a meal, but started to flag after a mile or two. The wind picked up and fat drops of rain slapped against his face. Eventually a horse and cart drew up next to him and Knox hopped up next to the driver. The man was making a delivery to the old hall. After a few initial pleasantries, they didn't exchange another word.

After about an hour the delivery man dropped him by the gates to Dundrum House but when he asked for his mother in the kitchens he was told that she was at home. No other explanation was offered and Knox started to worry that one of his family might be ill. Peter perhaps. Or maybe even his mother. Unlike most of the servants, his mother had been permitted to live away from the main house, perhaps because of the length of time she had served Cornwallis. The family cabin lay a few hundred yards from the gates on the edge of a parcel of land known as Fishpond Field. None of his memories there was a happy one, Knox realised as he made his way up the familiar track. Even the trees seemed gloomy and oppressive. After rounding the last bend, he saw an unfamiliar figure stooped over a wooden tub.

'I'm looking for Sarah and John Knox.'

The woman rose and stretched her back. She regarded him indifferently, taking in his uniform, then wiped her hands on her apron. 'They moved.'

Knox dug his hands into his pockets and glanced at the cabin. He was really worried now. His mother hadn't mentioned moving on his last visit. 'Where to?'

'Quarry Field. The new houses.'

Knox knew the cottages she had mentioned: they were airy, spacious and even had an outdoor privy.

It was a fifteen-minute walk, and when he entered the open door, Knox found his mother standing over the range. A pot of water was boiling and a line of clothes was hanging diagonally across the room. Peter, his youngest brother, was snoozing on a chair. As soon as she saw him, Sarah Knox rushed to greet her son, throwing her arms around him and kissing his cheek. Breathlessly, she explained that Cornwallis's agent had offered them this cottage for the same rent they'd been paying on their old place.

'I told you he wasn't such a bad man.' Her expression was both kind and defiant. 'He even gave me a day's holiday to move in.'

Peter had stirred from his slumber and as soon as he saw Knox he leapt up to greet him. This only augmented Knox's guilt, the fact that he hadn't visited his brother for such a long time. Peter was a frail boy with a thin face and droopy eyes that never quite focused on the person he was looking at. Knox ruffled his hair and let the boy hug him. He didn't look his fifteen years and he certainly didn't act them. Not for the first time, Knox wondered what would happen to his brother if and when their mother passed away, for he was quite sure it was her love – unconditional as it was – that had kept the lad going.

Peter knew how to talk but he rarely, if ever, spoke. Instead he would coo and murmur and gargle and their mother would interpret for him. This time he was silent and, having let go of Knox's midriff, he retreated back to his chair next to the fire. Knox thought about his other brother, Matthew, big as an ox, a labourer on the estate like their father, and wondered how they had all turned out so different. He tried to push from his mind thoughts about his brothers and the guilt he hadn't made more of an effort to get to know them. He had his own family to worry about now.

'So did his Lordship give you any reason for this unexpected turn of events?' he asked.

'He told me that it was a reward for loyalty.' His mother looked approvingly around the room. 'Your father did a little jig when he saw the bed next door. He's never even slept on a mattress before.'

Knox hadn't seen his father in more than three months and he wondered whether his mother knew that he tried to time his visits to Dundrum to avoid having to converse with the man. He knew it was cowardly, simply avoiding his father, but he hadn't been able to put memories of his youth out of his head, times when his father would return home drunk and full of rage and take it out on him with a leather strap. It had always been a surprise to him that the man treated Peter and Matthew with affection and Knox had never been able to reconcile this difference; the coldness of the man towards him with the warmth of his dealings with his younger children. It had bothered Knox for a long time – bothered him more than he had ever admitted to anyone, even his wife – but now too much water had passed under that particular bridge.

'Is that all Cornwallis said?'

His mother went over to join Peter by the fire. She patted the lad's head and smiled as his neck and back arched towards her, like a cat wanting to be stroked. Finally she turned back towards Knox. 'If truth be told, I got the feeling that it had something to do with you.'

'Why me?'

'The agent said something about his Lordship being . . . pleased with you. I didn't ask what he meant.'

'And he didn't say anything else?'

'I can't remember. I was excited. He just said you were a good fellow. And loyal. He called you loyal.'

Knox looked around the large, well-appointed room. It was dry, clean and warm – the kind of place in which his mother had always dreamt of living. And it would be a better home for Peter. 'I'm pleased for you, Mam.' Knox tried to smile. 'You deserve something good for a change.'

She gave him another hug and showed him around the rest of the cottage. Afterwards, she prepared a meal of corn, and while he ate, she told him what Matthew had been doing. Matthew was seventeen, only two years older than Peter. Knox had never asked why there had been such an age gap between him and his brothers but suspected it had something to do with their father's drinking. He had never understood why his mother hadn't walked out on his father; why she had remained loyal to him even when he vented his anger by striking her with his fists.

Knox scooped out the last of the corn with his finger. 'Cornwallis may be our friend today but what happens if he turns against us tomorrow?'

His mother put her hands into her apron. 'Why would he turn against us?' A note of caution entered her voice.

'I don't know.'

But Knox had never been able to hide anything from her. When she sat down on the bench next to him and pulled his face towards her, he tried to look away.

'Why, son?'

'Why do you think? He's a vain, capricious man who does things arbitrarily to suit his whims.'

'He'd have to have a reason to turn against us, Michael.'

'He's cruel, Mam. He likes to hurt people.'

'Don't talk nonsense. He's been good to us, hasn't he?'

Knox thought about his investigation. 'But for how long?'

His mother stared at him and sighed. 'I can see you're thinking about this errand his Lordship has given you. You think all of this is an inducement not to rock the boat.'

'Isn't it?'

Knox could see the confusion in her eyes but this time he waited for her to speak. 'I always brought you up to do the right thing so I can hardly ask you to do any different now.'

'But?'

'Look.' She pointed at Peter, curled up on the chair next to the fire. 'What would happen to him if we were evicted from this place? If your father and brother lost their jobs on the estate? If I were dismissed from my position?'

'I'll be careful, Mam. You don't have to worry about that.'

This didn't seem to settle her. 'It's not you I'm worried about.' Her gaze drifted across to Peter.

Knox didn't really consider himself to be Protestant, even though his mother and especially his father had brought him up to fear God and Catholics; to fear Catholics more than God. It had always felt odd, and not a little false, to hate in such an indiscriminating way, for there were many more Catholics than Protestants in Tipperary, and Knox had always tried to judge people according to their merits. These days, he couldn't say with any certainty that he hadn't been attracted to Martha precisely because she was Catholic; because she stood for everything he had been warned against. It helped that Martha was as unkind about Rome as he was about the Church of Ireland. But even though they had been married for five years, it sometimes struck him that neither of them had fully escaped their childhood indoctrination. In arguments, he always saw himself as the rational one; felt that her positions were oblique and hard to fathom. Only when he thought about it did he realise that Protestant ministers had always said the same thing about Catholic doctrine. Sometimes he wondered how she saw him. He knew she found him too literal-minded at times. 'Why is the wafer only ever just a wafer to you,' she would say during arguments. With this attitude came a kind of dogmatism; Knox often had trouble seeing things from a different perspective. He lacked imagination, though Martha always said he retained the ability to empathise with others. But when you believed so ardently in the rightness of your views, it was hard to compromise, even if someone like his mother wanted him to look the other way. Perhaps, he decided, it was simply pig-headedness: the one thing he had inherited from his father.

In the village, he entered the taproom of the New Forge Inn and wiped his boots on the mat. The New Forge was the only place that offered accommodation and it had been closed on his previous visit. He approached the counter and asked the pot-boy to fetch the landlord. While he waited, Knox noted the clumps of sawdust on the wooden floor and the black tallow rings on the low ceiling. When the landlord finally appeared, he was a man of about forty with dark black hair, a stocky figure with a pockmarked face. He addressed Knox in English.

Knox took out the copperplate and placed it on the counter. 'D'you recognise him? I'm wondering if he took a room here some time last week.'

The landlord peered down at the image.

'This would have been on Saturday or Sunday night,' Knox added.

'Aye.' The landlord shot him a wary look.

'You recognise him?'

'I think so.' He had another look at the copperplate. 'I was wondering when he'd be back or someone would come asking for him.'

'You rented him a room?' Knox felt his heart skip a beat. He hadn't expected his intuition to be right.

'He turned up on Saturday night and paid in coin for a week.'

Knox tried to rein in his excitement. 'Did he tell you his name? Where he was from?'

'I couldn't place his accent. But he wasn't from here. At a guess, I'd say he was an Englishman.'

Knox nodded, already wondering what he would do with this new information. 'But did he give you a name?'

'I'm sure he signed in. Wait just a minute.' The landlord went to fetch the visitors' book. Placing it on the counter, he opened it up and pointed to one of the entries. 'Didn't put down an address.'

The landlord swivelled the book around and pushed it towards Knox.

Knox scrutinised the entry. There was just one word, penned in a style that lacked ornamentation.

Pyke.

Nothing more.

'He didn't say what had brought him to Dundrum?'

'He didn't say and I didn't ask.' The landlord gave Knox a hard look. 'I'm assuming something's happened to him.'

'He's dead.' Knox waited a moment. 'But I'd appreciate it if you kept this information to yourself.'

The landlord nodded. Perhaps he'd been expecting this. 'I put him in the room at the back. He wanted somewhere quiet. I haven't checked the place since he took it. Maybe he left some possessions behind.'

Knox followed the stocky man up the stairs and waited as he unlocked the door to the dead man's room. There was a frock-coat and a plain, white shirt hanging in the wardrobe but no sign of a suitcase. The landlord opened one of the drawers and whistled. Knox joined him, staring down at the pistol and hunting knife that lay inside. He reached out and inspected them.

'I'd like to hold on to these,' Knox said, having ascertained that the pistol was loaded.

The landlord didn't raise any objections and they completed their search of the room without turning up anything else.

'So how did he die?' the landlord asked as they made their way down the rickety stairs.

'Froze to death.'

The landlord turned to face Knox. 'Wouldn't be the first to die that way, would he?'

Knox turned the corner of the newspaper and looked over at Jeremy Brittas, who was snoozing in his armchair. He had stopped to see his neighbour on his way home and had been pressed into performing his usual duties. But as soon as he tried to put the newspaper down, the old man's eyes opened. 'I'm listening, dammit.'

There was a letter in the paper entitled 'Free Trade Run Mad' and a longer piece – 'Mr Smith O'Brien's Concluding Letter to the Landed Proprietors of Ireland' – which Brittas would not want him to read. Knox surveyed the opening lines and found himself nodding his head in agreement.

'Read it out loud, man.'

'*If a foreign invader had subjugated your native land, and had imposed upon it the payment of an annual tribute amounting to four or five million sterling, in addition to . . .*'

'I don't want to know what some hot-under-the-collar Repealer thinks. Read me something else.'

'*Very large arrivals of Indian corn and barrel flour are reported in Sligo.*' Knox felt his ire begin to rise. '*There are large quantities in the hands of private speculators, many of whom never did business in the grain or flour trade before.*' As Knox put down the newspaper he noticed that his hands were shaking.

'What is it now?' Brittas peered at him through his wire-framed spectacles.

'Does no one else see the sheer lunacy of it all: putting the relief effort in the hands of jackals?'

Brittas sat forward, a puzzled look on his face. 'You're upset, boy. What is it?'

Knox gestured to the newspaper lying crumpled at his feet. 'It's just words and stories to you, isn't it? Opinions to be contested or corroborated.'

'That's what a newspaper is.'

'This . . .' Knox reached down and grabbed the newspaper. 'This has been sanitised for the likes of your good self.'

'Sanitised?'

Knox could feel tears in his eyes but he fought to keep them at bay. 'The other day I saw a pit full of bodies, fifteen or twenty of 'em, limbs intertwined. Today I passed a corpse lying in the hedge-row. I didn't stop.'

'But the *Tip Free Press* is a liberal paper,' Brittas said, still not grasping what Knox was saying.

Knox picked up the crumpled newspaper and threw it on to the fire. 'I think I should stop coming here for a while.'

'But I . . . how will I . . . I don't understand what's come over you.'

Knox wanted to say something pithy that would reassure his neighbour – whom he had always liked and admired – but there were no words left to him.

Knox often found himself staring down into the cot while James slept, amazed just by his existence, by his fingernails and little nose;

amazed that, in some small way, he had been responsible for creating a life. Since the autumn, he had spent more and more time watching his son sleeping, either as a way to forget about the terrible things he been forced to witness or to remind himself that the goodness in the world hadn't been entirely extinguished. Before Christmas, Knox had come across a mother and her baby lying by the road to Golden. It had been a beautiful morning – crisp, clear, the sky as blue as a painted plate. The mother and child were frozen as solid as bricks, the mother still clutching the infant tightly to her body in a pitiful attempt to keep it warm.

It had taken until noon for the bodies to thaw enough for them to prise the baby from the mother's grasp.

James had been the same age as that child and for days afterwards, Knox had lain awake wondering what had driven the mother to take refuge in a hedgerow, what her final thoughts had been before passing into unconsciousness; whether she had still harboured hopes that her baby might live if she held him tight enough. It helped having James, of course – being able to pick him up, hold him, feel the child's soft breath tickle his cheek – but it made him vulnerable too. The fear that something might happen to James would suddenly fill Knox's head and sometimes make it hard for him to breathe.

Knox left the cot and joined Martha in the front room. The dog was sleeping by the fire but it raised its head when Knox entered the room. He told her what he had said to Jeremy Brittas; that he didn't understand where his anger was coming from.

Martha kissed him once on the forehead. 'These are terrible times, Michael. If you weren't angry, I wouldn't respect you.'

'But you still think I'm risking too much, by not doing what Moore and Hastings want me to do?'

Martha didn't answer him at first. 'I understand that you have to do what you have to do. But it doesn't stop me from worrying about the consequences.'

Neither of them spoke for a while. Outside it had started to rain, and they listened to it beating against the windowpanes.

'I heard that Father Mackey's planning to denounce Asenath Moore from the pulpit on Sunday,' Martha said eventually.

Father Mackey was the parish priest of Clonoulty, and over the past few months he had taken to seeking Martha's opinion, even though she'd hadn't been to confession for about two years. Knox worried about his presence, worried that any dalliance with the Catholic Church on her part would harm their marriage.

He reached down and patted Tom on the head. 'So what's Mackey planning on saying?'

'He's livid that Moore is only offering relief to those folk who attend one of his Bible classes.'

'But he's not surprised, surely? Everyone knows that Moore has always tried to convert his workers.'

Martha shrugged. These conversations about Father Mackey were always sensitive. 'But Mackey's willing to put his neck on the block. Surely that's the point? I mean, who else has spoken up against Moore in public?'

Knox didn't have an answer but he couldn't quite bring himself to commend Mackey as Martha wanted him to.

'I think I know the name of the man who was murdered on Moore's estate,' he said, breaking the silence.

'Oh?'

Knox couldn't tell from her tone what she thought about this development. 'A man called Pyke.'

Martha brushed a strand of hair behind her ear. 'And what do you intend to do with this information?' She stood up and went over to the fireplace, feeding a little more coal into the grate.

'I don't know. Sometimes I think I'm stupid to be doing what I'm doing. I think how many people have died and wonder why I'm so concerned about this one body.'

Martha came over to where he was sitting and stroked his head. 'Do you have an answer?'

Briefly Knox thought about all the bodies he had seen since the start of the winter. 'Moore asked specifically for me.' He was trying to formulate in his mind what he wanted to say. 'He asked for me either because he thinks I'm incompetent and I won't find anything out or because he thinks he can bully me into holding my tongue.'

'Do you think Moore is afraid that something damaging might come to light?'

'I'm almost sure of it.'

SEVEN

Pyke had woken early that morning, his dreams formless and unsettling, and since he had not been able to get back to sleep, he dressed quickly and slipped out of the Castle unnoticed. He had gone to bed thinking about Cathy, trying to make sense of the coldness of her greeting. The air was cold and damp and smelled of smog and wet leaves, and the mountains rising up on all sides of the town were just about visible through the mist. Following directions he had been given by Sir Clancy Smyth, it took Pyke half an hour to find the place where John Johns lived: a crofter's cottage perched on the lower slopes of a hill. Farther up the hill Pyke could see another cabin, though it wasn't in as good a state of repair. He didn't try to conceal his presence and had travelled halfway along the track when a tall man wearing a black shooting jacket appeared from behind a tree and aimed a rifle at his chest. 'Stop right there, sir, and raise your hands above your head.'

Pyke did as he was told.

'Identify yourself.'

'My name's Detective-inspector Pyke. I'm from Scotland Yard in London.' He turned cautiously to face his interlocutor. 'I'm looking for John Johns. I was told by Sir Clancy Smyth that I'd find him here.'

'What's your business?' The man took a step away from the trees, still holding the rifle.

'I need someone to translate for me, someone who speaks English and Welsh.' Pyke paused, trying to decide whether he should be honest with Johns from the start.

The man holding the rifle was a head taller than he was, with broad shoulders and a muscular frame. He was about Pyke's age, wore gentleman's clothes and had thick, black hair that reached almost as far as his shoulders.

'Are you Johns?'

The man unbolted his rifle and let it fall to his side. 'Aye.' He took a couple of steps towards Pyke. 'You said Smyth gave you my name?'

'That's right.'

Johns held out his hand and waited for Pyke to shake it. 'Smyth's a decent sort. They're a rare breed in Merthyr.'

Pyke tried to place his accent. He didn't sound Welsh but he didn't sound English, either.

'So what brings you all the way from London?'

'A child has been kidnapped.' Pyke tried to assess whether this was news to Johns or not. Merthyr was a small town and some of the servants at the Castle could easily have told their family and friends.

Johns stared at him, his reaction giving nothing away. 'Aye, the Hancock boy.'

'So you know.'

'Clearly.'

'You heard who might have taken him?'

'I heard the Hancocks believe it might be some radicals, folks from the Bull perhaps.'

Pyke tried not to show his surprise. Johns' source of information was as good as his was. 'You don't think so?'

Johns turned his attention back to the rifle at his side. 'Far as I know, the Bull haven't been active in this part of the world for a few years now, certainly not in Merthyr itself.'

'I heard they were still organising in the mining villages farther up the valley.'

'It might make folk feel good about themselves, to blacken their faces and dress up in cow hides, but as far as serious political agitation is concerned, the Bull is a spent force.'

'Then why would someone want to make it seem as if they're involved?'

'I have no idea.' Johns looked up the hill to the farther hut.

Pyke sensed there was something he wasn't saying. 'I've heard the Hancocks aren't the most beloved employers in town.'

The skin above Johns' nose was knotted into a frown. 'A few years ago there was a strike at the Caedraw ironworks. It got nasty for a while. Perhaps you've already met Jonah Hancock? To keep the furnaces burning, he shipped over hundreds of workers from Ireland. That made the natives angry. They tried to picket the works. When that didn't work, they broke into the one of the buildings, barricaded themselves inside – a hundred men in total. Jonah Hancock decided to enlist the help of some men who wouldn't be afraid to crack a few skulls. There's a bully in China called John Wylde, calls himself the Emperor. Wylde and his men stormed into the building and battered the strikers with pick handles and brickbats. None of the strikers was killed but they didn't walk out of that building on their own two feet. The police stood by and let all of this happen. Hancock played his hand beautifully. The strikers had to grovel to get their jobs back, and he rewarded them with a massive cut to their wages.'

'And Wylde?'

'He's pretty much allowed to do what he likes. Now he owns all of the prostitutes in China.'

'So feelings ran high and a few heads were cracked. But would a veteran of that strike really have done something like snatch Hancock's child in broad daylight?'

'I don't know, I wasn't involved.'

Pyke sensed that Johns was still holding back. 'But you know some people who were?'

'You could ask in the Three Horse Shoes. That's where the Chartists and trade unionists have always gathered.'

'We could go there now, if you aren't busy? I could pay you a couple of pounds.'

Johns' gaze drifted again. Then he let out a deep sigh. 'Look, I appreciate the offer, really I do, and I could always use some additional money, but I don't want to get involved in anything that's going to put me at odds with the people of the town. I don't know how much Smyth has told you about my background but it's taken me a long time to earn the trust of the kind of folk who frequent the Three Horse Shoes.'

'He just told me you used to be a soldier.'

Johns watched a bird soar up into the gloomy sky. 'Does Newport and the forty-fifth regiment mean anything to you?'

'Wasn't there a disturbance there a few years ago?'

That made him smile. 'A disturbance? You could call it that. Folk around here call it a rising. Our regiment was the last line of defence, stationed inside the Westgate Hotel. When the mob tried to storm it, I shot and killed two men.'

Pyke could see the pain in the former soldier's eyes. 'You were only following orders. I do the same.'

'That may well be true but no one apart from me pulled that trigger. I'll always have it on my conscience.'

Pyke thought about Frederick Shaw and all the other men he'd killed. In that moment he felt he could trust John Johns a little more. 'I'd like to pretend I don't know what you're talking about.'

'You've killed men in the line of duty?' Johns looked searchingly into his face.

Pyke just shrugged.

Finally Johns said, 'You're wondering why I decided to settle here? Why I didn't go somewhere else, start afresh?'

'I've never left London.'

'Guess who gave us the order to fire on the mob?' Johns looked out across the valley.

'I have no idea.'

'Zephaniah Hancock. At the time he described the protesters as vermin. I don't imagine his opinions have changed very much.'

The Three Horse Shoes pub was situated on the east side of Market Square in the town centre. It occupied the ground floor of a stout, red-brick building with the taproom at the front and a private room to the rear. Johns accompanied Pyke into the taproom and made at once for Bill Flint, the Chartist Pyke had met on the train up from Cardiff. When it became clear that no introduction was necessary – and that he wasn't needed to translate – Johns went to join another man at the back of the shabby room.

Flint was wearing a blue-checked woollen shirt, open at the throat, canvas trousers, wooden-soled shoes and a red handkerchief tied around his neck. On the train, Pyke had let the man believe he was a journalist, intending to write a piece on the town in light of

Thomas Carlyle's description of it as the dirtiest place in the kingdom. Now Flint's guard was up and he wanted to know how Pyke knew Johns.

'I'm paying him to translate for me. He was recommended to me by Sir Clancy Smyth, the chief magistrate.'

Flint leant against the counter and called out to the barmaid. Pyke noticed that one side of her face was so badly scarred that her skin had turned black.

'Want to know how it happened?' Flint whispered. 'Once upon a time she worked for a man called John Wylde.'

'The bully in China?'

'I see you've been getting to know the place,' Flint said, nodding.

'What do you know about him?'

'Wylde runs all of the brothels in China. Meredith was one of his women. That is, until he found out that she was sleeping with his rival, Benjamin Griffiths. He poured hot oil down one side of her face and had one of his men hold her down while he whipped her with a cat-o'-nine-tails. Wylde did it to her in the street, in broad daylight, in view of a hundred witnesses. I suppose that was the point. To humiliate her publicly and show off his power.'

Pyke waited for the woman to serve him his ale and left a few coins on the counter to pay for it. 'I take it Wylde was never prosecuted,' he said, turning back to Flint.

The Chartist nodded vigorously. Before he could respond, Pyke added, 'I also heard Wylde and some of his men were responsible for breaking the strike at Caedraw a few years ago.'

Flint glanced nervously at the other drinkers. 'I wasn't there but I'm told there were forty of 'em, armed to the teeth with picks, coshes, machetes, brickbats, knives, whatever they could lay their hands on. Bobbies didn't lift a finger.'

'And now Wylde can do as he likes?'

'As long as he does as he's told.' Flint lowered his voice to a whisper. 'Now, every time we have a meeting, and word gets back to the Hancocks, Wylde and his bullies show up and try to put a stop to it.'

'It can't make Jonah Hancock a popular man in these parts.'

Flint shook his head. 'Actually he *is* popular at the moment.

Wages have never been higher and jobs are plentiful. Merthyr's booming and there's no appetite for a strike.'

'But among certain people – let's say those hurt by Wylde or one of his men – there must be some desire for retribution.'

'*Retribution?*' Flint shuffled a little closer to him. 'Let me explain something to you. We might complain bitterly about men like Hancock and Josiah Webb, promise to bring them to their knees, but if they were to walk in here right now, you wouldn't hear a single word of dissent. You have no idea of the power they wield over us.'

Pyke thought about what he'd been told and decided to push Flint a little harder. 'So what if I were to tell you that someone has committed a crime against the Hancock family?'

Flint's expression became suspicious and his body stiffened. 'You're not a journalist, are you?'

'I'm a police detective from London,' Pyke whispered. 'I just want to know whether anyone *you* know has decided to take matters into their own hands.'

Flint's expression hardened. 'I don't think I should say anything else to you, at least not in here.' His bloodshot eyes glittered in the gaslight.

He followed Pyke outside. 'So have the Hancocks actually accused us of something?' Flint sounded both angry and curious.

Pyke looked around and wondered whether Johns had seen them leave.

'If he has,' Flint said, 'ask yourself one thing: how does it serve his own ends? That's the only thing that matters to men like Hancock. Because whatever he claims we've done, he'll use it as an excuse to come after us.'

Pyke considered this. 'I want to talk to someone who was there at the works during the strike. Someone who's still there. Someone on your side.'

'Why?'

'I want to know what's going on at the ironworks. What the mood of the workers is right now.'

Flint considered the request. 'John Evans. He was a furnace-man; now he's training to be a puddler. If you put a straight question to him, he'll give you a straight answer.'

Pyke watched as Flint stumbled back into the taproom then went to join Johns, who had appeared from another door.

'Well?' Johns fell in next to him and they walked a few yards in silence.

'Jonah Hancock isn't the most popular figure in the Three Horse Shoes. Nor is John Wylde. But I'm pretty sure Flint didn't know anything about the Hancock boy.' Pyke let a drunken reveller barge past them. 'Isn't it about time you told me how you know about the kidnapping?'

Johns looked directly at him and said, 'Cathy Hancock is a friend of mine.'

Pyke tried to cover his surprise but he didn't do a good job of it. The fact that Johns would openly describe Cathy as his friend seemed – given their differing social stations – a breach of decorum. Either he felt he had no choice but to reveal their friendship or he didn't care what Pyke thought. Pyke wanted to ask how good a friend Cathy was but he knew Johns wouldn't elaborate. Instead, he turned his thoughts back to his conversation with Flint.

'Bill Flint said something interesting. Made it seem like the Hancocks might use this situation as an excuse to clamp down on dissent at the ironworks.'

Johns dug his hands into his pockets. 'What are you suggesting?'

'I don't know . . . Would you put it past the Hancocks to arrange the kidnapping, and then use it as an excuse to come down hard on whoever is suspected?'

Johns didn't have an answer but Pyke could see he'd struck some kind of nerve.

When he returned to the Castle, Pyke found Cathy Hancock taking tea on her own in the drawing room. Her blonde hair had been arranged into ringlets and she was wearing an elaborately brocaded pink silk dress with puffed sleeves and a waist gathered in by a whale-boned corset. She looked like she was there to ornament what was an otherwise masculine room. The paintings on the walls were of unsmiling old men and a pair of deer antlers hung to one side of the fireplace. When Cathy saw Pyke, she sat up straighter and smiled; a display of politeness rather than an indication of intimacy.

'Detective-inspector,' she said, taking care to avert her eyes from his. 'I believe you wanted to ask me some questions.'

Pyke sat down in the armchair nearest to her and whispered, 'Last night, why did you tell me I shouldn't have come?'

'*Did* I?' She lifted her blue eyes to his and smiled, two dimples appearing at the sides of her mouth. 'I'm afraid I don't remember.'

Pyke tried to find some indication of the person – the girl – he'd once known. 'You must have had a reason for saying it – even if you don't remember speaking the words.'

'This last week has been a stressful time for me. I'm sure you can understand.' She pulled a dainty woollen shawl over her shoulders.

'Quite so.' Pyke removed a notepad and a piece of charcoal from his pocket. 'Perhaps you could tell me what happened last week. I believe that you and William were returning from the cemetery at Vaynor.'

She nodded carefully. 'My husband and I had a daughter, Mary. She died two years ago. Every week I go there with my son to put flowers on her grave.'

'And your carriage was ambushed on the road back into town. You remember how many of them there were?'

She bit her lip gingerly. 'Four, I think. One of them held me down while another one snatched William.'

'Do you remember anything about the man who held you down?'

Cathy inspected her gloved hands. 'He was dirty – that much I do remember. His breath smelled of beer. He'd tied a handkerchief around his face, to hide his features, but I could see he had a beard and two small, quick eyes.' Until this point she hadn't displayed a modicum of sentiment but now her top lip began to tremble. 'It was horrible, quite horrible. Just the thought of it makes me quiver with fear.'

'I'll do everything in my power to ensure your son is returned to his home safely.'

'Thank you.' Briefly she raised her head and Pyke felt that she was truly looking at him for the first time.

'Am I to understand that my assistance was sought on your recommendation?' He let his gaze linger on the whiteness of her neck.

'Your ability as a detective is well known in this household.

Therefore when this terrible thing happened, it was naturally to you that my husband wrote.'

Pyke digested what Cathy had just told him, unsure what to make of it. It seemed to confirm what she had intimated the previous evening: that he was there at Jonah Hancock's insistence, not hers.

'Last night, your husband suggested I interview your son's former nursemaid, a woman called Maggie Atkins. Apparently she left under a cloud. Do you think I should bother with her?'

'Who . . . *Maggie*?' Cathy tried to laugh but the tension in her voice was clear. 'Not in a million years.'

'Then why would your husband tell me she should be a suspect?'

She looked down and fingered a frayed piece of lace on her dress.

Pyke decided to try a different approach. 'I met a friend of yours today. A man called John Johns.'

That was sufficient to puncture her façade. Her expression suddenly fell and she shot him a pleading look.

Pyke's eyes darted around the room, aware for the first time that someone might be listening to their conversation. He stood up quickly and stretched. 'That will be all for now. In the meantime, I'd just like to repeat what I said earlier. We will do our best to ensure that you and your son are reunited.'

As he went to leave, her eyes were moist and she mouthed a silent thank-you.

Dinner was an awkward affair; Jonah Hancock at one end of the table and Cathy at the other. Pyke was sitting opposite Zephaniah, who had to be fed by one of the servants. When Jonah wasn't speaking, the only sound in the cavernous dining room was the clinking of silver cutlery on bone china. Zephaniah didn't say much but his eyes didn't leave Pyke.

'In this household, Detective-inspector, we've always been assiduously reminded of your abilities.' Jonah looked directly at Cathy, whose stare remained fixed on the food on her plate, which she barely touched.

It had been a petulant remark and once again Pyke thought about Zephaniah's claim from the previous evening. *My daughter-in-law has always carried a torch for you.*

After dinner, the three men retired to the library to have their brandies and cigars, and discuss Pyke's plans for the rendezvous at the old quarry the next morning.

'You'll have to trust me to do my job. The letter instructed me to go there alone and so I will go there alone.'

Some of Jonah's bonhomie had returned and he nodded briskly. 'A sensible decision, sir. You have the hundred pounds?'

Pyke nodded. Zephaniah Hancock had given him the purse full of gold sovereigns before dinner.

'Let's just hope that tomorrow we'll be clearer about the second letter and whether or not it was sent by my son's kidnappers.' With a cigar in hand, Jonah Hancock blew a smoke ring up into the air. He watched it rise and then dissolve.

Zephaniah looked at Pyke and smiled, as though they shared a secret. 'I would trust the detective-inspector with my own life, son. He will do as he sees fit and we will support him.'

Jonah seemed perplexed by his father's changed attitude towards Pyke and it took him a moment to recover. 'Quite so.'

'Perhaps, sir,' Zephaniah said, still staring at Pyke, 'you would tell us your opinion of my radiant daughter-in-law?'

Pyke saw Jonah stiffen. The old man was evidently savouring his son's discomfort. 'In what sense?'

'Well, I believe you knew her when she was a girl. I was wondering whether you find her much changed.'

'I'm sure that anyone who knew me as a child would find me much changed.' Pyke took a sip of brandy and put the glass down on the table. 'But to answer your question, sir, I find Catherine a charming, well-mannered young woman.'

'Indeed so.' Zephaniah's eyes were glinting.

Pyke had had enough of the old man's games and announced he was ready for his bed. Jonah ushered Pyke to the door, patted him on the shoulder and wished him luck for the morning.

'Whatever you may think of me, Detective-inspector, and my father, I do love my son very dearly. That's all that matters here.'

Pyke had climbed the stairs and was halfway along the landing when he heard her whisper his name.

Cathy was waiting for him in an alcove, shrouded in darkness.

'I had to talk to you away from prying eyes and ears,' she

whispered breathlessly. 'My husband and father-in-law have made it their business to know who I talk to and what I talk about.'

Pyke could just see the whites of Cathy's eyes in the half-light produced by a candle. 'What is it they're afraid you'll say?'

She didn't answer.

'Why did you tell me I shouldn't have come?'

Cathy took a deep breath. 'I'd been drinking. I don't remember. Please don't hold it against me.' She tried to smile.

'I need to ask you a question, Cathy. Who do you honestly believe has your son?'

'I don't know.'

'Scottish Cattle?' Pyked waited and added, 'Maggie Atkins?'

That drew a snort. 'Maggie was a saint. Her problem was that she was too close to me, took my side, stood up to my husband. It's why they concocted that whole situation and threatened her with the police.'

'Being treated like that . . .' Pyke said, 'it could make a person bitter.'

'Not Maggie. You'd know what I mean if you met her. And she loved William, too. She would never do anything to put his life at risk.'

'Maybe I should talk to her, just to rule her out as a suspect.'

'You could do, but you'd have to travel to Scotland. She's working for a family in Edinburgh.'

Pyke considered what she'd said. 'Any other suspects?'

'My husband has made many enemies in his years as an iron-master. The same goes for Zephaniah, more so. He's always been more ruthless than my husband. In fact he treats Jonah with contempt, always describes him as weak and mollycoddled. It agitates my husband greatly, the fact that Zephaniah so clearly prefers his younger brother, Richard, and that spurs him to act in ways that belie his natural disposition.'

'I asked Zephaniah about your family. He didn't pretend he had much interest in your son beyond the fact that he's heir to the estate.'

Cathy's eyes darkened but she kept her thoughts to herself.

Pyke allowed his gaze to drift from her neck to her cleavage and immediately he saw that she'd noticed this. She smiled and touched his arm. 'I'm glad you're here.'

Pyke thought about her husband downstairs and the fact that both of them were old enough to be her father.

'It's late, I'm tired.' He looked into her cool, bloodshot eyes and felt the muscles in his stomach tighten.

It took Pyke a good hour to walk from the Castle to the ramshackle cottage near the old quarry but he left at five in the morning and made it there before sunrise, enabling him to slip into the cottage unnoticed. He didn't know whether the kidnappers – if indeed that was who had sent the second letter – were watching the cottage, but if they were, he didn't want his arrival to be spotted. By the time John Johns arrived at ten o'clock, to drop off the purse of sovereigns as Pyke had arranged, he supposed that someone would be watching them from the higher ground: they would watch Johns arrive with the purse and watch him leave without it and some time after that, they would venture down to the cottage to collect their booty. Pyke wanted to be there when this happened. He knew he was taking a risk – and potentially putting the Hancock boy's life in danger by not following the demands of the second letter – but he wasn't convinced that it had been sent by the real kidnappers.

It was easy to see why the cottage had been chosen as the site for the rendezvous. As a milky lightness appeared at the edges of the sky, Pyke saw that the place was surrounded on three sides by steep-angled hills, green and wet from the previous night's rainfall. Anyone perched on one of these hills would have a bird's-eye view of the cottage, and there was no way of sneaking up on it, in daylight at least, without being seen. Pyke peered out of the window. The previous night's mist had cleared and visibility was good. Farther down the valley, he could just about see the blast furnaces attached to the Morlais works; beyond them the town spread out like a canker on an otherwise pristine landscape. It was seven o'clock. If he could just bring the Hancock boy home, that would be enough.

Through the window of the abandoned cottage, Pyke watched John Johns wander up the mud track. Clouds had rolled in off the hills and Pyke could see the first drops of rain. Johns kept his eyes fixed on the cottage, as Pyke had told him to, his shooting jacket buttoned right the way up to his collar. He didn't bother to knock, just pushed open the door and entered the dark room. He dropped the purse on to the mud floor and brushed the rain from the shoulders of his coat.

'I think there are two of them up there.' He pointed to their approximate positions. 'One on each hill.'

Pyke nodded. He had suspected this. 'Do you think you could double back on yourself when you reach Anderson's farm road, and try coming at them from the other side of the hill?'

'Depends on how much time I've got.' Johns hesitated then added, 'And what you want me to do.'

'Just try to see who they are. But don't let them see you. That's the important thing.'

'Bet whoever comes here to pick up the purse will get the fright of their life when they see you.'

Pyke wondered whether Johns had meant this as a criticism.

'I should get going.' Johns peered out at the rain. 'That is, if you want me on that hill by the time someone arrives to pick up the money.'

They parted without exchanging another word. Pyke watched Johns make his way back along the mud track until he was a faint smudge in the distance.

When someone arrived about an hour later, he seemed nervous and distracted, not at all sure what he was meant to do. Peering into the abandoned cottage, the man waited on the doorstep for what seemed like minutes, perhaps trying to summon up the courage to step inside. Pyke had seen him from a distance and didn't recognise him. He was dressed as a labourer and walked with a determined stride. Pyke waited until the man was inside the cottage before he revealed himself, stepping out of the shadows behind the door. Startled, the man jumped back and before Pyke could grab him, he'd turned around and bolted for the door. He ran about ten or fifteen yards back down the track then stopped. He turned around and was about to say something when a loud crack echoed around the valley. Pyke watched as a flower of blood exploded on the front of the man's shirt. His expression froze and he stumbled forward with nothing to break his fall. Pyke raced over to the spot where the man had fallen. Looking up at the hill, he saw that Johns was gesticulating towards the spot where the shot had come from but the marksman was nowhere to be seen. The only sound was the wind blowing in the long grass.

A few minutes later, Johns appeared, red-faced, by the side of the cottage, a rifle in his hand. 'There were two of them all right. One of 'em must have seen me and decided to leave this behind.' He glanced down at the body, which was surrounded by a thick pool of blood. 'I saw they were armed but I never thought they'd turn their rifles on one of their own.'

'Whoever he is,' Pyke said, gesturing towards the corpse, 'he isn't, and wasn't, ever one of them.'

'As soon as the one on the farthest hill had got his shot off, they both ran away.' Johns held out the rifle that he had retrieved from the mountainside.

Pyke took it from him and looked it over. 'You recognise either of them?' It was a new Baker's rifle, one of the most expensive and accurate money could buy.

'No, but if I saw the one who fired the shot again, I might be able to identify him.' Johns looked up at the hill where the marksman had been positioned. 'To hit a man square in the chest from that kind of distance . . . you'd have to be a professional soldier.'

Pyke nodded. He'd had the same thought. A Baker's rifle was the weapon of choice for Her Majesty's infantry. 'There's a barracks near here, isn't there?'

'That's right. The Pennywenn barracks in Dowlais.'

'Maybe you could go there, see if any of the faces are familiar?'

Johns seemed uncomfortable with this suggestion but he didn't say anything. Instead, he pointed towards the dead man. 'Did he say anything to you before they shot him?'

'He took one look at me and fled. That's when he was shot.'

The blood had now seeped into the mud. Pyke knelt down next to the body and rummaged through the man's pockets. Apart from a few coins, the only item was a notebook. Standing up, he flicked through it. It was a rent book. The address had been handwritten on the first page.

'Where's Irish Row?'

Johns frowned. 'Dowlais, just around the corner from the Morlais works.'

Pyke held up the rent book. 'According to this, that's where he lived. Are you feeling strong?'

Johns wiped his hands on his coat. 'How far do we have to carry him?'

They took it in turns to carry the dead body and made it as far as a public house on the Pennydarren Road. There, Pyke paid a man a couple of shillings for the use of his horse and cart and they rode the additional mile to the Castle in silence. Pyke had decided to take the body to the Castle in the first instance because he wanted to know whether there had been news about the Hancock boy.

Johns just nodded.

As they neared the entrance, Pyke turned to Johns. 'So how well do you know Cathy?'

'Mrs Hancock? I met her after I left the regiment and decided to come here to Merthyr to live.'

Waiting a moment, Pyke said, 'Most people in your circumstances would've fled back to England.'

'A couple of the men left the regiment at the same time as me. Got out of Wales as fast as they could.'

'But you wanted to stay?'

'I think I saw it as my penance.'

'And what kind of welcome did you receive?'

'Most people didn't know; not at first. Not until old man Hancock let it be known who I was and what I'd done.'

'What you'd done on *his* orders.'

'That didn't seem to matter. I'd pulled the trigger. The blood was on my hands.'

'Why would he do a thing like that?'

Johns shrugged. 'I don't think he liked the notion of me settling in *his* town. It made him nervous. He tried to force me to go elsewhere. Catherine came to my rescue. I think she heard the two Hancocks discussing my situation and took pity. Managed to convince Jonah that I wasn't a threat.'

'And are you?'

'What . . . *me*? A threat?' Johns turned to face him, his hands

77

gripping the reins. They were nearly at the top of the hill, the Castle right in front of them.

They looked up and saw Jonah Hancock standing on the front steps. As soon as he saw the horse and cart, he rushed down the steps, his face creased with worry. 'Superintendent Jones has just paid us a visit.'

Pyke saw Cathy emerge from the entrance. Her hair was loose and blowing in the gusty wind.

'They've found a body under Jackson's Bridge, a young boy.' Jonah gasped for air. 'Jones thinks it might be William.'

PART II

*

Hinterland –

n. a region remote from urban areas

n. a remote and undeveloped area

n. unexplored territories full of mystery and danger

EIGHT

At the previous day's constabulary meeting Sub-inspector Hastings had read out new crimes that had been perpetrated. The post-car from Cashel to Thurles had been held up and robbed; a home in Mullinahoue had been burgled by a gang of masked gunmen; a man had been set upon about a mile from town and relieved of his purse and his double-barrelled fowling piece; and worst of all, a policeman had been shot and seriously wounded when he had tried to prevent a pay clerk being robbed in Caher. Hastings had told them that the situation was unacceptable and it was their job to find and punish those responsible. He'd slammed his fist on his desk and told them that if they were doing their jobs properly, people would be too scared to commit any crimes. Knox hadn't dared point out this was utter nonsense and crime was rising for the simple reason that people were desperate.

After the meeting, the sub-inspector had asked Knox how his murder inquiry was progressing. Knox had already decided not to tell Hastings that he'd identified the dead man and so he gave only a vague answer. The sub-inspector had grunted and reiterated his demand that Knox was to return to normal duty first thing on Tuesday morning. Cornwallis wanted the whole matter to go away and what Cornwallis wanted, men like Hastings endeavoured to make happen.

Therefore, when a note arrived at the barracks from the landlord of the New Forge in Dundrum requesting that Knox go there at his earliest convenience, he didn't mention it to the sub-inspector.

After breakfast on Sunday, Martha and James set off to visit her sister in town and Knox picked up a ride from a shopkeeper who was on his way to Dundrum Hall to deliver some provisions. They exchanged a couple of pleasantries and then lapsed into silence. The air had a wintry feel and halfway between Cashel and Dundrum rain started to fall as sleet, the sky grey and threatening like gunmetal.

Knox found the landlord sweeping damp sawdust into piles in the taproom of the New Forge Inn. This time the man's greeting was a little warmer. He offered Knox a nip of poteen, which Knox declined.

'The maid was cleaning the room we were in the other day and found these stuffed under the mattress.' He walked across to the counter and retrieved what turned out to be a thin bundle of letters.

Knox thanked the landlord and asked whether he could sit in a quiet corner and read them. 'And I'll take that poteen now, if you don't mind.'

He settled down at a table at the far end of the narrow room and laid out the envelopes in front of him. In fact, there were just three. Carefully Knox removed the letters and scrutinised their contents. Penned by the same hand, they were addressed to Pyke and signed by someone called Felix. The first and second letters had been sent to an address in London; the final one, to the station-house in Merthyr Tydfil in Wales. In each letter, the return address had been given as St John's church in Keynsham, Somerset. Knox took the earliest one, dated the fourth of August, and read it carefully once more. The author announced that he'd arrived safely and that he had been met at the train station by 'Martin' and was settling into his new accommodation very well. Everyone had been welcoming, he wrote, and he was looking forward to beginning his studies. He hoped that everything was fine at home and asked Pyke to pass on his best wishes to Mrs Booth and to give Copper – presumably a dog – a pat on the head. The letter was signed 'With love, Felix'.

Knox put it back in the envelope. The tone was warm but not overly familiar. Felix was clearly the younger party and the reference to 'home' made Knox think that Felix might be the dead man's son.

The second letter, dated the fourteenth of October, was longer and, Knox felt, more intimate. He focused on a passage from the middle.

I know you don't want me to but I pray for you every morning. You sounded sad in your last letter. I know you claim no affiliation or belief but this must mean you feel terribly alone and even lonely at times. When I am lonely or afraid I pray to God and He helps comfort me. I know, of course, that you are never afraid but I worry that your sadness is something you won't be able to alleviate on your own. You always told me that turning to someone outside of our family in times of need is a sign of weakness. I know Godfrey was a great support to you — and I hope I was too, though I was probably a burden as well — but now he has gone and I have moved here, who is there to help you? Who can you turn to in your hour of need?

Knox put down the letter and realised there were tears in his eyes. It wasn't so much what had been written that had affected him; it was the fact that Felix cared greatly for the dead man and would now have to be told that his father had been murdered. Briefly Knox thought about his own father and how he would not mourn the man's passing.

Further answers were provided by the final letter. This one was much briefer and to the point. Felix mentioned Pyke's visit to Keynsham, referred to a kidnapped child and said that he hoped the child had been found. He finished the letter by announcing he'd been given a few days' holiday from his studies and wanted to visit Pyke in Merthyr for a day or two. He said he would arrive some time on Sunday the twenty-second and stay with Pyke until the Tuesday morning.

Knox folded the letter and put it back in the envelope. He had another look at the address. *The station-house, Merthyr Tydfil.* When Knox had first noticed Felix's reference to an investigation, he'd assumed that Pyke was some kind of private agent but now it struck him that Pyke might be a policeman. The letter had also mentioned a kidnapped child. What if Pyke had been sent to Merthyr to try to find this child? Still, there was nothing in the letter that explained what had brought Pyke to Ireland — or who might have wanted him dead.

Knox looked down and saw that his hands were trembling. What if the corpse were a senior policeman from London? The situation made him feel ill.

Carefully Knox placed the letters in his coat pocket and thanked the landlord for the poteen he hadn't touched.

Outside the sleet had turned to snow. It was midday and he looked up and down the street for any sign of a carriage or cart. Folk would be coming out of church and he might be lucky enough to find a ride back to Cashel.

'Knox.'

He looked up and saw Maxwell hurrying across the street in his direction. Cornwallis's agent was red-faced.

'Someone saw you earlier and word got back to his Lordship. He has a problem and asked me to come and find you.'

Knox felt his stomach knot. 'What kind of a problem?'

Maxwell seemed to notice Knox's unease and appeared to enjoy it. He offered Knox a thin smile. 'His Lordship will explain.'

They found Cornwallis in the stables. The aristocrat was wearing tan breeches, black leather riding boots, a bright red waistcoat and a grey cutaway coat. He was pacing up and down outside a stable door.

'Your presence in Dundrum is most fortuitous, Constable. I presume you were visiting your family?'

Knox just nodded. He had no intention of telling Cornwallis the real reason for his visit.

'I would like to think they're happy in their new accommodation.' He glanced over at Maxwell. 'I imagine they will find things a good deal more pleasant where they are.'

Knox didn't want to agree because that would put him in Cornwallis's debt, but he didn't want to disagree and risk eliciting the old man's ire.

Cornwallis nodded impatiently. 'Anyhow, boy, now you're here, you can take care of a little problem for me.'

'Has something happened, your Lordship?'

Cornwallis removed a key chain from his one of his pockets and went to unlock the stable door. 'Maxwell here caught him red-handed. The brigand was trying to draw blood from one of my cattle.'

It took Knox a few moments to realise that he knew the man slumped on the wet hay. He was about the same age as Davy McMullan and they had known each other when they were children.

Knox had last seen him about three years ago, when they had crossed paths on the main street in Dundrum and exchanged a brief, cautious nod. This time, Davy McMullan looked up at him indifferently. If he recognised Knox, he didn't show it. His skin looked jaundiced, his whiskers were unkempt and his face was positively skeletal. His only item of clothing was a soiled smock-frock.

'We've long suspected people have been stealing from us,' Cornwallis said, triumphant, 'but this is the first time we've caught one of them red-handed.' He nodded for Maxwell to take up the story.

'Clever buggers, they are. They cut a vein in the cow's neck, draw off a pint or two into a jar, then stop the bleeding by putting a pin across the incision, holding it in place with a few hairs from the tail.'

Knox glanced at McMullan. He didn't look strong enough to stand up without assistance, let alone commit theft. Bending down, Knox whispered, 'When did you last eat a meal, sir?'

McMullan wouldn't look at him but murmured, 'Three days ago, I think.'

Knox stood up a little too quickly and felt dizzy. He turned to Cornwallis. 'This man needs a good meal, not further punishment.'

The aristocrat stared at him, hands on hips. 'I beg your pardon, man?'

'Can't you see this man is on the verge of starvation?' Knox was desperately trying to censor himself but he was also angry.

'And you think that's my concern? Or *your* concern, for that matter? Do you think it's unimportant that this man broke the law?'

Knox knew he'd waded into an argument he couldn't win. 'These matters are never *un*important . . .'

'But you think I should pat this man on the back and perhaps set a place for him at my table?'

'If he did, in fact, do as you said, he should be punished under the letter of the law. But anyone can see he's starving. I think we should treat someone like this with a little compassion.'

The old man's facial features seemed to shrivel into each other.

'Since when does a man of your lowly rank tell me – a viscount – what is and what is not appropriate behaviour?'

Knox knew he'd said too much and felt his anger turning to contrition. 'I'm sorry, your Lordship.' He bowed his head, not sure what else to say.

'If the law means nothing, perhaps we should permit people to rape and pillage as they see fit? Maim and murder, even. Is that what you would like to see, boy?'

'No.'

'But you still think I should show this wretch some compassion, even though he stole from me?'

'If he committed a crime, then he should be brought before the magistrate.'

'If?' Cornwallis's eyes narrowed. 'Are you doubting my word now?'

'What I meant to say, your Lordship, is that of course he will be brought before the magistrate.'

'See to it he is, boy. You'll take him with you back to Cashel and deliver him to the barracks there.'

Knox nodded. 'I'm afraid I don't have any transportation of my own . . .'

Cornwallis waved away his objection. 'Maxwell will provide you with a horse and cart. I'll send one of the stable hands to collect it from you in the morning.'

Knox stared down at the forlorn figure of Davy McMullan and felt as bad as he had felt in a long while.

Knox had long since become accustomed to other people's suspicions, their sullenness in his company. Not their open hostility; just the notion that he had picked the wrong side and thrown in his lot with the enemy. For a few years, he had entertained the fantasy that he and his fellow constables, Catholics to a man, were united in a desire not to punish and coerce the local people but to help them, Catholics and Protestants together, keeping alive the spirit of the United Irishmen movement. Such a notion had, of course, been hopelessly naive, and as soon as the second potato crop failed and desperate men and women started to attack grain barges bound for Waterford, his complicity in a system established to safeguard the rich was impossible to ignore. Before this, Knox knew that some of the constables overlooked minor transgressions, a pheasant poached here, a rabbit taken there, as he had done, but since the autumn, their orders had been clear: no mercy, no tolerance. Two weeks ago, McCafferty had been dismissed for refusing to arrest a man who had dug up his neighbour's turnips, and last week a second constable, Mearns, had been forced out for speaking his mind at a meeting.

As he led Davy McMullan to the cart, Knox wondered what would happen to him if Cornwallis ever decided to complain about his behaviour. The snow had stopped falling but an inch had settled on the ground and was already melting into a brown sludge.

While Jonathan Maxwell went to speak with one of his men, the stable boy sidled up to Knox.

'You the man who's lookin' into that dead body, one found not far from here?' he whispered.

Knox patted the horse on its nose, trying to appear bored, in case Maxwell saw them in conversation. 'That's right. Why? Did you see something?'

'I didn't see who done it, if that's what you mean.'

'But you have some information about the murder?'

'None of us likes the master but we're afraid of him. They say he's grown a tail. Promise me you won't tell 'im what I'm about to say.'

'I promise,' Knox whispered out of the corner of his mouth.

The stable boy went round to check the horse's reins. 'All I know is that his Lordship knows the fellow that died.' He looked around, making sure Maxwell was otherwise occupied. 'I was there when his Lordship first saw the body. His eyes near popped out of his head.'

Knox turned slightly but the stable boy had raced off as Maxwell strode towards the cart, his face red and blotchy. 'His Lordship will expect to see this man's name when the list of defendants at the next sessions is published in the newspaper.'

'Mam, this is Davy McMullan. He used to be a friend of mine. I've invited him to join us for lunch.'

Knox had cut off the rope binding the man's wrists before they'd reached the cottage and he now ushered McMullan into the warmth of the front room.

The news that there would be two additional mouths to feed sent his mother scurrying over to the pot of boiling corn but Knox knew she would find a way of making do. Knox was greeted with a hug from each of his brothers. Matthew was now taller than he was and his arms and shoulders had filled out from his work on the land. His greeting was warm but short-lived. Peter's arms remained around him and Knox stroked him gently on the head, the way he liked. Slowly Knox prised himself away from Peter and to his surprise the lad scurried over to where their father was standing and nuzzled against the older man. Martin Knox put his arm around his youngest son and for a few moments no one spoke. This was the first time the whole family had been together in months and Knox suddenly felt like an intruder, as though he had interrupted their domestic harmony and introduced tension into the air. Martin watched him carefully.

The previous winter Peter had fallen sick again, this time with a fever, and they had all taken turns to stay at home and nurse him, even Martin. In fact, their father had done as much if not more than anyone and Knox had struggled to reconcile this notion with the drunken ogre he had known as he grew up.

Davy McMullan shuffled across to the fire and held up his hands to warm them.

'Davy McMullan? We knew your ma and da, didn't we? You used to live not far from us.'

McMullan didn't seem to have heard Martin's question. He stared wordlessly at the fire.

'Laddie, I asked ye a question.'

'Let him eat first,' Knox's mother said, stirring the pot of corn with a wooden spoon. 'Look at him. He's nothing but skin and bones.'

'Man comes into my home uninvited. Is it too much to ask him to be civil as well?'

'I invited him. I'd ask you to treat my guest with respect, but clearly that's something you're incapable of.'

Knox stepped into the space between McMullan and his father. This was the first time he had openly confronted the man and he could barely control his shaking hands. His father hadn't actually struck him in a long while but memories of those encounters were seared into his brain. Knox had seen at first hand what violence did to its victims and perpetrators and had vowed never to strike another man in anger.

The injury registered on his father's face and he reddened. 'You watch it now, Michael. You're under my roof now.'

Knox didn't like to cause a scene in front of his mother – or Peter

– but his father's show of affection towards his younger brother had rankled. 'You may live here and throw in a few pennies towards the rent that you haven't pissed up against the wall, but this will always be Mam's house.'

His father took a few steps towards him, his fists curled up into tight balls. His face was scarlet and Knox could see the veins pulsing in his neck. 'I warned ye, lad.'

Trying to control his nerves, Knox stood his ground and to his amazement he saw that his father didn't know what to do.

Peter started to whimper and then scuttled over to their mother, who gathered him up into the folds of her apron. 'Please, both of ye.' Her tone was scalding and it brought them to their senses. She started to ladle spoonfuls of the steaming hot corn and buttermilk into bowls. '*There.*' She feigned a smile and placed one of the bowls in front of their guest, who had taken up a place at the small table. Uninvited, he picked up a spoon and started to eat.

Knox stared at McMullan, who continued to spoon the corn into his open mouth. He finished in what seemed like seconds and wiped the bowl clean with his little finger, then silently eyed the food that had been laid out for Knox. Knox told him to go ahead. He said that he'd already eaten that morning, which was a lie. McMullan looked at him, hollow-eyed. He didn't need another invitation. Tucking in with his spoon, he emptied the second bowl in a few mouthfuls. By now, even Martin Knox had taken an interest and was watching McMullan with a mixture of fascination and revulsion.

After he'd finished the second bowl of corn, McMullan sat there in a daze. Then he turned to look at Martin Knox. 'You were asking after my family, sir.'

Knox's father tried to stammer a response but the words got stuck in his throat.

'We were evicted from our cabin just before Christmas. By then the workhouse in Cashel had closed its doors. I thought I'd be able to get some relief work on one of the estates but the agents were hiring their own tenants. We stayed with a neighbour for a day or two but then one of the children was struck down with the fever and we all had to move out. After that, no one would take us in. Why would they? I did what I could, built a shelter outdoors, but I had no money for food, nothing at all. All I could do was forage for grubs.

My elder child died a week later. We buried her as best we could but by then our younger child had fallen ill and she perished a few days later. My wife took it all very badly as you can imagine. When I woke up the following morning, I found her lying next to me. She'd taken her own life. I buried her next to my beautiful girls.'

For what seemed like minutes no one in the room spoke. Knox looked up at his mother and saw that her eyes were damp with tears.

He went across to where Davy McMullan was sitting and placed his hand gently on the man's shoulder. 'I don't know what to say. But I'm sorry for all you've had to suffer.'

Knox's father looped his thumbs through the top of his trousers and sniffed. 'His Lordship's tryin' to run things the best way he knows how. You can't blame him. Sometimes these things happen. Bad luck.' He looked around the room for support.

His mother, who had made the same argument to Knox a few days earlier, walked over to where her husband was sitting and slapped him once around the cheek.

No one dared move. Knox prepared himself for his father's response but this time he wouldn't let the man lay a finger on his mother. Matthew stared down at the floor and Peter was weeping. Knox had once seen his father split open his mother's skull with the force of his blows but now the man just looked broken and lost.

'We should get going before the weather sets in.' Knox looked at Davy McMullan. He hadn't told them that he was transporting the man to prison.

His mother nodded dumbly, still in a state of shock. Knox went to hug her. 'Tell him if he lays a finger on you,' he whispered, 'I'll come back here with a warrant for his arrest.'

She flinched and withdrew from him.

Outside, Knox patted the horse and climbed up on to the cart. Listlessly McMullan joined him, shivering from the cold. They sat there next to one another, staring into the darkness.

'I'm not going to take you to Cashel, Davy. You don't deserve to be punished for what you did.'

McMullan nodded but didn't say anything.

'You're free to go.'

'Free?' McMullan stared at him blankly then shook his head.

Knox watched him trudge off down the track, leaving faint

footprints in the snow. Later it struck him that he should have offered the man his coat or some money but by then he was halfway back to Cashel and his thoughts had turned to what would happen when Cornwallis found out that McMullan's name wasn't listed among those to be tried at the quarter assizes.

NINE

The three of them were ushered into the living room of the station-house. The child's body lay on a walnut table covered by a white sheet. Jones closed the door behind him and remained where he was. Jonah Hancock and Cathy stared at each other and then at Pyke. Before they had left the Castle, Cathy had rinsed her face in cold water and of the two of them, she looked the more capable; Jonah Hancock couldn't even bring himself to look at the table. The two of them had barely spoken in the carriage but as they disembarked, she had offered Jonah her hand and he had taken it. Pyke didn't know whether this was just habit or some kind of coming together in the face of adversity.

Pyke strode towards the table. There was no reason to prolong the agony. 'Would one of you care to step up here?' His hand rested on the sheet.

Now Pyke could feel his own heart thumping against his ribcage. If the dead child was indeed their son, they would blame him – for not precisely following the orders of the second letter. And perhaps they would be right to do so. He'd taken a risk and it had blown up in his face. A man was dead and they still had no idea who'd taken the boy. Maybe, Pyke thought grimly, the kidnappers had decided to cut their losses, flee the town and kill the lad in the process. Of course, none of the money had changed hands.

Jonah Hancock waved his request away, indicating that the task was beyond him. That left Cathy. She stared at Pyke dry-eyed and tried to smile. 'Looks like it will have to be me, then.'

Pyke guided her to the spot next to him. Impressed by her fortitude, he touched her softly on the small of her back, not caring whether Jonah saw it. If her husband couldn't give her the moral support she needed, then he would.

'Ready?' Pyke's hand hovered above the sheet. Briefly he thought about the dead bodies he had seen. Most recent had been Frederick Shaw's. Pyke had held him as he'd died. He never believed that the dead looked at peace. It was usually a terrible sight, someone you'd known and perhaps even loved turned into a slab of mottled flesh.

'As I'll ever be.' Beside him, Cathy took a deep breath.

As Pyke slid the sheet off the boy's face, he tried to imagine how he would feel if this were Felix. Cathy looked down at the face, her expression hard.

'It's not him.' She let out a tiny gasp and turned to Pyke. 'It's not my William.'

Jonah Hancock barged Pyke out of the way and stared down at the corpse. His hands were trembling. 'By Gad, it really isn't him, is it?' Turning to his wife, he added, 'How could anyone think it was our son? This boy looks nothing like him!'

Pyke wanted to take Cathy in his arms and tell her that everything was going to be fine but he stood aside to let Jonah comfort her. Jonah simply patted her arm and said, 'Someone should go home and tell my father . . .'

'What you did was reckless, sir, and even worse, it needlessly endangered the life of my son,' Jonah Hancock said, once Pyke had explained what had happened on the mountain. One of the constables had escorted Cathy back to the Castle.

'I still don't believe that second letter was sent by the men who've kidnapped your son,' Pyke said, knowing this didn't wholly justify the decision he'd made.

'But you've no proof, have you? Admittedly it's not the same handwriting but that can easily be explained. One of the other kidnappers could have scribed it.'

Pyke looked uneasily at Superintendent Jones, who had said very little. He had to admit that Hancock had a point. 'What we need to do is find out who shot and killed that man up on the mountain. It couldn't have been one of the kidnappers. Why shoot one of their own?'

'So let's assume that someone else found out about the

arrangement and decided to try and put a stop to it. Shoot this chap and have done with it,' Jones suggested.

'Perhaps.' Pyke shrugged. 'I just can't see what was gained.' He turned to Hancock. 'Your son is still missing and we still have all of the ransom money.'

Jones nodded, similarly bemused. 'You said Johns saw the assassin? That he'd be able to identify the man again?'

'One of them, perhaps. He made a good point. It takes considerable skill to shoot a man at such a distance and kill him, so the person who pulled the trigger was a trained marksman. A soldier, probably.'

'Why on earth would a soldier want to kill one of my son's kidnappers?' Hancock said, angrily.

'For a start, we don't know whether the dead man was one of the kidnappers or not.' Pyke went to retrieve the rent book he'd found in the man's pocket. 'There's no name in here but it says the man lived in Dowlais on Irish Row.'

'So what are we waiting for?' Hancock said. The sweat on his forehead glistened in the candlelight.

'Irish Row?' Jones seemed unconvinced by this. 'You're saying this man is Irish?'

'There's only one way to find out,' Hancock said, rubbing his hands together.

Jones and Pyke shared a troubled look. It was the superintendent who spoke first. 'I think you'd better let us take care of matters from here, sir.'

Hancock's face reddened with indignation. 'It's two miles to Dowlais. If not by my carriage, how do you intend to get there? Walk?'

'Irish Row after dark?' Jones said dubiously.

Pyke looked at him, and then at Hancock. 'I don't see we have a choice.'

'They're a wild lot and they live in squalor you simply wouldn't fathom. But I still can't believe that an Irishman or a mob of Irishmen would do anything as bold or rash as kidnap Mr Hancock's son. That kind of undertaking requires planning and capital. Most of

94

the Irish here are just trying to survive.' Jones glanced at Hancock, waiting to be contradicted.

Pyke watched them, their wariness in one another's company, and thought about what Johns had told him: that the police had stood by while the bullies – bought and paid for by the Hancocks – ran amok among the strikers.

'What I don't understand is why a bunch of Paddies would want to pick a fight with us,' Hancock said. 'We've been damn good to 'em, shipped 'em over here and gave 'em work.'

Pyke looked out of the dirt-smeared window. Even with four horses, the carriage was struggling to negotiate the thick mud. 'I'm told you used Irish labour to break the strike a few years ago and drive down wages.'

'Nothing illegal in that.'

'No, but it must have caused resentment between the Irish and native workers.'

Hancock chose not to respond and crossed his arms.

This was Pennydarren Road, Jones explained, to fill the silence. It hadn't been metalled, which made it impassable at certain times of the year. Eventually it turned into Dowlais Road, with its string of squat terraced houses clinging to either side.

'And Dowlais is where the other great ironworks is located?' Pyke put the question to Hancock.

'Great, I think, is a misnomer, sir. They employ more bodies than we do at Caedraw but technically ours is a superior operation. With almost half as many workers, our output is nearly the same.'

Pyke nodded.

'The truth of the matter,' Hancock added, tapping his nose, 'is that Josiah Webb is too miserly to invest in new machinery. Instead he relies on manpower to do the work that the giant water wheels and steam engines perform at Caedraw.'

'To be fair to the Webbs,' Jones interrupted, 'they've been stymied by the issue of the lease at the Morlais works.'

Hancock glared at the superintendent but remained quiet.

'What issue?' Pyke asked.

'The lease is up for renewal at the end of this year but the landowner wants thirty thousand a year and Webb is only willing to pay ten. He says he'll close the works rather than pay thirty.'

'Lease or no lease, it's true that Caedraw employs fewer workers than Morlais but ours are more skilled, better paid and better motivated. Contrary to what you may hear, sir, we treat our workers with respect – and we pay them in coin, not tokens they can only spend in the company shop.'

They had turned off the main road into a narrow street. Children as young as three raced alongside the carriage, banging their fists against the wooden panels, trying to frighten the horses. Ash-tips were piled up in front of each house and feral dogs roamed in and out of open doors. It was the smell that was most noticeable, though: an eye-watering stench of human and animal faeces.

Irish Row was a miserable street running parallel to the main road, fronted on both sides by dilapidated terrace houses, just a single room up and down. Most were sinking into the mud. There were no pavements nor gas lighting but the street was thronged with people; some had just finished their shift and some were about to start. At the far end, the buildings were more substantial and given over to lodging houses and beer shops with names like the Exiles of Erin and the Shamrock. Shafts of light and raucous shouts spilled from half-open doors. Number fifty – where the murdered man had lodged, according to the rent book – was a block farther than the last of the beer shops.

The carriage came to a sudden halt and was quickly surrounded by children. The driver tried to shoo them away with his whip, to no avail. Some climbed on to the wheels and pressed their faces against the glass.

'You're to stay in the carriage,' Jones said to Hancock. 'Your driver will see that no one bothers you.'

Hancock nodded. Suddenly the idea of stepping outside his private cocoon didn't seem too attractive.

Jones removed his truncheon, and Pyke his pistol, and they opened the door, pushing their way through the crowd of children. Some tried to grab them, others begged for coins. Jones waved them off with his truncheon, then took a lantern from the carriage. Peering in through the front window of number fifty, Pyke couldn't see any light or sign of life.

They knocked and, when no one answered, Pyke tried the door and discovered that it was unlocked. They stepped into the low-ceilinged room. The air was dank and mouldy. Jones held up the lantern. There was a chest of drawers pressed up against one of the walls. The drawers themselves were empty or lying on the floor but the ashes in the grate were still warm. A brief search of the rest of the house confirmed that it was deserted.

'Looks like we just missed whoever was here,' Jones said, looking out at the children's faces pressed against the window.

But Pyke's attention had been caught by something in the corner of the room, hidden behind one of the drawers. Bending over, he reached out and retrieved a child's shoe and coat.

Back in the carriage, Pyke showed the items to Jonah Hancock. The ironmaster took the coat, pressed it up against his nose and sniffed. Trembling, he handed it back to Pyke.

'That's my son's.'

'I want all the stinking lodging and boarding houses in upper and lower Merthyr turned upside down and razed to the ground if needs be.' Jonah Hancock was pacing up and down in the drawing room. 'It's clear that some Paddies have taken my son and I want to know what you intend to do about it.'

'We don't know for certain that the kidnappers are Irish . . .' Pyke paused, trying to gather his thoughts. 'But it does seem likely that there are two gangs. Presumably the man who was killed, the one sent to collect the first bit of the ransom, didn't belong to the same gang as the marksmen who shot him.'

Jonah Hancock didn't seem to have heard him. 'I want every Irish pub and beer shop searched . . .'

'Wait a minute, boy,' Zephaniah admonished his son. 'Do we really want to be stirring up a whole hornet's nest of trouble?'

This seemed to bring Jonah to his senses. He stopped pacing for a moment and looked at his father.

'Relations between the Irish and the Welsh are tense enough at present,' Zephaniah croaked. 'Think what this could do.'

'Your father's right. We should sit tight for now – until we've had a chance to work out who's got your son,' Pyke added.

'That's easy for you to say,' Jonah spat.

'If we insist that the police ransack the home of every Irishman in town, do you imagine they'll accept the situation lying down? But they won't turn on the police. No, they'll vent their frustration on those nearest to them. And I can assure you, sir, that the natives won't turn the other cheek. We've had a fragile truce between our Welsh and Irish workers these last few years. This could set us back years.'

Jonah stared at his father, still unconvinced. 'You're talking as an ironmaster, sir. I am talking as a father.'

'Nonsense. I want the boy back just as much as you do. But tearing down the town for no good reason is only going to make matters worse.'

'*No good reason*? We found my son's coat and one of his shoes in a house on Irish Row. What more reason do you need?'

The older man dismissed this with a flick of his hand. 'Can you talk sense into my son, Detective-inspector?'

Pyke turned to Jonah. 'Just hold off for a day or two and let me do my job.' When Jonah didn't respond, Pyke turned back to the old man. 'Your son's right about one thing. The boy's life is more important than some industrial strife.'

'If I thought it would help, I'd rip apart the town with my bare hands.' Zephaniah held his hands up and tried to keep them steady. 'But even if some Irish mob has our boy, which I don't believe, stomping around Irish Row is only going to put the lad's life in even more danger.'

That seemed to cool some of Jonah's indignation. He turned to Pyke and said, 'So what do you propose to do, sir?'

'Right now, we're at the beck and call of the kidnappers. We're also at the beck and call of another gang who probably don't have your son. What we need to do is take charge of the situation. Remember: you've got something they want. Money. We need to use this fact to dictate *our* terms to *them*. No more jumping to someone else's demands.'

'And how do you suggest we dictate terms to people we don't know and can't – at the moment – identify?'

'We let it be known we want to get in touch with the kidnappers. What's happened has probably unsettled them and they'll be wary about bringing letters to the Castle. We need to find a third party, an intermediary.'

'What do you propose?'

'The local newspaper.'

'Go on,' Jonah said.

'We place a personal notice – an oblique one, of course – and wait for a response. Then we make it clear what *we* want: for example, the terms under which we are prepared to pay the ransom.'

The tautness in Jonah's face had disappeared. He turned to Zephaniah. 'What do you think, Papa?'

'Listen to the man.' Zephaniah arranged the blanket over his legs. 'He speaks a lot of sense.'

A scribbled note from Cathy had been slipped under the door, asking him to meet her outside in the garden next to the fountain.

Tired but intrigued, Pyke retraced his steps back down the stairs, then passed out of the Castle unnoticed and hurried around the building to the small, enclosed side garden. Cathy was standing under a tree, a black cloak obscuring her face. Startled, she looked up and tried to fall into his arms. As he caught her, Pyke checked to make sure that no one could see them from the Castle. Up close, her eyes were puffy and sore and her lips were stained with wine.

'I had to see you,' Cathy whispered. 'I had to know whether you found anything in Dowlais.'

'One of your son's shoes – and his coat.'

She gasped and then was silent for a short while. 'You're quite sure men from that part of the town have my son?'

Gently, Pyke tried to extricate himself from her grasp. 'At the moment, I'm not sure about anything. Look at me, Cathy.' This time he was rougher and pushed her away so he could see her face. 'I want to know why – when I first saw you – you said I shouldn't have come.'

'I don't remember what I said . . .'

'You'd been drinking. I could smell the wine on your breath. You barely recognised me.'

She gave an unpleasant laugh. 'Did it dent your pride?'

Pyke tried to make sense of her erratic behaviour, flirting with him one moment then humouring him the next. 'Something isn't right here, and I'm not just talking about the fact that your son is missing.'

'I don't know what you're talking about.' She stopped fidgeting and stared at him, her eyes glinting in the moonlight.

'Both the man who was shot and the men who shot him had to have known about the kidnapping and the second ransom letter.'

'How so?'

'One group has your son, the other group doesn't. How did they *both* know about the arrangements?'

'I don't know.'

Pyke let her go but she remained where she was. 'Why did your husband write to me, Cathy? Why *me* and not someone else?'

'You'll have to ask him. I can only speculate. But I do know word of your success at Scotland Yard has travelled.' She was shivering slightly in the cold.

'But you didn't write to me, did you?'

Cathy avoided his eyes and let out a small sigh. 'Perhaps you're unaware of the division of duties and responsibilities in a marriage. I could never have proposed such a thing without my husband's sanction.'

Pyke reached out and touched Cathy's cheek. When she still refused to look at him, he moved his finger down to her chin and gently lifted her face. 'Who do you think has your son, Cathy?' He knew what he was thinking was a bad idea, but he couldn't deny he found her attractive and he could see that she was drawn to him. It was a dangerous combination, her vulnerability and his loneliness.

A flash of anger lit up her eyes. 'Do you really think I wouldn't have told you if I had my suspicions? If I was forced to guess, I'd say it was someone my husband had wronged in business. But that would be pure conjecture.'

Pyke watched as Cathy slipped the cloak back over her head. 'It's getting late,' he said. 'We should go back to our rooms before we're missed.'

Cathy's eyes fell to the ground. 'Of course. My husband will be wondering where I am.'

Pyke started to walk back towards the Castle but then stopped and turned around.

Cathy still hadn't moved. 'If you find my son and bring him back to me safely, I'll be indebted to you for the rest of my life.'

The following morning, Pyke collected Johns in the Hancock's open-topped phaeton and backtracked first of all to Caedraw before turning on to Pennydarren Road and following it up the hill to Morlais. In the phaeton next to them was the body of the Irishman who'd been shot and killed up near the old quarry. Briefly Pyke told the former soldier what he intended to do. Once he'd listened to Pyke's proposal, Johns rubbed his chin.

'You think this is a good idea?'

Pyke shrugged. 'Someone must know who he is.'

'But it's not treating the dead man with much respect, is it?'

These words echoed around Pyke's head as he lugged the corpse into the first beer shop they came to on Irish Row and dumped it on to the floor.

The beer shop was called the Exiles of Erin and reeked of stale bodies and gin. A few sullen-faced men dressed in ragged clothes stood near the counter. They watched as Pyke turned the body over, so that the dead man was lying face up.

'I want a name.' No one looked up at him and no one uttered a word. Johns stood in the doorway, arms folded.

'Who is he?'

When no one answered again, Johns barked a few words at them in what Pyke presumed was Welsh. One of the men looked up at Pyke and then at Johns and suddenly darted for the back door. He was too quick for either of them so instead of chasing after the man, Pyke took out his pistol and let the rest of the men in the beer shop see it.

'This man was shot and killed up near the old quarry. Apparently he lodged at a place here on Irish Row, number fifty.' As Pyke waited for Johns to translate, he tried to assess the reactions of the men standing in front of him. They watched him carefully, not moving, not even looking at each other.

Eventually a man at the far end of the counter – tall with broad shoulders and sandy-coloured hair – took a step forward and peered down at the dead body. When Johns asked him something, he hesitated then rattled off a few sentences.

'His name's Deeney. Just off the boat from Dublin, came here like everyone else to look for work. Kept himself to himself, no family, no real friends, a loner.' Johns turned from Pyke to the man who'd told him this. 'Apparently the dead man didn't lodge at number fifty. No one does. Place has been unoccupied for months.'

But if this was true, why did the rent book indicate to the contrary? Pyke had inspected the rent book carefully; it hadn't given any details about the landlord. He had another look at the corpse, just a grey slab of flesh. A man just off the boat, presumably escaping the ravages of the famine in Ireland. So how had he become involved in the kidnapping? Perhaps he had simply been used as an errand boy, paid a few coins to go up to the old quarry and pick up the purse, then been shot and killed for his troubles.

Outside, as they carried the body back to the waiting phaeton, a small crowd had gathered. The mood wasn't pleasant.

Johns leapt up on to the carriage, took the reins and geed up the two horses. Pyke joined him, pistol in hand. The phaeton lurched forward through the mud and a path cleared for them. Turning around, Pyke kept the barrel of his pistol aimed at the crowd. It wasn't until they had turned back on to the main track that they felt able to relax.

'Dead men have souls too,' Johns said, after a few moments' silence.

Pyke nodded. 'It was lucky for us that man spoke Welsh.'

Johns turned briefly to look at him and then returned his stare to the muddy track. 'We weren't talking in Welsh.'

Pyke hadn't expected this. 'So you speak Irish as well?'

'I am Irish, or at least I was. I was born there, left when I was seventeen. I haven't been back since.'

Later that afternoon, Pyke presented himself at the ironworks' offices and told one of the agents – Dai Jenkins – that he wanted to talk to John Evans, the man that Bill Flint had suggested. Jenkins was a squat, ugly man with jug-handle ears and a cropped haircut. He wanted to know whether Evans had done anything wrong. Pyke shook his head but refused to let the agent know what his business was. In the end Jenkins shrugged and instructed Pyke to follow him.

They crossed the river using a pedestrian bridge and came to a row of blast furnaces, vast brick-built edifices towering seventy feet into the air. Men at the top were feeding barrows of coke and iron ore into the furnace mouths, the materials having been levered up there by an enormous water wheel. Behind them, one side of the mountain had a scorched look, hot cinders cascading down into the valley. Pyke and Jenkins entered the forge, an enclosed building where the molten ore, having been released from the furnaces, was directed into channels cut into the earth.

Jenkins went to find Evans and when he finally returned, it was clear that the puddler wasn't going to say anything of significance in his presence. Pyke told the agent he wanted to speak to Evans alone and waited until Jenkins had retreated to other side of the forge.

'I was told by Bill Flint that you were involved in the strike here at the ironworks a few years ago and that you were part of the group that was set upon by John Wylde and his men.'

Evans looked at him cautiously. Still a young man, he had strong forearms, weathered skin and wore a handkerchief wrapped tightly around his head to keep his hair out of his eyes while he worked.

'And who are you, sir?'

'Detective-inspector Pyke from Scotland Yard.'

'A long way from home. You come all this way to rake over ancient history?'

'Ancient history? It was only three years ago. As far as I understand it, Wylde and some bullies from China, bought and paid for by the Hancocks, charged into the crowd and smashed a few skulls. After that, I heard, the strike collapsed.'

Evans readjusted his handkerchief. 'What is it you want to know, Detective-inspector?'

'Last week Jonah Hancock's son, William, was seized by kidnappers. Two ransom notes, apparently penned by Scottish Cattle, were sent to the Castle.'

Evans' eyes opened wide. His fear, and surprise, seemed genuine. 'And you think that had something to do with me?' He looked around the forge. 'With us?'

'The Hancocks couldn't have endeared themselves to you that day. Perhaps this is your chance to get revenge.'

The puddler shook his head violently. 'You're not going to put this one on me, sir. By no means.' He grew more agitated. 'Do you think any of us would *dare* pull something like this? Have you lost your mind?' He realised he was almost shouting and tried to calm down.

'Perhaps not you personally, but what about Scottish Cattle?'

'The Bull would never go after a five-year-old boy to settle their score with Jonah and Zephaniah Hancock.'

'So there are scores to be settled, then?'

Evans shook his head. 'Not here, sir. Not any more.' His stare was defiant.

'All's rosy in the garden?'

'Compared to three years ago it is.' He sniffed. 'You might not believe it but in the last six months, Hancock has given us everything we've asked for. Better contracts, higher wages, the chance for men like me to learn a new trade. They've even cut back on the work offered to the Irish.'

'And that's a good thing?'

'Too right it is, sir. No one wants their wages driven down by hordes of unskilled workers.'

Pyke made a mental note of this volte-face. Three years ago, the Hancocks had made a point of shipping over workers from Ireland in order to break the strike and keep wages low.

'Doesn't this sudden display of generosity make you a little suspicious? The Hancocks are hardly known for their charity.'

'It's a boom year, so it is. Orders are flowing in. There's no way they could cut wages.'

Pyke decided to ignore the remark. 'I also heard Hancock pays the China bullies to stamp on the slightest sign of dissent before it has the chance to spread.'

Evans regarded Pyke for a moment. Then he leant a little closer and whispered, 'As long as the Hancocks've got the bullies at their beck and call, no one's gonna say a word against them. Folk are too frightened to open their mouths.'

'Are you trying to tell me *you're* too frightened to say what's really on your mind?'

Evans didn't reply.

Pyke watched as white molten ore hissed and spat its way along the channels carved into the earth. 'A personal notice has just been placed in the *Merthyr Guardian*.' Pyke turned his attention back to the puddler. 'I want you to look at it and tell all of your fellow workers to look at it, too.'

If Scottish Cattle had snatched the Hancock boy, he wanted them to see the notice.

Pyke left without another word and went to rejoin Dai Jenkins on the other side of the building. Jenkins had been talking excitedly to another man and when he turned to look at Pyke, his face was gleaming with anticipation. 'I don't expect you've heard the news, then.'

'What news?'

'The Peelers have closed off Jackson's Bridge.'

Pyke waited for him to continue.

'They're going door to door along Quarry Row and Bathesda Gardens, turning folk out of their homes.'

Pyke swore under his breath. Jenkins saw this and grinned. 'Paddies aren't goin' to like it. Trust me. There'll be trouble, sure as night follows day.'

TEN

Michael Knox was not a superstitious man. In fact, it was the superstitions and myths associated with Celtic lore that he most despised. If people chose to put their trust in fairies or leprechauns, it meant they weren't paying attention to important questions such as political representation and public accountability. He didn't believe that the Rock of Cashel had fallen out of heaven nor that Asenath Moore had grown a tail. But after he had left the horse and cart back at the stables and paused to look up at the ancient house, its windowpanes gleaming in the morning sun, his mind turned to the local men who, thirty years earlier, had torn down a military barracks a few miles away in Ballack, and their ancestors who, two hundred years back, had fought Cromwell's Ironsides while resistance in nearby Fethard and Cashel had crumbled without a shot being fired.

Knox knew it was probably just wishful thinking but as the north wind blew and he stared out across the estate in the direction of Ballack, where one of the rebels had been hanged, he thought – just for a moment – he could hear the murmurs of the men who'd fought and been killed or who'd been transported to Van Dieman's Land for their part in the uprising.

This time, Knox entered the old house through the poor door and found his mother chopping carrots in the kitchen. He hadn't warned her of his visit and he could see by her expression that she was worried. Maybe, he decided later, it was merely that she didn't want to be reminded of what had happened the previous day at the cottage. Knox kissed her on the cheek and told her that Martha and James were both well. Secretly he was relieved to see her there at work, unscathed. Knox had been worried that his father might have drunk himself into a violent rage and taken it out on her. He asked whether there was somewhere they could talk in private and followed her as she led him into one of the pantries.

'Well, what is it, love?' She tried to smile but it came across as forced.

Knox removed the daguerreotype from his pocket and handed it to her. She hesitated and then looked at the image. When she handed it back to him, her hand was trembling slightly.

'He was the one they found on the estate.' Knox waited for a response. 'The murder I was told to investigate.'

His mother nodded, as though she'd suspected this. 'Why did you bring this here, love? I mean, what would his Lordship say if he knew . . .'

Ignoring her concerns, Knox lowered his voice. 'You've been here longer than anyone. I was just wondering whether this face was familiar to you.'

'Me?'

Knox looked into her eyes. He hated putting her on the spot. 'Someone told me that when Moore came upon the body, he nearly collapsed from the shock.'

She dug her hands into the folds of her apron. 'I don't want you to drag me into this business, Michael. Please. I don't want to rock the boat, not now, not when his Lordship has been so good to us.'

'The impression I got was that Cornwallis knew the man who was murdered.' Knox looked around the pantry, the shelves buckling under the weight of all the food.

'I wish I could help you, Michael, but I don't know anything. And even if I did, I need to think about Peter. It would kill him, if we were forced out of our home.'

'This is important to me, Mam. I don't expect you to understand but I think Cornwallis asked for me because he thought he could bully me into doing nothing.'

His mother's gaze fell to the floor. Knox could tell she was torn.

'His name is Pyke. He has or had a son called Felix. I suspect he might be a policeman from London. That is, before someone stabbed him.'

This drew a tiny gasp from his mother. 'I don't know anything about a policeman, really I don't. I've never left the county, let alone the island. I don't know anyone from London.'

Knox took her trembling hand in his and squeezed it gently. 'The man has a son, Mam. A young son. Don't you think that lad has a right to know his father is dead?'

His mother squeezed his hand back and looked up into his face. 'You're a good boy, Michael. Always were. It's why I love you. But I'm begging you to leave this matter be. For all of our sakes. Especially yours. I don't know anything about this business and I don't want to. If his Lordship has told you to let the matter lie, what do you imagine he'll do if he finds out you've been sniffing around?'

Knox didn't have an answer for her. Deep down he knew she had a point.

She leant forward and kissed him on the cheek. 'All folk like us can think about right now is surviving. Right and wrong don't come into it.'

Knox had just stepped through the poor door when a voice called out his name. Startled, he turned around and saw the figure of Lord Cornwallis hobbling down the steps towards him.

'One of the stable boys told me you were here,' he said. He took a moment to catch his breath. 'Just seen your mother?'

'I thought I should return the horse and cart.' Knox made a point of not looking at the aristocrat.

'Good boy,' Cornwallis said, trying to smile.

'Least I could do, your Lordship,' Knox muttered.

'And the brigand I placed in your custody?'

Knox felt his stomach cramp. 'All taken care of, your Lordship.' He stared down at the ground. More than anything in the world, he wanted to be as far away from the man – and Dundrum House – as possible.

Cornwallis nodded and sniffed the air. He stared at the grounds, a perfect frost making everything appear pristine. 'You're turning out to be quite a man. More of your mother in you, I'd reckon, than your father.'

It was a casual remark – meant both as compliment and warning –

but Knox took it to be the latter. It underlined that the affairs of his family were well known to Cornwallis.

The old man patted him on the shoulder. 'I'm glad we've had this little chat.' He turned around and retreated halfway up the steps. 'If you ever run into difficulties, see that you contact me first. I always like to reward loyalty.'

The authorities had ceased being able to keep up with the dead. Bodies were slung without grace or ceremony into hastily dug pits. Record-keeping lagged well behind. But every day the police were briefed not about the famine and the dead but about ambushed food convoys and burglaries. Knox could see the senselessness, even the absurdity, of the situation but he kept his thoughts to himself.

After returning to the barracks, he found an empty room and took a pen, an inkwell and a piece of foolscap. His report was due. He cleared his mind and thought about what Hastings would want him to say: no progress had been made; the victim was a vagrant; and his identity would remain unknown. Knox began to write, the nib of the pen scratching against the foolscap. *My inquiry has failed to determine the identity of the victim. The victim is most likely a vagrant who had gone to the estate looking for work.* He blinked and glanced down at the paper. *He was most likely robbed at knifepoint by another vagrant who has now absconded to parts unknown. A struggle ensued and the victim died of a stab wound to his abdomen.*

Knox looked over what he'd written. It was short and to the point and might even earn him a promotion. He blotted the paper and put it to one side of the desk. Tearing off another piece of paper, he dipped the nib in the inkwell. *Dear Felix* . . . How did you tell someone that their father was dead? *I am afraid I am the bearer of terrible news. I believe your father – Pyke – was murdered by a person or persons unknown on the fourth night of January in the grounds of Dundrum House, County Tipperary.* He stared at the few words on the page. What else was there to say? That the body had been buried along with fifteen or twenty others in a famine pit outside the town? He reached into his pocket, retrieved the letters Felix had written to Pyke, and copied out the return address given on one of the envelopes. Then he added a few more words of condolence to the letter and signed it.

Knox left his report with one of the sub-inspector's clerks, then made his way up Main Street to the post office from where the mail coach would shortly be leaving for Dublin. At the counter, he paid the postage and dropped the letter into the mail sack.

Fatigue hit him only on the walk home. He skirted around the Rock and by the time he had reached the top of the lane where he lived, across from the ruined abbey, he was exhausted. From there, it would take him another twenty minutes to reach the cottage. This time, he didn't bother to call in on his neighbour, as was his custom. He couldn't face reading the old man his newspaper.

Martha was upstairs in their bedroom singing to the child. He kissed them both and sat on the chair at the end of the bed.

'Are you unwell?' Martha touched his forehead, concern etched on her face. 'Do you want to lie down?'

'No, I'm just a little tired.'

'Are you sure? You look terrible.'

'Thank you.' He smiled weakly.

'Did anything happen today?'

'No, Martha, I'm just tired.'

James started to squawk in the crib.

They ate dinner in silence. Afterwards, Knox scrubbed out the pot in the yard. He patted the dog on the head and stared up at the dark cloudless sky. It was bitterly cold but he hardly noticed. When he let himself back into the house, he saw that Martha had already gone to bed. The dog scratched on the door to be allowed inside but Knox ignored it. Upstairs, he undressed in the dark and climbed into bed.

Martha had turned her back to him but he knew she wasn't asleep. They lay in silence. What was there to say?

'Oh, Michael.' Martha turned to face him. Her body felt soft and warm. He wanted to cry. 'You seem so sad and lost.'

He could just about see the outline of her face. 'I'm sorry.'

'Sorry for what?'

'I'm just sorry.' He wanted to fall asleep and never wake up.

'What is it, Michael? What happened today?'

'I need to sleep.'

Next to him, he heard Martha sigh. 'It's hard sometimes, I know, to keep going.' She reached out in the dark and gently touched him on the cheek. 'But we have to. We all have to.'

ELEVEN

Quarry Row was a short walk from the centre of the town but going there was like stepping into a different world. The street ran adjacent to the River Taff and was like a bog, wheel-tracks cut deep into the mud, making it all but impassable to vehicles. Cinder heaps and mounds of human excrement sat in piles outside most houses and wolfish dogs scavenged for scraps. The terraces had been thrown up by unscrupulous speculators using the cheapest materials and many were already sinking into the mud. It was the kind of street that ought to have been razed to the ground, yet each week the numbers grew, the poor and destitute arriving from famine-hit Ireland in search of a job and a new life. These same people were now being thrown on to the street by constables, while soldiers waited in the shadows.

Pyke found Superintendent Jones co-ordinating the search at the far end of the street. The constables were moving from house to house in pairs. On the street, small knots of young men shouted at them as they passed. A rock was thrown and a window shattered.

'Who gave the orders for this to happen?'

Jones turned to face him. 'Ah, Pyke. I sent word to the Castle but you had already left.'

'Was it Jonah Hancock?'

'Hancock?' He screwed up his face. Farther up the street, they heard another pane of glass break.

Pyke took Jones by his coat lapel and pulled him closer. 'Is this your response to what we found on Irish Row in Dowlais? Why not go door to door there? Who told you the Hancock boy might be here?'

Jones tried to push himself away but Pyke's grip was firm. The superintendent was clearly angry at being manhandled in public. 'I do what I'm told, sir. If you don't like it, go and see Smyth.'

'Smyth gave the orders?' Pyke let go of Jones' coat. They both looked up, jarred by the sound of a chest being dropped from an upper-floor window. Anyone could see that they were minutes away from losing control of the situation. One of the constables blew his whistle.

'I need to answer that call.'

Jones tried to push past Pyke but he held his ground. 'The Hancocks are prepared to pay the ransom. We should be helping them to bring their son home, not putting his life in greater danger.'

'I'm just following orders.'

Pyke looked at the angry faces of the men yelling abuse at the policemen. Suddenly he'd had enough of this miserable town and its dirt-poor population.

'If the Hancock boy turns up dead as a result of this pathetic circus, I'll hold you – and Smyth – personally responsible.'

Pyke found Sir Clancy Smyth in the living room at the courthouse. The magistrate was directing one of his servants to shovel more coal on to the fire.

'Ah, Detective-inspector, glad you dropped by,' he said, standing up. He offered his hand but Pyke pushed it away.

'I want to know why you ordered Jones and his men to search all the houses on Quarry Row and Bathesda Gardens.'

Smyth reddened and gestured at the servant to leave them. 'I would remind you who you're addressing, sir.'

Pyke took a deep breath and tried to work out why Smyth might've taken it upon himself to order the police to the Irish stronghold of lower Merthyr. Sir Richard Mayne had described him as a good sort, a view supported by Johns, but this decision seemed careless to the point of recklessness.

'If you don't order your men to pull back, there will be a full-scale riot. Is that what you want?'

Smyth's face whitened. 'That bad, eh?'

'You need to rescind that order, send word to Jones immediately. Then you can tell me why you took the decision.'

Clearly Smyth didn't like his authority being questioned but the thought of presiding over a riot was even less appealing. He called in a clerk and whispered a few words in his ear. When the man had left, he turned back to Pyke. 'There. Are you satisfied now?'

'But why did you send your men to lower Merthyr? Why not Irish Row in Dowlais?' Pyke thought about the body they had identified there, a man called Deeney.

'I don't need to share my information, or my reasons, with you.' Smyth wandered over to the window.

'As far as I understand, the family has agreed to pay the ransom. Why put the boy's life at risk by trying to capture the gang before any money has changed hands?'

Smyth turned around, a frown etched on his face. 'And you think that's right? To cave in to criminals?'

'If it were my son, I'd pay to get him back. Then I'd go after the men responsible and make them wish they hadn't been born.'

Smyth didn't seem to have heard him. 'Places like Quarry Row and China are blots on the landscape. Perhaps if they were destroyed, a new Merthyr could rise up from the ashes.'

Pyke shook his head, incredulous. 'And in the meantime, a young boy's life is hanging in the balance?'

'I had my reasons, Detective-inspector. For the moment that's all I'm prepared to say.'

'And if the boy turns up dead?'

'I'm happy to live with the consequences of my actions, sir. Now if you'll excuse me.' He gestured at the door.

Pyke remained where he was. 'We should be on the same side, you and I, but standing here, all I can think about is that I find more common ground with the Hancocks.'

Ignoring him, Smyth went to open the door, but Pyke wasn't quite finished. 'Did you know that the Hancocks paid a bully from China to break the strike a few years ago and the police stood by and did nothing? And now that same man seems to be able to operate in China with impunity.'

'If I had the manpower, Detective-inspector, China wouldn't even exist and men like John Wylde wouldn't have a stone to hide under.' Smyth paused then added, 'One moment you seem to be defending the Hancocks, the next accusing them. Perhaps, sir, it is you who needs to work out what your intentions are.'

'Tell me more about John Wylde.'

John Johns rubbed his chin. They were in the taproom of the Bunch of Grapes on Castle Street. 'What do you want to know?'

'I was told he owns all of the brothels in China.'

'He's carved up the territory with Benjamin Griffiths. Wylde has seized control of prostitution, Griffiths the gambling. Wylde likes to regard himself as the emperor, though.'

'Emperor?'

'Of China.' Johns looked around the crowded taproom. 'It's a self-appointed title.'

Pyke took a sip of his ale. It tasted like mud. 'I've been wondering why people call the place China.'

'No one really knows. The Celestial Empire. It's somewhere . . . different, alien. Where the normal rules don't apply.'

'There's this woman who serves behind the counter at the Three Horse Shoes. Perhaps you've seen her. She used to *belong* to Wylde. Then he found out she was fucking Ben Griffiths and he poured hot oil over her face.'

Johns shrugged. 'Irrespective of their business arrangement, I do know there's no love lost between Wylde and Griffiths.' He sat forward, arms resting on the table. 'Question is, why are you so interested in him?'

'You were the one who put me on to him,' Pyke said. 'You told me the Hancocks used him and his men to break the last strike.'

'I thought you were here to find the Hancock boy.'

'I am – and I keep coming back to the two ransom demands, both apparently from Scottish Cattle.'

'No one I've talked to believes the Bull would do something like that.'

'I know. That's what I've heard too. But think about it. If they haven't got the boy, then someone's trying to blame them. If they *do* have the boy, the Hancocks must have done something to provoke them. Either way, this is about more than a five-year-old child. I've tried to get people – workers – to talk to me but they're scared.'

'Because of the Hancocks' influence with Wylde and his men?'

Pyke nodded. 'If we could give Wylde something else to worry about, I might have more success persuading folk to talk to me.'

'I'd say they're more afraid of the Hancocks than they are of a bully like Wylde.'

'Maybe so, but there's something rotten in this whole business, and the sooner things are out in the open the better.'

Johns didn't disagree. 'By the way, I went back to Dowlais yesterday afternoon, this time to the barracks there. I'm afraid I didn't come across the man I saw up on the mountain that day.'

'You're sure he wasn't there? Perhaps you just didn't see him.'

'I watched their drill. The full regiment was present, no absentees. Believe me, I would've recognised him.'

'Well, thanks for trying.'

Johns acknowledged this with a small nod. 'It seems to me that what you're actually looking for is a way of rattling Wylde's cage.'

'That's right. I was trying to think of a way of setting him and Griffiths against one another.'

Now Johns was smiling. 'May the best man win?'

'Exactly.'

They waited for the pot-boy to hurry past them.

'Actually, I've heard a rumour that Wylde keeps some of his money hidden under floorboards in the back room of a beer shop in China.'

Pyke saw the gleam in Johns' eyes. 'Who in their right mind would try and take it?'

'Exactly,' Johns said, running the tip of his finger around the rim of his empty beer glass.

'What's this place called?'

'The Boot. You could gut a pig on the floor without causing any noticeable change in the surroundings.'

'Sounds delightful. What do you say we go there and take a look?'

John Wylde scratched a boil in the centre of his forehead but didn't for a moment take his small, quick eyes off the pistol Pyke was aiming at him. He seemed comfortable despite the situation, the fact that Pyke and Johns, both with large black handkerchiefs pulled up over their faces to conceal their identities, had stormed into the pub brandishing pistols. He was a smaller man than Pyke had been expecting and was rather nondescript in person. Still, it was clear that every man in the taproom deferred to him and when Pyke jabbed the end of his pistol into Wylde's neck, it was as if the entire room gave a collective gasp of astonishment. No one treated the emperor in this fashion, certainly not on his own territory. For his part, Wylde took the invasion in his stride, but Pyke could see that the small man was just biding his time, waiting for a momentary lapse in Pyke's concentration.

While Pyke kept Wylde occupied, he could hear Johns tearing up floorboards at the back of the building. Pyke's presence in Merthyr was not a secret and perhaps a man as well connected as Wylde would have heard about him, but Pyke doubted whether he would have thought a policeman capable of carrying out this kind of robbery in broad daylight. For the plan to work, Wylde had to think that he and Johns were emissaries of his rival, Ben Griffiths.

Pyke took his eye off the so-called emperor only for a few seconds but it was all the man needed. Wylde lunged at him brandishing a cudgel that had suddenly appeared in his hand. He missed with his first swing, which gave Pyke just enough time to raise the barrel of his pistol and pull the trigger, the ball-shot almost taking off Wylde's hand at the wrist, and spraying the counter behind him with tiny fragments of blood and bone. The bully's screams filled the room but no one else moved. He had fallen to one knee and was clutching his shattered hand.

Johns appeared at the doorway and held up a leather satchel. Pyke let him go first and then followed him through the front door. They walked quickly to the end of the alley then ran. A minute or two later, they were out of China and crossing Jackson's Bridge.

'I took what I could fit into the satchel,' Johns said, panting, once they had crossed the bridge.

'There was more?'

'We got most of it,' he said. 'Enough to send Wylde into a frenzy.'

'He'll have to recover from his pistol wound first.'

Lines appeared across Johns' forehead. 'What happened?'

'He took a swing at me with a cudgel. I shot his hand.' Pyke shrugged. 'It will work in our favour.'

'He'll tear China apart looking for his money.'

'All we have to do is make sure he finds what he's looking for.' Pyke gestured at the leather satchel.

Johns looked down at the river flowing beneath them. 'You realise we've opened Pandora's box?'

Pyke joined him at the iron rail. 'It couldn't be done any other way, not without the sanction of the magistrate and the police.'

'We'll have blood on our hands before this thing is finished.' Johns turned to Pyke. 'Are you ready for that?'

'To be honest, I can't remember a time when there wasn't blood on my hands.'

Jonah Hancock was apoplectic when he heard about the police action in Bathesda Gardens and Quarry Row and spent a few minutes pacing around the drawing room in ever decreasing circles, venting his spleen. Had the police found his son? Who had authorised the action and why had no one consulted him? Didn't the police understand that the raid could put the boy's life in danger? Rumours were sure to circulate regarding the object of the search. Soon they would be inundated by possible sightings and people trying to claim that they had taken the boy.

'Sit down, it's exhausting just looking at you,' Zephaniah barked from his armchair. 'This all came from Smyth, didn't it?' The question was directed at Pyke, not his son.

Pyke nodded. 'He would have learned of our discoveries at the house on Irish Row from Jones.'

'This was a shot across our bows,' Zephaniah said quietly. 'It had nothing to do with finding the boy.'

Pyke explained that he'd persuaded Smyth to order his men back before the situation had spiralled out of control. 'But it did make me wonder about the enmity that exists between him and your family.'

Jonah exchanged a wary look with his father. Eventually it was Zephaniah who said, 'Perhaps it's a simple case of envy – and money. At one time, I suppose, his would have been the foremost family in the town.'

'I got the impression he thinks that the ironmasters aren't contributing enough to the general well-being of the place.'

'We pay the rate. It's up to the Board to determine how it's spent.'

Pyke thought about the lack of civic amenities but decided not to say anything more.

'I take it they didn't find anything,' Jonah said. 'Anything to indicate my son's presence on Quarry Row . . .'

'Not as far as I know.'

Jonah started to pace again. 'So what do we do now?'

'We wait.'

'For someone to respond to the notice in the newspaper?'

'For the kidnappers to get back in contact.'

'Meanwhile my son has to spend another lonely night in some godforsaken place . . .'

'We'll hear something soon.'

'And if we don't?'

Pyke didn't answer.

Pyke knew that sleep was beyond him and decided to take some night air. He found his way to the walled garden and sat down on the bench. The night was clear and cold and the sky was filled with stars. Within a minute or so, he heard footsteps crunching on the gravel path. Without turning, he knew who it was. The first thing he smelled was the gin on her breath. Wordlessly she sat down next to him. They remained silent for a moment or two.

'Sometimes I look at myself and think I'm not a good person.' Cathy edged a little closer to him.

'I'm not sure I've ever judged people on the basis of their moral fibre.' Pyke half-turned and saw her profile silhouetted in the moonlight.

'I married him when I was eighteen. I agreed to the marriage because he was wealthy. Isn't that a terrible thing?'

'Why don't you leave him?'

'I've thought about it. I might have come close to actually doing it. But I wouldn't go without my son, and Jonah would never let me leave with him.'

'And now this has happened.'

An owl hooted in the distance. 'In one sense, I suppose, it has brought us closer.'

'And in another?'

Cathy laughed softly. 'In my good moments I know my husband wouldn't do anything to jeopardise our son's life.'

Pyke said nothing, waited for her to continue.

'In others, I wonder whether my father-in-law may be trying to use the situation to his advantage.'

'In what sense?'

'I don't know.' She turned to Pyke and tried to smile. 'My husband has a complicated relationship with his father. He's the elder but Zephaniah always makes it clear he favours his younger brother, Richard. As a result Jonah is always trying to prove himself. I suspect Zephaniah regards Jonah, and by extension our son, as weak. I know for a fact he's always frowned on the way William cleaves to me.'

As Pyke listened, he tried to work out how the situation might benefit Zephaniah.

'You do believe he's out there, don't you?' Cathy added, turning to him. 'That my son is still alive.'

Pyke could feel the warmth of her breath on his neck. Sensing what was happening, he tried to move away. 'We can't let ourselves believe otherwise. Your son is valuable to the kidnappers only as long as he's safe and well.'

'I do know that.' She squeezed his hand and edged closer to him again. 'But it's nice to be reminded.' Their shoulders were practically touching.

'I've often thought how it would be if you ever came here to visit: what it would be like between us.' She threaded her arm through his.

Pyke exhaled quietly. 'I knew your father a long time ago.'

'So?'

'Whatever you think you might feel for me, it's just nostalgia – and loneliness.'

Turning fully towards him, she slipped her arm around his neck, brushing her fingers through his hair. 'Don't say anything,' she whispered, guiding him into an embrace.

It was a scalding, breathy kiss and its effect was like a kick to the guts. She pulled away and looked at him, her eyes shining. 'Were you speaking for yourself just now?'

'I meant I'm old enough to be your father.' Pyke didn't say it was just plain lust on his part, which would have been closer to the truth.

'So's my husband.' Her lips were wet. She reached out and touched him on the cheek.

Suddenly he heard a twig snap and whatever had existed between them in the moment was broken. 'Someone's out there.'

'*Where?*'

'Over in those trees.' Pyke saw something move in the shadows. He jumped up but whoever it was had disappeared by the time he reached the first line of trees. Once he had satisfied himself that this person wasn't simply hiding near by, Pyke went to rejoin Cathy on the bench.

'Are you quite sure it wasn't just an animal? A fox, perhaps?' Cathy was shivering from the cold.

'No, it was a man.'

'And do you think he saw us?'

'I don't know.' Pyke turned to look at her.

Cathy seemed to have come to her senses and stood up, placing her cloak back over her head. 'I should go.'

Pyke nodded but said nothing.

'Come with me,' Cathy said. 'If we go back inside through the main entrance, even at different times, my husband will know.' She led Pyke around to the very back of the building, the slope rising up behind them to their right, and came to a halt next to a door, concealed by a hedge, which seemed to lead not into the Castle but the side of the mountain.

Cathy opened the door and said, 'Jonah doesn't know I know about this. It's how the prostitutes he fucks are smuggled into the Castle. When the place was constructed, his father had it included in the plans.'

Pyke followed her into the darkness, but once they were inside, she turned to him and said, 'There was something I meant to ask you.'

'Yes?'

'It was a coat you found at the house on Irish Row, wasn't it?'

'That's right. A winter coat.'

She nodded, as though she'd been expecting this answer. 'I remember it was a mild day, unseasonably so.'

'The day William was kidnapped?'

'Yes.' Cathy bit her lip. 'I tried to make him wear a coat but he wouldn't.'

'You're saying he wasn't wearing that winter coat when the kidnappers seized him?'

'I'm almost certain of it.'

'But it was his coat? The one that turned up on Irish Row?'

'Yes, I think so.'

'So how did it get there?'

They stared at one another for a moment or two. Cathy didn't have an answer for him.

TWELVE

WEDNESDAY, 27 JANUARY 1847

Cashel, Co. Tipperary

After a week, Knox managed to put the letter out of his mind. He hadn't forgotten about it entirely but there were too many things to do; too many things to worry about. So when, more than two weeks after he'd sent it, he still hadn't received a response from the son, he started to relax. Perhaps the letter had never arrived; perhaps Felix had moved address; or perhaps Knox had misunderstood the exact nature of his relationship to the deceased. Initially, when he'd heard nothing, Knox had considered writing another letter, this time to Scotland Yard, but he decided on reflection that this would have been pushing the matter too far. He had done his duty and his conscience was clear. In actuality he was glad that he'd received no letter from the son. It meant he didn't have to worry about what Hastings would say – if and when he found out what Knox had done. Knox had been lucky not once but twice. In addition to the son's silence, he had not been reprimanded for letting McMullan go free. Cornwallis must have forgotten to look at the list of defendants at the quarter sessions.

As January wore on, the weather remained cold and the ground frozen solid. This made digging new graves and burial pits next to impossible and meant a temporary cessation of most of the public works which, in turn, put new strain on the workhouses and the shambolic relief effort. Fifteen people died in the parish in the third week of the month – from disease, starvation or just from the cold – and by the end of the month the situation had deteriorated further. Each day, the newspapers would report on the arrival of a new shipment of corn from America, but what little of this made it to the depot in Cashel was too expensive for most people to buy. It was the same story right across the island. Knox had read in the *Tip Free Press* that folk were dying in their tens of thousands and that no one in Dublin or London was doing a damn thing about it. Anger had given way to despair – and while the government ignored their suffering, the landowners squabbled among themselves about who would pay for the non-existent relief effort. The only ones who prospered were traders and undertakers.

Knox had received a letter from his mother informing him that all was well at home and that Peter was thriving in the new cottage. Though she hadn't said so, the message seemed clear enough: carry on doing nothing. He'd wanted to visit them but his shifts at work hadn't permitted this, and in any case he had his own family to worry about. Despite the food shortages, the constabulary were well provided for and James continued to grow. He seemed healthy and Knox felt as content as the circumstances permitted.

During the days, Knox and the other constables found themselves deployed away from the town, patrolling the lanes and fields of nearby estates in order to crack down on poaching and sheep-stealing. Aristocratic families like the Pennefathers and the Moores had complained to the authorities about the theft of game and livestock from their land, unable to acknowledge the link between their greed and short-sightedness and the worsening public order. If the great and the good refused to provide, the land would have to: snails and frogs were fried, hedgehogs baked, crows feathered and roasted, and foxes stripped to the bone and boiled for soup.

One evening, after a particularly long and gruelling day, Knox had come across a poem in the new edition of the *Nation*, sandwiched in between stories about the famine and a dispute between Daniel O'Connell, long seen as leader of Ireland's quest for independence, and Young Ireland, a group who believed – unlike O'Connell – that blood would have to be spilled before Britain relinquished its grasp over the island. The poem mocked the 'proud soldiers' who guarded their 'masters' granaries', and as Knox sat with Martha and the dog in front of the kitchen fire, it struck him that he was one of the poet's targets.

Knox had spent much of his adolescence and the early part of his manhood trying to be good. It had been one of his mother's earliest admonishments and certainly the one he had tried hardest to respect.

And it was true: Knox did try to be good. But what did that really mean? How good was he and did goodness matter when so many folk were dying? Was it *good* to uphold public order? Was it *good* to humble yourself before men like Asenath Moore? Surely to be good, in such a situation, was to resist such men. And yet each morning, in front of the sub-inspector, he nodded compliantly as he and the other constables were berated for failing to arrest more poachers and thieves.

The following morning, Knox prepared breakfast as usual and sat with Martha while she breastfed James. It was a clear, bitterly cold day and another flurry of snow had fallen during the night. Standing by the upstairs window, he looked out at the hedgerows shagged with ice. There would be more bodies today. He turned and watched Martha and James. 'Sometimes I dread going to the barracks. I dread what might have happened in the night.'

Martha looked up from her breastfeeding. 'I forgot to tell you. I came across a body yesterday at the end of the lane. Birds had pecked out the eyes. When I came back later, it was gone.'

'Yellow Bill probably heard about it and carted it off to the burial pit.'

'It wasn't anyone I knew.'

Knox nodded. He knew it was only a matter of time before one of them came upon the corpse of a friend or neighbour. He put on his coat and took his time buttoning it up. 'I was being foolish, wasn't I? Getting myself worked up over that man they found on Moore's estate.'

'You were just doing what you thought to be right.'

Knox picked up his hat. For some reason, he hadn't told Martha that he'd sent a letter to the dead man's son. It wasn't an outright lie but he was uncomfortable about having withheld this information. Perhaps, Knox decided, it wouldn't matter now.

Martha carried James to where he was standing and kissed him softly on the cheek. 'I do love you, Michael. And it won't always be this bad.'

Knox carried these words with him as he walked into the town. The sky was clear and bright and it was easy to believe they were true.

'Constable Knox,' one of the clerks said to him, as soon as he'd set foot inside the barracks. 'The sub-inspector wants to see you in his office immediately.'

Knox felt the muscles in his stomach tighten. He murmured his consent and shuffled up the stairs.

Hastings' office was at the top of the stairs and enjoyed an uninterrupted view of the Rock. Knox knocked on the door, waiting for the sub-inspector to answer. Hastings opened the door himself and greeted Knox with a nod of his head. 'Come in and sit down, Constable.' He stood to one side and let Knox enter the room. There was someone Knox didn't recognise sitting behind Hastings' desk. A chair had been set out for him but Hastings opted to stand. He gestured to the other man. 'This is the County Inspector.' *No name.* Knox inhaled sharply. The County Inspector was based in Clonmel.

The man in question had a thin, cadaverous face, a beaked nose and a widow's peak that swooped dramatically down his forehead. His eyes were fixed on Knox. 'Constable Knox.' He gestured for Knox to sit down.

'I have just received this letter from one of the commissioners of the Metropolitan Police.' He held it up for Knox to see. 'In it, he describes how one of my constables, namely you, has identified the body of a man who was murdered in the grounds of Dundrum Hall three weeks ago as one Detective-inspector Pyke – from the aforementioned Metropolitan Police.' The County Inspector let the letter fall to the desk.

'I wrote to the deceased's son in Somerset, to inform him that his father had likely died in the circumstances you just mentioned.'

The County Inspector stared at him impassively. 'And yet I also have in front of me the report you penned and submitted to the sub-inspector here, in which you made it clear that you could *not* determine the deceased's identity.' His mouth hardened.

Knox saw his mistake. If he'd come clean about his discovery, they would not have been able to touch him. After all, he could claim to have done what he had been told to do. But he had lied – and now he had been caught in that lie.

'I couldn't be certain that this man was who I thought he was. The letter I sent to the son was written in a personal capacity. I felt I couldn't let him live his life not knowing what had happened to his father.'

'But you just said you couldn't be wholly certain that the deceased was, in fact, the lad's father.'

'I had no idea the man was a policeman from London.' Knox had lied again but they wouldn't catch him in that lie if they didn't get to see the letters Felix had written. He would tell them he'd thrown them away.

'Surely you must have considered making some mention of this discovery in your official report.'

'I did, sir.'

'And yet there is no mention of it in the report. Can you explain why this might be?'

Knox lowered his head. He was sweating profusely; his only hope was to throw himself at their mercy. 'I took from Lord Cornwallis that it would probably be best if nothing came of my investigation.'

The County Inspector exchanged a fierce look with Hastings. 'This is a most serious allegation, sir. Are you suggesting that his Lordship tried to exercise undue influence over a police matter?'

Knox sat bolt upright, suddenly aware of what he'd said. 'No, not for a minute, sir. His Lordship's actions were absolutely proper throughout . . .'

'He didn't tell you how to conduct your investigation?'

'No, sir.'

The County Inspector nodded. 'But you assumed he would not have wanted anything arising from your inquiries to damage his estate's reputation.'

'I tried to approach the matter with the utmost caution. I understand that murder is a very sensitive subject.'

'And yet – in spite of whatever assurances you may have given his Lordship – you went ahead and wrote to the son of the deceased.'

Knox tried in vain to swallow. 'It seemed like the right thing to do.'

'And did lying to the sub-inspector in your report seem like the right thing to do?'

'As I tried to explain, sir, I wrote to the son as a father.' He hesitated, trying to clear his mind. 'On the subject of the investigation,

I have to admit I was a little surprised that a man of my lowly rank would be given such responsibility.'

The County Inspector's eyes narrowed. Knox knew he'd made a good point. It would be hard for them to discipline him for his failings as a detective because to do so would be to admit their own culpability – dispatching a constable with no experience to investigate a murder.

As if to underline this point, Knox added, 'I wasn't told whether the report should be what I absolutely knew to be true or what I thought *might* be true. In the end, I used the former standard.'

Below in the yard, a horse and cart rattled to a halt. The County Inspector waited for silence. 'I can see that mistakes were made on all sides.'

Knox ignored the sweat spilling down his face.

'I am concerned, however, about the lingering taint on the good character of Lord Cornwallis.'

'As I tried to explain, sir, his Lordship conducted himself with absolute propriety at every juncture . . .'

'I am pleased to hear this. I would like to be able to say that his Lordship feels the same way but I'm afraid to report that he has made a rather serious accusation about your conduct as a policeman.'

Knox felt his blood run cold. 'I'm sorry . . .'

The County Inspector consulted another document. 'Were you summoned to Dundrum Hall on Sunday the tenth of January this year?'

'It's possible. I would need to think about it . . .'

'Perhaps I can jog your memory, Constable. Were you, or were you not, asked by his Lordship to transport a man by the name of McMullan, who'd been caught stealing blood from the estate's livestock, to one of the cells at the barracks to stand trial for theft?'

The room started to spin. Knox tried to sit up straighter but it didn't seem to make a difference.

'Please answer the question, Constable.'

'Yes, sir . . . I was.'

The County Inspector nodded. 'And yet this man never appeared at the barracks.'

'No, sir,' Knox muttered, trying to plan a new defence for himself.

'Would you care to tell us why not?'

'The man in question broke free of his restraints and escaped. I searched but wasn't able to find him.'

'I see.' The County Inspector glanced across at Hastings. 'Were you made aware of this fact?'

Hastings shook his head.

The County Inspector turned back to Knox. 'So you didn't feel the matter was important enough to report it to the sub-inspector?'

'On the contrary, I realised what a big mistake I'd made. I was too ashamed to admit I'd failed.' Knox bowed his head and exhaled. He could feel the thump of his heartbeat.

'A pattern of deception is beginning to emerge.' The County Inspector looked at the document in his hand. 'Is there anything else you wish to add?'

'Nothing, sir – aside from my humblest apologies.' Knox waited, not daring to breathe. Perhaps all they wanted him to do was grovel.

'You don't, for example, wish to make it known that you were acquainted with the thief?'

'I knew who he was but that's not surprising, given the size of the community we both grew up in.'

Hastings coughed. 'Constable Knox was given special dispensation to serve in his county of birth, sir.'

'Ah, I see. But I'm assuming you didn't treat this man, this suspected thief, any differently to others you have taken into custody.'

'No differently, sir.'

The County Inspector smiled for the first time. He picked up the piece of paper he had been consulting. 'I have here a letter, signed by your own father, stating that you took the thief, Davy McMullan, back to your family's dwelling that same day, and presented him to them as a friend in need.'

It was as if the air had been sucked out of the room. Knox had to stop himself from retching. The worst of it was that his own flesh and blood had betrayed him; he didn't know where to look.

'Is it true, Constable? Did you introduce McMullan to your father as a friend rather than your captive?'

Knox didn't have the capacity to lie any more. He nodded listlessly.

'Speak up, Constable.'

'Yes, it's true.'

'And is it also true that you allowed McMullan to go free because you felt sorry for him?'

Knox could feel the tears in his eyes. 'Yes.'

The County Inspector shoved another piece of paper across the desk. 'That's good, Constable. You will sign this document, if you don't mind.' He held out a pen and indicated that Knox should approach the desk.

Knox tried to stand up but his legs buckled. 'What is it?'

'It's a legal document. By signing it, you will be recognising that the decision I have taken regarding your situation has been informed solely by your behaviour towards Davy McMullan – and is in no way related to your regrettable errors in the matter of the murder investigation.'

Dazed, Knox went over to the desk, picked up the pen and signed his name. 'What decision have you taken, sir?'

The County Inspector took the document and inspected it. Eventually, when he was satisfied that everything was in order, he said, 'Your employment at the constabulary has been terminated with immediate effect.'

Knox just managed to make it back to his chair before his legs gave way.

'Once you leave this room, you will change out of your uniform and you'll present it to the sub-inspector along with any other items belonging to the constabulary.'

'How will I pay my rent? How will *I live*?' His thoughts turned to the weekly ration of corn.

'That is no longer our concern.' The County Inspector gestured to the door. 'Now, if you'll excuse us . . .'

'I have a wife and a young child. This is all I have, sir. All that's standing between us and . . .' Knox couldn't bring himself to finish the sentence.

'Then, sir, you should have considered your responsibilities more carefully before you appointed yourself judge and jury in the matter of Davy McMullan.'

Knox thought about throwing himself on to the floor and begging for his position. '*Please*, sir . . .'

The County Inspector stared at him dry-eyed and held up his hand. 'That will be all.'

He didn't know how far he had walked, or for how long, but by the time he arrived home, it was dark. He was greeted at the gate by the dog. Martha must have heard the barks because the door opened and her face appeared. She saw at once that something was wrong. Ushering him into the cottage, she sat him down next to the fire and then pressed her warm hands against his icy cheeks.

'What's the matter, my darling? You look terrible and you're so cold.' She stared at him, her expression guileless and loving.

It made him despise himself even more; the stupidity and selfishness of his need to be good. 'I'm fine.' He smiled weakly. 'I've just had a long day.'

Martha took a step back and studied him. 'You don't look fine, Michael. You look sick.'

'Really, I'm fine.' He had kept his uniform for the day as he'd had nothing to change into. 'I just need to sit for a while and get warm.'

'When I opened the front door and saw you by the gate, I thought you were about to cry.'

Knox could feel his grip on the situation begin to loosen. He knew he would have to tell Martha what had happened in time – but not before he'd come up with a plan. He had two pounds in savings – hidden under the ground in the yard. This would pay for the rent and keep them in food until some time in March. If he could find alternative employment, news of his dismissal wouldn't be so devastating.

'It was just one of those days.' He corrected himself. '*Another* of those days.'

'Are you sure that's all it is?' She looked at him dubiously. 'You don't seem your usual self.'

More than anything Knox wanted to tell her the truth, tell her that he'd been dismissed, because this was what they had always done – tell one another the truth – but he felt too frightened and too ashamed. 'Really, Martha, I'm just tired down to my bones.'

She didn't appear convinced but decided not to push it any further. 'Well, I'll just put on the water for supper.'

Nodding silently, Knox thought about their dwindling supply of corn. 'Just give me half of what I'd usually have. They fed us today.'

She came over to where he was sitting and touched his forehead. 'You don't have a fever.'

'I feel fine, Martha, really I do. I'll just go upstairs and look in on James.'

'He was asking for you earlier.'

As soon as he reached the top of the stairs, Knox had to steady himself by holding on to the banister. His lip started to quiver. Looking up, he saw James, fast asleep in the cot, and he started to weep.

Knox woke early, before it was light, and slipped out of bed without waking Martha. He dressed quickly in civilian clothes and a pair of old boots and went downstairs. There, he lit a candle and let himself out into the garden, where he was greeted by Tom, who had forgotten the indignity of being locked out in the cold and jumped up at him, wagging his tail. It was drizzling and most of the snow had melted, which meant the ground was no longer frozen. Watched by the dog, Knox found a shovel in the coal shed, went to the spot under one of the birch trees, and sliced the blade into the earth. It took him less than a minute to dig up the pouch he'd buried there. Brushing it, he emptied the coins into his hand and counted out two pounds and twenty shillings. He put the two pounds back in the pouch and then buried it again, patting the mud into place with the back of the shovel. With the twenty shillings in his pocket, Knox let himself back into the cottage, followed by Tom. There, he swept out the grate, prepared the fire and lit it with a match.

While he waited for the fire to catch, he retrieved the daguerreotypes and the letters he'd hidden at the back of the dresser. Had all this been worth losing his position for? Knox stared into the grate, trying to work out how long two pounds, twenty shillings would last. It would have to pay for coal, food and of course the rent. Would it be possible to see out the rest of the winter on such a sum? Perhaps only February, if he was frugal, Knox decided. A more immediate concern was what he would tell Martha. Part of him couldn't bring himself to deliver the bad news. This wasn't *just* because she would be angry with him but because he didn't want to lose her opinion of him, to see himself reduced in her eyes to the status of pauper. After her anger had abated, she would pity him, and most of all he couldn't bear to see this because he deserved to be punished for what he had done. He had put his family at risk, and for what? So that a boy he'd never met would know that his father had perished.

Knox filled a pot with water and placed it over the flames. When it had boiled he poured a cup of Indian corn into the water and gave it a stir. His mind drifted back to a time – two summers earlier – when Martha had been expecting and he had fattened her up on a diet of buttermilk and potatoes, unaware that the first blight lay just around the corner. The corn kept them from starvation but it was a poor substitute for milk and potatoes, and Knox fantasised about the creaminess of this mix on his tongue. One morning in October, he'd stepped out into the garden. The stink had hit him first, even before he'd realised that the crop had turned black. About a month later James had been born.

After breakfast, Knox would go into Cashel, pay the rent and use whatever was left to buy more corn. Perhaps he would also make a few discreet enquiries about the possibility of finding work. As he watched the corn bubbling, he started to feel guilty again, the fact that he was sneaking around the cottage, not wanting his wife to ask where his uniform was and why he wasn't wearing it.

Knox didn't imagine that he would be affected by the public shame of losing his post but as soon as he entered the town and people noticed him out of uniform he immediately felt self-conscious, as if everyone knew that he had been dismissed. At the bottom of Main Street, he hurried past the entrance to the police barracks and continued up the busy thoroughfare, past the Palace and Town Hall, as far as Friars Street, where the office of the agent for the Brittas family – Mr Warburton – was located.

Knox usually paid his rent on a Friday but he didn't imagine the agent would mind getting his money a day early. He waited on the other side of the street for Warburton to arrive and gave the man a few minutes before entering the office.

The same age as Knox, Warburton was about as fair a man as you were likely to find in his position. He sat behind a cheap wooden desk, hunched over a stack of paper. When Knox entered, he looked up, startled.

'Knox.'

'I've come to pay the rent.' Knox shoved ten shillings on to the desk and took a step back.

Warburton nodded, as though he'd been expecting Knox to say this. 'Sit down,' he said, gesturing to the chair opposite him. 'Please.'

Knox did as he was told but he could tell that something wasn't right.

'I don't know how to put this, Knox, so I'll come straight out with it.' He tried to smile. 'I've always liked you as a tenant. You've never missed a week and you're always polite.'

'What is it you have to tell me, Mr Warburton?' Knox could feel the bile rising in his throat.

'Last night, I was visited by Mr Brittas himself. He instructed me personally on this matter.'

'What matter?'

'I'm afraid you will have to vacate Mr Brittas's property and land by the end of the week.' Warburton couldn't bring himself to look at Knox.

'The end of *this* week?' When the agent just nodded, he said, 'But it's already Thursday.'

'I put this point to Mr Brittas and he told me to inform you that you would be able to stay until Saturday morning, but you must be gone by midday.'

'Go where? That's our home. We've lived there all of our married life.'

'I'm sorry, Knox. You're a good man and I have no idea what you've done to anger Mr Brittas, but I'm afraid to say it's none of my business.'

'I've paid my rent on time every week, never missed a week in five years, not even once.'

'I'm just a humble messenger, sir. But Mr Brittas did want me to emphasise that his decision is final.'

'I have a wife and a young child. I've just lost my position at the constabulary and I've nowhere else to go. If you could just talk to Mr Brittas, remind him that I've always been a good friend to his father. His father is nearly blind and I read to him whenever I can.'

'I'm sure Mr Brittas's father is grateful, and maybe he could speak on your behalf, but I can do no more.'

'But why? What have I done?'

Warburton said nothing but stood up and walked slowly to the door.

Knox had never dreamt that Cornwallis's influence extended this far but he didn't doubt that the aristocrat was behind this latest indignity. He was amazed that Cornwallis could be so vindictive or that he cared so much about what Knox had done, but then the man had always had a mean streak and Knox had gone behind his back and done the very thing he had been instructed not to do.

'Saturday lunchtime, then.'

Knox nodded silently and left the office.

Jeremy Brittas was sitting, as usual, in his worn armchair, staring listlessly into the fireplace. Having let himself into the lodge and announced his arrival from the doorway, Knox stepped into the room.

'I thought you'd come running to me as soon as you heard the news.' Brittas seemed to be relishing the situation.

'So you knew?'

'My son came here to tell me. He knows you sometimes visit me, though you've not been here in the last week, I've noticed.'

'He wants to *evict* us from our home. I thought you could talk to him, persuade him to let us stay.'

'His mind's made up. He made that very clear to me. He warned me against trying to help you.'

'Did he say why?' Knox was desperate.

Brittas rearranged the few strands of white hair on his liver-spotted head. 'Let me tell you something about my son. At bottom, he's a weak, capricious man who has mismanaged this estate and allowed it to fall into disrepair. I can say all this because he is my son and I love him none the less. But I do know he has been troubled by his creditors. It's my understanding that some of these debts have been cleared, on the proviso that he deals with your situation quickly and ruthlessly.' Brittas paused. 'It would appear you've upset some fairly important people, young man.'

'Lord Cornwallis asked me to perform a small service for him. I didn't do as I was told.'

'Cornwallis, eh?' This time Brittas's expression was serious. 'A nasty one, and that's no lie.'

'I lost my position in the constabulary yesterday.'

He considered this, rubbing his bony, bristly chin. 'Martha know?'

'Not yet.'

'If you want my advice, you'll go home now and tell her everything. No good has ever come from keeping secrets.'

'And tell her what? That we're to be forced out of our home the day after tomorrow? That we have nowhere to go?'

'You'll find somewhere.'

'Will I? I have about two pounds to my name and no likelihood of employment. If Cornwallis has bullied your father into banging his drum, he'll do his best to spike my chances with anyone else I go to.'

'Look, if you and your family need somewhere to put your heads down for the next few days, you can stay here with me.'

Knox looked at the old man. 'But your son has made it clear you're to have nothing to do with me.'

'Let me deal with my son.'

Farther along the lane, almost in front of their cottage, was a lacquered brougham attended by liveried footmen. The four horses that drew it were stationary, snorting in the breeze. As Knox approached the brougham, the door swung open and Cornwallis leant out of the shadows. He beckoned Knox to join him.

The interior smelled of damp clothes and pipe tobacco. There was a layer of hay on the floor. Cornwallis was wearing riding boots, tan breeches and a black velvet frock-coat.

'I'm sorely disappointed in you, boy. Sorely disappointed. I thought that you and I had an understanding.'

Knox stared down at the wet hay. He knew that whatever he said would only make a bad situation worse.

'Well, what's done is done and now we'll all have to live with the consequences of your stupidity.'

'I've lost my position at the constabulary and I'm to be evicted from my home.' Knox looked up at the aristocrat. 'How does your predicament compare to that?'

'I'll not be spoken to in such an impudent manner, boy. Nor do I have to justify my decisions to someone of your station.'

Knox was about to ask Cornwallis what he was so afraid of – why he had tried so hard to bury the murder inquiry – but he managed to stop himself.

'What I do need to know is how is you were able to identify the deceased as a police detective from Scotland Yard.'

Knox shuffled uncomfortably on the cushionless seat. 'You've taken my job and my home. Why should I help you now?'

Cornwallis broke into a gummy grin. 'You're forgetting my benevolence towards your mother and father.'

'You would throw them out too? A woman who's served you loyally and without question for forty years? What kind of a monster are you?'

Cornwallis's eyes narrowed, his mouth hardening. 'Now I'm prepared to overlook your impetuous behaviour just this once. Next time, I won't be so forgiving.'

Knox fell into a sullen silence. The aristocrat had him in the palm of his hand and they both knew it.

'Your misfortunes are wholly self-inflicted, but it would be remiss of me if I didn't also say that they bring me deep personal anguish.' Cornwallis waited. 'I asked you a question, sir. I should like an answer.'

Knox stared out of the mud-stained window, wondering whether Martha was at home. If she was, she would have seen the horses and brougham.

'The deceased took a room at the New Forge Inn in Dundrum. I found letters there, written to him by his son.' Knox decided not to mention the pistol and knife which he'd also found, or the two daguerreotypes.

'I should like to see those letters.'

Knox looked at the old man and felt pure hatred welling up inside him. 'Why are you so concerned about the death of a man you dismissed as a vagrant?'

Cornwallis's face seemed to shrink. 'One word from me, boy, and your mother will be driven from her home. Please don't underestimate my willingness to do what is necessary.'

Knox reached inside his greatcoat and produced the letters. He had intended to keep them from his superiors at the constabulary but that didn't matter now. Better to try to limit the damage, make certain that his mother and brothers didn't suffer the same fate that would befall Martha and James. Cornwallis took the letters but didn't inspect them.

'If I find you've held anything back from me, I'll be seriously displeased. Your family will learn of my displeasure also.' Cornwallis used his walking cane to bang the roof of the brougham.

The door swung open and one of the footmen appeared. 'Now get out of my sight.'

'You've taken my livelihood. At least allow me to remain in my home.'

'That, sir, is a courtesy I am already bestowing on your family. Do not expect me to extend the same generosity to you.'

Knox climbed out of the carriage. As soon as he'd done so, the door slammed closed and the driver took up the reins and shouted at the horses. The brougham lurched forward and Knox watched as it rattled away down the track.

Martha was waiting for him by the front door.

'God, Michael. What have you done?' She looked him up and down, noticing his shabby clothes.

Knox blinked and stood by the gate, not wanting Martha to see that he was on the verge of tears.

THIRTEEN

Jonah Hancock announced that a letter had been delivered that morning to the offices of the *Merthyr Guardian* and that the editor – who had been told what to do but not why – had forwarded it to the Castle. Pyke took it from Hancock and carefully inspected the writing. The style matched that of the original letter. The message was simple. Twenty thousand pounds in banknotes was to be left in the first-class carriage of the train for Cardiff departing at nine o'clock on Monday morning. The man delivering the suitcase of money was not to travel on the train. Failure to follow these instructions would result in the death of William Hancock. If these instructions *were* followed, William would arrive at Merthyr station on the eleven o'clock service from Cardiff. Pyke read the letter again. There was no reference to Scottish Cattle.

'My guess would be that it's genuine,' Pyke said, glancing around the dining-room table.

'That's what we thought, too,' Zephaniah said. 'Same handwriting as the initial letter.'

'So what do you think? What do you want to do?' This time Pyke directed his question at Jonah Hancock, but it was Cathy who answered.

'My husband says he wants to move the rendezvous spot to China – of all places.' Her frustration was palpable.

'*China?*'

Jonah Hancock reddened. 'There's one way into China and one way out. This way we can get enough men on the ground to control the territory.'

Pyke shook his head. 'Out of the question. First, it's too

dangerous. I heard that one of the bullies, Ben Griffiths, robbed John Wylde at gunpoint yesterday. Shot off his hand, too. Wylde will try to retaliate. There's no way we can guarantee your son's safety in that kind of environment.' Clearly Jonah Hancock hadn't heard about the trouble. He looked appalled.

'And second?' Zephaniah said, stirring milk into the coffee that one of the servants had poured.

'This is a good arrangement – for all concerned.' He turned to Jonah. 'What you don't want is anything that will make the kidnappers nervous. The railway station is perfect. There will be lots of people, plenty of distractions.'

'But what my son is saying, Detective-inspector, is that we cannot keep a public place of that size under surveillance.'

'And the kidnappers *know* that.' Pyke looked at Jonah. 'That's why they've chosen it. But you read the letter. If you decide to put a man on every entrance and exit, and on the train, and the kidnappers realise what you're doing, then your son's life will be put at risk.'

'That's exactly what I've been trying to make clear,' Cathy said, from the other end of the table.

'So we just leave a suitcase containing twenty thousand pounds in the luggage rack of the first-class carriage and wait? Hope they'll do as they say, and send my son back here on the next train?' Jonah said.

'I don't see what other choice you have – that is, if you've agreed to pay the ransom.'

'We're going to pay,' Zephaniah said, a trace of irritation in his voice. 'I thought we made that clear.'

'You have the money?'

'We've had it on deposit at the bank ever since we received the first letter.' The old man took a sip of coffee. 'Don't worry, Detective-inspector. We've no plans to upset the apple cart, at least not until we know the boy is safe.'

Pyke went across to the doors and closed them. 'No one else is to be told about these arrangements. I mean *no one*. Not the servants, not the police. Is that clear?'

They all nodded but Pyke wondered whether they would be able to keep the news from spreading. He thought again about the boy's coat and Cathy's suspicions – that William had not been wearing it

139

on the day he'd been kidnapped. In which case how had it ended up on Irish Row? And why had the coat and a shoe been left at a house that the dead man, Deeney, hadn't even lived in? The whole situation struck Pyke as a set-up, but by whom and for what end?

Pyke decided not to push the point. Instead he said, 'Unless anyone has an objection, I'd like to be the one to take the suitcase to the railway station.'

Zephaniah nodded. Cathy said, 'Yes, I'd feel much better if you handled it.'

'This trouble in China,' Jonah said, when they had finished and were making their way out of the room. 'Did you hear what might have set it off?'

'I heard that two masked men held up a beer shop at gunpoint. They escaped with most of Wylde's money.'

Pyke watched the skin tighten around the ironmaster's pale eyes.

'Why do you ask?' Pyke stared at the man's flabby face. 'Surely you have no interest in the affairs of a couple of bullies?'

Jonah Hancock muttered a response and left Pyke standing alone in the entrance hall.

Pyke was about to mount a horse that had been prepared for him, when Cathy joined him outside. She was wearing a woollen coat and a lace bonnet and locks of blonde hair flapped around her face in the breeze.

'I wanted to thank you,' she said, walking beside him to the other side of the chestnut gelding.

'For what?'

'For talking sense into my husband.'

Pyke mounted and they walked down the first part of the driveway in silence. 'Was he really pushing for the rendezvous to take place in China?' he asked.

'Until you put him straight,' she replied.

'And Zephaniah?'

'He kept his opinions to himself.'

'It'd be much easier to go after the kidnappers if you could somehow hem them in and China would be perfect for that. That's why the kidnappers would never have agreed to the proposal.'

They went as far as the lodge. In the weak sunlight, Cathy's skin glowed and her hair assumed a golden hue.

'About last night . . .' She stared down at the ground and appeared to blush.

'Cathy, you don't have to say anything.' Pyke was thinking about the man who'd been spying on them and whether word of their brief embrace had made it back to her husband.

'Whatever happens, Pyke, don't think badly of me,' she whispered, then turned back towards the house.

As he watched her walk up the driveway, Pyke wondered whether she was using him in a way he hadn't yet realised.

Pyke had always had a flexible attitude towards violence. He had tried to measure the merits of any course of action not against some abstract standard but according to what it might be able to achieve. He knew this meant that his moral compass was, at times, shaky and that, hypothetically speaking, heinous individual acts could be justified according to the common good. This explained his decision to rob Wylde at gunpoint, and as such he should have been ready for the sight that greeted him as soon as he, and John Johns, set foot in China.

It was the smell of charred flesh that hit Pyke first. He could taste it at the back of his throat. An entire row of houses was smouldering, smoke still drifting out of forlorn, blackened window frames. The thatched roofs had been destroyed in the fire and two bodies were laid out in the mud, covered by a dirty sheet. The fire had been extinguished not by human hand but by the rain that had swept in off the nearby mountain. Men and women huddled in doorways, pointing at the corpses. No one seemed to know what to do.

'Who were they?'

'Prostitutes.'

Pyke felt the rainwater leaking down the back of his neck. 'Wylde's?'

'Wylde's men tore apart the Green Dragon on the Pennydarren Road. I hid the money there because Griffiths is sleeping with the landlady. They found the money and killed Griffiths's mistress by way of punishment. I'm guessing this was Griffiths's retaliation.'

Pyke became aware of an ache that stretched from one side of his chest to the other.

'This wasn't our doing.' He looked over at Johns, aware of how hollow his words sounded. 'We didn't set light to that roof and we didn't beat Ben Griffiths's mistress to death.'

Johns turned up his collar and stared at the darkening sky. 'You think it's going to get better after this? Wylde has probably already made his next move.'

'What's done is done.' Pyke tried not to look at the charred remains of the two women. 'Nothing we can do about it now.'

'No? So we just let Wylde and Griffths tear each other apart and butcher women like this in the process?'

Pyke's throat was dry and scratchy. 'This would've happened, this fight over territory, sooner or later. We just lit the touchpaper.'

'And now two innocent women are dead.'

Pyke was about to say that no one was innocent, not in a place like China, but he realised how callous that would make him sound. 'If you prefer we can go out there, find Wylde and Griffiths, execute them, and have done with it.'

Johns looked at him, trying to work out whether he was serious or not. 'That how it works in London?'

'Look, this is about the Hancock boy, remember. Now Wylde's attention has been directed elsewhere, perhaps someone will talk to us.'

Johns considered this. 'If it is just about the boy, why not let the Hancocks pay the ransom and leave it there?' He gestured at the corpses. 'You're doing this because you don't like the notion of the Hancocks and a couple of bullies carving up the town for their own gain.'

Pyke was surprised by the acuity of Johns' insight. It was quite true: he was working for the Hancocks but at the same time he was tempted to rein in their influence, to clip the wings of people like them.

'It's time we left. People are starting to notice us.' Johns waited for Pyke to catch up with him, then they retraced their steps out of China and eventually came to a halt on Jackson's Bridge.

'I like you, Pyke, and I'd like to be able to trust you.' Johns looked down at the murky water.

'But?'

'I see a little of myself in you. You look at the world as it is and a part of you wants to destroy it.'

'I'm just here to make sure nothing bad happens to the boy.'

'In which case, why get involved in the matters of China?'

'Because I think they're related. That's how an investigation works. You learn to trust your instincts.'

'And Cathy?'

The question took Pyke by surprise.

'What about Cathy?' he said.

Johns turned to him suddenly. His face was glistening. 'You're not here for her?'

'I don't understand why you're asking me about her.'

Johns' eyes narrowed. 'She's been a good friend to me. I don't want to see her get hurt.'

'And I *do*?'

Johns ignored the question and set off across the bridge. This time Pyke didn't try to follow him.

That night, Pyke took his supper in a pub in town and slipped back into the Castle without interrupting dinner. He'd been in his room for about an hour when he heard a knock on his door.

Cathy was wearing a nightgown and slippers. She had combed her hair and her eyes were bright and clear.

'I saw you come in.' She stepped into the room and waited for Pyke to close the door. 'Jonah and Zephaniah didn't. I heard them talking just now. They still think you're out.'

She walked towards him then stopped just in front of him. He let his gaze drift from her azure-blue eyes down her slim nose to a freckle just above her mouth. Something about this felt wrong but he was lonely and a little drunk and she hadn't come to his room simply to talk. Pyke didn't want to talk to her, either. He knew what he wanted and it seemed she wanted it too: not love, not marriage, but simply gratification.

Quickly he pulled her into an embrace, and the force of it seemed to take them both by surprise. Pyke touched her skin and felt his hand quiver. He pulled the nightdress up over her head as she loosened his trousers. Cathy lay down on the bed, her golden hair spread across the white pillow. Pyke didn't bother to take off the rest of his clothes, and as soon as he was inside her, he felt an overwhelming urge not just to pleasure himself but to annihilate her. But the harder he went at it, the more she seemed to enjoy it, until it was as if they were both pounding away at one another, a carnal act with little or no affection behind it.

Afterwards, they lay next to each other, staring up at the ceiling. All Pyke could think about was the twenty years that separated them and the fact that he'd complicated an already complicated situation. What would Jonah Hancock do, Pyke wondered, if he found out that he had been cuckolded?

'I sometimes wonder what would have happened if I had married you – and not my husband.' Her skin smelled of sweat and sandalwood.

'Me?' Pyke tried to laugh. He didn't really believe that her feelings for him ran deep but what she'd said made him uneasy. What if she really was holding a torch for him, as Zephaniah had suggested?

She tapped him playfully on the arm. 'Is it really such an abhorrent idea?'

Pyke sat up slightly and turned towards her but before he could say anything, she reached out and pressed the tip of her finger against his lip. 'Please don't say it.'

'Say what?'

'That you think what we just did was a mistake.' Smiling, Cathy got up, picked up her nightgown and slipped it on.

Pyke watched her for a few moments. 'I saw John Johns earlier today. He asked me about my intentions towards you and told me he didn't want to see you get hurt.'

Hearing this, she stiffened slightly and turned away, so he couldn't see her face. 'He's just concerned about me, as a friend.'

Pyke sat up and pulled the sheet over his waist. 'It made me wonder whether he likes you as more than a friend.'

'Who, John? Surely not.' But her laugh wasn't quite convincing.

'It also made me think about the man who was spying on us the other night.'

'You think it might have been John?'

Pyke watched her cross the room, to the door, her hand resting on the handle.

'No, not necessarily. But I thought I'd mention it.'

She ran her fingers through her hair and smiled. 'John isn't interested in me for myself. Deep down, I think he despises my husband and father-in-law and sees me as a way of getting at them.'

'Why would he think that?'

But Cathy had already slipped out of the room and closed the door behind her.

FOURTEEN

Knox lay next to his wife, listening to her sleep, the sound of her breathing soothing him. It was early, barely light, but he had been awake for hours, thinking about what might happen to them. Closing his eyes, he remembered their wedding night and the day James had been born, the happiest of Knox's life. They had tried to pack things up but the reality of their eviction hadn't sunk in. He'd told Martha everything and she had let him talk, calm, not rushing to judge him. They'd both cried, then Martha had berated him, but in the end she had come around. She told him that she understood why he'd done what he'd done.

Just before they had turned in for the night, she had gripped him, tears in her eyes. 'Oh, Michael, what are we going to do? We've got no roof over our heads, no money, no work. And we have James to look after.'

'I'll get work,' he'd said. 'I'll do what I have to. We'll get by. You'll see.'

'*How?* How will you get work, Michael? People are dying in their thousands. There is no work.' She had paused then, perhaps aware that her tone had been harsher than she'd intended.

Now he sensed Martha stirring next to him and held his breath. He didn't want her to wake up, not just yet. They had six hours to clear the cottage and Warburton would treat them humanely; and Jeremy Brittas had offered them a bed for the night. That would do until they found somewhere else.

'But where, Michael?' Martha had said yesterday, once it became apparent that no one would even rent them a room.

Knox had spent the afternoon knocking on doors and Brittas's was the only offer made to him. Somehow Cornwallis had poisoned everyone in the town against them.

Martha rolled over to face him now, eyes still closed. 'Hold me,' she whispered. 'Just hold me and don't say anything.'

Knox put his arms around her and pulled her close. It was warm under the blanket, warm and dry. All the things he had taken for granted.

'Why didn't you say anything to me before, Michael? What did you imagine I'd do?' Her tone was inquisitive rather than accusatory.

'I was ashamed. I couldn't stand the thought I'd let you down. Let us down. James, especially.'

'So what do you think Moore's trying to hide?' Martha said, suddenly. She broke their embrace and rested her head on her elbow.

'One of the labourers at the estate told me that Moore knew the dead man. Said that when Moore first saw the body, his eyes nearly popped out of his head.'

'Does Moore know you know this?'

Knox shook his head.

'The only way out of this mess may be for you to keep digging.' She pulled the blanket up over her shoulder. 'You've nothing left to lose.'

'No. What I need to do is forget about Moore, forget about the murdered man. I'll find work and a new place for us to live.'

Martha's smile was sad. 'Don't you get it, Michael? Moore's seen to it that no one will rent us a home. Who on earth will give you a job?'

Knox nodded mutely. He had said what he thought Martha wanted to hear but he had reached the same conclusion.

'Yesterday, when you went into town, I took James to see Father Mackey in Clonoulty.'

Knox sat up. Her visits to Clonoulty were the only thing they really argued about. He just didn't understand why she kept going, when she professed to be ambivalent about the Church. 'You didn't mention that yesterday.'

'I'm not the only one who's kept their silence, am I?' Her stare was defiant but there was no real anger in her tone.

'So why did you go to see Mackey?'

'Because he said if we were ever in need, his door would always be open.'

'And is it?'

'He's not in Asenath Moore's pocket.'

Knox felt his indignation weaken. 'He'd even take in a dirty Protestant like me?'

'No one's outside of Moore's reach, Michael.' Martha bit her lip, wouldn't look at him. 'Not even a man like Father Mackey.'

'What are you trying to tell me, Martha?'

'Father Mackey denounced Moore from the pulpit. Since then, his home's been broken into, his horse stolen and the windows of his church shattered.'

Knox was starting to see where this was going. 'Let me guess. He said he'd take you and James in, but not me.'

'It would just be for a few weeks, Michael, until this whole thing has blown over. You could use the money you've saved . . .'

'What about old man Brittas? Remember, he offered us a roof over our heads, too.'

Martha smiled and shook her head. 'You can be so naive, Michael. He's an old man. As soon as Brittas finds out we're staying at the lodge, that'll be that. He'll have us out of there in no time.'

Knox felt a wave of bitterness swelling up inside him. 'So you go to Father Mackey and I sleep in a hedgerow.'

'Better you in a hedgerow than our son. You think he'd survive even one night out in the cold?'

Knox fell silent, another pang of shame. Martha saw it and reached out, touched his cheek. 'I'm sorry. That came out wrong. I love you, Michael, I really do. And it would just be for a few weeks.'

'And in the meantime, I take myself off to Dundrum to find out what connection the deceased had to Moore?'

'We won't have a moment's peace in this town until you do. Moore's frightened of you, Michael. Of what you already know and what you might find out. That's why he's done what he's done. If you find out what that something is then you can hold it over him.'

Outside in the lane, Knox heard horses' hoofs and the jangling of harnesses. He got out of bed and went to the window. A carriage pulled by four horses came to a halt. Knox was already halfway down the stairs.

The rain outside was torrential, the sky black as ink. Four men were standing in front of the gate, all wearing hats. Jeremy Brittas was gesticulating at the others while Warburton, his agent, pointed to the cottage.

'You still here?' Brittas said gruffly when Knox opened the front door. On the few occasions Knox had met him before, he had always been perfectly civil.

'Excuse me, sir,' Knox said, 'but Mr Warburton assured me I would have until midday to clear out my possessions.'

Brittas ignored him and barked orders at the two men he'd brought with him. Warburton refused to look at Knox.

'I have a wife and child, sir. Please have some mercy.'

Finally Brittas acknowledged him. He had always struck Knox as a kindly man, perhaps even a little meek for his own good, too much in his father's shadow. Now his eyes were dead. 'I'm afraid, sir, my mind is made up. You have fifteen minutes.'

'Fifteen minutes? You don't understand how much there is to do. We have a young child.'

Brittas looked at his pocket watch. 'It's seven now. I'll give you till quarter past.'

'Please, sir. We've nowhere to go, nowhere to take our possessions. Don't you have an ounce of compassion?' Knox turned around and saw Martha standing, arms folded, on the front step.

'You have fifteen minutes,' Brittas repeated.

Knox grabbed his wrist. 'I've been a good friend to your father, haven't I? I've visited him nearly every day, read the newspaper to him. Doesn't that count for anything?'

Brittas pulled his hand free and looked around for his agent. He didn't want to answer Knox's question.

'Please, sir, I beg you to reconsider . . .'

But one of the labourers shoved Knox to one side and said, 'We have orders to tear the place down.' By this time, Brittas had turned and was heading back to the carriage.

'We have to clear out what we can,' Knox said, moving around the room grabbing pots and pans.

'And do what with it, Michael? We have nowhere to take our things.'

'In less than fifteen minutes, those men will start to pull this place apart. We need to gather what we can and put it outside.'

'In this weather?'

'Either that, or they'll tear the place up and we'll lose everything.'

Martha began to cry. Knox took her in his arms. 'Go to Mackey's now, Martha. Take James, and whatever corn you can carry.'

She looked up at him, her face smudged with tears. 'What about all our things?'

'I'll do what I can. We can stack our possessions outside, in the lane.'

'But everything will be ruined.'

'We have no choice, Martha. If we have to leave some things behind, then so be it. It's more important that you get James to Father Mackey's.'

Martha bit her lip and nodded. 'So where should I start?'

'You go upstairs and find whatever we can carry to Clonoulty, whatever you think you might need. I'll start down here.'

Martha went over to the window and peered out at the rain. 'What kind of animals are those men? Did you tell them we have a child?'

'I would've taken off their boots and licked their feet if I thought it would've made a difference.' Knox was throwing the cutlery into the pots. He looked up and saw Martha still staring out of the window.

'We have to get going. We've only got ten minutes.'

As Martha went upstairs, Knox looked at the dresser, the neatly stacked piles of books and newspapers. Martha was right. Everything they took outside – the bedlinen, candles, coal, firewood, clothes – would be ruined. He had brought this upon them. He had done this to them. Taking up a teapot, Knox hurled it against the wall, watched it smash into a thousand pieces.

An hour later, their worldly possessions were piled up in the lane outside the cottage, a pathetic assortment of kitchen utensils, china, pots, pans, books, clothes, blankets and sheets. Knox had left the belongings there and walked Martha and James to the end of the lane, where the driver of a passing horse and cart had agreed to take them to Clonoulty. Too shocked to talk, they'd embraced quickly and Knox had watched as Martha and James had climbed up next to the driver, wondering when he would see them again. About fifty yards from the cottage he was joined by Tom, who wagged his tail, oblivious to what was happening. The two labourers were discussing what to do and Warburton was overseeing the operation. Lengths of chain and a collection of levers and hooks were laid out in front of them.

The two men fixed one end of a large iron chain to the horses' harness and attached a hook and a lever to the other end. Then one of them carried this end to the front window and looped it around and through the frame. Knox sank to his knees. Shivering, the dog curled up next to him and started to whine. This was clearly a well-drilled operation. When everything was in place, Warburton appeared with a whip in his hand and cracked it over the horses' heads. As they bolted forward, some of the front of the cottage came with them. The two men went to inspect the damage and attached the hooks and levers to another part of the wall. This time, when the horses bolted forward, part of the roof came crashing down, brick dust fanning out across the yard. Knox stared at the damage, disbelieving. The only home he'd truly loved, and where he'd spent the happiest years of his life, lay in ruins.

He pictured himself standing at the front door, Martha carrying James, just born, in her arms. More memories: Martha sitting on the back step quietly singing while he hoed the patch of land at the rear; James giggling while the dog poked its wet nose into his face. Knox remembered the bad times, too, but suddenly they didn't seem so bad. The stink of the first potato blight; a time before when Martha had miscarried their first child. Then, he had been sad, disconsolate even. But this was sheer devastation.

The men had picked up their crowbars and sledgehammers and now set to work on what remained of the cottage. The rain had eased. Knox watched as the last wall was felled. A few minutes later there was nothing left, just a pile of bricks and stones, the thatched roof lying forlornly on top of the rubble.

It took them another five minutes to dismantle the chains and hooks. When everything was cleared away, the two men trudged back to the carriage. Warburton appeared at the gate to assess the damage. He gave Knox a contrite look.

'For what it's worth, sir, I'm sorry for what we did.'

Knox waited for the carriage to depart and then there was silence, just the sound of the wind in the branches.

Knox had thought he might be able to rescue some of their possessions but now this idea struck him as hopelessly naive. Where would he take them? If, and when, Martha was settled in Clonoulty, perhaps he could store some of their possessions there but even this, he knew, was unlikely. Soon enough people would learn what had happened and scavengers would turn up; a pan could be exchanged for a bowl of corn, their blankets could be dried and used. The books would be ruined but who wanted to read?

Better to think they had lost everything than cling to false hope. Knox looked at the wet dog, shivering against his legs. What would he do with Tom?

Knox moved a few of the pots and pans, and the blankets and clothes, to the coal shed, which hadn't been destroyed. Then he took the shovel and dug up the cloth purse in which he'd hidden his last remaining coins. He had also buried the daguerreotypes, and the dead man's pistol and knife. Holding one of the copperplates in his hand, Knox stared at the silvery image. It struck him, then, that he had not heard from the son, Felix, and that the letter he'd sent to Somerset had ended up at Scotland Yard. Knox supposed it didn't matter. Nothing would bring back the man, he mused bitterly. And now his own life lay in tatters.

Knox inspected the pistol and realised it was loaded. He held it in hand and curled his finger around the trigger. *You have to answer for what you've done, Moore.* He imagined firing it, the noise and the smell of powder. He felt Tom brush past his ankles and his mind was yanked back to the present. The dog couldn't come with him. It would make him too conspicuous and he had nothing to feed it. The kindest, most humane thing would be to aim the pistol and fire. Knox knelt down and let the cowering mutt lick his hand. Knox had named the animal after Thomas Davis, who had died a year earlier. At the time, one newspaper had called his death 'the end of Ireland's hope', unaware how prophetic these words would become. What hope would the dog have, left to fend for itself?

Knox stood a step backwards, then raised the pistol and aimed at the mutt's brown face. Tom started to whine. Sweating, Knox lowered the barrel and wiped his forehead with his sleeve. He couldn't do it; he couldn't pull the trigger. Unaware of how close he'd come to being shot, the dog stayed contentedly at Knox's side while he gathered up the daguerreotypes.

When Knox reached the end of the lane, the dog was still following him, but at the junction with the mail coach road to Dundrum, the dog stopped and sat down in the middle of the track. Perhaps it thought Knox was simply going to work, and would be back as usual later that day. Knox thought about calling out to it one more time, giving it a farewell pat on the head, but he decided a clean break would be better. He turned and walked twenty paces along the road to Dundrum before looking behind him. Tom hadn't moved but his head was cocked slightly to one side. Knox knew that it was no time for sentiment but it struck him that he'd done the dog a disservice by not putting it out of its misery.

FIFTEEN

The next morning Pyke woke early and decided to walk into town. The overnight rain had cleared and the air smelled clean. At the station-house, he asked for Jones, but the superintendent hadn't yet arrived. One of the constables recognised Pyke and explained there had been more trouble in China: he didn't know the details or whether there had been any more fatalities. Outside the station-house, a red-faced clerk caught up with Pyke and thrust a letter into his hand.

The writing was Felix's. Pyke tore open the envelope and pulled out the letter. All seemed to be well in Somerset. This calmed him a little. Felix made reference to his visit there and to the kidnapped child. Pyke then diverted his attention to the last few lines. *I've been given a few days' holiday from my studies. I plan to visit you in Merthyr for a day or two.* He stared down at the page. *I'll arrive some time on Sunday the twenty-second.* He went to check the date at the head of the letter. The seventeenth.

Pyke took a moment to compose himself. Today was the twenty-second so Felix would be arriving in Merthyr some time that day. He would almost certainly travel up on the train from Cardiff, but how many services were there on a Sunday? Pyke followed the clerk back into the building.

'Will you be on duty for the rest of the day?'

Startled by the change in Pyke's tone, the clerk took a moment to answer. 'Yes . . . yes, I will.'

'All day?'

'All day.'

'My son Felix may turn up here looking for me. If he does, I wonder if you could keep him here and send word for me up at the Castle.'

The clerk gave him a bemused nod. 'That shouldn't be a problem, sir.'

Pyke thrust a silver coin into the man's reluctant hand. 'Write me a note, to be opened only by me. Please don't just pass on a verbal message.'

Just to be on the safe side, he didn't want anyone at the castle to know Felix was visiting him. He didn't yet know who were his friends, and who were his enemies.

At the railway station Pyke was told there was just one service from Cardiff and it would arrive at four in the afternoon. He was now looking forward to Felix's visit. He hadn't been aware of how much he missed home until he'd received the letter. He missed the comfortable feel of their house, its smell, the presence of his three-legged mastiff, now almost fifteen and blind in one eye. He missed drinking wine in his armchair, pulled up close to the fire. He missed his son, too, but Felix had been gone for a while.

What kind of home, he wondered as he entered the Castle, had this been for Cathy and her son? He didn't imagine it had been a happy one. As he crossed the hall, he remembered his dream from the previous night. Frederick Shaw had been in it. Felix as well. Something terrible had happened, but he couldn't remember what. He'd woken before dawn, his back bathed in sweat. The room still smelled of Cathy, of what they had done.

But Cathy wasn't waiting for him now. Instead Jonah Hancock appeared from the library and beckoned him over. The ironmaster's face was full of fury and Pyke feared the worst.

There was a newspaper laid out on the table. The *Merthyr Chronicle* – the town's other newspaper. Without speaking, Jonah pointed at the report in the far left-hand column. *Riot in Merthyr*.

It described the events of Friday afternoon – the door-to-door search by the town's constabulary. It reported that there had been minor disturbances and, right at the end of the piece, it speculated that the police had been searching for a missing child. It didn't mention the Hancocks by name, nor did it say that the child belonged to one of the town's eminent families.

'I can see why you're angry but there's no mention of your family or William here. No one will think to connect this to you.'

'No?' Jonah Hancock scrunched the newspaper into a ball and hurled it across the room. 'The fewer people who know what's happened to William, the safer he will be. That's what you said.'

Pyke watched the blood rise in the ironmaster's face.

'Think about it. There's no way the newspaper could have found out about the exact reason for the search,' Pyke said, hoping to placate Hancock. 'But this is a small community and I'm afraid that word of what's happened to your son is bound to spread sooner or later. Can you be *absolutely* certain that none of the servants has mentioned that William is missing to a friend or family member?'

Hancock told him that the household staff had all been sworn to secrecy, although he seemed to know as well as Pyke that people were bound to gossip.

Pyke looked at the shelves stacked high with books and wondered how many of them the ironmaster had actually read. It struck him, too, that no one had told him very much about William. No one had talked about what kind of a lad he was, what he liked to do, what made him laugh, what made him cry. Pyke tried to remember Felix at the same age. What had *they* talked about? Felix had always been a warm-hearted boy but Pyke hadn't been an especially attentive father.

'By the way, I was wondering whether you'd managed to locate my son's former nursemaid,' Jonah Hancock said.

'You mean, as a possible suspect?'

The ironmaster shrugged.

'I put this point to your wife. She assured me it would be impossible as Maggie Atkins has found work far away from here.'

Hancock gave him a look he couldn't quite interpret. 'Since you're here, we should go to my study to discuss arrangements for tomorrow.'

Pyke followed him back through the entrance hall and along a wide passageway to a large oak-panelled room at the back of the Castle. There, Jonah Hancock unlocked the door of a safe, built into the wall. Reaching inside, he scooped up a large cloth sack, then turned around and emptied its contents on to the desk. There was, he said, a thousand pounds in coins and nineteen thousand in Bank of England notes. He urged Pyke to count it.

Pyke stared at the pile of gold coins and the neat stacks of notes held together with string. 'I'm sure that won't be necessary.'

Hancock stood beside the desk, his hands resting on the edge. 'In my original letter I promised you a certain fee.'

'We can talk about that when your son is returned to you safe and well.'

Hancock returned to the safe and took out a much thinner stack of banknotes, then slid them across the desk. 'A thousand, just as I promised.'

Pyke stared at Hancock. 'I wouldn't usually expect to be paid until my work was finished.'

'Take it.' The ironmaster ran his hand through his hair and made an effort to smile. 'I'm happy with what you've done.'

Pyke let his fingers rest on top of the stack of notes. 'But what if, heaven forbid, something were to go wrong tomorrow?'

Hancock was gathering up the twenty thousand and putting it back into the cloth sack. 'I think it's best I settle my debt now, don't you? If something bad were to take place, and I hope and pray for all our sakes that it doesn't, I'm not sure that doing so would be foremost in my mind.'

Pyke loitered in the entrance hall as long as possible, waiting for Cathy to return, but eventually he set off down the driveway, hoping to stop off at the station-house before meeting the four o'clock train from Cardiff.

He saw the man – a priest, in fact – waiting outside the gates, but as he hurried by, a voice called out, 'Detective-inspector Pyke?'

The man had grey hair, a round face and a ruddy complexion. He was wearing a long black cassock and a miniature wooden cross dangled from a gold chain around his neck. He introduced himself as Father Carroll and explained he was parish priest at the Catholic chapel in Dowlais.

'How can I help you, Father?' Pyke glanced up at the clouds gathering above them and felt a spit of rain on his face.

'I wanted to talk to you about the disturbances the other day in Bathesda Gardens and Quarry Row.'

'Oh yes?' Pyke decided not to say anything more. He wanted to find out what the priest knew.

'I read in the newspaper that the police were searching for a missing child.' Father Carroll turned and looked up at the Castle. 'I also heard a rumour that it was the Hancock boy who was missing.' He spoke in a soft brogue.

'Who told you this?'

'So it's true, then? The Hancock boy has been taken?'

'I didn't say that. I just asked who had relayed this information to you.'

The priest looked away and shook his head. 'I can't exactly say. It's just a rumour I heard. The point is, I was told you were lookin' into the matter and I felt it was my duty to reassure you that no right-thinkin' Irishman would attempt such a stupid thing.'

'Perhaps I could ask who told you I was looking into the matter?' Pyke searched the priest's face.

'That would be Sir Josiah Webb, sir,' he said, without hesitation. 'In fact, he was the one who suggested I come and talk to you.'

Pyke digested this information. Webb owned the Morlais ironworks.

'I see. Then can I assume Sir Josiah shares your thinking and your concerns on this subject?'

'I'd say so, but for different reasons.'

'Go on,' Pyke said. He had a quick look at his pocket watch. It was already a quarter past two.

'You'd be amazed how quick a disturbance like that can spread. Last night the windows of the Catholic chapel were smashed.'

Pyke stared at him, trying to work out how the two events were related.

Father Carroll must have seen his confusion. 'Maybe you don't know how uneasy things are at the moment between the Irish and the Welsh, sir. You not being from around here.'

'And you suspect that what happened to your chapel was retaliation for . . . ?'

'Welsh folk don't much care for the Irish. Mostly I'd say they're afraid we'll take their jobs.' He looked up at the rain clouds. 'Relations haven't been good these last few years, and, well, if the locals thought some Irishmen had kidnapped a little boy, they'd do something about it.'

Pyke looked at the priest, interested now. 'And that's why you think your windows were smashed?'

The priest sighed. 'No one gains when something like this happens; when Irish and Welsh folk fight among themselves. That's what Sir Josiah said, too. And that's why he's worried. If the fighting spills over into the works, well, it wouldn't be good for business.'

Now Pyke understood why Father Carroll had been summoned to see Webb, and why Webb had sent him here. Both men wanted to make it clear that no Irish gang would do something as stupid or desperate as seize the Hancock boy.

'I'm afraid I have to go, Father. I have an appointment in town.' Pyke had another look at his watch. 'But I'm pleased you came and I promise to treat what you told me with the utmost seriousness.'

But as he went to leave, the priest reached out and grabbed one of his wrists. 'Mark my words, this whole town is ready to go up in flames, and it will, if people like you let it happen.'

Pyke found the clerk in the storeroom of the station-house and reminded him about Felix's arrival. On the front steps of the building he ran into Sir Clancy Smyth, who was swaddled in a greatcoat, muffler, top hat and gloves.

The chief magistrate greeted Pyke warmly, in spite of their fractious encounter the day before. 'I was informed your son is expected here at some point today. We'll make him quite welcome, of course,' he added.

Pyke had hoped to keep news of Felix's visit secret but the clerk had clearly informed Sir Clancy.

'But I do have some worrying news – about our mutual friend John Johns.' He rubbed his hands together and watched Pyke's reaction. 'According to witnesses, he was set upon by a gang of ruffians at the top end of High Street. They dragged him into one of the alleyways. I've had my men out looking for him ever since but they've found nothing.'

'Are they sure it was Johns?'

'He's a tall man and well known around here. One of the witnesses was quite sure of it.' Smyth looked up and down the street. 'I was wondering whether he said anything to you – whether he knew of anyone who would want to attack him?'

Pyke's thoughts turned immediately to what they had done to John Wylde, but they had both been disguised. Still, Johns *was* a tall man and perhaps someone in the beer shop had recognised him.

Pyke raised his eyes to meet the magistrate's. 'No, I'm afraid not. Johns kept his thoughts to himself.'

Smyth nodded. 'It's just I regard John not simply as an acquaintance but also a friend. I'd like to think he's safe.'

Pyke tried to remember what, if anything, Johns had said about Smyth, and wondered whether their mutual dislike of the Hancocks explained their friendship.

'There are hundreds, if not thousands, of my countrymen here in Merthyr but I've only ever talked about the old country with him. You know he came from the same county as I did?'

'He told me. Left at seventeen.'

'To join the army.' Smyth blew on his hands to warm them. 'Both of us Tipperary men. Protestants in a Catholic country.'

'I'll have a look for him.'

'I'd appreciate that.' Smyth's smile vanished as quickly as it had appeared. 'One of the witnesses thought the men who'd attacked him were part of a China mob.'

If Pyke's expression revealed anything, it would have been only for a few seconds, but Smyth was watching him carefully.

'What business did Johns have in China?'

'I don't know, Detective-inspector.' Smyth moved off down the stone steps and added, almost as an afterthought, 'That's why I asked whether he'd said anything to you.'

When Pyke went looking for John Wylde in China, he found that the Boot beer shop had been set upon with sledgehammers and crowbars. There was nothing left of it and no one wanted to talk about what had happened. Pyke had watched, for a moment, while a hawker tried to push his barrow through knee-deep mud and caught sight of a man, trousers around his ankles, fucking a woman against a brick wall. Across the alleyway, another man had collapsed and was muttering to himself, too drunk to stop a boy from emptying his pockets. A stray pig stopped briefly next to the inebriated man, sniffed him, and moved on.

By the time he made it back to the railway station in lower

Merthyr, it was almost four and the platform had started to fill up with people waiting to greet the service from Cardiff. Compared to the giant concourse at Paddington, the station was a drab, squalid affair, with a low ceiling, built from wood rather than iron. Pyke took a moment to think about what might happen when he brought the suitcase the following morning. He looked for the entrances, the nooks and crannies where people might be able to hide, the food stalls, the ticket office, and where the porters liked to stand.

At about five minutes past four, the train appeared around the bend, steam billowing from its engine. It chugged slowly into the station, coming to a halt with a violent hiss. The doors opened and the first passengers stepped down on to the platform. Pyke scrutinised the faces as they appeared through the mist. There was a man wearing a fustian jacket carrying his own suitcase; a woman dressed in a crinoline leading a porter who was struggling with a large chest. More passengers emerged: Pyke watched as an older man wearing a shooting jacket and billycock hat embraced a younger woman, perhaps his daughter. A young man stepped down from the first-class carriage and Pyke thought for a moment it might be Felix. He went to greet him but soon realised that the man looked nothing like his son.

After another five minutes, the crowd thinned out and then it was just him and the vendors on the platform, with a lone couple loitering at the far end. Pyke went to check the carriages but there was no sign of his son. He had another look at the letter, to make certain he hadn't misread it, but there it was. Felix had said he'd arrive on the twenty-second. If that was the case, then where was he?

As he looked up and down the empty platform it struck him that perhaps Felix hadn't travelled to Wales after all.

SIXTEEN

SUNDAY, 31 JANUARY 1847

Dundrum, Co. Tipperary

Knox had slept rough in a deserted crofter's hut, with nothing but a blanket for protection against the cold. He hadn't eaten a meal for two days, which meant he felt weak and light-headed. The walk from Cashel had sapped his strength: an arduous, cross-country trek as he tried to remain hidden from the road. He hadn't wanted anyone to warn Cornwallis of his likely presence in Dundrum. The rain had petered out some time in the night and the clouds had moved on, but that meant the temperature had plummeted. Knox tried not to think about Martha and James, what they would be doing. It upset him too much. Father Mackey would insist they accompany him to mass and he pictured his wife and son sitting on one of the rock-hard pews, staring up at a statue of Christ. Would she take the sacraments?

The sun had been up for an hour by the time he reached the outer edges of the village. He'd already skirted around Oughterleague and the perimeter of Castle Killenue and had passed the police barracks and the school. It was early on Sunday and both places were locked. He heard horses' hoofs in the distance and hid in the hawthorn bushes. It was about eight o'clock, perhaps half-past eight. Knox knew his parents and brothers attended the ten o'clock service and the walk to the church from their new home would take about half an hour. But he was close by now, less than ten minutes away, and already he could feel the blood pumping in his veins.

Knox had walked this road a thousand times but today it felt unfamiliar, threatening in a way he couldn't put his finger on. Sunlight filtered through the branches of the trees and cast shadows across the track. Ahead the road swept around to the left and he could see the Gatlee mountains in the distance. He was nearing the house now and could see a thin plume of smoke drifting up from the chimney. They would all be there; Peter, Matthew, their mother and father, a family shielded from the ravages of the famine because of the man they worked for.

Knox took off the blanket, wrapped the daguerreotypes inside it, and left it in front of the cottage. Opening the door, the first thing that hit him was the warmth.

Knox's father, Martin, was sitting by the fire. His mother was hanging up clothes. There was no sign of his brothers. He hadn't knocked and his parents' surprise was palpable. Knox saw his father's expression change. His mother said something but he didn't hear. Instead, he walked straight past her towards his father, who was struggling to his feet. Knox threw a punch, caught him on the jaw, then threw another punch with his other fist, this time grazing the man's cheek. The first punch had done the damage, though. Wiping saliva from his mouth, he saw the light disappear from Martin Knox's eyes, heard the breath rush from his lungs. Knox hit him again, this time on the nose, and felt the bone crunch, his father staggering blindly, hands cupping his nose. Knox punched him again, even though the man was about to fall over, then he felt someone pinning his arms from behind. Struggling free, he turned and saw Matthew. Somewhere in the room Peter was wailing. Over the sound of his sobs, his mother was screaming at Knox to stop. Knox looked around the room, aware for the first time of what he had done, what he'd become, no better than the man he'd just beaten and whose face was now a bloody mess. He felt a sudden stab of shame.

Knox staggered to the door, pulled it open and stumbled outside. He hadn't gone far when he felt someone tug on his sleeve.

'Dear God, Michael, what have you done?' His mother's voice was shaking.

Knox tried to gather himself. 'He signed a statement to the police against me.'

She stared at him, not blinking. Something in her expression had changed. She let out a long sigh.

'I've been dismissed from the constabulary and we've been forced out of our home. I had to watch while my landlord and his men reduced the cottage to rubble.'

'Oh, Michael.' Instinctively she reached out and touched him.

Knox bit back the urge to weep. 'That man I brought here. Davy McMullan. He'd been caught stealing blood from one of Moore's cattle. You saw him. You heard what he'd suffered. So I let him go.' He pointed at the cottage. 'And that man signed a statement saying I'd put our family at risk, bringing a criminal into his home.'

There were tears in his mother's eyes. 'Michael, it's me you should be angry with. I'm the one you should have struck.'

Knox tried to comprehend what she'd just said. 'You?'

'His Lordship summoned me. He gave me an ultimatum. Either I agreed to his demand or he would evict us from our home.' Tears were streaming down her cheeks.

'You made my dad sign that statement against me? Your own flesh and blood?'

His mother tried to grab his wrist but Knox pushed her away. 'God, Michael, please don't make this any harder for me. You know our family's circumstances. You know Peter wouldn't last a night if we had to sleep rough, not in this weather.'

Knox could see Matthew out of the corner of his eye. His younger brother was standing by the door, Peter next to him, mute and shivering.

'All along I've just tried to do the right thing, be good as you taught me. We've always stuck together, you and me, Mam. But now even you've turned against me.'

'I had no choice, son. Don't you see? Don't you see the position I was in? Please. I did the only thing I could. Cornwallis would have dismissed *all* of us, me, your father, your brother, then driven us from our home. I couldn't let that happen.'

'And so we've been forced out of our home instead. Me, Martha and James. We've lost everything. Is that what you wanted?'

'No. Dear God.' His mother wailed.

'Moore's used us – you and me – from the start. Don't you see that? He asked for me, a novice, someone who'd never investigated a murder before. Why? Because he thought he could tell me what to do. And why did he think that? Because of the power he wields over you, over my family here.'

His mother stared him, dry-eyed now. Perhaps she understood the logic of what he had just said.

'You've always defended him, Mam, but he's a monster. A cold-hearted monster, with no qualms about forcing a baby out of his home.'

This time his mother offered no defence of her master.

'What is it that he's so afraid of, Mam? Who was that dead man? Why was Moore so keen to bury the whole matter?'

Through her sobs, his mother said, 'I don't know, son. All I know is that people like us should never try to interfere in the business of men like Cornwallis.'

'I showed you the daguerreotype and something registered in your expression. You know something, don't you, Mam?' Knox was clutching her wrists and staring into her terrified face.

'Haven't you heard a word I've said, Michael? I love you, always have done and always will. I've never said so but I've always felt closer to you than anyone. But I have to put Peter's needs first. What I did was terrible, unforgivable even. I know that, but I didn't have a choice. I couldn't put Peter's life at risk.'

Knox felt as if his innards had been scooped out. 'Moore's turned the whole of Cashel against us, Mam. No one will rent us a room, we're finished. My only hope is to find out what Moore is afraid of and use it to get back what's rightfully mine, what's been taken from me. To do that, I need your help.'

'I don't know anything, Michael. I'm just a servant. I know my place, do as I'm told.'

'And what about doing what's right?'

His mother wiped her eyes with the sleeve of her dress. 'This is no time for principle, son. Not now, while death is so close.'

The crowd at the counter of the New Forge in Dundrum village was two deep, men in their best clothes, fresh from the Sunday service. Some would know him, know who he was, but Knox no longer cared. These were the lucky ones, still in work, who could afford a mug or two of stout. In his civilian clothes, no one paid him much attention. Knox waited at one end of the counter for the landlord to notice him: the news of his dismissal wouldn't have travelled this far.

His mind turned back to what had just taken place, the fight with his father and the argument with his mother. Knox had always felt *different* from his family. The ten-year age gap between him and

Matthew didn't help but it was more than that. His mother had always loved him with a fierceness he couldn't quite comprehend – which was why her rejection of him was so bewildering. His father had always treated him with caution and, if he'd been drinking, with undisguised hostility. Knox could still recall a night when his father had returned from the pub. This would have been before Matthew was born, and Knox had been asleep in his mother's arms. His father had woken him up and had taken a leather strap to him, hitting him over and over, stopping only when his mother jumped on his back and toppled him to the floor.

'What can I do for you, Constable?' The landlord stood there, arms folded across his apron.

Knox took out one of his precious shillings and placed it on the counter. 'I wonder if you could tell me where I might find the Doran family. The mother, Maria, used to work up at the big house.'

Maria Doran had once been his mother's closest confidante and, until her dismissal, had been the longest-serving member of the household after his mother. Knox didn't know the reason for her dismissal – his mother had never talked about it – but as soon as it happened, no one ever mentioned Maria's name again.

'Done something wrong, has she?'

'I just need to talk to her, that's all.'

The landlord glanced down at the silver coin and licked his lips. 'Only Dorans I know have a smallholding just north of Ponds Cross Roads, left-hand side.'

Nodding, Knox shunted the coin towards the landlord. 'And I want to buy some food. A bird, if you have one.' He saw the man's expression. 'I'm not interested in where it's come from, if that's what you're worried about.'

They both knew that any bird the landlord might be able to procure had been poached from the Cornwallis estate.

'I've got a partridge, plucked and ready, but it won't be cheap.'

'How much?'

'Ten shillings.'

Knox took a deep breath. Before the famine, you could have picked up a bird for a tenth of that amount. 'Eight.'

'Only one I've got. I won't let it go for less than ten.'

'Throw in a bottle of porter?' Knox got out his purse and rummaged around for the coins.

Maria Doran had aged in the two years since he'd last seen her, so much so that he might not have recognised her if they'd passed in the street. She was a few years younger than his mother but now looked ten or fifteen years older. Her daughter had been reluctant to let him into their one-room cabin but Maria had brushed away her objections. Now her children had been banished outside and been told not to disturb them. Maria Doran was sitting on the room's only chair, as close to the fire as she could get.

'You're Sarah Knox's boy, aren't ye?' Maria Doran had spoken to her daughter and son-in-law in Irish but addressed him in English. All of Cornwallis's servants had to speak English. It was a condition of service.

Knox nodded. 'Michael.'

'Come closer, let me have a proper look at you.'

Knox did as he was asked, knelt down next to her, and let her run her bony fingers over his cheeks.

'I remember ye. Always your mammy's favourite.'

He decided to let the comment pass, tried not to think what his mother had said to him, what he'd said to her.

'I don't know whether you heard about the recent murder on the estate,' he began. 'A man in his forties, perhaps, stabbed in the stomach.'

'She never spoke to me again, after Moore made his accusations.' Maria Doran stared at him, reproachful.

Knox nodded. He had never before thought of his mother as flawed but now it was hard not to. Of course, he didn't know the circumstances behind Maria's dismissal but he was inclined to believe anything that showed Moore in a vindictive light.

'I'm guessing they weren't true.'

'Oh, they were true, all right, I pilfered a little food, but no one stopped to ask why.'

They were silent for a while, both watching the fire glowing in the grate. 'Just now, I asked about a murder on the estate . . .'

'Now I've seen ye, satisfied my curiosity, you can get out of my sight.'

'You want me to go?'

The old woman looked away. 'Tell your mam I haven't forgotten, haven't forgiven either.'

'Then you won't be needing this.' Knox held up the bird he'd been hiding in his coat. 'Or this.' He showed her the bottle of porter.

Maria Doran gasped and stared, open-mouthed, at the bird. He could sympathise. He couldn't remember the last time he'd eaten meat.

While the daughter prepared the bird, placing it on a spit over the open fire, with a pan underneath to catch the fat and juices, Maria Doran told Knox she hadn't heard a thing about a murder and said she didn't know why Asenath Moore would be so keen to cover up his association with a policeman from London. She was at a loss to help him, and she seemed to feel bad about it, now that Knox had provided such a feast for her and her family. They talked briefly about the people they knew, the ones who'd died. 'The lucky ones,' Maria called them.

'Moore always treated your mammy different,' she said, reminiscing. 'Been with the family longer 'n anyone.'

Knox waited: he wanted to steer her away from the subject of his mother.

'Can you think of *anything* at all that Moore would want to keep secret?'

The smell of the cooking bird had filled the room, making it hard to concentrate. He swallowed the juices in his mouth.

'Man like that, done plenty of bad things, but nothing we got to hear about.'

It was dark outside now and the daughter and son-in-law had joined them at the fire. Knox uncorked the bottle of porter, took a gulp and passed it to the daughter. The sweet taste lingered in his mouth, the alcohol warming his stomach. An invitation to stay for supper, and overnight if needed, had already been offered and accepted.

'Does anything stick out in your memory?' Knox asked. 'Something that made Moore angry, perhaps?'

The old woman laughed. 'Moore was always angry.' She took the bottle and drank a swig of the porter.

'Mam tell you why he dismissed her?' This time it was the daughter who'd spoken. She was plain and dumpy, her skin pitted with pockmarks.

As Knox turned to her, Maria Doran sat up. 'Actually there was something, a long time ago.'

They both turned their attention back to Maria. 'I was just a wee slip of a girl. Hard to believe, isn't it?' She took another gulp of the porter, then handed it to the son-in-law. 'This would've been a month or so after I started.'

Knox felt the policeman in him return. 'Do you remember the date?'

'Spring, twenty-five. I'd just had this one,' she said, gesturing at her daughter. 'My mam was lookin' after her.'

Knox glanced over at the daughter. 'So what happened?'

'This young man in military uniform turned up at the hall one day. He went to see his Lordship, had this blazing row. Afterwards, Moore was angrier than I'd ever seen him. He threw a wineglass at the wall while I was in the room, claret, then made me scrub it up, and pick up the glass with my fingers.'

'Did anyone find out what the row was about?'

'Not this one.'

'And did anyone know who the soldier was?'

'I didn't, of course, but I'd only just started there. Afterwards, I was told he was the gatekeeper's lad. Apparently Moore had big plans for him but the lad had gone off and joined the army.'

'And what happened to the gatekeeper?'

'Died, long time ago. The wife lived a little longer but she's been dead for ten years now.'

'Any other children?'

'Not that I know of.' The old woman sniffed.

'What was the gatekeeper's name?'

Maria Doran's attention switched to the nearly cooked bird as her daughter turned it on the spit. The room was warm and the smell was incredible. Knox thought of the small fortune he'd spent, and then about Martha and James, what, if anything, they'd had to eat. He missed them with an intensity that shocked him, a physical craving that hadn't let up since he'd watched them disappear around a bend in the track on their way to Clonoulty.

'The name?'

The old woman turned towards him and frowned. 'Johns.'

'John what?'

'Johns,' she said, still scowling. 'That was the family name.'

Knox made a mental note of it and wondered whether he wasn't wasting his time.

Later, as he lay on the mud floor under his blanket listening to the others sleep, he knew he was fortunate, to have a full belly and to be protected from the cold, and that by the morning, countless others across the island would be dead.

SEVENTEEN

Pyke glanced out of the carriage window as they crossed Jackson's Bridge and then looked over at Jonah Hancock and Cathy, sitting at either end of the bench opposite him. The suitcase containing the money had been set on the floor between them. They hadn't spoken since leaving the Castle and Pyke hadn't seen Cathy since she'd come to his room. Huddled in the carriage, she refused to look at him.

'So you're to take the suitcase and put it in the luggage rack in first class and then return to the carriage where we'll be waiting for you.'

Pyke nodded. Jonah had been through this four or five times already. 'If all goes to plan, William won't arrive at the railway station until eleven. Perhaps you should go back to the Castle or to a hotel, wait there,' he suggested.

'We're not moving from the front of the railway station,' Cathy said, looking at Pyke for the first time.

They had turned from Market Square on to High Street and passed the chapel on the left-hand side. Pyke checked his pocket watch. It was already half-past eight.

'After I've left the suitcase on the train, I have some business to attend to in the town.' He paused, looked at Jonah. 'I'll find you in front of the station concourse at around ten.'

'What kind of business?' Jonah Hancock was frowning.

Pyke ignored his question. 'Just so I know. You haven't made any secret arrangements to position some of your men inside the railway station or on the train?'

'I hope not,' Cathy said quickly. She shot her husband a vicious look.

Jonah shook his head. 'This is my son's life we're talking about, sir. I've done *exactly* as the letter demanded.'

Pyke didn't pursue the matter but somehow he didn't quite believe that the Hancocks were about to give up twenty thousand pounds without a struggle.

The train was due to arrive at 8.45 and leave again at nine. It was a stopping service from Cardiff and there was no way the Hancocks, even with their resources, could put a man at every station between Cardiff and Merthyr. The only other option was to hide a man on the train itself, but Jonah Hancock had assured Pyke he wasn't about to imperil William's life.

They had reached the bottom of High Street. Ahead of them, across a stagnant stretch of water, was the railway station. Pyke studied the faces milling around in front of the building as the carriage juddered to a halt. It was twenty minutes to nine.

Jonah Hancock picked up the suitcase and thrust it into Pyke's hand. 'Back here at ten, then?'

'I don't need to check it's all there?'

'I counted it myself this morning.'

'Well, then.' The door swung open. Pyke looked first at Jonah and then at Cathy. 'Wish me luck.'

As he was alighting, Cathy touched him gently on the arm and whispered, 'Please bring my son back.'

Pyke entered the station through the main door, the suitcase in his left hand. Straight ahead was a book-stand and the ticket office. He followed one of the porters to the platform where the service from Cardiff was due to arrive, then stopped and had a look around. A man with a pale face and red-rimmed eyes shuffled past him, closely followed by a boy with a bow-legged gait and malnourished cheeks. Pyke's gaze shifted to a well-dressed woman who was carrying a small dog in her arms. He couldn't see Felix anywhere, but he didn't see any of Hancock's men lurking in the shadows either.

A crowd had gathered at one end of the platform and in the distance Pyke saw plumes of white steam rising up and heard the sharp iterations of the engine's pistons. The locomotive came into view and pulled into the station, crunching against the buffers, the carriages and trucks clanking together. Porters swarmed towards the first-class carriage. Pyke waited while the passengers disembarked, the trickle becoming a steady stream. Momentarily forgetting why he was there, Pyke studied their faces for any sign of Felix but once again his son wasn't among them. A newsboy walked by him, inadvertently knocking the suitcase, and his attention was wrenched back to the present.

He was keeping an eye out for his son but he was also being a policeman, looking for people who were acting suspiciously. Policemen always looked at the world in a different way, never trusting what they saw, never mistaking the apparent for the real. He thought about Frederick Shaw for some reason, the debacle in the warehouse. He had seen something on that occasion and fired his pistol, shouted a warning and then squeezed the trigger. He had trusted his eyes, his judgement, but both had been shown to be faulty. Nothing in the station was making him nervous. But could he trust his intuition?

Taking his time, he had another look around the building to make sure he wasn't being followed then started along the platform towards the front of the train where the first-class carriage was located. A porter appeared from one of the doors but Pyke strode past him, confident, as if he knew where he was going. He reached the first-class carriage and stopped. There was no one inside.

It was ten to nine and the first passengers for the service back to Cardiff were starting to appear. At the far end of the platform, Pyke heard someone announce the forthcoming departure. Yanking open the door, he climbed into the carriage. The luggage rack was directly in front of him. As expected, it was empty. Pyke put the suitcase down and decided to have a quick look inside. He tried one of the catches then realised it was locked. Jonah Hancock hadn't mentioned anything about a lock. Pyke jiggled it again, to no avail. With a little more time, he could have picked the lock, but looking up he saw the first of the first-class passengers pass by the window, heard the door swing open. Peering over the seat, Pyke studied the new arrival, but he didn't recognise him. Another passenger joined them, much older. He sat down and picked up his newspaper. Pyke shoved the suitcase into the luggage rack and waited. More doors opened and slammed shut.

You couldn't get from the standard-class to the first-class carriage while the train was moving. Pyke had already checked. Perhaps the man charged with collecting the money planned to join the train at the next station.

Reminding himself that this was not his concern, Pyke stepped out on to the platform. The porters' shouts were louder, the departure imminent; a handful of late arrivals hurried along the platform, clutching their possessions, then boarded the standard-class carriage. There were only two men in first class and neither of them had displayed any interest in the suitcase.

The shrill blast of the whistle cut through the air and without warning the engine and carriages clattered forward. Running alongside the first-class carriage, Pyke peered through the rough glassplate and saw that no one else had joined the train. He stopped, hands on hips, and took a moment to catch his breath.

As the train disappeared around the bend in the track, he checked the time. Five past nine. That gave him almost an hour to walk to the police station and still get back for ten.

It took Pyke fifteen minutes to get to the police station on Graham Street. This time, a different clerk was on duty, but as soon as Pyke asked whether his son had arrived, the man's face brightened.

'You're Detective-inspector Pyke?'

Pyke looked at the man, surprised. 'My son's arrived?' He had come to the conclusion that Felix hadn't travelled there after all.

'About an hour ago.'

'Can I see him?'

'He said he didn't want to stay here. Said he would take a room at the Southgate Hotel on High Street.'

High Street ran perpendicular to Graham Street. Pyke turned left, as he'd been told to, and saw the Southgate Hotel on the other side of the street. Not a salubrious place at all. It didn't seem like the kind of hotel his son would choose.

The entrance hall was a depressing spectacle, with peeling wallpaper and tallow rings on the ceiling. Pyke waited at the desk but no one came to meet him; the entire downstairs was deserted. He couldn't picture his son arriving at a place like this and wanting to stay. Why hadn't he just waited at the station-house? Perhaps this was all the lad felt he could afford and he'd wanted to assert his independence.

A narrow staircase corkscrewed up to the first floor. Pyke took the steps two at a time. A single lantern hung on the landing wall.

'Felix?' Pyke's voice echoed down the corridor. None of the rooms appeared to be occupied. Perhaps Felix had already left, tried somewhere else. Somewhere above, on the upper floor, he heard footsteps, floorboards creaking. Pyke called out again. 'Hello?'

Someone coughed. The sound came from a room at the other end of the passageway. Pyke moved towards it. Everything was quiet, eerily so. He heard the cough again and now he could see a weak shaft of light emerging from the room. 'Hello?' Pyke walked towards it, suddenly not feeling at all comfortable. 'Felix?'

He approached the partly open door, knocked twice and waited for a response. He heard footsteps behind him, on the landing. Turning, he saw a figure silhouetted against the half-light of the lantern.

'Do you run this place?'

Pyke took another step back along the landing, then saw the man raise what looked to be a blunderbuss.

He bolted back towards the half-open door but now the man who'd been coughing stepped on to the landing. John Wylde was grinning, a pistol in his hand. Pyke was trapped, with nowhere to go.

Wylde fired first, the blast lighting up the corridor, and deafening in the confined space. Pyke threw himself against one of the doors, felt the frame splinter. He fell into the room, but not quite in time. He knew he'd been hit but he didn't know how badly, although his whole left side was suddenly wet. He staggered to his feet, nothing else on his mind but survival. Wylde's accomplice stood in the doorway, his blunderbuss raised, about to fire. Running, Pyke hurled himself against the window and crashed through the glass just as the ball-shot from the heavy gun peppered the wall beside him. Moments later, he landed on his back, fell through the flat roof of the building below and found himself on the floor of what looked like the back of a shop. His mind went blank. He might even have passed out. What saved him was that Wylde and the other man had no clear shot from the window above.

When Pyke came around he tried to stand up. His legs wouldn't hold him, not at first. Touching the left side of his stomach, he felt the wetness and saw that his fingers had turned crimson. Finally on his feet, he looked around the storeroom and staggered towards the door. It hurt to move but at least the blood wasn't gushing from the wound. He reassured himself that it hadn't been a direct hit. Forcing open the door, Pyke stepped into the alley, and started to hobble away, trying not to think about the pain. Behind him, he could hear noises, screaming. Ahead was a dead end, so he kicked down one of the side doors and stepped into someone's backyard, then passed through the house. Out on the street, Pyke looked right and left, but he didn't see Wylde or the other man. He turned left and limped on for twenty yards. Behind him, the shouts were getting louder, closer. Someone's front door opened and Pyke lurched towards it, falling into the room and clutching his stomach. He heard a woman gasp and looked at her terrified face. 'Close the door,' he spluttered. She did as she was told, even though he found out later that she didn't speak English. Pyke rummaged in his pocket and produced one of the banknotes Jonah Hancock had given him.

'That's a hundred pounds.' He waited for the woman to take it.

A man had joined them. He barked something at Pyke in Welsh.

'Please help me.' Pyke gave them a pleading look and held out his hands. He didn't know whether they'd understood him or not.

The woman drew the curtains and Pyke felt his eyelids flutter.

EIGHTEEN

MONDAY, 1 FEBRUARY 1847
Tipperary Town, Co. Tipperary

The driver of a coal-cart dropped Knox in the middle of Tip Town at half-past nine the following morning, and from there it took him less than five minutes to find the barracks, the most imposing building in the town. It was a bitterly cold day, perhaps even colder than the previous one, and on the ride over from Dundrum they had passed another corpse slumped in the hedgerow. Knox had stared at the frostbitten landscape, and thought about Martha and James, whether they were awake yet, what the day held in store for them.

In the courtyard, Knox asked a soldier in uniform to direct him to the clerks' office. The soldier pointed to a door on the far side of the courtyard. Knox entered a long passageway and stopped outside the third door on the left-hand side, as he'd been instructed.

Knox explained to the clerk that he was trying to find his long-lost brother and that the only thing he knew about the man was he'd left home in the spring of 1825 and joined the army.

The clerk gave him a sympathetic smile. 'No word from him since?'

'I have no idea if he's even still alive.'

A silence settled between them, while the clerk considered how to proceed. 'Do you know which regiment he joined?'

'I'm afraid not.'

The man let out a pained sigh. 'You see, sir, there is no permanent regiment based here. The soldiers serve a period of time here, a year, sometimes longer, and then move on.'

'But you could find out which regiment was based here in the spring of that year?' Knox laid a five-shilling coin on the clerk's desk.

The clerk eyed it carefully but didn't pick it up. 'If I really *had* to, I suppose I could.'

'And if you were able to settle upon a regiment, there would be a record of all new recruits, I presume?'

'Somewhere, perhaps. Among all this paperwork. But as you can probably imagine I'm very busy this morning.'

Knox considered his rapidly shrinking purse and wondered whether this was just a case of throwing good money after bad. How much Indian corn could he buy with five shillings? With ten?

Rummaging around in his pocket, he produced another five-shilling coin and let the clerk see it before closing his fist around it.

The clerk looked around the small, dusty room. 'Why don't you come back in about an hour, sir? I'll see what I can do.'

As he left, Knox saw that the clerk was inspecting the coin he'd left on the desk.

An hour later, the clerk was sitting at his desk, a giant ledger book open in front of him. He beamed at Knox and even stood up and shook his hand.

'The Twenty-ninth Regiment was stationed here in the spring of 1825.' He patted the ledger. 'Fortunately for you, military men are assiduous record-keepers.'

'Do you have a list of new recruits?'

The clerk smiled and patted the book again. 'Your brother's name?'

'Johns.'

Carefully the clerk ran his finger down the list of names scribbled in black ink. He came to a halt about halfway down. 'John Johns. Date of birth, March tenth 1806. Forty years old now, nearly forty-one.'

'Is there any other information?'

The clerk looked puzzled. 'Such as?'

'Whether he's still part of the regiment? Or a date of discharge, perhaps?'

'The Twenty-ninth have long since moved on. We wouldn't have that information here. But I *do* happen to recall that this particular regiment was stationed in South Wales for a while. Got themselves tangled up in some nasty business in Newport about seven or eight years ago, had to turn their rifles on civilians.'

Knox thought about the letter sent by the son to the deceased while he was in Merthyr. That was in South Wales, wasn't it?

Frustrated, he paid the man another five shillings and retraced his steps to the town centre. There, he counted the coins left in his purse: one pound and eight shillings. The previous night's banquet was now a distant memory but he resisted the urge to spend any more of his money on food.

It took him the rest of the day, most of it spent waiting by the side of the road, to travel to Clonoulty.

Knox knew something was wrong the moment he saw Martha. A grim-faced maid had met him at the front door and led him through the house to a room at the back.

Martha's sleeves were rolled up, and her hair was pinned back. She didn't hug him. Instead, she said, 'It's James.' She looked pale and exhausted.

Knox felt as if he'd been kicked in the stomach. 'What's the matter?'

'He started to cry just after we left you, he wouldn't stop, and before we got here, the driver had to pull over and wait while I cleaned him up. There was shit everywhere. The night before last he was sick four times and now he's running a fever, poor little mite, wailing and sobbing. There's nothing I can do.' There were tears streaming down her face.

Knox went to comfort her but she pushed him away. 'Father Mackey's gone to fetch a doctor.'

'Can I see him?'

'He's sleeping now, first time in two days. I don't want you to wake him.'

'I just want to see him.'

'Later, Michael.' She tucked a strand of hair behind her ear. 'I know it's not fair of me to blame you but you weren't here.'

'This is my fault?'

'It was a terrible journey. James was in a state by the time we arrived here.'

'So what you're saying is our son got sick because we were evicted from our home?'

'No. Lord, I don't know. Listen to me. I haven't slept in two days, Michael. I blame myself. Of course I'm going to blame you as well.'

'If I could just see him . . .'

Martha's face reddened. 'I said I didn't want him woken. It's taken two, three days for you to get here and all of a sudden you're making demands.'

'You made it quite clear I wasn't welcome here, Martha. I wasn't needed. That Mackey's invitation didn't extend to me.'

'*I* needed you, Michael, but you weren't here. I needed you to hold me and tell me our son is going to get better.'

Knox stared at her, chastised and angry. She'd never spoken to him like this before.

'I'm here now, aren't I?'

Martha bit her lip and nodded, her eyes welling up. 'When the doctor arrives, he'll expect to be paid.'

'I have money.' Knox pulled out his purse and jangled the coins. He felt pathetic.

'And when that's all gone?'

'Whatever it takes, Martha. I'll walk on water, if I have to.'

That made her smile. 'What if it's too late? What if he's caught something and there's nothing we can do?'

Knox opened his arms and this time she allowed him to hug her.

Knox had always believed he was a good father, and since James had been born he'd tried never to raise his voice in his son's presence. He remembered what it had been like to hear his parents rowing, see his father raise his fists, trying to intervene and getting his eye cut or lip split in the process. Perhaps as a result, he'd always been careful to treat his wife and son with kindness and understanding. But as he watched his son from the doorway, the boy's tiny frame wrapped up in a blanket, Knox felt that he'd failed.

The doctor had been and gone, told them what they already knew – that James was gravely ill. He'd promised to return in the morning but hadn't said anything about his fee.

'I'm sorry about earlier.' Martha squeezed Knox's hand. 'Some of the things I said.'

Knox touched her forehead. 'You must be exhausted. Why don't you try to sleep? I'll wake you if there's any change.'

'I might do that.' She smiled bravely. 'You didn't tell me what you've been doing.'

'Another time.'

Martha nodded. Perhaps she understood why he didn't want to talk about it, didn't want another argument.

They heard a bang at the door and wondered whether the doctor had forgotten something. Then they heard voices, unfamiliar voices, and footsteps, determined ones. Mackey knocked first and then opened the door, his face pale.

'The police want to talk to Michael.'

Knox exchanged a wordless glance with Martha.

In the hallway, Sub-inspector Hastings was flanked by two constables, Morgan and O'Hanlon. Knox hadn't expected to see someone of Hastings' rank. The constables averted their eyes.

'How did you find me?'

Hastings looked at Martha. 'Your wife was seen in the village by one of our constables and word came back to us at Cashel. A man was posted outside the house.'

Knox nodded, tight-lipped. It was a small, often oppressive world: everyone knowing everyone else's business. But that didn't explain why they had been looking for him; or why a man of Hastings' rank had come all this way to see him.

The sub-inspector coughed. 'We'd like you to accompany us back to the barracks.'

Knox wasn't afraid, not any more. 'My son is very ill. I'm not leaving this house.'

Hastings faltered. 'I'm afraid I have my orders.'

Knox tried to think how his actions could have warranted such a reaction. 'I don't care if you've got orders from the Queen. I'm not leaving this house. I have to tend to my son.'

Hastings licked his lips, not sure how to proceed. Looking at the constables, he gathered his resolve. 'My orders are to bring you to the barracks. I'm authorised to use force, if that's what it takes.'

'Haven't you caused me enough agony? Didn't you hear what I said? My son's gravely ill.'

'I'm sorry about your son.' Hastings turned to O'Hanlon and

Morgan. Reluctantly they stepped forward and clasped their hands around his shoulders, one on either side. Knox tried to shake them off but they wouldn't let go. He hadn't spoken to any of his former colleagues since being dismissed but now it was clear that he was to be treated as an enemy. Knox felt his resistance wither; he would go with them because he had no choice.

'At least let me say goodbye to my wife and child.'

Hastings pursed his lips together and nodded. The constables let him go. Martha threw her arms around him.

'James will pull through, Michael. You'll see. We'll be here waiting for you.'

Knox felt the daguerreotypes, heavy in his coat pocket, and tried to remember what he'd done with the deceased's pistol and knife, where he'd put them. Then he remembered they were wrapped up in the blanket which he had left in the coal shed at the back of the house.

'Can I have a moment with my wife?'

Hastings and the two constables withdrew to the door but kept it open. Turning his back on them, Knox clasped his wife's hands and held them. 'Keep him safe. I'll be back as soon as I'm allowed.'

Martha let him hold her but she wouldn't look at him. 'I'm afraid, Michael. I'm afraid that our son won't make it.' She was shivering in his arms.

'We just have to be strong,' he muttered, trying to sound convincing.

NINETEEN

Pyke woke up and had no idea what time it was, whether it was day or night. He touched his wound, as gently as possible, gasping out loud from the pain now that the effect of the gin and laudanum had worn off. Looking down, he noticed that the blood was still fresh. Upstairs he could hear the family moving around. He would have died without their kindness, the fact they'd hidden him from Wylde and had fetched him what he'd needed: gin and laudanum for the pain, bandages and something to pick out the lumps of ball-shot. Pyke had imbibed the gin before going to work on the wound, and when he'd removed the last of the shot, he'd used a hot poker to close it. That had been the worst bit, the part that had caused him to scream with agony. Later, he'd slept and now he was awake. Awake and still alive. Peeling back the bloody bandages, he inspected the wound. It looked grim. At least there was no sign of infection, no gangrenous smell. He changed the bandages and then tried to sit up.

Pyke had offered five hundred pounds to the person who could bring Felix to him. He had made the offer to the family and told them to pass the word on to their friends, the people they trusted, but as yet no one had found him. Pyke hoped this meant Felix hadn't travelled to Merthyr after all, and he had already sent a message to Martin Jakes in Keynsham. What bothered him was the clerk's conviction, when he'd asked for his son at the station-house. Yes, Felix had arrived. Yes, he'd taken a room at the Southgate Hotel. Pyke had been set up, that much was clear. But who had given the orders? Wylde had been waiting to ambush him at the hotel, but how had he found out about Felix?

Pyke hadn't been a good father. He hadn't been there for Felix as often as he should have. His uncle, now deceased, had helped to bring up the boy. Pyke had spent too much time away from home. The lad had forgiven him but the scars were there for all to see. Pyke had driven him into the arms of the Church. He hauled himself into a sitting position, bolts of pain coursing up and down his left side, almost causing him to bite off his tongue. He had finished the laudanum hours earlier and there was no gin left either. Sinking back to a horizontal position, Pyke stared up at the ceiling, trying to work out how Wylde had found out about his role in the burglary or indeed whether this had been the reason for the ambush. His thoughts turned to the Hancock boy.

Pyke had heard nothing about him either. He had sent a message to the Castle, that he had delivered the suitcase, as requested. All being well, William Hancock had arrived back – in one piece – at eleven o'clock the previous morning. But what if the boy hadn't materialised? The Hancocks would be frantic and they would be blaming him.

Briefly his mind turned to Cathy, her soft, smooth skin, the way she'd yielded, dug her fingernails into his back.

When he woke up again, the family were downstairs, trying to go about their business. They were talking in Welsh. Noticing he was awake, Megan, the wife, knelt down next to him and touched his forehead. She had kind eyes. Smiling, she said something to John, her husband.

'Felix? My son?'

They understood that much. John shook his head, frowning.

Pyke wanted to ask them about the Hancocks, whether they'd heard anything about the boy, but he didn't think they'd understand him.

There was a bang on the door and Megan went over to the window to see who it was. She went to the door and opened it. Must be someone she knew, someone she trusted. Pyke listened. They spoke in Welsh. The woman at the door was agitated, excited even. The husband joined in the conversation, and then indicated to Pyke that he would go next door and fetch their neighbour, who spoke some English. Pyke could tell from the tone of their conversation that something was wrong.

The neighbour came and knelt down next to him. 'They've found a body in Post Office Field.'

'*Who?*' Pyke felt as if he had been winded and panic spilled through him, the news he hadn't wanted to hear.

'I don't know.'

'How far is Post Office Field?'

'From here? A few minutes.'

Pyke didn't have to think about it. He staggered to his feet, the pain now a welcome distraction.

A large crowd had built up near the entrance to Post Office Field, an acre of scrubland surrounded by houses. A constable Pyke didn't recognise was blocking the only route into the place.

Men and women were whispering to one another in a mix of Welsh and English, curious shopkeepers mingling with labourers from the ironworks.

The neighbour turned to him. 'A woman over there knows the man who found the body. He reckons it's a young boy.'

Pyke experienced a giddy surge of relief, and then guilt. His thoughts turned to Cathy; he wondered whether she'd heard the news. He heard someone say, 'Hancock.'

'It could be the master's son.' The neighbour was a Caedraw worker, a furnace-man. He was terrified by the notion.

Pyke imagined the scene, a handful of constables huddled over a corpse, frozen almost solid. He thought about the Hancocks, the worst news a family could receive, the rage and the grief, the devastation they would be feeling. It was the most heartbreaking thing that could happen to a parent, having to bury your child. Nothing would be the same again.

They heard the horses, the rattling of a harness, before they saw the brougham. It turned into the dead end from Victoria Street, the crowd clearing a path before it. It came to a halt, and the driver climbed down and opened the door. There was Jonah Hancock, but no sign of Cathy. Hancock took no notice of the crowd, his expression blank, the muscles of his face clenched tight. The constable let him through; they watched as he crossed the first part of the field.

Pyke reached inside his coat and touched his wound. There was fresh blood on his fingers. He could hardly feel the pain, though. Why had the kidnappers taken the boy's life?

The crowd had grown and a hushed reverence had come over them. Death was a regular occurrence for the poor but not for a family like the Hancocks.

Pyke's thoughts turned to Cathy. She would be distraught, inconsolable. He wanted to see her, comfort her, but he knew this was out of the question. Would the family blame him?

The crowd looked up and everyone was quiet: Jonah Hancock in the distance, carrying the body of his son. Someone next to Pyke began to sob, another joined in. Hancock was closer now, striding carefully, his son's legs and arms dangling down. Pyke watched his hard expression and wondered whether he could have managed such composure, such dignity, if the corpse had been Felix's.

Approaching the brougham, Hancock handed the body to the driver, then climbed into the carriage and reclaimed it. The door closed and moments later the brougham rattled off in the direction of Victoria Street.

As soon as the brougham had gone, the mood turned ugly, grief turning to anger. Later the neighbour explained that the people had been talking about the police search of Bathesda Gardens and Quarry Row. Hadn't they been looking for a child? A few people had put two and two together and had come up with an answer. An Irish mob had killed the Hancock boy. Most of the people there worked, or knew someone who worked, at Caedraw, and it was as if an outsider had come into their community and killed one of their own. No one seemed to like Jonah Hancock but he was the ironmaster and deserved their loyalty.

By the time Pyke left, some of the crowd were shouting for vengeance.

That night, still with no word from Felix, Pyke lay in the downstairs room, imagining the worst. Perhaps it had been seeing William Hancock's corpse, seeing a father carry his dead son.

John and the neighbour had paid one of the police constables a considerable sum of money. The man had told them, *reassured* them, *promised* them, that Felix wasn't being held in the station-house, and had never been there. Pyke had given them a physical description of the clerk who'd directed him to the Southgate Hotel. They were told that the man hadn't shown up for work. Asked for his home address, the constable had given it to them, but when they had gone there to look for him, they found that the room had been vacated.

Later in the night, Pyke heard the rioting and thought about Felix, possibly out there, alone in a strange country. Pyke could almost feel the hatred, the resentment, the ugliness vibrating in the air. Dosed up on laudanum, he drifted in and out of consciousness, asleep when awake and awake when asleep; shapes, faces, memories moving in and out of focus, their meaning just beyond his reach.

In the morning, the family was told that a mob of more than two hundred, mostly from the Caedraw ironworks, had marched on Quarry Row and Bathesda Gardens. Taken by surprise, the police had been unable to stop them from setting light to the houses. No one seemed to know how widespread the rioting had been but people had died.

Soldiers from the barracks were now patrolling the streets and reinforcements had been summoned from Brecon.

The disturbances had spread to the works themselves, Caedraw *and* Morlais. Someone reported that all of the blast furnaces had gone quiet, the first time this had happened since the strike.

Shops had been attacked and ransacked; rubble and broken glass littered the streets. The town centre was deserted. Two had died. Five had died. Ten had died. More. No one knew. Even in the house, the air smelled of charred wood.

The husband had procured a horse and cart and Pyke had driven to the Castle, each bump, each rut, causing him to wince. The entrance was blocked and Jenkins, one of the agents, was giving orders to two men armed with rifles. Pyke waited for Jenkins to leave and then hobbled up to one of the guards. Thrusting an envelope into the man's hand, he instructed the man to deliver it at once to Catherine Hancock. The guard asked who he was but Pyke turned without answering, and limped back to the horse and cart.

'All kinds of rumours, place is wild with 'em,' the neighbour said, grim-faced.

The husband was sullen and wouldn't look at Pyke. They were standing across from each other in the downstairs room.

'Such as?'

'A man who worked for the Hancocks made off with twenty thousand, meant to be for the kidnappers.'

Pyke assimilated this news without reacting. So the kidnappers hadn't received the money; and the Hancocks blamed him. Understandable in light of his 'disappearance'. He thought again about Cathy, whether she'd got his letter, what she must be going through.

'Apparently the man in question is a policeman from London.'

John tugged the neighbour's sleeve, said something in Welsh.

'He wants to know where your money's from,' the neighbour said, by way of translation.

Pyke understood now that they thought he was the one who'd stolen from the Hancocks. They were frightened, feeling let down. He looked at the neighbour. 'Tell him, on the life of my own son, I did not steal any money, nor have I broken the law in any way, shape or form.'

The neighbour stared at him, trying to work out whether or not to believe him. 'You didn't answer the question.'

'Hancock paid me what he'd originally promised.'

'To negotiate the safe return of his son?'

Pyke nodded. He could see how bad it looked.

The neighbour and John exchanged a few words in Welsh. The former was about to translate, for Pyke's benefit, when the noise of horses' hoofs interrupted their conversation. A carriage pulled up outside one of the houses farther up the street, a place Pyke knew to be empty. It was the address given on the note he'd left at the Castle for Cathy. At the window, they watched as four men leapt out of the carriage, smashed through the door with crowbars and stormed into the tiny house. About a minute later, they emerged, clearly agitated, not sure what to do next.

'Those men were sent by Jonah Hancock.' Pyke turned to the neighbour. 'They're looking for me. If you really think I had something to do with the Hancock boy's death, or I stole the ransom money, I won't stop you from going out there and telling them where I am.'

The neighbour translated and the two men discussed what to do, their eyes darting between Pyke and the activity outside. As they talked Pyke thought about the presence of Hancock's men and what it indicated – either that Cathy had read his note and passed it on to her husband or that his letter had been delivered directly to Jonah Hancock.

It also told him that the Hancocks were baying for his blood. The police would be looking for him, too.

John spoke. The neighbour waited for him to finish then turned to Pyke. 'He says you can stay – for the time being.'

Pyke felt another bolt of pain streak up one side of his body. He took a breath and had to steady himself against the wall. In other circumstances, he would have been relieved by this offer, but all he could think about now was his son.

TWENTY

In the police wagon, the journey to Cashel took a little under two hours. It was a bumpy, uncomfortable ride made worse by the silence, the two constables not wanting to acknowledge Knox or too afraid to say anything in Hastings' presence. For his part, the sub-inspector was in a foul mood and refused to tell Knox why he'd been summoned back to the barracks. Knox was too worried about his son to care about his own predicament. Cornwallis had taken his post and his home. What else could they do to him now? Lock him up? Knox tried to think what they might be able to use against him. In his pocket, he felt the two copperplates rattling around and realised his mistake. If they threw him in a cell, they would search him and find the plates. It was difficult not to be overwhelmed by the injustice of it all.

At the barracks, he was led into the front of the building by O'Hanlon and Morgan, but they hadn't handcuffed him and they didn't take him to the cells. Instead, they led him upstairs and waited with him in the corridor while the sub-inspector went into his office. Knox heard voices. Then the door opened and he was beckoned inside.

To his surprise, and despite the lateness of the hour, the County Inspector was there, together with a man Knox didn't recognise.

'You know the County Inspector, of course,' Hastings said, once he'd settled into his chair behind the desk. He turned to the stranger. 'This is Benedict Pierce, the Assistant Commissioner of the Metropolitan Police.'

Pierce nodded at him and even tried to smile. He was a neat, well-groomed man in his late forties, with short dark hair, a cleanly shaven chin and small, quick eyes.

'The Assistant Commissioner has made the arduous journey from London to look into your unsubstantiated claim that the man found on the estate in Dundrum was one of his men, Detective-inspector Pyke.'

Knox felt his chest tighten. 'I was given the task of investigating this murder, sir,' he said to Pierce. 'I'm a lowly constable with no experience of such matters. I was told I could have four days and it was made clear that I was not to do much. Get rid of the body and let the whole thing drop . . .'

'That's a deuced lie, sir,' Hastings spluttered, almost knocking over the inkwell on his desk, 'and I'll ask you not to repeat it in such august company.'

'When it became clear I hadn't followed these orders,' Knox said, ignoring Hastings, 'and after it was discovered I'd identified the dead man and contacted his son in Somerset, I was called in here and dismissed.'

'You were dismissed, as you put it, for aiding and abetting the escape of a suspected thief, and I'll remind you that such an action could land you in prison, if we were inclined to prosecute.'

The Englishman held up his hand. 'I'm not here to judge the rights and wrongs of your disciplinary procedures. I just want to know how and why this gentleman came to believe that the corpse was that of one of my men.'

Knox tried to assess whether Pierce would be sympathetic to what he had to say.

'Perhaps you could tell me about your investigation,' Pierce said, looking directly at him.

Knox did as he'd been asked and described each stage of his inquiry. He was as frank as he felt he could be, but he didn't mention his suspicion that Cornwallis had known the dead man. He also didn't say anything about the daguerreotypes.

'So do you still have the letters you found in the lodging house – the ones written by Pyke's son?' Pierce said, once Knox had finished.

'I'm afraid not. I was made to give them up to Lord Cornwallis.'

'What's his interest in the letters?' Pierce asked, curious now.

Hastings and the County Inspector had suddenly gone very quiet.

'I don't know. You'll have to ask him,' Knox said, gesturing at Hastings.

Pierce ignored the insinuation. 'And the pistol and knife you found there?'

'I still have them. I left them at Father Mackey's house in Clonoulty.'

Pierce looked over at the County Inspector. 'I will need to inspect them, of course.'

'I fear you've come all this way for nothing,' Hastings said. 'I mean, there's no hard evidence that the deceased was one of your men. By his own admission, Constable Knox is not the finest investigator in the land.'

Pierce considered this. He seemed angry. 'I could, of course, order the exhumation of the body . . .'

Hastings shook his head warily. 'It was buried with countless others in a pit at the workhouse. There's no way you'd be able to tell any of them apart now due to the decomposition.'

'In any case,' the County Inspector said, 'as I understand it, we have no idea whether this man, Pyke, even travelled to Ireland . . .'

Knox coughed. 'It's my guess he was looking for someone called John Johns. Johns was born in this part of the world but he joined the army and ended up in Wales. I might not be the finest investigator in the land but I do know that Pyke had come here from Merthyr and he'd gone to Wales to investigate the kidnapping of a child.' Knox could see straight away that he'd scored a hit. Hastings and the County Inspector could see this too and went quiet.

'It would seem,' Pierce said, turning to Hastings, 'that your former employee is not the dim-witted investigator you perhaps believed him to be.'

The sub-inspector reddened but said nothing. Pierce gestured for Knox to continue.

'I knew I had to identify the victim,' he said, deciding to play what was his strongest card. 'But I also knew that, untreated, the corpse would quickly decompose beyond recognition. I put it to Sub-inspector Hastings that we should either pay someone to embalm it or arrange for a daguerreotype image to be fixed on a copperplate.'

Pierce glanced across at Hastings, scowling. 'I'm assuming your suggestions fell on deaf ears.'

'That's unfair, sir,' Hastings blustered.

Pierce cut him off. 'Pity your ideas weren't taken up.'

Knox saw a faint glimmer of hope. 'The sub-inspector made his position clear. But I chose not to listen to him.' He waited for the implications of what he'd just said to sink in.

Pierce sat forward. The atmosphere in the room had changed in an instant. 'Did I hear you right?' the Englishman asked.

'I know a shopkeeper who has an interest in daguerreotypes and I asked him to help me. He agreed. Of course, I had to pay him out of my own pocket.'

'And did he capture an image of the dead man?'

Knox nodded. 'Two, in fact. It's amazing how good – how *clear* – the images are.' He was almost enjoying himself now.

'Do you still have them?' There was wariness in Pierce's tone now. This revelation had thrown him too.

'Yes.'

'Where are they?'

'Here.'

'Here? *Now?*' Pierce seemed almost panicked by this notion.

Knox reached into his pocket and retrieved both copperplates.

Pierce eyed him carefully. 'I presume this shopkeeper will corroborate your story?'

'I expect so.' Knox glanced over at Hastings. 'He doesn't have any reason to lie.'

'Do you think I could see the daguerreotypes, please?' Pierce held out his hand.

Knox passed them to him and watched as Pierce, hands trembling, inspected the images. His expression remained inscrutable.

Pierce then passed the daguerreotypes to the County Inspector. 'I have known Detective-inspector Pyke for the best part of twenty-five years. I wouldn't say we were friends and I might even confess that I've never cared for the man, although he is undoubtedly a fine detective.'

Knox tried to read some kind of inference into this but couldn't.

'Perhaps I should say he *was* a fine detective.'

Knox stared at him, felt his heart skip a beat. 'Was?'

'It would seem that my journey over here has not been in vain.' There was a curious smile on his lips.

'It *is* Detective-inspector Pyke, then?'

'As I said, I've known Pyke for half my life and I can say without a shadow of a doubt that man in the picture is him.'

Pierce turned to Hastings and the County Inspector. 'It would seem that one of my detectives was murdered in your jurisdiction. I would like to know what steps you have taken to find and apprehend the guilty party, sir, aside from handing over the inquiry to a constable with no experience of these matters.'

Flustered, the County Inspector looked over at Hastings, spectacles perched on the end of his nose.

'*Well?*'

'I assumed – wrongly, as it turned out – that the deceased was a vagrant, a poacher . . .'

'That's what Lord Cornwallis told you to assume,' Knox said, then to Pierce, 'Cornwallis also wanted me to investigate the murder. That way, he supposed, nothing would come to light. He assumed he could intimidate me. When his Lordship realised what I'd done, that I'd betrayed his trust, he made sure I lost my job here at the constabulary and arranged to have me evicted from my home.'

Pierce regarded Knox for a moment. 'These are very serious accusations. But I can't see that it is in anyone's interest for these matters to be aired in public. As such, I'd like to propose that I work with Constable Knox to have another look at the murder and bring the affair to a more satisfactory conclusion.'

Constable Knox. Pierce had just referred to him as *Constable* Knox. 'Does that mean I've been reinstated?'

'You should remember that Knox was dismissed for an entirely separate, and highly grievous, incident.' This time it was the County Inspector who'd spoken.

'Indeed,' said Pierce, 'but *you* should remember, sir, that gross procedural irregularities have been committed by all parties, including yourself.'

Knox felt light-headed. Suddenly his future seemed much less bleak. But almost at once, he had another far less palatable thought. What would happen when Pierce returned to England? Would Hastings honour his commitment to give him back his job? The man had been humiliated and Knox knew just how dangerous a wounded beast could be.

'Far be it for me to be awkward, sir, but it would be remiss of me not to ask under what or whose jurisdiction you intend to conduct this investigation?' The County Inspector looked at Pierce.

'I wouldn't advise you to make life any more difficult for yourself than it already is,' Pierce replied.

The County Inspector and Hastings fell silent. It was clear that Pierce had won this particular skirmish.

'One of my best detectives has been killed. The fact that I didn't like the man is not the issue here. One can't simply murder a policeman and expect to get away with it.'

The County Inspector muttered, 'Of course, *of course.*' But the strain on his face was evident.

'From what I understand, you've been considerably inconvenienced as a result of your investigation,' Pierce said to Knox. Then he turned to Hastings. 'I'd like to propose that Constable Knox be recompensed to the tune of, let's say, ten pounds for the time being? That should be enough to get him back on his feet.'

Knox's thoughts now turned to his fever-stricken son. 'I will need to be driven back to Clonoulty tonight.'

'That shouldn't be a problem.' Pierce raised his eyebrows. 'Should it, Sub-inspector Hastings?'

'Not at all,' Hastings said. He looked pale and beaten.

'But you're to report to the barracks first thing tomorrow morning. I want to get to the bottom of this business before I leave.'

Outside, as the carriage was being prepared, Pierce sidled up to him. 'I'm sorry to hear about your son's illness. Please pass on my best wishes to him, and your wife.'

Knox nodded. 'Thank you for what you did in there.'

The Englishman acknowledged his gratitude but didn't speak for a few moments. 'Why do you think this murder has unsettled them so much?'

'I don't know but if I had to wager, I'd say it has something to do with this man, Johns.'

Pierce agreed. 'You were right, by the way. Johns lives, or rather lived, in Merthyr Tydfil.'

'And something brought him over here?'

They waited while the horses were led out of the stables. 'How much do you know about what happened in Merthyr?'

'Nothing, really. Only what was mentioned in the letter.'

'Which was?'

'That the deceased had gone there to investigate the kidnapping of a child.'

The Englishman stared up at the cloudless sky. 'You might have read about it in the newspaper. Something went very wrong and the child was killed.'

Knox thought about his own predicament. 'You think it had something to do with Pyke coming over here?'

'I think Pyke followed Johns – and a magistrate called Sir Clancy Smyth. He's another Tipperary man.'

'So was Johns involved in the kidnapping?'

'I don't know. I'm guessing Pyke blamed him for what happened afterwards. After the boy was found dead.'

'And what *did* happen?'

Pierce didn't answer right away. 'You know the letter you sent to Pyke's son, Felix, informing him of his father's death? He never got it.'

'Why not?'

'Because Felix had gone to Merthyr to see his father.'

'What about when he returned to Somerset?'

Pierce gave him a strange stare. 'You really don't know, do you?'

'No, I don't.'

'He never returned to Somerset.'

TWENTY-ONE

He entered the old courthouse via the back door, which was unlocked. Inside the air smelled fetid and stale, and nothing moved. The only sound was the wooden shutters rattling against their jambs. Pyke stood at the bottom of the stairs and called out, 'Hello,' but no one answered. Sir Clancy Smyth had not been seen in Merthyr for a number of days, at least according to Superintendent Jones, who'd shared this information with John, the man who'd shielded Pyke from both the police and Hancock's emissaries.

Pausing to catch his breath, Pyke touched his wound and winced. He could walk unaided, albeit with a pronounced limp and considerable pain, but it was slow work and his recovery would be long and arduous. None of this concerned him, though, not compared to his desire to find Felix or determine once and for all that he was safe and hadn't travelled to Merthyr in the first place. Pyke had written to Jakes in Somerset and was still waiting for a reply. In the meantime he'd scoured the town for his son. He had even tried to sneak into the Castle to speak to the Hancocks, but the grounds had been too heavily patrolled and, as he had later found out, the entire family, including Cathy, had now left Merthyr, having buried William alongside their deceased daughter at the Vaynor cemetery. They were said to be mourning in private at their family estate in Hampshire. From what Pyke had heard, the police were still looking for him in connection with the kidnapping and therefore believed he might have been involved. Pyke wasn't concerned what the police – or the Hancocks – thought of him, but it bothered him that Cathy might think that he had knowingly put her son's life in danger.

Pyke ascended the staircase, listening for sounds above him, but there was nothing except the creaking of floorboards under his feet. To lose one child to illness must be hard enough, but to lose another? Pyke couldn't comprehend her grief. Would William's death have brought her closer to her husband? It was always possible, he supposed. They could both blame him – for running off with the money and letting their beloved son perish at the hands of his vengeful kidnappers – but to Pyke, this explanation rang hollow. He still had no idea what had happened, but he didn't see how it would profit the kidnappers to execute the lad in cold blood, even if they hadn't actually received the ransom money. Why not just try again? Why murder the boy and throw away any chance of getting the twenty thousand? Pyke also didn't know what had happened to the suitcase he'd left on the train departing for Cardiff.

On the landing Pyke paused again. Smyth had lived in this building for – what? – ten years, before moving to a bigger pile a couple of miles south of the town. The decor was dated and the wallpaper peeling. It certainly wasn't a place to inspire envy in others, to show off the owner's wealth and social standing. Instead it was the residence of a man who had fallen on hard times, where nothing had been attended to for years and where neglect was visible everywhere you looked; the old courthouse was no longer a functioning seat of law and the entire building conjured an air of decay.

Pyke had expected there to be servants or at least an ancient retainer, someone to keep the place from total rack and ruin, but the upstairs, like the downstairs, appeared to be entirely deserted. It was true that someone had hastily thrown white sheets over some of the furniture, but this didn't explain where Smyth was or where he had gone. As chief magistrate, would he really have cut and run at the time when the town needed him most? When riots and rioters had necessitated calling in the army? Smyth had presented himself as someone who loved the town, despite its flaws.

Outside, a cart clanked passed the building and farther down the street he could hear a dog barking. The army had re-established control of the town and the streets were more or less empty. Still, the damage to property was extensive and people had been killed – Pyke didn't know how many. Workers from Caedraw and Morlais had turned on one another, but mostly the violence had been sectarian, Welsh against Irish, Protestant against Catholic. Pyke had witnessed the aftermath: shops destroyed, churches burned to the ground, homes ransacked.

He tried the first door off the landing, peered into the gloomy room. It was a study of sorts and like the rest of the building it was unoccupied.

'Smyth?' His voice echoed off the walls.

The next door he tried was a bedroom; the curtains were drawn but a few cracks of light seeped in around the edges. Pyke saw the dresser first and caught a glimpse of the bed in the looking glass. Feet on the bed. Quickly he crossed the room and tore back the curtains, let the daylight flood in; he turned and saw a figure sprawled on top of the bed, fully dressed. It took his eyes a few moments to adjust to the light; blinking, he moved towards the figure, panic rising in his chest. Standing over the bed, Pyke stared down, open-mouthed, at Felix.

A hot spike of bile spewed from his mouth. Instinctively he reached out and shook the boy; his son's skin was as cold and stiff as marble. At once he knew; he didn't need to check for a heartbeat. There wouldn't be one. Felix had been dead for a while, at least a day. The body didn't even look like his son; the cheeks were pale and wax-like, the eyes like those of a dead fish. Pyke opened his mouth and fell to his knees, but what came out was more of a strangled cry than a scream. His son was dead; Felix, dead. He could see the truth of the words but he couldn't accept them, accept that Felix would never walk or smile or talk or argue with him ever again. Pyke fell on top of his son, enveloped his body in his arms, his cry becoming a sob, and he imagined just for a moment that he was dreaming, that none of this had actually happened. But Felix was real, his son's corpse was really in his arms, and then it struck him, the finality of it, that Felix wasn't ever coming back.

Numb and sobbing, Pyke lay on top of Felix's lifeless body, hugging it, hugging *him*, no longer sure how long he had been there, time a blur. This was the moment he had been dreading ever since Felix was born, that his son would die first, that he would have to bury the lad and live the rest of his life knowing that he had somehow let Felix down; that he had, wittingly or otherwise, caused his son's death, either through neglect or as an unintended consequence of the way he lived his life, the kind of universe he existed in, a sordid, violent world in which life was cheap.

A while later, Pyke laid Felix down on the bed. How had the lad died? Pyke's mind was working like a policeman's, almost in spite of himself. There was no blood, no obvious wounds. Had he died on the bed or had someone carried him there? It took Pyke five minutes to remove Felix's clothes, the body limp and pathetic on the bedcovers. There was bruising around the neck but not the kind that would indicate the boy had been strangled. The room continued to spin around Pyke, all of it unreal, the fact that he was in Merthyr, far from home, staring down at his beloved son's naked corpse. Pyke had long since reached the conclusion that God was little more than a fancy but Felix had given over his life to the Church and this was how he had been repaid. Hands still trembling, Pyke dressed Felix again, as best he could.

Briefly his thoughts turned to his long-deceased wife, Emily, and the day she'd given birth to Felix. He was aware of the fact that he, the most unworthy one, had outlived them both, and was now totally alone. He felt his legs buckle, and had to take a few deep breaths, the physicality of his pain almost too much to bear. Again he stared down at his son's corpse and realised that he was still crying, tears that were hot and salty and full of such utter desolation that he wanted nothing more than to curl up next to the lad and take a knife to his own wrists, to let the blood seep out of his wounds until he drifted out of consciousness.

PART III

*

Requiem –

n. a song or hymn of mourning composed or
performed as a memorial for a dead person

TWENTY-TWO

It was Sunday morning and Market Square was deserted, just a few soldiers standing outside a tent, blowing into their hands to keep themselves warm. Everyone else was at church or at home. The previous night had been quiet, with hardly anyone on the streets. The violence had dissipated, the need for retribution giving way to collective revulsion.

The wind was blowing off the mountain, an easterly blast that rippled the tops of the puddles. Next to the police station-house was a grocer's and farther along was the undertaker where, two weeks earlier, Pyke had taken his son's corpse. He told them to preserve it as best they could, and make a coffin, so that he could accompany his beloved son back to London and bury him in Bunhill Fields next to his uncle. It was hard to remember everything through the fog of grief, a pain so unbearable that Pyke had thought, more than once, about turning his pistol on himself. Each morning, when he woke up, there it was, a canker that made it difficult for him even to move. He had wept during the funeral, a short service attended by a handful of people, but not since, as though a veil had come down, shielding him from his grief. Martin Jakes had wanted to bury Felix at Keynsham but Pyke had refused to sanction a Christian burial even though it was what Felix would have wanted. There was no way Pyke could listen to Christian homilies about God and the afterlife. Jakes had come to the funeral in London because he was a good man and he had loved Felix, but they hadn't spoken after the ceremony.

Pyke had been waiting on Graham Street for two hours and he was finally rewarded for his patience when Superintendent Jones emerged from the station-house and headed in Pyke's direction.

Jones didn't notice him until Pyke fell in beside him. 'I heard you have John Wylde in custody. I need to see him.'

It took Jones a few seconds to realise who was standing next to him. '*Pyke.*' He didn't seem to believe Pyke was there.

'I want to see Wylde.'

'I didn't think we'd see you again, at least not here, not after what you did.' Jones glanced nervously up and down the street.

Pyke didn't respond immediately but it confirmed that people still assumed he'd taken the twenty thousand pounds and left the Hancock boy to his fate.

'*What I did?*'

Jones shook his head. His brow was beaded with sweat, despite the cold.

'I was shot.'

'Shot?'

'By Wylde.'

Jones regarded him carefully but said nothing.

'I was told by one of your clerks, Jim Massey, that my son had arrived and taken a room at the Southgate Hotel. I went to meet him. Wylde and his men were waiting there to ambush me.'

'Massey's dead.'

'I know.'

Ostensibly he had been another victim of the violence that had briefly spiralled out of control. His body had been found in Glebe town two weeks earlier.

'Do you want to know what I think?' Pyke looked up at the snow-covered mountain. 'If they'd killed me, buried me in an unmarked pit, it would have been easy to blame me for running away with the ransom money.'

'Public opinion has tried you in your absence and found you guilty.'

'I didn't come back here to defend myself.'

'Where have you been?' Jones shot him a sceptical look. 'Apart from recovering from your so-called pistol wound?'

Pyke unbuttoned his greatcoat, peeled back his frock-coat, and pulled up his shirt, to expose the scar, which was still raw. 'Satisfied?'

'If you didn't steal the twenty thousand, why wait so long to come forward?'

'I had to go back to London.' Pyke hesitated, trying to decide whether or not to tell him the truth. 'I went home to bury my son.'

Just saying the words made Pyke wince. He had come back to Wales and now all he felt was the crushing sense of his own failure. Whereas once upon a time he'd trusted in his ability to turn any situation to his advantage, now he realised how impotent he really was and how little he could determine his own fate. Felix was dead; so was William Hancock. Many others had been killed in the rioting – and for what? The blast furnaces were still burning. And when it was all over the dead would be forgotten about by everyone except their close family. And the town would still be in the grip of men like the Hancocks and Josiah Webb.

Jones hadn't known about Pyke's son. No one had known.

'I'm sorry.' Jones' concern appeared genuine. 'How did he die?'

'I don't know.' Closer inspection had revealed bruises on his hands, neck and chest, but Pyke still had no idea how Felix had sustained his injuries.

'Where did you find him?'

'The old courthouse.' Pyke paused, let the implications of this information sink in. 'In one of the upstairs rooms. Someone had laid him out on the bed.'

'The old courthouse?' Jones shook his head. 'Sir Clancy hasn't been seen for two or three weeks.'

Making the obvious connection between the courthouse and Smyth, just as Pyke had done.

'I went to his house, Blenheim, down in the valley. His butler told me Smyth has left for Ireland.'

'He never told me he was going.' Jones gestured towards the soldiers huddled outside their tent. 'Sir Clancy abandoned the town to the soldiers. Now a captain called Kent is in charge. We weren't able to keep a lid on things. Kent's taking orders directly from Sir Josiah Webb.'

Pyke didn't know for sure whether Smyth knew about, or had been responsible for, his son's death, but he had fled the town suddenly without revealing his plans to anyone; and that, to Pyke at least, indicated a troubled state of mind.

'I need to know what happened to my son.' It was why he'd

travelled back to Merthyr and was the only thing that got him out of bed in the morning.

Jones nodded, the suspicion returning to his eyes. 'I bet Jonah Hancock feels the same way.'

'What happened to his son, to mine, it's part of the same thing.'

'And you think John Wylde has the answers you need?'

'There's only one way to find out.'

Wylde was sitting on the floor of his cell, back against the wall, arms curled around his knees. His wounded hand was swaddled in a bandage.

After the door had swung open, Pyke entered the cell, closely followed by Jones. The bully glanced up, saw who it was, and his upper body stiffened, although there was nowhere for him to go.

'Who gave the order to assassinate me?' Pyke could feel the anger building inside him, a knotted ball in the pit of his stomach which was hard to distinguish from his grief.

He listened while Jones translated but the superintendent's words made no impression on the bully. When he didn't answer, Pyke said, 'Who told you to go to the Southgate Hotel?' Again Jones translated but received no response.

This time Pyke went across and knelt down next to Wylde, almost gagging from the smell of him. Before Wylde could react, Pyke grabbed his bandaged hand and squeezed it hard. A sickening yell echoed around the tiny room.

'I want to know how you knew that I was going to turn up at the Southgate Hotel.'

Pyke didn't expect Wylde to answer but almost immediately the bully looked at Jones and rattled off a few sentences.

'He says he received an anonymous letter telling him you would be there,' Jones said.

Pyke regarded Wylde, trying to anticipate what the man would say next. 'And you just decided to go there and kill me?'

Wylde looked at him, sullen, and barked a few words at Jones, then held up his bandaged hand.

'He says he knows it was you who shot off his hand and then robbed him.'

'Who told him that?' Pyke knelt down again and this time hit Wylde around the face. 'Who?'

This time the bully didn't need a translation.

'The same letter.'

Standing up, Pyke turned to Jones. 'He's lying. He knows who gave the orders.'

Jones glanced down at the prisoner, suddenly uneasy. 'Is he telling the truth? *Was* it you who shot him?'

Ignoring Jones, Pyke reached down and grabbed Wylde's throat, pressed him against the wall. '*Who?*' But he hadn't counted on the bully's strength, his speed, and didn't react quickly enough. Wylde lunged, his mouth open like a rabid dog, and bit Pyke on the hand. Pyke gouged his thumb into the bully's eye. Wylde's jaw went slack and as Pyke pulled out his thumb, wet with blood, the bully began to convulse. But Pyke hadn't finished. Instead he felt his fingers around Wylde's throat and he kept on squeezing, shouting at Wylde to tell him about his son, anger and grief pouring out of him until he was hardly aware of what he was doing.

'Christ Almighty. What kind of monster are you?' Jones threw himself on top of Pyke and managed to pull him off Wylde. He was panting, shocked.

But Pyke wasn't concerned by Jones' moral righteousness. All he could think of was his dead son and the guilt that was growing inside him like a tumour.

It took him an hour to walk from Market Square to Morlais House, a mostly uphill trudge along the Pennydarren Road. When he presented himself at the front door, the butler led him through to the drawing room. Pyke had told the man his name and even though he'd not met Sir Josiah Webb, the ironmaster seemed to know who he was and shook his hand, as if Pyke had come there at Webb's invitation.

Webb was a robust, rosy-cheeked man in his fifties, with snow-white hair and a full, almost portly figure. In other circumstances, he might have struck Pyke as an almost grandfatherly character but he had heard that Webb was every bit as ruthless as Zephaniah Hancock.

There was an oil painting of two young boys on one of the walls, perhaps Webb's sons. It made Pyke think about his own situation; that he would never see Felix marry, never know what it was like to have grandchildren. Briefly Pyke's thoughts returned to the burial ceremony, not one reference to God or Jesus, a decision borne of his own guilt and rage and one that didn't reflect the decisions Felix had made during his brief life. Pyke had put a notice in *The Times* and had made a point of writing to the people who'd known his son. He hadn't wanted to be secretive about the ceremony because Felix had done nothing wrong. If Pyke was ashamed of anything, it was the world that *he* had chosen to inhabit, a base world where a young man's life could be sacrificed for no reason. But now Pyke saw Jakes had been right; the service should have been a Christian one. It was what Felix would have wanted. Maybe he would rectify his mistake when all of this was finished.

'I've been hoping we might have this conversation, Detective-inspector,' Webb said.

Pyke tried to clear his mind, focus on the task at hand. Somehow it was jarring, to be addressed by his title. He no longer thought of himself as a policeman. The title, the sanction, the law itself: all of it was irrelevant. He knew he would never go back to his old position. He had said as much to Jack Whicher, one of his detective-sergeants, who'd seen the notice in the newspaper and attended the ceremony.

'You may feel differently later,' Whicher had said.

'That's just it. I don't feel anything.' He had been about to say something else when he remembered that Whicher too had lost a son.

'Pierce also saw the notice. I'm surprised he's not here. He's demanded that you return to Scotland Yard at once.'

'Pierce knows he wouldn't be welcome here.' Pyke had paused, looked up at the winter sky. 'He's read about the rioting?'

'And the death of the industrialist's son.'

Pyke had known his superiors would find out about the carnage sooner or later but now no longer cared. 'I'm going back to Wales.'

'Look, Pyke, Pierce knows that I'm close to you and he told me to tell you there will be no immunity from prosecution.'

Pyke hadn't expected to be treated any differently but the barely concealed threat hardly registered.

Webb's throaty cough brought him back to the present. 'I heard this wild rumour, that you had absconded with the ransom money.'

'Not true. If I had taken the money, why would I bother coming back to this godforsaken town?'

Webb considered this, his lips pursed together.

'I was shot by John Wylde. Maybe you've heard of him. He calls himself the emperor of China.'

'Wylde? The name's familiar. If I'm not mistaken, I believe my friends up at the Castle formed an acquaintance with him a few years ago, used him to break a strike.'

Pyke nodded. He wasn't surprised that a man like Webb knew such things. 'I think someone paid him to assassinate me.'

'What a terrible business,' Webb said, shaking his head. 'Then again there has been so much brute ugliness over these past few weeks I hardly recognise this town.'

Pyke strode across to the window and looked out at the small courtyard and garden. 'I understand you've been forced to halt production at the Morlais works.'

'Temporarily, I hope. Now that the soldiers have restored order, I expect to be back in business in a day or two. To be perfectly frank, my future depends on it.' Webb tried to laugh but there was tension in his eyes.

'I'm told you're close to Captain Kent, the man who's billeting at the barracks and is in charge of the soldiers.'

'Who told you that?'

Pyke opted to ignore the question. 'Does that mean you're co-ordinating the clean-up effort?'

'Kent's his own man but it's true that I've made my wishes known to him.' Webb was clearly uncomfortable with the line of questioning.

They stared at one another for a moment. 'Why did you have to close the works?' Pyke said, finally. Earlier he'd passed Caedraw and had seen plumes of smoke spurting from the top of the blast furnaces.

'The atmosphere was too poisonous, given what happened: the violence, the riots, the beatings.'

'I understand there are no such problems at Caedraw, though?'

Webb took out a handkerchief and mopped his forehead. 'I would gladly choose my current predicament, as desperate as it is, over the ordeal that my friends from the Castle have had to endure.'

Pyke thought again about what had happened to the Hancock boy, the sheer needless tragedy of it.

'I do know that the Hancocks, *père* and *fils*, have drastically reduced the number of Irish workers at Caedraw. As a result, they haven't been faced with the same difficulties as we have.' Webb shrugged. 'With the benefit of hindsight, it seems like a clever decision.'

Pyke left the window and joined Webb in front of the fireplace. 'The reason I came to see you was because I thought you might know where I could find Sir Clancy Smyth.'

'Me? Why would I know that?'

'He hasn't been seen for a number of weeks. I'm told he's gone back to his family pile in Ireland.'

'That may be so, but I'm afraid Smyth and I haven't been on speaking terms for some months.'

'Oh?'

Webb sighed. 'I've had troubles with renegotiating the lease at Morlais. It runs out at the end of this year; in a couple of weeks, actually. To begin with, the landowners, the Thomas family, wanted thirty thousand a year. That's sixteen more than I'm currently paying but the order books are full and I would have agreed to their demands. Then out of the blue Thomas came back and said he wanted fifty thousand a year. *Fifty thousand pounds.* At fifty, I'd be broke within months. It's outrageous . . . pure greed.'

'What's any of this got to do with Smyth?'

'His hands are all over it. He's good friends with the Thomas family, sees himself as a defender of traditional values against parvenus such as myself and, I suppose, the Hancocks.'

Pyke thought about the rancour that existed between Smyth and the Hancocks. 'I see, but where's the profit for him – and for the Thomas family – in driving you out of business?'

'That's a good question but I'm afraid it's one I can't answer. It's very simple, really. I need to meet a sizeable order currently on the books from Russia if I'm to pay the rent they want to charge. But because of what's happened, the trouble, I'm behind on production and I've heard that the Russians are looking around for alternative sources.'

'And if you don't meet the deadline?'

'If I don't meet the deadline and the Russians don't pay for the iron that we've already produced, well . . .' Webb shook his head, more sad than angry. 'I'd have to shut down the works for good.'

'So when did Thomas have this change of heart and demand fifty instead of thirty thousand?'

'About a month ago.'

'At Smyth's bidding – or so you think?'

Webb looked around the simply furnished room, seemingly lost for a few moments. 'If you want my opinion, Detective-inspector, I don't believe he's gone back to Ireland.'

'Why not?'

'He's too involved with every aspect of what goes on in this town. He wouldn't leave all of it behind, not willingly anyway.'

But what if something had gone terribly wrong and he'd found himself with the body of a sixteen-year-old boy on his hands?

'If he decided to stay here, but he wanted to hide, who would put him up? You say he's close to the Thomas family?'

Webb's eyes brightened. 'I was planning to visit them later this morning, plead my case one final time. Perhaps you would like to accompany me?'

In Webb's company, William Thomas assured Pyke he knew nothing about the whereabouts of Sir Clancy Smyth, and when Pyke questioned the servants and stableboys, he was told that no one matching Smyth's description had been seen in or near the house.

Later Webb told him that he'd struck a deal with Thomas to pay thirty thousand a year, on the assurance that the full amount would be paid on the first of January.

'Now I just need to meet the deadline for the Russian order, make sure they pay on time.'

Webb dropped Pyke off in the middle of the town. As he had the previous night, Pyke intended to sleep in John Johns' cabin and wanted to get there before the light disappeared. The track took him past the Caedraw works and the Castle.

Had it really been only a few weeks since he had first set foot inside that Gothic monstrosity?

It was hard to recall what he had expected on that occasion, what he had wanted to do, his hopes and fears. Pyke felt a gust of rage swell in his stomach but he did his best to quell it. He was thinking about Jonah and Zephaniah when he noticed there were still men posted at the gate. Without really thinking about what he was doing or why, Pyke slipped into the grounds and made his way up the slope to the walled garden where he had embraced Cathy. That seemed like a lifetime ago. Still not sure what he hoped to find, Pyke followed the route she'd shown him to the back of the building and the hidden passageway into the Castle. His boots may have been made from the best leather but Pyke had long since lost any feeling in his toes, and the left side of his stomach – where he'd been shot – ached, in spite of all the laudanum and gin he'd consumed.

Earlier it had snowed and Pyke could see that farther up the mountain it had started to settle.

Entering the passageway, he paused, waiting for his eyes to adjust to the darkness. He had a box of matches in his pocket and it took him a few moments to retrieve it and light one. Briefly the match flared, illuminating the dank passageway. Pyke looked ahead and sniffed; he'd expected the air to smell of damp but a thicker, riper scent invaded his nostrils. Instinctively he knew what it was. Lighting another match, he took a few nervous steps forward and saw what looked like an old sack directly ahead. But he knew it wasn't a sack; he knew what it was and the closer he edged towards it the more certain he became.

Kneeling down, Pyke could see it was a human body and it was clear to him that the flesh had begun to rot. The air was so obscene that it took every ounce of his self-control not to vomit. Chivvying away a rat, he reached forward and felt his fingers touch flesh; cold, decomposing flesh.

It was hard to tell who the corpse belonged to at first; maggots had eaten some of the flesh and the face and hair were covered in mud. Holding the match with one hand, he scraped away some of the mud from the face and felt a sudden jolt of panic. Her lips had turned blue and her eyes were as small and hard as stones. Both her wrists had been slit and next to her corpse lay a knife, the blade covered with dried blood.

As he stood there, Pyke wondered what had passed through Cathy Hancock's mind just before she had cut her own wrists.

*

By the time he had stumbled the mile or so from the Castle to John Johns' cabin, Pyke ached from tiredness. It was now completely dark and all he could think about was Cathy's crumpled form. He tried to remember her as she'd been, the time they had lain together, beautiful, coquettish. It was such a waste of a life. But she had lost her daughter and then her son and she was trapped in a loveless, moribund marriage. What did she have to live for? Pyke blamed himself – for not doing more to ensure her son's safe return and for abandoning her in her moment of need. Perhaps if he hadn't been shot, he could've found her, reasoned with her, reassured her. But what would he have said? What did you say to someone who'd just lost their son? Words were useless in the face of grief. Pyke knew this better than anyone.

Looking around, it struck him he would need to forage for wood, light a fire. He didn't need food, he wasn't hungry, but the cold was intense.

An envelope had been shoved under the door of the cabin. He saw it as soon as he stepped into the room. His name was scribbled on the front. Straight away, he recognised the writing, the same hand which had penned the first and last ransom demands. Quickly he tore it open and studied the contents.

Vaynor cemetery. Tonight at nine.

At the bottom of the page, there was a name, a signature. It took Pyke a few moments to place it.

TWENTY-THREE

TUESDAY, 2 FEBRUARY 1847

Clonoulty, Co. Tipperary

Knox stood over James' cot, watching his son sleep. It was five in the afternoon and nearly dark, the first time James had slept in almost twelve hours. Martha was also asleep, on the floor, exhausted. She hadn't put her head down in nearly three days. The doctor had visited again that afternoon and his prognosis wasn't good. He had been especially concerned by the fact that some of James' skin, especially on his back, had turned blue-black and he was still running a fever. James hadn't eaten in two days, wouldn't take any food, and for most of the day he was curled up in a ball. The doctor had mentioned cholera. When he'd left, they had gone back to the cot and stared down at their son, hoping for a miraculous transformation. Father Mackey had gone to the church to pray for James. A while later, the boy finally drifted off to sleep. Knox had ordered Martha to do likewise. A long night lay ahead of them.

Martha had tried to reassure James, tried to talk to him, comfort him. It had worked to some extent but the lad was still very weak. Knox listened to his breathing, reassured, looking at his little hands.

'Should we wake him?' Martha said, about an hour later, after she'd splashed water on her face.

'The doctor said sleeping was good.'

She nodded, bit her lip. 'He is going to be all right, isn't he?'

'The next two days will tell.' This was what the doctor had said.

Smiling, Martha reached out and touched his face. 'Thank you for staying with me today.'

The previous night, Knox had returned – euphoric – following his trip to Cashel and had told her about the exchange between Hastings, the County Inspector and Pierce, the policeman from

England. Told her what he had said and done, played up his triumph, and that Pierce had forced his superiors to reinstate him in the constabulary. They would be able to eat, he'd said. They would find a new place to live. James would get better. Everything would go back to how it used to be. In the night, however, James' fever had worsened and the cramping in his stomach had become more severe. By the morning, Knox hadn't wanted to leave James' side and no mention was made of his appointment in Cashel.

Now it was evening and James' condition had improved a little, Knox found himself thinking about Benedict Pierce, whether he'd travelled to Dundrum House alone and, if so, what kind of a welcome he'd received.

'You're worried about something. I can tell.' Martha stroked his hand.

'I'm worried about our son.'

'But you're thinking about what you missed today, whether it'll count against you.'

'We need to eat, pay the rent. I just wonder what will happen when this Englishman leaves.'

'If James has a better night, you should go and find this man Pierce tomorrow.' Martha gave his hand a squeeze.

Knox looked at her and nodded. She was a good wife. 'Some day we'll look back at this and smile.'

'God, I hope so.' She leant forward and kissed him on the cheek.

Knox set off for Cashel before dawn. James had slept all night and his temperature was lower. The lad had even managed a smile, the first in three days. That was when Martha had told Knox to go. He had prevaricated but her certitude and James' improved condition were enough to convince him. He would travel to Cashel and find the Assistant Commissioner; between them they would determine what had happened to Pyke.

Knox had to wait for an hour before the first cart heading in the direction of Cashel appeared. The driver, a shoemaker from Tip Town, didn't hesitate to pick him up and they talked about the weather, their families, the countryside, anything but the famine.

The sun had risen above the Rock by the time they entered the town, the shoemaker dropping Knox off by the fountain at the bottom of Main Street. Farther up the street, a brewer's dray had pulled up outside the King's Head and two men were unloading barrels of ale.

As Knox entered the station-house, Sub-inspector Hastings was coming down the stairs. He saw Knox and stiffened slightly. 'A word, if you please, Constable.'

Knox followed the man back up the stairs to his office. At least the sub-inspector had referred to him by his rank.

As soon as Knox shut the door, Hastings said, 'Assistant Commissioner Pierce has had to return to London. He left last night on the stagecoach for Dublin.'

Knox felt a tightening across his chest, not sure what this would mean for him. 'Did he . . . ?'

'He wanted me to give you this.' Hastings took a letter from his desk and handed it to Knox.

While Knox opened the letter, Hastings said, 'A special coroner's inquest was held yesterday afternoon. The deceased's name was officially recorded. A verdict of murder by a person or persons unknown was entered.'

Hands trembling, Knox read the short missive. It thanked Knox for his diligence and hard work but pointed out that it would not be in the public interest to pursue the inquiry any further.

'Did he go to Dundrum and pay Lord Cornwallis a visit?'

Hastings affected a look of indifference. 'Yes, I believe he did. What's that got to do with anything?'

How had Cornwallis convinced Pierce to drop the investigation? Knox wondered. A threat perhaps? Or a bribe? The aristocrat had connections in London. He could help a man like Pierce. In any case it didn't matter. Knox had missed his chance. The letter made no reference to the precariousness of his situation.

It would not be in the public interest. Anger replaced consternation. Who determined what was, and wasn't, in the public interest?

Hastings strode across to the door and opened it. 'You don't imagine that your old position has been kept open, do you?'

Knox was too dumbfounded to answer. When he reached the top of the stairs, he heard Hastings say, 'Good day, *Mr* Knox.'

His future had been decided in a matter of minutes. They hadn't regarded him as a threat. Once again they had taken his home and his job and now they were slamming the door in his face.

From Cashel, Knox had to walk as far as Pubblehill, about five miles, before he got a lift. Knox sat listlessly next to the driver, a wire-maker, hardly able to talk, too stunned by what had happened, another reversal of fortune. He sat there, arms around his knees, thinking about a decision he'd already made. It was time to confront Moore in person, find out once and for all what he knew about the dead man, about the murder, and why he'd tried so hard to bury the whole matter.

The wire-maker dropped him on the High Street and Knox walked the remaining few yards to the Anglican church. There was no Catholic church in the village. Moore had seen to that.

The church was locked but Knox found the vicar tending to one of the graves in the yard. He was a middle-aged man with a stern face, ink-black hair, deeply inset eyes and a striking Napoleonic nose.

'I wonder if you could help me. I'm looking for my birth certificate.' Knox waited for the vicar to stand up.

'And you are, sir?'

'John Johns.' Knox had heard from his mother that the vicar was relatively new in the parish. Knox had never met him before and he wouldn't have known about Johns. Or indeed Johns' mother and father, both of whom were long deceased.

'Gordon Marks.' He offered his hand and waited for Knox to shake it.

Knox did so. 'Do you keep the records here?'

'It depends how far back you want to go.' Marks rubbed the dirt from his palms. Then he realised that he'd made Knox shake his muddy hand. 'Sorry about that.'

Knox indicated it was quite all right. '1806. March.'

'They might go back that far.' Marks looked at him. 'So you were born in the parish?'

'That's right.'

'Perhaps I know your family?'

'My mother and father are both dead.'

'I'm sorry. Where did they live?'

Knox didn't want to say the lodge-house as that might alert the vicar's suspicions. 'A cabin on Castle Field.'

'And when did they pass away?'

'Ten years ago.'

The vicar rubbed his jaw. 'Well, then, let's see what we can find out.' He led Knox into the church. Knox hadn't been inside it for years and it was like stepping back into his former life. Even the smell was familiar; it reminded him of sitting next to his mother.

In the vestry – a high-ceilinged room at the back of the church – Knox waited while Marks consulted some leather-bound tomes stacked on wooden shelves behind a large desk. His thoughts returned to the old days, sitting next to his mother on one of the rock-hard pews, his father at home, sleeping off the ale from the night before. Knox was surprised how much he cherished these memories, a time before Matthew and Peter, when it was just the two of them.

'1806, you say?' Marks had heaved one of the volumes off the shelf and put it on the desk.

'March.'

The vicar nodded and turned over a page, then another, then another. Knox peered over his shoulder.

'Perhaps you'd permit me to consult my birth certificate in private,' he said, afraid that the vicar might see something that would alert his suspicions.

Marks looked up, a little flustered. 'Oh, yes, I see.' Aware it was a delicate matter, he stood up and pulled down his cassock. 'I'll wait outside.'

Knox sat down and turned the pages until he'd found the entries for March. He saw Johns' name near the bottom of the page. He could hear his own heart thumping.

Born on the tenth day of March eighteen hundred and six.

He let his finger drift across the page but there was no entry in the column for the father's name. It had been left blank. Fighting back the disappointment, Knox checked to see the mother's name.

He blinked, couldn't trust his eyes, had to look again. But it was just as he'd seen it the first time.

Sarah Jane Maguire. His mother's maiden name.

TWENTY-FOUR

Pyke came upon the churchyard from the path and looked beyond the headstones at the church itself, boxy and deserted. Cathy Hancock had visited regularly, to tend the grave of her deceased daughter. Now she and her son were also dead. Perhaps William Hancock had been buried next to his sister, Pyke thought, whereas Cathy had been left to rot in an underground passageway built by her father-in-law as an escape route, and used by her husband to smuggle prostitutes into his bed. Did Jonah and Zephaniah Hancock know that Cathy had committed suicide? Pyke didn't know for certain that Cathy had, in fact, killed herself, but all the evidence pointed towards it; the slashed wrists, the blood-crusted knife. Jonah and Zephaniah had taken off for England. Maybe they had looked for her and hadn't been able to find her; but then again perhaps they had found her and decided that she wasn't worth burying. This was where she ought to rest, Pyke decided. When it was all over, he'd come back for her, give her the burial she deserved.

An owl hooted and then something rustled in nearby bushes. A disembodied voice said, 'Detective-inspector Pyke?'

In the gloom, a figure came into view. Maggie Atkins took a couple of steps towards him. She was wearing a dirty white cotton dress and a woollen shawl but looked cold and bedraggled, her hair dangling over her face.

'Cathy talked about you a lot. I saw you once – a month ago – at John's cabin and then again last night, same place. That's why I left the note.'

Her cheeks were pinched, her figure almost skeletal.

'I've just come from the Castle.' Pyke waited for a moment. 'I found Cathy's body there. I think she killed herself.'

Maggie Atkins gasped softly and then covered her mouth. 'She . . . she blamed herself . . .' Tears welled in her eyes.

'Her wrists had been slit. I found her in an underground passageway at the back of the building.'

William's former nanny tried to fight back the tears. 'I tried to talk to her, reason with her . . .'

'Why did she blame herself for William's death?'

There was a wild look in her eyes. 'You don't know? Cathy always thought you'd find out.'

'Find out what?' Pyke's mind was racing, trying to make the connection.

'There was no kidnapping – at least not a genuine one. It was staged to appear genuine, for the benefit of the driver and ultimately Jonah Hancock.' Maggie's head was bowed and her tone was disconsolate.

Pyke's mind drifted back to the first words Cathy had said to him. *You shouldn't have come.* She hadn't asked for him, hadn't wanted him there. Cathy – and others, including Maggie – had set the whole thing up with the intention, no doubt, of extorting twenty thousand pounds from her husband. And then what? For a moment Pyke wondered at the recklessness and naivety of the scheme. There was no way men like the Hancocks would have allowed such a thing to take place without exacting retribution. His mind turned to her body. Perhaps this was what had happened.

'Tell me about it, Maggie.'

She nodded once. 'I suppose Cathy had had enough of her husband's boorish ways, his infidelities, her father-in-law's interference. She knew he'd never consent to a divorce, at least not one that allowed her to keep William. And she couldn't afford to leave just like that. In any case, she'd put up with the Hancocks for five years, and she believed she deserved something for her efforts.'

Pyke thought about Cathy's unhappiness and what it must have taken to drive her to do such a thing. 'And you and John Johns agreed to help?'

Maggie stared at him and then nodded. 'I saw at first hand how terrible her husband and her father-in-law could be.'

'And Johns? Was he her lover?'

Maggie blushed a little, perhaps taken aback by the bluntness of his question. 'Some of the time. I think he liked her more than she liked him. But he had his own reasons for wanting to get back at the Hancocks.'

It made sense now, Johns' occasional diffidence towards him; he would have seen Pyke as a rival for Cathy's affection. Perhaps Johns had been spying on them the night he and Cathy had embraced in the garden.

'So they concocted this plan? Execute the kidnapping and then send a ransom note to the Castle from Scottish Cattle.' Pyke waited and said, 'You wrote the first letter – and the last one.'

Maggie tucked a strand of hair behind her ear. She was shivering from the cold. 'That was John's idea, Scottish Cattle. He did it to confuse the Hancocks; no one's heard from the Bull in years.'

'You didn't send the second letter, though? The one directing me up to the quarry.'

She shook her head.

'Know who did?'

'No.'

Pyke studied her expression and decided he believed her. 'But you – *Cathy* – must have believed Jonah would pay.'

'I was nursemaid and nanny to that boy for four years. Jonah had his faults, plenty of them, but he loved his son.'

'It would have been cruel, then, what you all planned to do. Take his son away from him, presumably start a new life with the twenty thousand?'

'Let me put it a different way. He loved the *idea* of his son. But most of the time he hardly saw William.'

Pyke considered this. It made him think of his own failings as a father. The same accusation could have been levelled at him. 'What happened, after Johns set up the kidnapping? Where did you keep the boy?'

'That hut, up the slope from his cabin.' Maggie's cheeks coloured slightly. 'I think I saw you from the window one day . . .'

So the Hancock boy had been there the first time Pyke had visited. No wonder Johns had poked a rifle in his face.

'Did Cathy say whether Jonah or Zephaniah suspected anything?'

'That was her main worry. She thought one of them, especially Zephaniah, would work it out. But she didn't think they had, even at the end.'

'So what went wrong with the kidnapping?' He was starting to form an impression of Maggie Atkins: a devoted servant who had seen Cathy's unhappiness and decided to help.

'John had this notion that someone was following him. There were people he trusted, radicals, the ones who'd helped him carry out the kidnapping. So the day before the rendezvous at the railway station, he had them stage an ambush in the middle of town – to check whether anyone really was following him, and make people think he'd disappeared. He wanted to lie low for the night, make sure no one knew where he was. His task was to collect the ransom money – meet the train at Cwmbach, collect the suitcase and then jump off between there and Fernhill.'

So it hadn't been Wylde and his bullies who had snatched Johns in broad daylight. But Smyth had known about it because that was how Pyke had found out.

'What was your part in the whole affair? You were looking after William, right? All being well, he was due to arrive on the eleven o'clock train.'

'The night before, Johns took me and the boy to Fernhill. We stayed in a room near the station. He said he would let me know if all went well; then all I had to do was put William on the train.'

'Weren't you worried the boy might say something to his father afterwards? He would have been part of the deception, or at least he would have had to play along with it. Wasn't that too much of a burden to put on his shoulders?'

'You never met William, did you?' Maggie's eyes started to mist up again.

'No.'

'He was a thoughtful, intelligent boy. In all honesty, he hated his life at the Castle, hated to see his mother so sad. His father was an abstraction to him and he cried whenever Zephaniah tried to take him in hand. Cathy was his life, and when she asked him if he'd be happy to move somewhere else, start again, he said yes. He could be cunning if necessary. And stubborn, too. He knew what was at stake.'

'So Cathy's plan was to take William back to the Castle for a while, pretend everything was fine. Then what? Disappear one night and never return.'

'Something like that.' Maggie wiped her eyes on the sleeve of her dress. 'Cathy felt it was too risky, fleeing straight away. Better to let the dust settle, pick her moment. Perhaps when Jonah and Zephaniah went to London on business or their home in Hampshire.'

Pyke considered the plan and tried to work out whether it was stupid, foolhardy or brilliant in its own way.

'So what happened? What went wrong?'

'That night, I was in the room in Fernhill, with William. Neither of us slept much, as you can imagine. As it was getting light I heard voices, whispers, outside the window.' Maggie had to pause, the rawness of the memories still too much for her. 'I'm sorry.'

Pyke looked around the barren churchyard, the headstones. 'Take all the time you need.'

Maggie nodded forlornly. 'I rushed over to the window. That's when I saw him: he was standing outside, face clear in the dawn.'

'Saw who?'

'Sir Clancy Smyth.'

Pyke stared at her; he hadn't expected this. He still didn't know how the magistrate was implicated in Felix's death but he hadn't suspected Smyth's involvement in the kidnapping.

'You knew who he was?'

Maggie nodded. 'I'd seen him at the Castle a few times.'

'But he wasn't on his own?'

'No.' She took a breath, trying to control her emotions. 'There was another man with him, someone I couldn't see properly. A moment or two later, his man kicked down the door. He was wearing a handkerchief over his face. He picked up William with one arm and there was a pistol in the other hand. He was as close as you are. He aimed the pistol at me and I think I screamed. Then at the last moment, he turned, fired it into the wall. William was shouting, trying to wriggle free, but the man's grip was too strong. He took the boy and I heard the carriage leave. That was the last time I saw him.' Tears were flowing down her cheeks.

Pyke offered her his handkerchief but she declined. He was trying to make sense of what she'd just told him, the unidentified man firing but deliberately, it appeared, missing her.

'So what did you do next?'

'I didn't know what to do. I panicked. I didn't dare get on the train. I thought they might be waiting for me at the station. So I walked – ran, actually – back to Merthyr, picked up a ride that took me to Caedraw, and from there I went to the cabin, I didn't know what else to do.'

'And did Cathy and Johns come and find you?'

Maggie nodded. 'Eventually. John came. I told him what had happened. He said the suitcase wasn't on the train.'

'I left it there, in the first-class carriage. I saw the train pull out of the station.'

'Well, according to John, it was gone about five minutes later, when he joined the train at Cwmbach.' Pyke thought about the two men in the first-class carriage. Perhaps one of them had taken it after all.

'Did he say who he thought had taken the money?'

Maggie wouldn't look at him.

'Maggie?'

Slowly she lifted her head to meet his gaze. 'Your name was mentioned. Then I told him what I'd seen, who I'd seen. That changed things. He left and I didn't see him again.'

'And Cathy?'

'She came later; she was out of her mind with worry. When I told her what had happened, she broke down.' Maggie took another deep breath.

Gently Pyke placed his hand on her shoulder. 'And?'

'She didn't tell me what she planned to do. I assumed she was going back to the Castle. We agreed that it was no longer safe to hide at John's cabin. I told her I would come up here, to an abandoned stone cottage near the cemetery. She promised she'd come and find me.'

'But she never did.'

Maggie shook her head. 'A little later, I heard about William, that his body had been found in the town.'

'You assumed Smyth and the other man must have killed him.'

'Yes.'

'And you've been living up here ever since?'

'I didn't know where else to go. Every so often, I went back to John's cabin, to see if anyone had been there. I thought John might return. Or Cathy.' She shook her head. 'Yesterday, when I saw the light, the fire, I thought it must be one of them. I crept up and saw you in the window. That's why I left the note.' She looked at him, her eyes glistening with tears. 'Who do *you* think killed the boy?'

'I don't know. It's hard not to point the finger at Smyth, though.' Yet Pyke couldn't see what the magistrate would have to gain from it, apart from using the death as an excuse to send in the troops.

'I don't know what to do, sir. I don't know whether I should go to the police and tell them what I know, or . . .'

Pyke shook his head. 'The fact that this man didn't shoot you doesn't mean you're safe. You need to stay here a while longer, wait for me. Where exactly is this abandoned cottage?'

After she'd told him, Pyke took off his greatcoat and put it around her shoulders. 'You're clearly a brave woman, Maggie, but you need to lie low for a while longer. What you know could still be dangerous. I'll come and find you when I think it's safe.'

She wrapped the coat around herself and smiled. 'Cathy liked you a lot, you know.'

Pyke looked at her, not sure what to say.

'I think a part of her imagined – *hoped* – that you and she . . . might, I don't know, find each other some time in the future.'

Pyke's mind turned to Cathy's decomposing corpse, her wrists slit open. A bloody winter, he thought. Another needless death.

It took him the best part of an hour to walk back into the town. He couldn't see more than a few yards in front of him. Bill Flint was drinking in the taproom of the Three Horse Shoes but he denied helping Johns, said he didn't know where the former soldier had gone.

'Apparently there was no kidnapping,' Pyke said, scrutinising Flint's reaction. 'The wife planned it with Johns, hoped to squeeze twenty thousand out of the Hancocks.'

If Flint was surprised by this, he didn't show it. 'Why are you telling me this?'

'He was helped by some of his friends – radicals.'

Flint's eyes narrowed. 'Trying to blame us for the boy's death now, eh?'

'I just want answers.'

The Chartist looked around the smoke-filled room. 'Then you'll want to hear what this young soldier has to say. He came in here looking for you a few weeks ago. We've been hiding him ever since.'

'Hiding him from?'

Flint shrugged. 'I'll let you work that one out.'

'Who is he?'

'Just a soldier.' Flint sniffed. 'Deserter now, I suppose.'

Outside, the cold was piercing.

'Didn't expect to see you again, to be honest,' Flint said as he led the way along an unlit alley.

'Think I made off with the ransom money?'

'Wouldn't be the first corrupt copper I've come across. So where have you been? Why did you come back?'

'Recovering from a pistol wound.'

'Someone shot you?'

'John Wylde.'

Flint stopped and turned around. His chalky face was partly illuminated by the light from a half-open window. 'Wylde tried to kill you?'

'Didn't succeed, though.'

'I can see that.' Flint turned and continued along the passageway, then came to a halt outside a door which led into a backyard. 'Come back to settle some debts, then?'

Pyke tried to put Felix out of his mind. 'Something like that.'

In the yard, Pyke waited while Flint knocked on the door of the house and whispered a few words to the man who greeted him. They were ushered into the back room, where another man wearing a dark blue woollen shirt was playing cards with a soldier still in uniform. The soldier was young, with cropped hair, pockmarked skin and a thick, almost square face. He stood up and greeted Pyke with an awkward shake of the hand.

'I served in the Forty-fifth regiment, until I left two weeks ago. We were billeted in Brecon.'

'What's your name?'

'Richard Considine.'

Pyke noticed that Flint and the other man had left them alone. 'What made you leave?'

'What they made me do . . .'

Pyke nodded, decided to let the younger man talk.

'They wanted me to kill someone I'd never seen before, never done us any harm, a civilian.'

'Let me guess. The shooting took place up near the old quarry, just off the Anderson's farm road.'

The soldier eyed him warily. 'Did one of the radicals tell you that?'

'I was hiding in the cabin at the time. I heard the rifle. The man you shot died in my arms. His name was Deeney. He was an Irishman, lodged in Dowlais.'

'No one told me his name. Nor what he'd done . . . to deserve . . .' The soldier's voice started to crack.

'I guessed you were a trained marksman. A professional. I had a friend look for you at the barracks in Dowlais.'

'I was never stationed here in Merthyr.'

'Probably why you were chosen. Clearly you're good with a Baker's rifle, too.'

'The sergeant-major always said I was the best shot in the regiment.'

'So why did you agree to do it?'

The former soldier didn't answer immediately. 'I got into some trouble with a woman, wife of a councillor. I was told I was going to be thrown out of the regiment. Stupid, really.'

'And all you had to do to clear your name, wipe the slate clean, was to come to Merthyr and do as you were told.'

'It didn't seem like too much at the time.'

'Killing an innocent man?' Pyke didn't say this to judge the young soldier, just to indicate that he knew what it meant to take a life. He tried to remember that awful, hollow sensation he had felt after he'd killed for the first time.

The soldier nodded, his expression pale, haunted. 'Captain said he was a criminal.'

Pyke shook his head. 'Not true. My guess is that he'd been paid a few coins to go to that cabin and pick up a purse. Just his bad luck he was Irish.'

He now understood what had happened. Someone had planted

the rent book on the dead man, directing them to Irish Row and the shoe and coat belonging to William Hancock. Clearly this person had wanted them to suspect an Irish mob.

Considine nodded. 'That's what this big fellow told me after he'd tracked me down in Brecon.'

Pyke described John Johns and asked whether this was the man who'd found him.

'That's right,' Considine said, surprised he had been able to identify Johns so quickly.

'And he persuaded you to come back to Merthyr?'

'He told me he'd been in my shoes once.' The young soldier wiped the sweat from his forehead. 'Said he knew how it felt, to kill a civilian in cold blood, made me see what I'd done. He said that I wouldn't be able to live with myself 'less I tried to put things right.'

Pyke thought about Johns and his friendship with the radicals. He would have known the second letter – directing them to the quarry – hadn't been sent by the real kidnappers and he'd always had his suspicions that one of the marksmen was a trained soldier.

'Do you know where that man is now?'

'Now?' The soldier shook his head. 'I just met him once, that time he came to Brecon.'

'There were two of you up the mountain that day.'

'That's right. Me and Captain Kent.'

It took Pyke a moment to place the name. He was the man who'd imposed martial law in Merthyr. 'Was he the one who gave the orders?'

The soldier nodded. 'He'll deny it, of course. He'll claim I deserted because of what I did, the affair.'

'Depends who asks.'

'You don't understand,' the soldier said, openly showing his fear for the first time. 'He won't stop looking for me and when he finds me, he'll kill me.'

'Let me worry about him.'

Considine shot him a puzzled look. 'Why? What do you intend to do?'

'That's my business.' Pyke kept his expression blank. 'Kent's now in Merthyr with your regiment. Apparently he's taking his orders from a man called Josiah Webb.'

Considine frowned. 'Only one person Kent ever took orders from.'

Pyke had expected the soldier to jump at the mention of Webb's name but he hadn't. 'Let me guess. Sir Clancy Smyth?'

The young soldier looked at him, still puzzled. 'Never heard of him.'

Pyke felt his world tilt on its axis and suddenly he saw it; saw what he'd been missing, saw who had killed William Hancock and why. It was all so obvious.

'Hancock,' Considine said, 'Zephaniah Hancock.'

TWENTY-FIVE

The rain was falling as sleet and there were no stars or moonlight to guide Knox, but he knew the track well, knew it as he knew everything else in Dundrum. He fought back another wave of anger. Usually the walk from the church to Quarry Field might have taken him half an hour but Knox covered the distance in ten minutes, running more than walking, impervious to the sleet and cold.

He didn't knock. He just opened the door and stumbled into the front room, red-faced and out of breath. His mother was knitting by the fire, a woollen shawl draped over her knees. His father appeared from the bedroom, wearing trousers held up by braces, and an old vest. There was no sign of his brothers.

'What is it, Michael?' His mother could see his expression, see that all was not fine.

'I have two words to say to you, Mam. John Johns.' Knox saw her flinch as if he had struck her.

She put her hand to her mouth and gasped. Knox's father remained rooted to the spot, unable to say anything.

'Born eighteen hundred and six. March the tenth. You would have been eighteen at the time.'

She stared at him, the edifice of her life beginning to crumble around her.

'This would have been before you married him.' Knox pointed at his father.

'Michael, please . . .' His mother's voice sounded weak, alien.

'Perhaps this was before you even knew him. But he wasn't the father, was he? Otherwise there would be no reason to leave his name off the birth certificate.'

'No good will come of this, Michael. Please, I beg you, don't take this any farther,' she muttered, her hands trembling.

'No, Mother, I will *not* leave it. You'll tell me the truth. What I've been doing these last few weeks, why my life has been destroyed.'

Sarah Knox began to weep.

'Moore's the father, isn't he?' The words filled Knox with revulsion, the thought of his mother, his own flesh and blood, lying with that man.

'Oh, dear Lord.' His mother gasped for air.

'Did he force himself on you? Was that it?' Knox waited, light-headed, dizzy. 'No, that couldn't have been it. You wouldn't have stayed in his service for forty years. *He* wouldn't have let you.'

'He's not the monster you think he is . . .'

Knox grabbed his mother by the shoulders and shook her, more violently than he'd wanted to. 'That man paid some thugs to destroy our home, giving us no time to clear out our possessions, taking to it with crowbars and sledgehammers.'

Disturbed from his sleep, Peter stumbled bleary-eyed into the room and scurried over to where their mother was sitting. Instinctively she opened her arms and allowed the lad to nestle against her.

'If not for me, son, then for Peter's sake. *Please.* Just let sleeping dogs lie. I'll tell you all you want to know in time. But not now, not like this.'

Without knowing what he was doing, Knox slapped her around the cheek, once, the noise echoing around the small room. 'Our child, *your grandson*, is desperately ill with a fever he picked up after we'd been driven from our home.' He stared at her, then at his hand, unable to comprehend what he'd done.

Peter was wailing in her arms, sobbing and shaking uncontrollably.

'Little James is ill?' She had been trying to console Peter but all of a sudden she looked up at Knox through bloodshot eyes.

'I want to hear you say it, Mother. Tell me to my face. John Johns is Moore's son. *Your* son.'

She bowed her head and nodded.

Knox never thought the day would come when he hated his mother but in that instant he felt nothing but contempt for her; contempt for the life she'd built, a life built on lies.

'Yes, Michael, he's *our* son,' she whispered, not looking at her husband, who hadn't uttered a word. 'There. Are you satisfied?'

Our son. Hers and Moore's.

'I've lost everything, Mother. My position, my home, maybe even my child. You could have helped. You could've said something. But you just let it happen.'

Peter had calmed down a little but she still wouldn't look at Knox, wouldn't meet his eyes.

'And if I'd told you, what do you think Moore would have done? That he wouldn't have tried to evict us? And how long do you think your brother would have lasted, living hand to mouth, sleeping rough?'

This took the sting out of Knox's anger but it didn't dissolve it completely. 'He asked for me, Mother, for me. Because he knew he could lord it over me. Knew you would keep me in line. He asked for me because he thought I was weak, pathetic, that I'd roll over and let him get away with it, just like this family's been doing for the last forty years.'

Tears were flowing down his mother's cheeks again and Knox began to feel a pang of sympathy for her. 'You don't think I'm proud of myself? That I don't hate myself for turning my back on you? What I did, I did for your brother's sake alone. But every night I went to bed and prayed for you, Michael, prayed that God would keep you safe.'

Knox felt another spike of anger. 'You prayed? You think God – if there is a God – is listening? Folk are dying out there in their thousands. If God cares so much, why doesn't he do something about it? I don't need your prayers.' Disgusted, Knox looked across at his father. 'You knew about this, didn't you? That she'd given birth to Moore's bastard. And yet you went ahead and married her.'

But Martin Knox didn't say a word. Instead his mother rose and moved into the space between them. 'Michael, I'm begging you, please go. I'll meet you in a day or two, we can talk then, I'll tell you everything . . .'

Knox stared at his father. The man's lips were dry and flaky, and his eyes were empty. There was something else, something they knew, his mother and father, something they'd both wanted to keep from him.

Knox turned back to her, afraid now. 'He was here, wasn't he? John Johns. He came to see you.' The reality of what he'd done – striking his mother – was starting to sink in and Knox knew he was capable of worse, knew it because it ran in his blood.

'I told him he couldn't stay.'

'He's your son; he came to you in his hour of need. And what did you do? You turned your back on him, just like you turned your back on me.'

'*NOOOO.*'

They stopped and stared at Peter, who had bellowed this, the loudest sound Knox had ever heard coming from the lad's lips.

Sarah Knox gathered him up into her arms and held him. 'Whether you can understand or not, Michael, I did what I did, I made the choices I made, to ensure this one would have a roof over his head.'

'What did Johns want? Why did he come here? It has something to do with the man who died, doesn't it? Did Johns kill him?'

'I don't know, Michael. *Please*, I can't do this. *Not now.* Not like this.'

'Well, does he look like me?'

That drew the first sound from his father's lips. It came out like a strangled laugh. For the first time, Knox saw there were tears flowing down his cheeks too.

He had a terrible sense of foreboding.

'What is it you're not telling me?' Knox looked first at his mother, and then at his father. 'This is me you're talking to, Mam. If you turn your back on me again, I'll walk out of that door and never come back. Is that what you really want?'

'I don't know what I want any more.' This time, she shouted, her face red and blotchy. 'I want what's best for everyone but I know I can't have that.'

His father turned and withdrew into the bedroom. His mother went to follow him but Knox grabbed her wrist.

'You don't understand. I need to talk to him . . .'

Sarah Knox managed to free herself from his clutch. When Knox joined her in the bedroom his father was sitting on the edge of the bed, weeping. Knox tried to summon pity for the man but he couldn't. He thought about all the times his father had beaten him, with a leather strap, with a cane, with his fists.

'I'm not your real father,' the man said listlessly. 'Moore is.'

His mother had collapsed on the bed and was weeping. Somewhere in the other room, Peter was screaming. Numb, Knox looked between his mother and father, still trying to assimilate what his father had said. His father, who wasn't his father. The truth of it was beginning to dawn: why his father had always hated him, the living embodiment of his wife's infidelities.

His mother was still sobbing and was trying to catch hold of his father's hand. 'All this time you knew?' she kept saying.

'Is it true?' Knox felt dizzy, the room spinning around him. 'Is it true, Mam?' he whispered.

She stared at him, her hands cradling Martin Knox's almost unrecognisable face. Knox tried to digest what he'd been told, the fact that his mother had never told his father that Knox wasn't his, that she'd kept this from him and believed – wrongly, as it turned out – that the man was unaware of Knox's real parentage. That she'd continued the affair with the father of her first child after their marriage.

Sickened, bewildered, Knox lurched towards the door.

Outside, he felt a blast of cold air against his face. He stumbled down the steps, looked around him and started to run, with no idea of where he was going. He ran until his lungs gave up and he fell down on to the muddy ground.

TWENTY-SIX

Pyke had seen the men guarding the front gate before but he had thought nothing of it. Now, though, he knew why they were there. The Hancocks hadn't decamped to Hampshire to mourn William's death. They had never left their fortress, and if Pyke had pushed on into the Castle, after finding Cathy's body, he would also have found father and son hiding away in their dusty rooms. As before, he approached the Castle from the mountain. There were no lights burning in any of the windows but this didn't mean the Castle was deserted. The shutters and curtains were thick enough to block out the light from a few candles. Aided by the moonlight, Pyke moved down the slope, oblivious to the cold and the discomfort of his wound, and found the entrance that Cathy had shown him at the back of the building.

His thoughts turned to finding Cathy's corpse in the dank passageway, a lump of waxy flesh. What had gone through her mind, he wondered, as she had drawn the razor across her wrists? The fact that her son had died? The guilt at the part she might have played in his death? And would he move her now that he knew the full story?

Now he was there, Pyke questioned again why he had come back. What good could he do? Except it wasn't a question of righting wrongs, he told himself. He needed to know what had happened to Felix. It was as simple as that. Pyke had no illusions any more about the law or his role in trying to enforce it.

The interior of the Castle was cold and draughty: a fire would create smoke, would let people see that the building was occupied. He slipped quietly along the polished wooden floors from drawing to dining room. The rooms were all deserted. No sounds anywhere in the building, just the wind howling outside. He moved towards the staircase and ascended, one step at a time, careful not to make any noise. At the top of the stairs, he looked along the landing and decided to try Jonah Hancock's room first.

The hinges groaned as he opened the door but Pyke needn't have worried. Jonah Hancock was lying, fully clothed, face down on his bed, an empty bottle of gin next to him. Pyke prodded him and the ironmaster grunted once but didn't come around.

Looking at him, Pyke felt a twinge of something, sympathy perhaps. Whatever else the man had done, he had lost his son, and Pyke knew well enough the utter desolation he must be feeling. To have something, someone, you loved snatched away from you – Jonah Hancock knew what that felt like, the hole it left.

At the far end of the passage, Pyke tried the door to Zephaniah Hancock's bedroom. Despite the lateness of the hour he found the old man lying in bed reading a book, a pair of spectacles perched on the bridge of his nose. As soon as he saw who it was, Zephaniah let the book fall to his lap and fumbled for something under the sheets.

Before he could retrieve his pistol, Pyke hit the old man on the mouth, heard his jaw snap.

'When did you find out that the child wasn't Jonah's?' While he waited for Zephaniah to recover, he inspected the pistol. It was loaded and ready to fire.

The answer had come to Pyke almost as soon as he'd found out that Zephaniah had ordered the assassination of the Irishman up on the mountain. Everything had followed from this simple truth: the child wasn't Jonah's, so Zephaniah, who had never much cared for the boy and who had another heir waiting in the wings, had devised a scheme to turn Cathy's kidnap plot to his own advantage.

'In the summer,' the old man croaked finally.

'Who was the father? Johns?'

Zephaniah nodded. 'I intercepted a letter she wrote earlier in the year. It confirmed what I already knew: that the boy wasn't a Hancock – too meek, cried a lot, no backbone.'

Pyke didn't try to hide his revulsion. 'The boy was only five years old. For five years, he was your grandson, your son's son. Blood can't change how you feel about a person overnight.'

'Can't it? That boy was an impostor. This way the estate can pass to Richard's eldest, my other son in England. A fine chap, strong and clever as a whip.'

The idea that Zephaniah would knowingly arrange the murder of a five-year-old boy, a boy he'd thought of as his grandson for five years, was almost too appalling for Pyke to take in. Worse still was his seeming lack of regret.

'But Jonah didn't see it that way, did he? This was your doing, not his? He loved that boy, whether he was the father or not. Right now he's passed out on his bed, a bottle of gin at his side.'

A frown spread across the old man's haggard face. 'I'm afraid my firstborn has always been a disappointment to me.'

'Because he's capable of some degree of empathy and still possesses a modicum of humanity?'

'He could see the logic of what I proposed but baulked at the implementation. But he didn't build up the ironworks to what it is today. I did – and I found out that the world isn't a nice place. Wolves eat dogs, sir, but I'm sure a man of your various experiences knows this.'

'You arranged to have a five-year-old butchered in cold blood and you imagine you can lecture me about the state of the world?'

'You're a woolly little lamb, aren't you? Do you have any idea how many men and women died at the works last year? Because they fell or their equipment failed or due to accidents, explosions, unforeseen circumstances. Am I to be held accountable for their deaths too? If so, perhaps the works should simply close down. But if this were to happen, thousands would lose their positions and the town would go into terminal decline.'

Pyke hesitated and took a deep breath. He would never get a man like Zephaniah Hancock to examine his heart and find it wanting. What he needed to do was get him to talk about what had happened. The truth about Felix would be in there, whether Zephaniah had a direct hand in that death or not.

'Perhaps you need a lesson in biology, sir,' Zephaniah continued. 'But the boy wasn't my flesh and blood and therefore had no claim over my estate.' Zephaniah must have seen Pyke's expression because he added, 'If you think me cold-hearted and lacking in sentiment, be that as it may. I make no apologies for who or what I am.'

'Tell me, then. When did you learn that Cathy and John Johns were behind the kidnapping? Before it had even happened?'

'Of course,' the old man wheezed. 'She should have known that nothing happens in this house without my knowledge.'

'So you knew she was planning the kidnapping and you decided to turn the situation to your advantage.'

'Stupid bitch thought she could get away with stealing money from under our noses.' Zephaniah's pink tongue brushed his dry, shrivelled lips. 'The whore didn't know that we knew, of course.'

Now Pyke understood what had happened. The Hancocks had lost a son and grandson – or so he'd thought. Being victims had put them above suspicion.

'So when Cathy came home that day and told you William had been snatched, you had everything in place. You were the one who sent the second ransom demand. You arranged for Captain Kent and Considine to be up on that hill, paid some poor, innocent Irishman to pick up a parcel from the cabin, sacrificed him; planted a rent book in his pocket, a few of the boy's clothes in a house on Irish Row, and let rumour and insinuation do the rest.'

'Just details,' the old man purred. 'You're not able to see the whole canvas, what we've been able to achieve.'

Zephaniah seemed almost proud of what he had done. Pyke had to use all of his self-control not to tear the man's throat out with his bare hands.

'You consider what's happened in the town – the deaths, the rioting, the hatred – an achievement?'

The old man shook his head. 'Now you're talking like my son, the sentimental fool. I'll tell you what I told him – the good of the works comes first. First, second and third. Nothing else matters. Is that too hard-hearted for you? I'll put it in plainer English. There was no way on earth I was going to allow that bastard to inherit what isn't, wasn't, his. Now, at least, the future of the works is assured and it will pass to someone with bona fide Hancock blood running through his veins.'

'Let's talk about the whole canvas, then.' Pyke looked into the old man's watery, bloodshot eyes.

Zephaniah sighed. 'You seem to have all the answers, sir. Why don't you enlighten me.'

'Set up the Irish as scapegoats so that when news of the kidnapping, and eventually the boy's death, spreads, the natives will turn on them. But because you'd already cut back on the number of Irish workers, Caedraw wouldn't be too badly affected. Not so with Morlais, though. That was the point, wasn't it? To drive the competition out of business. Because of the rioting, the fighting, the bad blood, Webb's been forced to close Morlais. After all, about a third of his workers are Irish. But at the same time he needs to *increase* his productivity – if he's to meet this order from Russia by the end of the year. That was the first front you opened against Morlais. For the second one you needed Sir Clancy Smyth.'

'Everyone has a price, sir. Even you.' Zephaniah managed the thinnest of smiles.

'You used Smyth's friendship with Morlais' landowner to force up the rent. In the meantime, you got Smyth to work for you, used him to do your dirty work, with house-to-house searches of Quarry Row, stories of an Irish mob seizing William fed to the local newspaper. What did it take? How much? Ten thousand?'

'As I said, everyone has their price. Smyth's estate has fallen on hard times. But when this blows over, *if* it blows over, he'll get what he wants. The troops will have brought order to the streets, the town will have been cleaned up, China a shadow of its former self . . .'

All cleaned up and ready to go to the dogs again, Pyke thought. Cut off one head, two heads even, and more will appear. Zephaniah Hancock was not long for this world but Pyke knew it was a futile act, one that would have little bearing on the lives of most of the people in Merthyr. In that sense, Zephaniah was right: the ironworks did come first. And in the end men like Smyth always bent to the ironmasters' will.

'Smyth didn't see you were using him, did he? That he was being lined up as someone to blame for the boy's death in case you weren't able to deal with Johns – or me.'

'I never wanted you here in the first place. That was Jonah's idea, a stupid one. Plenty of other people we could have given that suitcase to. Someone to blame, someone greedy, who wouldn't think twice about running off with the twenty thousand. The public and police would need a reason why the boy was murdered. If they believed you'd absconded with the money, left the kidnappers with nothing, well, that would have been enough.'

'That was why he wrote to me?' Pyke felt sick, knowing he *had* been lured down there by the promise of money in the first place.

A thousand pounds; Jonah Hancock had paid him too. Blood money. If it had meant nothing to him, he would never have come. Felix would never have come. His son would still be alive.

'Offered some astounding sum, he knew you'd come here sniffing, either for Cathy or the money or both. He was right about that, but I saw straight away you'd be dangerous. I couldn't talk him round, though. For years, he'd had to endure that bitch's taunts – that he was a lesser man than you. This was his chance to sully your name and rub Cathy's face in it.'

Pyke felt himself shrivel up inside.

'Jonah didn't know I intended to kill the boy, of course. And when he found out about the death, he went berserk, threatened to kill me, kill himself. In the end, I made him understand.'

'And Cathy?'

'That's where Smyth was useful to us. I wasn't too concerned about Cathy but I didn't want that brute John Johns coming after me. That's why I made certain that her nanny, that Atkins woman, saw Smyth when we snatched the boy, why we let her live. Sure enough, she ran back to Cathy and Johns and blabbed, as she was meant to do.'

'But Cathy must have suspected that you had something to do with her son's death?'

'Why? A woman she trusted with her life saw Smyth with her own eyes. And she knew that Smyth hated this family.' Zephaniah grinned to reveal raw, bloody gums. 'I was able to break the news to Cathy, tell her the boy had died at Smyth's hands and, best of all, that you'd absconded with the ransom money.'

'I found her body in the underground passageway. You as good as put the knife in her hand.'

Zephaniah nodded blankly as though he'd just been told the latest stock prices. 'It was Jonah who found her first. He wanted to give her a proper burial, in spite of what she'd done, what she'd been planning to do. I talked him round. Told him the rats would get her if we left her there long enough.'

Pyke closed his eyes. So she had died believing that he had turned his back on her, sacrificed her son's life for a tidy sum.

'And William?'

'What about him?'

'Who actually killed him?' Pyke realised that he didn't know how the boy had died.

'Does it matter?' Zephaniah shrugged. 'The point is, his death tipped the scales, set the fuse.'

'Did Smyth ever realise you'd set him up?' he asked eventually.

'Didn't have to have the conversation. I was going to suggest to him that he lie low for a while, perhaps go back to Ireland for a month or two, and then I heard he'd fled the town of his own accord.'

'To?'

'Ireland, I believe.'

'Do you know why?'

Zephaniah shook his head. 'Perhaps he realised what he'd become a part of. It worked out perfectly for us, though. Johns went after him, of course. Johns and Smyth, both out of the way, Johns blaming Smyth for the boy's death. The Hancock family devastated by the loss and above suspicion.' The old man eyed the pistol in Pyke's hand. 'Listen to me. Why don't you put that thing down and we can have a proper conversation?'

Pyke watched the old man, listened to him talking, so pleased with himself and with his cunning. He rammed the barrel of the pistol into the old man's cheek.

'So why stay here? Why not get out, and come back when the dust had settled?'

'You're a funny fellow, aren't you? *Leave?* When there's business to be done? Last week I met with the Russians, promised them the iron, the full order, as Morlais won't be able to produce it in time. When the deadline elapses, the Russians will tear up their contract with Webb and come over to us. Our iron is ready and waiting. Morlais will be forced to close, at least temporarily. But once Webb has gone, the works will reopen under new owners, *us*, and Caedraw will become the biggest ironmaker in the world.' The old man took a breath. 'It's why money isn't an issue. I'll give you whatever you want. Let's say fifty thousand, to make you go away?' He seemed certain that Pyke would agree to his price or name a higher one.

'I want to know about my son.'

'Your son?'

Pyke tried to assess whether the bluff was genuine; whether Zephaniah really had no idea about, and therefore no hand in, what had happened to Felix.

'My son arrived in Merthyr on or around the twenty-third of November to visit me. A few days later, I found his corpse laid out on a bed at the courthouse.'

This was another thing he hadn't been able to work out – why someone had left Felix's corpse for him to find, rather than burying it in an unmarked grave up on the mountain. It was almost as if someone had *wanted* him to find the body.

Doubt had crept into the old man's eyes. This was something he hadn't expected, something that altered the balance of negotiations. 'I didn't know.'

'Felix would have gone to the station-house to find me. I'm guessing Smyth snatched him and took him to the courthouse.'

'I had no idea you even had a son.'

'Smyth didn't share this information with you?'

Zephaniah tried to swallow. 'Not with me, not with my son.'

'I buried my son in London and I've come back here for answers.'

'As I said, Smyth has fled to Ireland.'

'Then I want the address of his estate.'

Zephaniah looked at the pistol, still in Pyke's hand. 'His family own land in Tipperary, near a place called Lisvarrinane.'

'And Johns?'

'All I know is that he grew up on an estate in Dundrum.'

'Nothing else?' Pyke took the pistol, aimed it at Zephaniah's head and waited.

'That's all I know.'

'Then it looks like our business is done.' He lowered the pistol, and tucked it into his belt.

'You're going to let me live?' There was a hint of incredulity in Zephaniah's voice.

'Did I say that?'

Turning suddenly, Pyke clenched his fist and smashed it against the old man's face, felt his bones crumble under the impact. Zephaniah passed out.

Downstairs, Pyke found a tin of lamp oil in the pantry and took it upstairs to Jonah's room. He doused the curtains with half of it, and took the other half to Zephaniah's room and did the same. Then Pyke lit a match and tossed it on to the curtains. Flames shot up the fabric. In Jonah's bedroom, he did likewise and waited to make sure the flames spread.

By the time he'd retraced his steps down to the cellar and out through the passageway, smoke was pouring out of the upstairs windows, and when he'd climbed up the mountain and turned around to inspect his work, flames had engulfed an entire wing of the Castle, plumes of orange lighting up the night sky.

As he stood and watched the fire, Pyke tried to feel something, anger, despair even, but nothing would come. He would go and find Captain Kent.

TWENTY-SEVEN

Knox had wandered for most of the night, not really knowing where he was, where he was going, only vaguely aware that he was heading north and west in the direction of Clonoulty. The sound of his father's sobs echoed in his ears, except that he wasn't Knox's father, Asenath Moore was. At one time, his mother had willingly lain down next to the man and had borne him two children – John Johns, who she had given up to the childless gatekeeper, and *him*, the child she'd kept. Time and again, he thought about his childhood, his mother keeping him close to her, protecting him against his father's drunken rages, his mother the saint, his father the devil, all of it now turned upside down. As he walked, Knox saw his father through new eyes; he understood his anger, his hatred of his wife, his self-hate, his self-pity. Knox hadn't asked about his two brothers but he didn't need to. They looked like their father and it was clear he loved them; loved them in a way he had never loved Knox. But how could he have loved another man's child? His father had suffered in silence, drowned his anger in alcohol, taken it out on him and his mother, a broken man before he had become a broken father. How had it been for him, knowing that each day his wife went to work in the kitchens of a man she had slept with, a man whose children she had secretly given birth to?

His mind turned to one of his recent visits to the house, Martin Knox comfortable in the presence of his two sons, his real sons, a gentle man embittered by circumstances.

As the first skeins of milky light gnawed at the sky, Knox stumbled almost by accident on the flint track, Clonoulty just a few miles farther along.

By the time he reached Father Mackey's house, the sun was pale and orange in the east. He paused on the doorstep, remembering for the first time in hours that his son was gravely ill. He let himself into the house, careful not to make any noise. It didn't matter. One of the servants met him in the hall.

Knox stepped into the drawing room where he could hear voices. He saw Mackey first, standing by the window. Then he saw Martha, both of them up, despite the early hour. He saw her face, the deadness in her eyes, and felt his stomach lurch.

'Is James . . . ?'

'The doctor thinks he'll make it.' Relief flooded her face. 'It was touch and go for a while but the fever has passed. He doesn't think it was cholera after all, just a fever.'

Knox went to hug her but she pushed him away. 'I had to go through all of this on my own, Michael. Do you know how lonely I've been? How afraid? You said you were only going to the barracks . . .'

Already exhausted, Knox blinked, not knowing what to say; how to make this better. 'Can I see him?'

'Is that all you've got to say, Michael?'

'I . . .' Knox wanted to tell her what he'd found out, about his father, about Moore, but the words wouldn't come.

When he tried to take her in his arms for a second time, tried to hug her, to comfort her, she pushed him away. 'You just weren't here, Michael. You haven't been here for a while.'

Mackey coughed and then excused himself – he couldn't get out of the room quickly enough.

Martha's face was like a suit of armour. 'Where have you *been*, Michael? What could have been more important than being here with us?'

Knox felt light-headed. All he could see was his father's face; all he could hear were the man's sobs.

'You made your choice, Michael. You chose to chase after a dead man, find justice for a corpse.'

What he wanted to say was: there is no justice. Not at this time. Not in this land.

'I don't know you any more, Michael. I don't know who you are, what you believe in. I want to be by myself for a while.'

'But James is going to live. He's going to pull through. Isn't that the important thing?'

Martha stared at him. She wanted him to say something else, to reassure her, to be the husband she hoped he still was. Knox could see this, see how much she needed him.

I am not who I thought I was. This same thought kept racing through his mind. He tried to find the words but they wouldn't come. A tear rolled down his cheek.

Martha's expression was sorrowful, yet also defiant. 'I think you should go, Michael.'

Knox looked at her and again tried to summon the words he wanted to say, the words she wanted to hear. None came to him.

'What's happened to you, Michael? What's happened to all the goodness that used to be in there?' She tapped his chest.

His mother had always told him to be good. Never tell a lie. He could hear her say it. *My good little boy.* It was all a sham.

Martha looked at him, bemused. 'How can we have fallen apart so badly? We were always the strong ones.'

Knox thought about all the dead bodies he'd seen, the needless suffering, the families torn apart, the lives sacrificed. What he'd done had been a protest, small and insignificant as it was, against the affairs of men like Asenath Moore. *His father.* The man who'd driven families from their homes and left them to die. How could Knox have sat back and done nothing?

'I'd like to come back tomorrow.' Knox tried to remember who he was, who his wife was. It was like looking at a stranger.

She followed him to the front door, and when he had opened it and let himself out, she stood there on the step, puzzled and sad, perhaps wondering how they had been reduced to so little.

'Michael?'

He turned around and looked at her, expectant.

She smiled, her face softening. 'Come back tomorrow morning. You can see James then.'

The Queen Anne mansion rose up out of the mist. Knox approached it from higher ground to the east, having to cross a bog and then the river, close to the place where they had found the body. He'd wandered aimlessly for most of the day and now it was almost dusk. The pale sun had dropped below the Galtee mountains and the temperature had fallen but Knox hardly noticed. He followed the path of the stream, the water black and empty, aware that anyone looking out of the front windows would see him. But he wasn't con-cerned about that. Staring at the stately house, he wondered where his mother and Moore had lain together, where he'd been conceived – perhaps in the pantry next to the pots and pans, Moore's trousers around his ankles.

The fields to his left were barren and marshy, the wind blowing from the east, icy and insistent, carrying with it the voices of those who had fought and died; the fourteen who'd ransacked a barracks in Ballack at the end of the Napoleonic war and who'd been punished for their insurrection, the O'Dwyers of Kilmanagh and their faithful who'd held out for days against Cromwell's Ironsides.

The famine dead. The fallen. Ghosts.

Knox entered the house through the poor door and made his way up the stairs. The house felt cold and empty but he knew Moore would be there. It was dusk, which meant he would be dressing for dinner. Knox knew the man's routine as well as his own – his family life had been determined by it. He'd always wondered why his mother had been allowed to live away from the house when the other servants, maids and kitchen-hands, lived in quarters in a nearby annexe. Now he knew why she had been granted special privileges. And wasn't it true that she'd asked Moore to put in a good word for him with the constabulary? What Moore had given, he'd also taken away. Knox's whole life had been shaped by the whims of this one man. His father. Knox found this notion repugnant.

Moore's bedroom was at the back of the house: Knox had ceased to think of him as Lord Cornwallis. Without knocking, he entered and found the man half undressed, sitting in front of a looking glass. A fire crackled in the grate. Moore saw Knox's reflection in the mirror and turned around.

'What's the meaning of this, boy?' His expression was indignant but Knox could see he was worried.

'I've just come from visiting my mother.' Knox held the aristocrat's stare. 'She told me the truth about my parentage.' He approached the dresser where the older man was sitting.

'What's all this about, boy? You're talking a load of damned nonsense. Barging in here like this. I'll have you whipped if you're not careful.'

Undeterred, Knox said, 'My mother was a fine-looking woman. She still is, in fact. It's no wonder she caught your eye.'

In that instant he could see that Moore knew. The bluster left him and he was quiet. Knox thought about the times he'd been cowed by Moore's rank and status, the things he hadn't said.

'You may have lain with my mother but you'll never be my father, at least not in the proper sense of the word.' As he said this, Knox thought about the man he'd always looked to as his father and wondered what this new revelation made him.

'I don't know what you're talking about . . .'

Moore had turned around and Knox slapped him once across the cheek. He saw the shock register on the aristocrat's face, the fact that a man of Knox's status had insulted him in such a manner.

'You sired another child with my mother. His name is John Johns. He was brought up by your gatekeeper. But none of this is a surprise to you, is it?'

Moore sought to recover lost ground. 'You'll go to prison for this. The scaffold even. Don't think I wouldn't do it. Even if you are . . .'

'Even if I am . . . ?'

'What is it you want, boy? Some money perhaps, to get yourself back on your feet? All right, I'll let you wet your beak.'

'Money? You think I'd touch your money? Tainted with the blood of all those people you've allowed to die?'

'What poppycock . . .'

Knox had heard enough. He grabbed the old man's throat, pressed his fingers into the wrinkly flesh, and began to squeeze. It felt good, better than he had expected. 'Say it,' he hissed.

It was hard to let go, to stop. Eventually he did. Moore was spluttering, his face the colour of beetroot. 'Say what, you fool?'

'How many times did you fuck my mother? Twice? More?'

'What do you want me to say, boy? That I loved your mother? Well, I did. There. I was young, she was beautiful, but poor, a servant. There was no way we could have made a life together. But what's done is done. I looked out for you, didn't I? I got you your position and Johns a commission in the army.'

Knox stood there, hardly able to fathom the self-justification coming from the man's mouth. 'You evicted my family from our home. My son caught a fever and nearly died. And I'm supposed to feel grateful?'

Moore didn't have an answer. Perhaps for the first time, Knox saw something resembling contrition in the man's face. His voice was suddenly quiet. 'I was hurt, boy, hurt that you'd gone behind my back. I thought you of all people would obey me . . .'

'Because I'm your son?'

Moore wouldn't look at him.

'I want only what you took from me; nothing more, nothing less.' Knox waited. 'I want my position back at the constabulary – a promotion to head constable – and I want you to rebuild my cottage, the one you had Brittas tear down.'

Moore straightened up, all his indignation gone. 'And you'll keep your mouth shut?'

Knox nodded, but he still didn't know whether he'd abide by any agreement they reached. 'The man who was killed, the police detective from London . . .'

'What about him?'

'Why did he come here?'

'Something had happened in Wales. I don't know what. Johns didn't tell me and I didn't ask. Johns came here begging for money – said there was a policeman looking for him. He said he wouldn't come back, that he had a debt to settle in Lisvarrinane, and after that, he promised to disappear for good.'

'When you laid eyes on the body for the first time, you were taken aback. Someone said your eyes nearly popped out of their sockets.'

'Johns came back to see me that night. He told me what had happened; that there had been a struggle – that he'd stabbed and killed this man, a police detective from London. But he didn't say where the struggle had taken place. I was shocked when I heard how close the body was, when I saw it with my own eyes.'

Knox stared down at the old man's rheumy eyes and hairless, oval head and tried to see something of himself in his face.

'So when the body was eventually discovered, you decided to ask for me, demand that I take charge of the investigation, to make sure nothing ever came to light about your link with the murderer.'

The old man nodded. There was nothing else to say. It was just as he had supposed. Moore had hand-picked him for the task because he knew that Knox and his family were beholden to him.

For what he'd done, for his callousness, his indifference to the suffering of others, Moore deserved to die, but Knox wasn't a murderer, didn't want that on his conscience as well. And he needed what Moore could give him: his former position and his home.

As he left, again using the poor door, he wondered where his mother was, whether she was working in the kitchens. And he wondered whether he would ever see her again.

Knox walked from Dundrum to Clonoulty; his mind was clearer now that he had stood up to the aristocrat and watched him cave in, his father who wasn't his father. With each step, he felt a sense of perspective return. James was alive and that was all that mattered. Martha still loved him and he loved her. She would forgive him for abandoning her. He knew she would; she had a good heart. They would rebuild their lives and there would be nothing more that Moore could do to harm them.

The journey from Dundrum took hours but Knox didn't care. He would've walked to Dublin if he had to. It was still dark when he arrived in Clonoulty and he didn't bother to knock when he got to Mackey's house.

Despite the lateness of the hour, candlelight was visible in the front window. Opening the front door, Knox entered the hall. He found his wife sitting in the back room. She didn't look up when he entered. He sat down next to her on the bed and sighed.

'I'm sorry, Martha. I'm sorry I haven't been here for you, that you've had to endure this on your own. I don't have the words you need to hear, there are no words . . .' Knox paused. 'But James is going to get better. We can rebuild our lives. Isn't that what counts?'

Martha didn't move, didn't even flinch. They sat next to one another, each contemplating their situation in silence.

'There's nothing left for us here, is there?' Martha's voice cracked as she spoke. 'I'm so grateful that the Lord spared our son but there's nothing left for us in this place, is there? Here, in this land, our country.'

Nothing left for *us. Our* country.

Knox reached out, put his hand on hers, and squeezed it. Martha didn't take it but she didn't spurn it either.

TWENTY-EIGHT

MONDAY, 4 JANUARY 1847

Dundrum, Co. Tipperary

Dundrum High Street was a collection of four or five buildings on either side of a mud track; the only place to stay was a ramshackle inn where the landlord rented him a simple room for a few shillings. Pyke didn't intend staying any longer than necessary.

He had travelled from Merthyr to Newport and from there to Cork City by ship. The crossing had been quiet and the ship nearly deserted. No one wanted to travel to Ireland. On the ship, he heard stories of destitution and loss, heartbreaking stories, villages wiped out by starvation and disease. From Cork, he journeyed by mail-coach to Cashel and from there he walked the remaining ten miles to Dundrum. The journey had taken a week and then it had taken him another week to track down Johns to a cabin between Dundrum and Oughterleague. That night he had followed Johns to the village's great house and watched from the stables as Johns slipped into the house via the servant's entrance.

Pyke had found the travelling arduous but comforting; the notion of going somewhere at least gave his existence some purpose, time spent on trains, boats and stagecoaches affording him the opportunity to think about Felix, to grieve: not simply to berate himself, but to remember his son. Now he just wanted to find out how Felix had died – he owed his son that much. Johns was his last chance for enlightenment. Before coming to Dundrum, Pyke had also made the journey to Lisvarrinane to confront Smyth, but evidently Johns had beaten him to it. He had been told that a fire had ripped through the big house and that the master, who'd only recently returned from Wales, had perished in it.

At just ten years of age, Felix had taken one of Pyke's pistols and used it to scare a boy who had been terrorising him, waved it in his face, finger poised on the trigger. The pistol had been loaded. Pyke tried, in vain, to reconcile this memory of his son with a more recent one, the Bible open in front of him, talking about forgiveness, contrition and God's grace. Perhaps you quite simply couldn't reconcile such things, Pyke decided. You just accepted that you couldn't reduce people you loved to one thing or another, that they would always go ahead and surprise you.

At bottom, he couldn't believe that Felix was dead. He would wake up each morning and, in those few seconds before consciousness seized him, he could still entertain the fantasy that Felix was alive, that he had his whole life in front of him. But as he opened his eyes, reality would invade the space of his dreams and the edifice he'd constructed in his mind – the hope, the yearning – would crumble. In those moments, he would experience a level of rage and self-loathing he'd never known, even after Emily's death, and nothing, not gin nor laudanum, could alleviate the pain.

Pyke also thought about his own life, what he had left to live for. After the burial at Bunhill Fields, he'd gone home and told the housekeeper, Mrs Booth, that he no longer needed her services. Then he'd taken his pistol into the garden and finished off his two pigs, one at a time, and buried them next to their sty. That just left Copper but Pyke couldn't consign his beloved mastiff to the same fate. Instead he had taken the three-legged dog to Jo, Felix's former nursemaid, now married with children of her own, and persuaded her to take him.

As Pyke stared up at the windows of the mansion, the curtains drawn inside, he wondered about Johns' connection to the man who lived there, a tyrant by all accounts.

The night was clear and bitterly cold. Since arriving in Cork, he'd seen death everywhere and he had found it hard not to think about how needless it was, how easily relief could have been provided, and therefore how deliberate it was too: a decision made somewhere by grey-haired men with full bellies and bulging purses to teach the poor a lesson. *Free will and free trade.* Let the market decide who lives and who dies. Pyke had passed putrefying bodies but he hadn't stopped to bury them. No justice for them. Not in this land. Not in these times. What could one man do in the face of so much horror, so much death?

Half an hour after Johns had entered the house, he appeared through the same door. Pyke was waiting to the right of the driveway, closer to the river than the stables now, and he didn't make his move until Johns was almost alongside him.

'John.'

Startled, the man turned and peered into the darkness. Then, realising who it was, he started to run.

TWENTY-NINE

MONDAY, 8 FEBRUARY 1847
Passage West, Co. Cork

Every paddle-steamer and lighter leaving from Cork City for Passage West was full to capacity and the narrow roads from Raffeen and Monkstown were thronged with carts, cabs, drays and pedestrians, the poor and the destitute heading for the seafront in the hope of securing passage on one of the ships leaving for Canada or the United States. It seemed to Knox that the whole county had descended on this thin strip of land; everyone looking to leave, each with their own stories of pain and loss; the walking wounded and the nearly dead.

Initially Knox had wanted to stay; he had tried to convince Martha that Asenath Moore would be true to his word – that Knox would be reinstated in the constabulary and that everything would go back to how it had been before. But Martha had been adamant that men like Moore and Hastings would never give them what they wanted; the liberty to live their lives as they wished. They had argued for hours, for days, and in the end, he had come around to her way of thinking. Best to start a new life somewhere else. This was why he had travelled to Cork and why he planned to travel much farther afield; Knox would go ahead and find a job, a place to live, and when he was settled, he would send for Martha and James.

He had purchased his passage – in steerage, all he could afford – from a broker in Cork City the previous morning: on the *Syria*, sailing that afternoon for New York. It had cost him ten pounds, up from five a week ago, someone had told him. Traders always made money out of death. He could have gone to Quebec for half that amount but he preferred the sound of New York, and in any case the St Lawrence river might still be frozen by the time they'd crossed the Atlantic.

With the ticket in his pocket, and ten shillings to buy some salt meat for the crossing, Knox was carrying all he possessed: his wedding ring, a letter Martha had written to him, a lock of James' hair. Martha would stay with Father Mackey until she heard from him and then she would make this same journey. Still, now he was at the seafront, staring out at the ocean, Knox couldn't help but wonder whether he would ever see Martha again, whether she would, in fact, come when he sent for her, and indeed, whether she would survive the famine. They'd talked about whether they should leave together, for this had been Knox's preferred option, but Martha had dug in her heels and told him that he should find a job first. Now, on the edge of the Atlantic Ocean, Knox felt alone and scared, and wished that Martha had come with him, so that they could comfort and reassure each other.

At William Brown's dockyard, he stared out at the slime-coloured water and saw the brig – the *Syria* – a small, squat, wooden vessel with three masts and an ugly tangle of rigging. A lighter was transporting cargo out to it, stevedores on deck loading crates into the hull. It didn't look as if it could make it as far as Liverpool, let alone New York.

His thoughts turned to James, how the boy liked to sleep on Knox's chest after he had been fed, his contented face, eyelids closing, soft little breaths. Yes, it was a miracle that James was alive, but Knox didn't believe that God had made it happen. Too many others had died for this notion to make sense.

The only reason for staying would be to find his brother. His *other* brother. John Johns, last seen heading west to Lisvarrinane. Knox hadn't been back to the cottage, hadn't said goodbye to his mother, father or his brothers. He hadn't wanted to see them. That part of his life was finished.

From the dock, he looked back towards the main street and then up at Carrigmoran hill, emerald green, a narrow track cut into it. He had always loved his country, had never imagined leaving it. Looking up at that hill, he felt overwhelmed and even a little sentimental, but there was nothing left to do now but wait.

THIRTY

He couldn't get used to the rocking of the brig, especially down in the hold where most of the steerage-class passengers congregated, so he spent his time up on deck, watching the crew work, staring out at the drab horizon. He was told that two hundred would be making the crossing but there had to be nearer to three hundred on board, the young and old, the sick and soon-to-be-sick. That was another reason why he spent as little time as possible below deck. A doctor had inspected the passengers before embarkation but only cursorily, and the first night he had been kept awake by the sound of a child moaning quietly next to him. The following morning, he found out that the child had perished in the night. Another death, but there was nothing to be done. He kept himself to himself, listened to the voices speaking Irish, glad of the anonymity, of the chance just to stand there on deck and watch the waves breaking against the ship and think about everything he had left behind.

A wave crashed over the side, splashing his feet, washing over the deck, but he didn't mind that his shoes were wet, because he was looking at a point on the horizon, far, far away, and trying to remember the day that Felix had been born and the nursemaid had passed him the mewling baby. The day Pyke had held his son for the first time.

THIRTY-ONE

'I didn't do it,' John Johns said, backing away towards the river. 'I didn't kill your son.'

Johns had bolted and Pyke had pursued him through the long grass until the former soldier had been caught out by the bend in the river, with nowhere left to run.

It had been more than a month since Pyke had last seen the big man and he seemed different. Less sure of himself, skittish. He looked thinner, too.

'Who did?'

'Apparently it was an accident.'

Pyke felt the skin tighten across his temples. 'Apparently?'

Johns glanced behind him at the river, black, cold and silent. 'I found him at the courthouse, at the bottom of the stairs.'

'You're saying he fell?'

'My guess is that Smyth had been keeping him there against his will. I can only assume your son tried to escape and fell down the stairs, broke his neck.'

'So who picked him up and put him on the bed upstairs?'

'I did.' Johns looked down at the frozen ground. 'I found the letters he'd written to you and realised he was your son.' Johns tapped his coat pocket. 'I brought them with me.'

'Why?'

'I didn't want anyone else to identify him. I knew you'd go there eventually, that you'd find him. I wanted you to find him, to be able to bury him, and grieve. But I couldn't stay in Merthyr . . .'

Pyke felt a stabbing pain in his chest, a sharp ache from the pointlessness of it all. 'And Smyth?'

'He's gone.'

'You followed him here?'

'He killed William Hancock.' Johns looked into Pyke's face. 'Or he as good as killed the lad.'

Pyke nodded blankly. He could let Johns carry on thinking that Smyth was guilty but at the same time the man deserved to know the truth. 'That night at Fernhill, Maggie Atkins was meant to see Smyth. It's why they didn't kill her. So that when the Hancock boy turned up dead, she would be able to implicate Smyth.'

Johns stared at Pyke, still trying to take in what he'd said. Pyke just felt immensely sorry for the man, sorry for the news he was about to break and the terrible hurt it would cause.

'Zephaniah Hancock arranged to have the boy killed. He knew William wasn't Jonah's son.' Pyke tried to smile. He had travelled for weeks, across land and sea, for this moment, and now all he felt was exhaustion and pity. 'He was yours, wasn't he? You, Cathy and the boy, you were going to start a new life together?'

Johns nodded but said nothing. Cathy was dead and so was his son. Both their sons were dead. Pyke wanted to tell Johns that he understood, but at the last moment held his tongue. What did it matter that someone understood? That wouldn't change anything.

'I'm sorry.'

Johns looked up at him. There were tears in his eyes. 'I'm sorry, too.'

They waited for a moment while the wind gusted, wet leaves blowing all around them. 'What did Smyth say when you confronted him?'

'Nothing.' Johns' expression didn't change. 'Didn't get a chance; as soon as he realised he was trapped, he turned his pistol on himself and pulled the trigger. The fire was to cover my tracks.'

Pyke considered the implications of this. 'So I've got to take your word for it – that my son died falling down the stairs?'

'Is knowing for certain going to bring him back?' Johns reached into his pocket. It took Pyke a second or two to notice the blade of a knife.

'What are you going to do with that?'

Johns didn't seem to have heard the question. In a nearby tree, a blackbird twittered, but there were no other sounds except for the breeze and the quiet flowing of the river.

'I found Cathy's body. She'd taken her own life, slit her wrists. I suppose she felt that she'd caused William's death.'

'If we hadn't gone ahead with the scheme in the first place, our son might still be alive.'

'Perhaps – but do you really imagine that Zephaniah Hancock would have let you leave and live happily ever after?'

'I suppose not.' Johns waited and added, 'What happened to the Hancocks?'

'Didn't make it.' Pyke shook his head. Then he gestured at the knife in Johns' hand. 'Put it away, John. No need for anyone else to die.'

Johns looked around at the barren landscape. 'You know, I was born here. Grew up in the gatehouse. Only when my father was on his deathbed did he tell me I wasn't his son.'

'Who was?'

'My father?' Johns laughed bitterly. 'That old coot who lives in the big house. Asenath Moore, Lord Cornwallis. Fucked a kitchen-hand. She was engaged to be married so I was given away.'

Pyke thought about his own father, who had died in a crowd stampede when he was a boy, and about Godfrey, who had rescued him and brought him up.

'Before you arrived in Merthyr,' Johns said, 'she'd finally agreed to come away with me. A new life, just the three of us.'

'Before *I* arrived?'

'She'd always carried a torch for you.'

Pyke bowed his head. 'Give me the knife, John.' He took another step towards the former soldier.

'*What?* Do you want to shake my hand, pretend we can be friends? Shake hands and go our separate ways, let ourselves believe that everything has worked out for the best?'

'Did I say that?'

'See here? People are dying because they can't afford to eat.'

Pyke took another step towards him and held out his hand. 'Give me the knife, John.'

'The rich get richer and the poor are buried in a pit.'

'There's no way men like us can change things. Not now, not any more. We've seen too much, done too much. For that to happen you need someone younger, their ideals intact.'

'Dinosaurs.' Johns almost looked amused.

Pyke took another step. 'The knife.'

Johns managed a smile and then took the knife in his other hand, turned it on himself and drove it into his belly. He fell to his knees and Pyke had to wrestle his hands off the handle in order to pull it out, blood spurting from the wound. Pyke cradled Johns' head in his lap, stroked his hair and waited for the man to die.

THIRTY-TWO

WEDNESDAY, 10 FEBRUARY 1847
Lisvarrinane, Co. Tipperary

Knox had walked for most of the day, stopping anyone he passed and asking them whether they had seen or heard of a man called John Johns. No one had. Knox described him as best he could but his description jolted no memories. A few told him about the fire at the big house – and that the recently returned absentee landlord, Sir Clancy Smyth, had perished in it.

When Knox asked where Smyth had returned *from*, and was told Wales, it pricked his interest. He was tired but the walking relaxed him, and because he had sold his boat ticket at a profit, he had the funds to pay for food and shelter. He'd bought a good pair of boots, too. Knox didn't know how Martha was going to react when he turned up on Father Mackey's doorstep in a day or so, whether she would be pleased to see him or devastated that he hadn't sailed for the New World. In the end, it was simple; he hadn't been able to. It was a physical thing. He needed to be with his wife and child. But on the journey back from Cork, Knox had begun to think about his brother, the man he knew as John Johns, the murderer of a London policeman, and he had taken a detour to Lisvarrinane, the last place where Johns had been seen. The trail had gone cold now and he was keen to get back to Clonoulty as quickly as possible.

Knox wanted to get back to Clonoulty, but he was afraid of what he'd find there, afraid that Martha would be angry or, worse, indifferent.

So he decided to walk, to give himself time to prepare himself, and as he walked, he let his mind wander. He crossed from Cork into Tipperary, and to pass the time, he bought a notebook and a pencil. During breaks, he would scribble down his thoughts, his impressions of the folk he met, their suffering, their fortitude. Knox liked the idea of bearing witness, recording what he saw, not for any particular reason or because people would necessarily want to read what he had written, but because it was the worst of times and someone needed to document it so that much later, others would know how bad it had been.

Just outside Ballyporeen Knox came across two men groping for eels in a river – they swore him to silence and offered him a meal of eel cooked over an open fire. The next day on the road to Clogheen, he came across a family who'd left the nearby village the day before. The woman told him that the sickness – *an droch-thinneas* – had killed three families. Close by the village of Ardfinnan he stumbled upon a corpse, maggots feasting on the flesh, and as he neared Cahir, Knox came across a dog, a large mongrel, carrying what looked like human flesh in its jaws. He noted these things without outrage or moral indignation: this was just the way it was. Some nights he slept rough, other nights he lodged with families. He spoke in Irish. No one attacked him; no one tried to rob him. As he neared Clonoulty, he found himself longing for the open road. What was the saying? Better to travel hopefully than to arrive. That was how he felt, but to reassure himself, he would lie awake at night, either under the stars or in strangers' cabins, and remember the way James smiled, remember the laughter lines around Martha's eyes, and in those moments he knew that, regardless of what he found at home, he would find the strength to endure.

THIRTY-THREE

TUESDAY, 2 FEBRUARY 1847

Dublin, Co. Dublin

Pyke stood by the window of his lodging-house room, looking down on to the street below, a solitary gas lamp illuminating the wet cobblestones.

Two days earlier, Benedict Pierce had come to this same address. Pyke had written to him to let him know where he was staying.

At that first meeting, Pierce had muttered threats about arresting Pyke and taking him back to London, but he had listened to Pyke's proposal and in the end he had done what Pyke had asked him to: travel to a small town in Tipperary and convince the authorities there that he, Pyke, was dead; that the body discovered on the estate of Dundrum House was him. Pyke had done his best to lay the groundwork, and make it appear as if he, and not John Johns, had been killed – he'd even left his pistol and precious letters from Felix in the room he'd taken in Dundrum village and paid off the landlord there. Still, he needed Pierce's help.

'I wrote to you because I want you to help me disappear.'

Pierce had looked at him strangely. 'Why would *I* want to help *you*?'

'If you do, I'll never return to London, never set foot in Scotland Yard again.'

That had been when Pierce understood. He had nodded once, and he might even have smiled.

Down on the street, Pyke watched as a young boy hurried to catch up with a woman dressed in fine clothes, his mother perhaps. For days now, it seemed, he had wandered the labyrinthine streets of this unfamiliar city, with only his memories to comfort him.

Returning his gaze to the street below, Pyke saw a dog trot past and heard the wheels of another carriage, a hansom cab this time, grinding to a standstill under his window. Pierce emerged from the cab, told the driver to wait, and looked up at the shabby building. Instinctively, Pyke stepped back from the window; he didn't want Pierce to see he'd been waiting for him. He listened as Pierce's footsteps came up the staircase and waited for the knock on the door.

Pierce had taken off his hat and was cradling it in his arms.

'It's done,' he said, removing a piece of paper from the pocket of his black frock-coat. 'Coroner's report. You died – wilful murder by a person or persons unknown – on the fourth of January 1847.'

Pyke took the piece of paper and inspected it. So that was it. He was a ghost, a non-person, which was exactly how he felt.

'Any difficulties?'

'The constable who investigated the murder looked like he might be getting close to the truth. He knew about Johns and talked about confronting the lord of the manor – Johns' father, I discovered. I paid this man a visit – Lord Cornwallis. He was only too keen not to rock the boat. He promised to stop the constable from asking any more questions. The official story is that Johns killed you and then fled.'

So it was done. Arthur John Pyke, rest in peace. Pyke tried to summon up something approaching sadness.

'Once my house is sold, you can keep half of the proceeds, and put my half into a bank. I'll write to you once I know where I'll be.'

That had been another part of their agreement. Pierce would never have turned down the chance to feather his nest. Their lives had paralleled each other for many years, Pyke thought, first as Bow Street Runners and latterly as policemen for the Metropolitan Police. Pierce had once been head of the Detective Branch, too. Perhaps, Pyke decided, they were more alike than he had ever cared to admit.

'And where will you go?'

'It's probably too late for me to start over.' Pyke shrugged. 'But I can't stay here and I can't go back to England. Too many memories.'

Pierce nodded.

'There are ships leaving every day for Canada and the United States. I fancy New York City.'

'Where they used to transport convicts.' Pierce managed a smile.

'Appropriate, then.'

Pierce passed his hat from hand to hand. Pyke could see he didn't want to be there. 'I suppose I should go. My cab is waiting.'

Pyke opened the door and waited for Pierce to pass through. At the last moment, Pierce turned around. 'I'm sorry about what happened, your son . . .'

Pyke nodded: there were no words. Instead he shook Pierce's hand and then watched him disappear down the stairs.

Much later, Pyke lay on his bed and listened to the sounds from the street. It was an end, he thought, this place, this time. But perhaps in another country he would learn to live again.

FRANKLIN COUNTY LIBRARY
906 NORTH MAIN STREET
LOUISBURG, NC 27549
BRANCHES IN BUNN.
FRANKLINTON, & YOUNGSVILLE

AFTERWORD

Thanks to the local history librarians at Merthyr Tydfil and Thurles and to Austin Crowe, owner of the Dundrum House Hotel, for giving me their time and advice and for pointing me in the right direction. I am sure they will be horrified at the liberties I have taken with their carefully arrived at notions of what happened in the 1840s but I am happy to offer a wholly fictionalised account of the past in order to get at some larger historical truths; about the famine in Ireland and the ways in which ironmasters in Wales exploited differences in order to keep their workforces divided and weak. Thanks also to the team at Weidenfeld & Nicolson and Orion, especially my editor Kirsty Dunseath, for helping to put this book together and promoting it and the rest of the Pyke novels. Particular thanks and much love to Debbie who has lived with Pyke at every moment of his journey and wielded her red pen with rigour and humour, and to Marcus and Sadie who have come into our lives and turned things upside down in the best way possible. This book is dedicated to them.